CONTENTS

WESTERN CLASSICS

Graphic Classics® Volume Twenty

ILLUSTRATION ©2011 CYNTHIA MARTIN

Out Where the West Begins *by Arthur Chapman, illustrated by Al Feldstein* 2

Riders of the Purple Sage
by Zane Grey, adapted by Tom Pomplun, illustrated by Cynthia Martin 4

Knife River Prodigal
by Robert E. Howard, adapted by Ben Avery, illustrated by George Sellas 52

The Right Eye of the Commander
by Bret Harte, adapted by David Hontiveros, illustrated by Reno Maniquis 74

The Holdup
by Clarence E. Mulford, adapted by Tim Lasiuta, illustrated by Dan Spiegle 86

La Perdida
by Gertrude Atherton, adapted by Trina Robbins, illustrated by Arnold Arre 102

The Last Thundersong
by John G. Neihardt, adapted by Rod Lott, illustrated by Ryan Huna Smith 110

El Dorado
by Willa Cather, adapted by Rich Rainey, illustrated by John Findley 120

About the Artists & Writers 142

Cover illustration by Cynthia Martin / Back cover illustration by Ryan Huna Smith

Western Classics: Graphic Classics Volume Twenty / ISBN 978-0-9787919-9-5 is published by Eureka Productions. Price US $17.95, CAN $22.50. Available from Eureka Productions, 8778 Oak Grove Road, Mount Horeb, WI 53572. Tom Pomplun, designer and publisher, tom@graphicclassics.com. Eileen Fitzgerald, editorial assistant. *Knife River Prodigal* ©2011 Robert E. Howard Properties Inc. ROBERT E. HOWARD and related names, logos, characters and distinctive likenesses thereof are trademarks or registered trademarks of Robert E. Howard Properties Inc. All rights reserved. Compilation and all original works ©2011 Eureka Productions. Graphic Classics is a registered trademark of Eureka Productions. For ordering information and previews of upcoming volumes visit the Graphic Classics website at http://www.graphicclassics.com. Printed in USA.

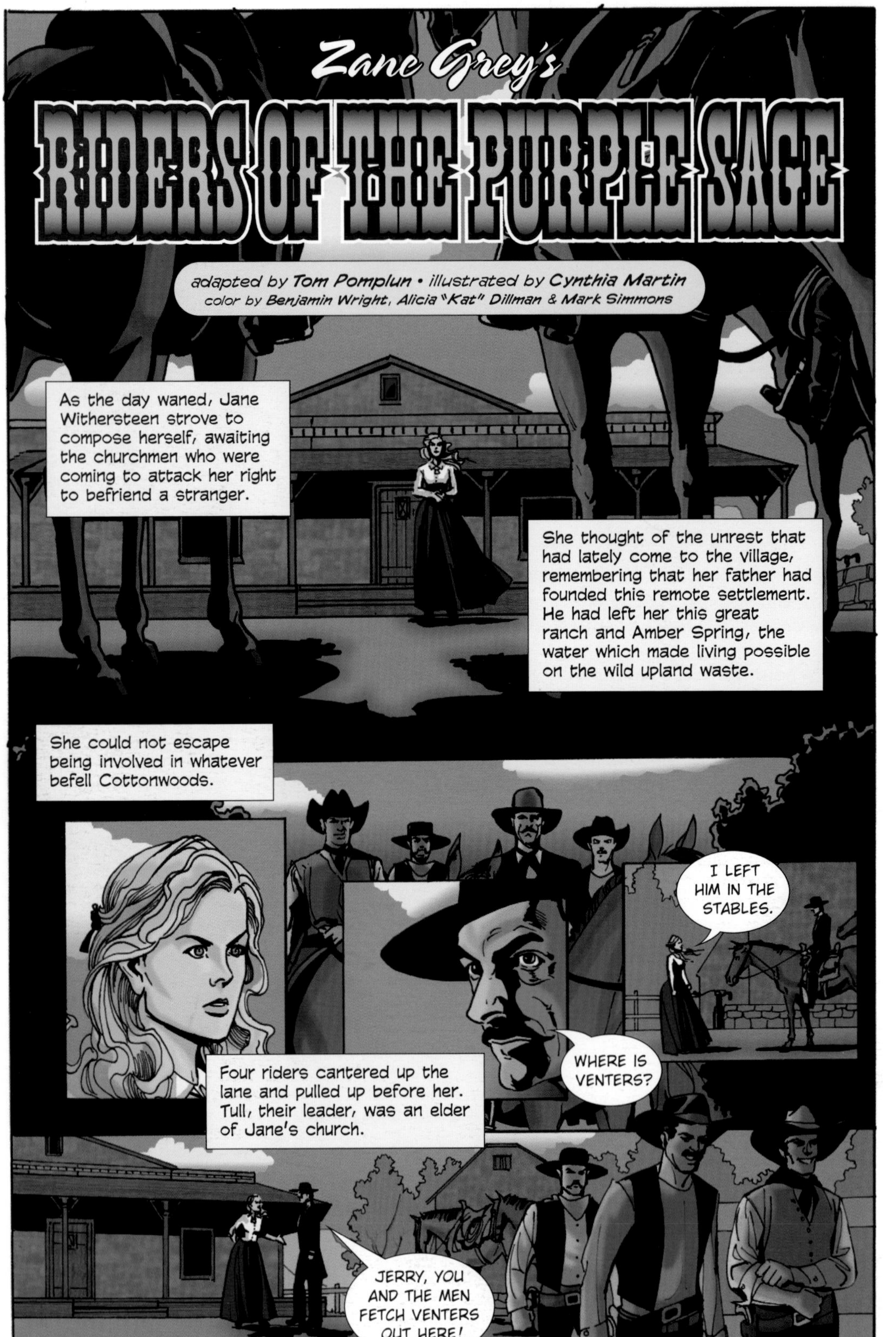

Zane Grey's
RIDERS OF THE PURPLE SAGE
adapted by Tom Pomplun • illustrated by Cynthia Martin
color by Benjamin Wright, Alicia "Kat" Dillman & Mark Simmons
As the day waned, Jane Withersteen strove to compose herself, awaiting the churchmen who were coming to attack her right to befriend a stranger.
She thought of the unrest that had lately come to the village, remembering that her father had founded this remote settlement. He had left her this great ranch and Amber Spring, the water which made living possible on the wild upland waste.
She could not escape being involved in whatever befell Cottonwoods.
Four riders cantered up the lane and pulled up before her. Tull, their leader, was an elder of Jane's church.
WHERE IS VENTERS?
I LEFT HIM IN THE STABLES.
JERRY, YOU AND THE MEN FETCH VENTERS OUT HERE!

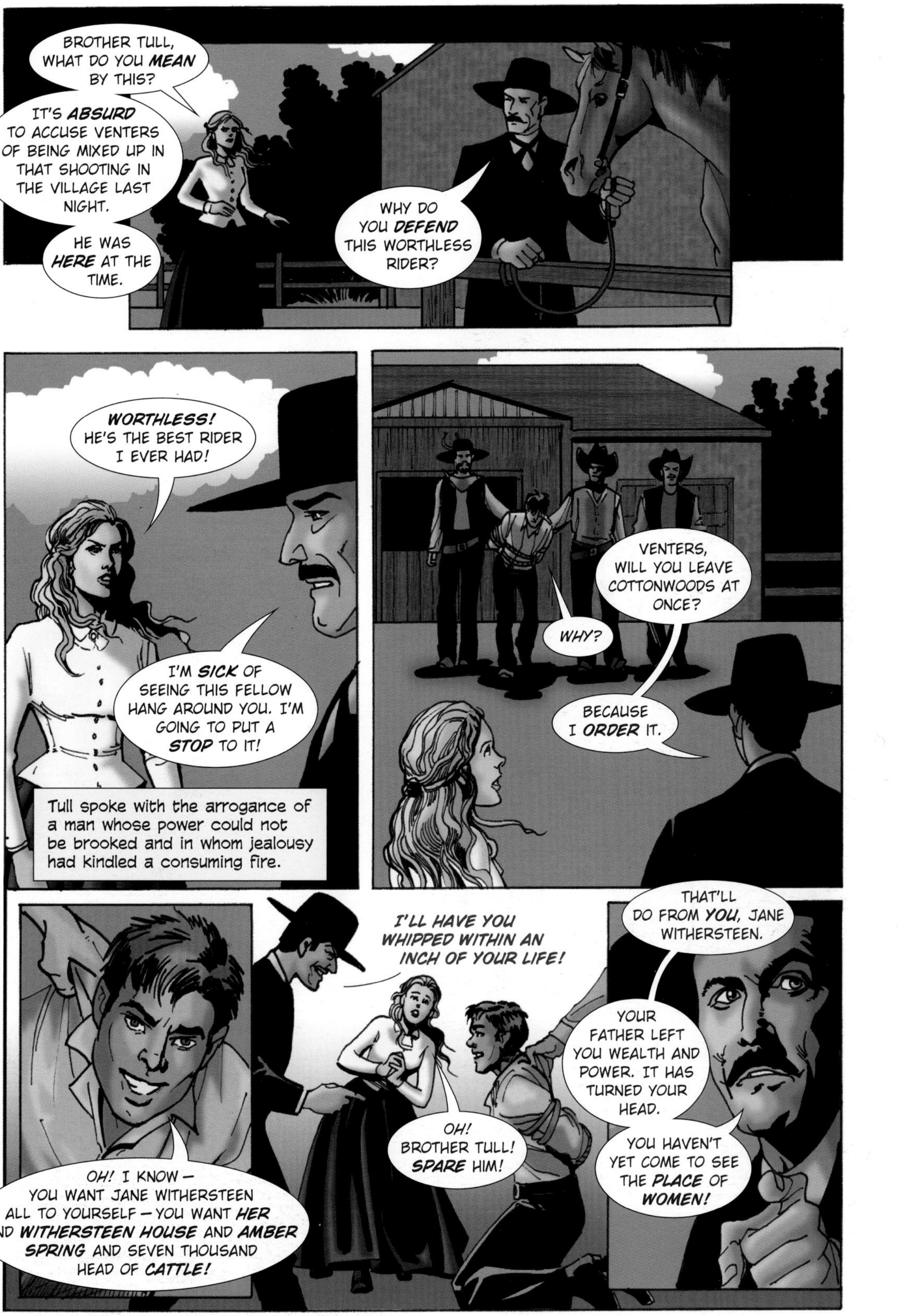
BROTHER TULL, WHAT DO YOU MEAN BY THIS?
IT'S ABSURD TO ACCUSE VENTERS OF BEING MIXED UP IN THAT SHOOTING IN THE VILLAGE LAST NIGHT.
HE WAS HERE AT THE TIME.
WHY DO YOU DEFEND THIS WORTHLESS RIDER?
WORTHLESS! HE'S THE BEST RIDER I EVER HAD!
I'M SICK OF SEEING THIS FELLOW HANG AROUND YOU. I'M GOING TO PUT A STOP TO IT!
Tull spoke with the arrogance of a man whose power could not be brooked and in whom jealousy had kindled a consuming fire.
VENTERS, WILL YOU LEAVE COTTONWOODS AT ONCE?
WHY?
BECAUSE I ORDER IT.
OH! I KNOW — YOU WANT JANE WITHERSTEEN ALL TO YOURSELF — YOU WANT HER AND WITHERSTEEN HOUSE AND AMBER SPRING AND SEVEN THOUSAND HEAD OF CATTLE!
I'LL HAVE YOU WHIPPED WITHIN AN INCH OF YOUR LIFE!
OH! BROTHER TULL! SPARE HIM!
THAT'LL DO FROM YOU, JANE WITHERSTEEN.
YOUR FATHER LEFT YOU WEALTH AND POWER. IT HAS TURNED YOUR HEAD.
YOU HAVEN'T YET COME TO SEE THE PLACE OF WOMEN!

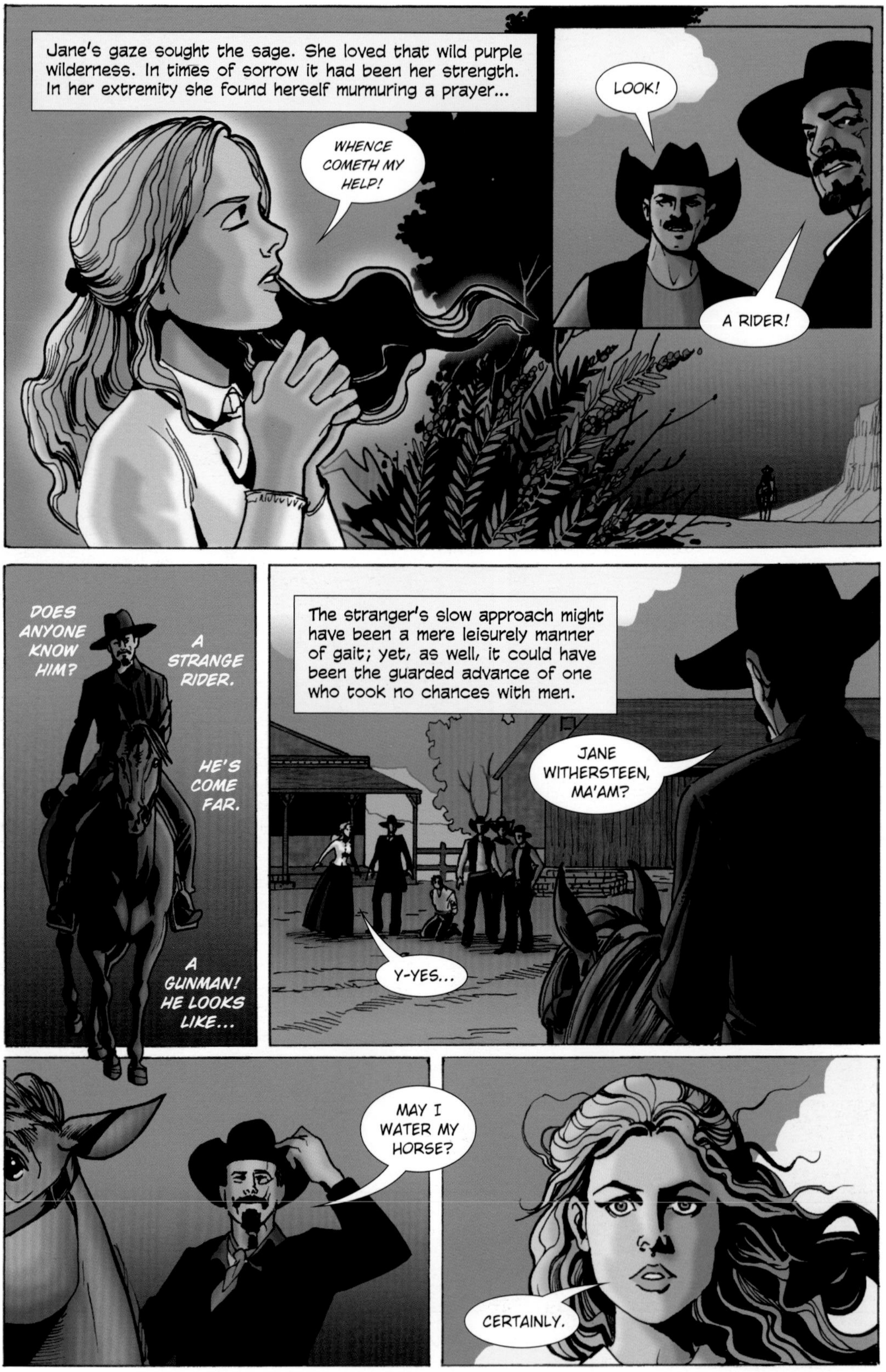
Jane's gaze sought the sage. She loved that wild purple wilderness. In times of sorrow it had been her strength. In her extremity she found herself murmuring a prayer...
WHENCE COMETH MY HELP!
LOOK!
A RIDER!
DOES ANYONE KNOW HIM?
A STRANGE RIDER.
HE'S COME FAR.
A GUNMAN! HE LOOKS LIKE...
The stranger's slow approach might have been a mere leisurely manner of gait; yet, as well, it could have been the guarded advance of one who took no chances with men.
JANE WITHERSTEEN, MA'AM?
Y-YES...
MAY I WATER MY HORSE?
CERTAINLY.

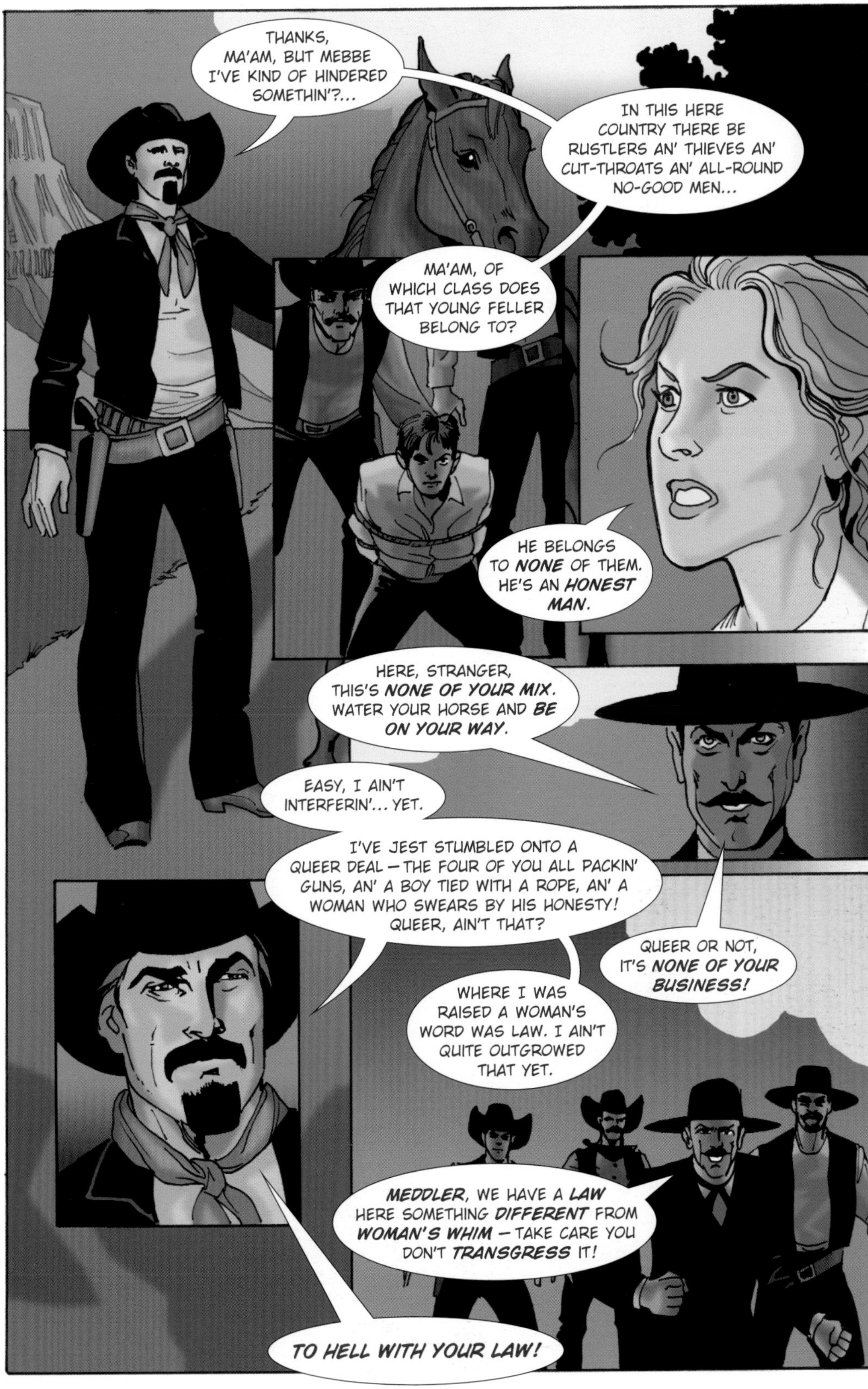
THANKS, MA'AM, BUT MEBBE I'VE KIND OF HINDERED SOMETHIN'?...
IN THIS HERE COUNTRY THERE BE RUSTLERS AN' THIEVES AN' CUT-THROATS AN' ALL-ROUND NO-GOOD MEN...
MA'AM, OF WHICH CLASS DOES THAT YOUNG FELLER BELONG TO?
HE BELONGS TO **NONE** OF THEM. HE'S AN **HONEST MAN**.
HERE, STRANGER, THIS'S **NONE OF YOUR MIX**. WATER YOUR HORSE AND **BE ON YOUR WAY**.
EASY, I AIN'T INTERFERIN'... YET.
I'VE JEST STUMBLED ONTO A QUEER DEAL — THE FOUR OF YOU ALL PACKIN' GUNS, AN' A BOY TIED WITH A ROPE, AN' A WOMAN WHO SWEARS BY HIS HONESTY! QUEER, AIN'T THAT?
QUEER OR NOT, IT'S **NONE OF YOUR BUSINESS!**
WHERE I WAS RAISED A WOMAN'S WORD WAS LAW. I AIN'T QUITE OUTGROWED THAT YET.
MEDDLER, WE HAVE A **LAW** HERE SOMETHING **DIFFERENT** FROM **WOMAN'S WHIM** — TAKE CARE YOU DON'T **TRANSGRESS** IT!
TO HELL WITH YOUR LAW!

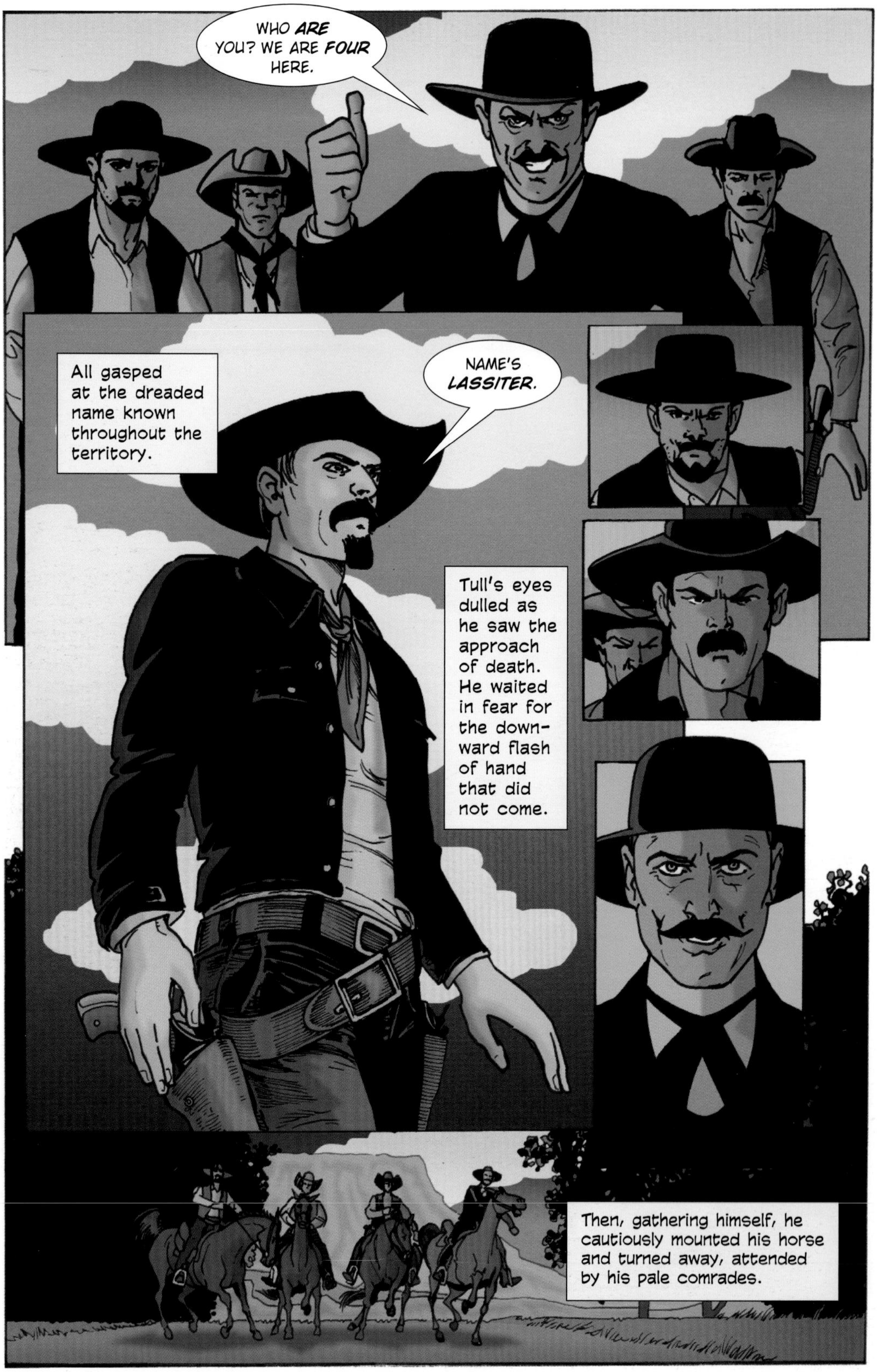
WHO **ARE** YOU? WE ARE **FOUR** HERE.
All gasped at the dreaded name known throughout the territory.
NAME'S **LASSITER.**
Tull's eyes dulled as he saw the approach of death. He waited in fear for the down-ward flash of hand that did not come.
Then, gathering himself, he cautiously mounted his horse and turned away, attended by his pale comrades.

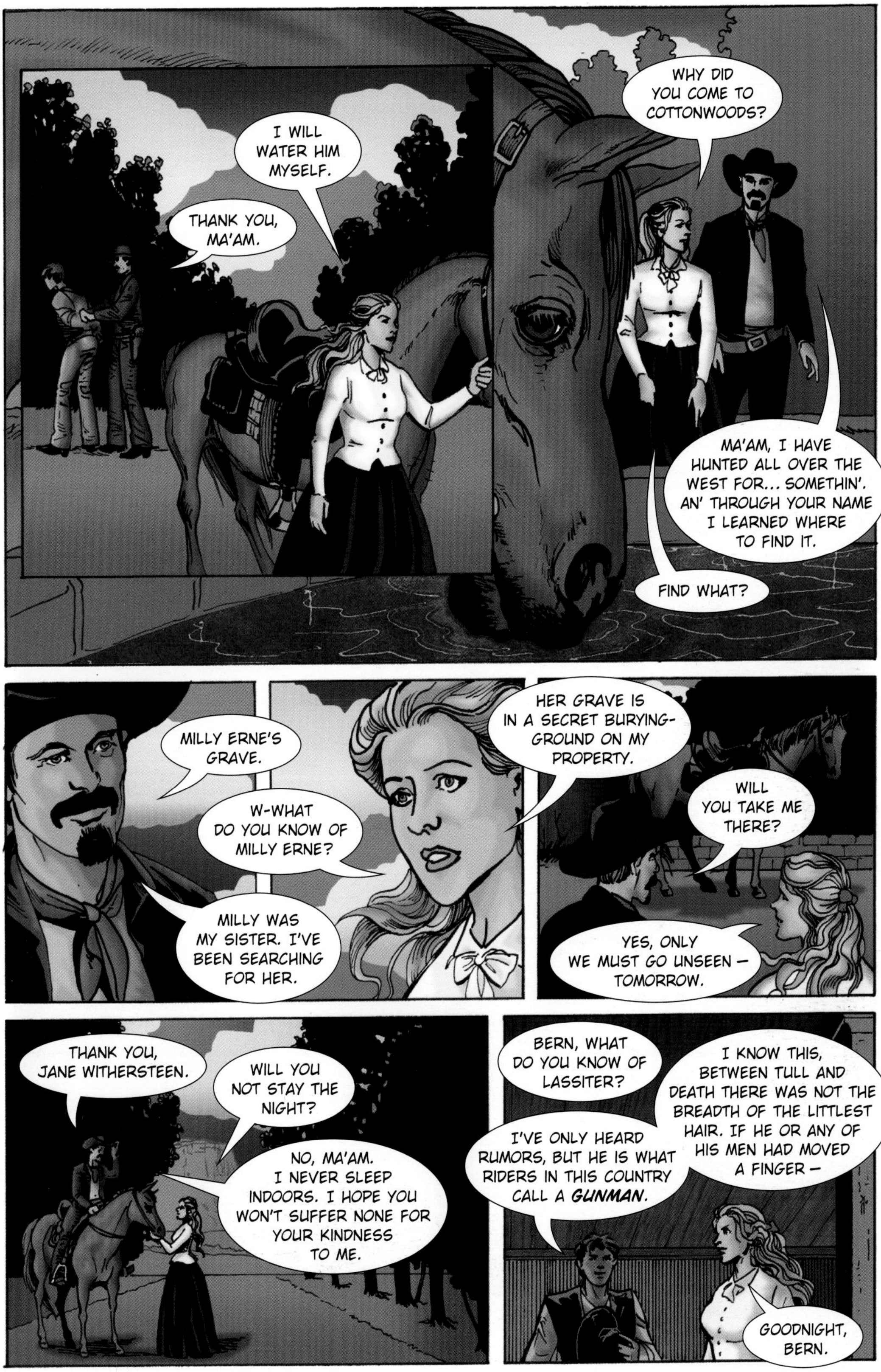
THANK YOU, MA'AM.
I WILL WATER HIM MYSELF.
WHY DID YOU COME TO COTTONWOODS?
MA'AM, I HAVE HUNTED ALL OVER THE WEST FOR... SOMETHIN'. AN' THROUGH YOUR NAME I LEARNED WHERE TO FIND IT.
FIND WHAT?
MILLY ERNE'S GRAVE.
W-WHAT DO YOU KNOW OF MILLY ERNE?
MILLY WAS MY SISTER. I'VE BEEN SEARCHING FOR HER.
HER GRAVE IS IN A SECRET BURYING-GROUND ON MY PROPERTY.
WILL YOU TAKE ME THERE?
YES, ONLY WE MUST GO UNSEEN — TOMORROW.
THANK YOU, JANE WITHERSTEEN.
WILL YOU NOT STAY THE NIGHT?
NO, MA'AM. I NEVER SLEEP INDOORS. I HOPE YOU WON'T SUFFER NONE FOR YOUR KINDNESS TO ME.
BERN, WHAT DO YOU KNOW OF LASSITER?
I'VE ONLY HEARD RUMORS, BUT HE IS WHAT RIDERS IN THIS COUNTRY CALL A ***GUNMAN***.
I KNOW THIS, BETWEEN TULL AND DEATH THERE WAS NOT THE BREADTH OF THE LITTLEST HAIR. IF HE OR ANY OF HIS MEN HAD MOVED A FINGER —
GOODNIGHT, BERN.

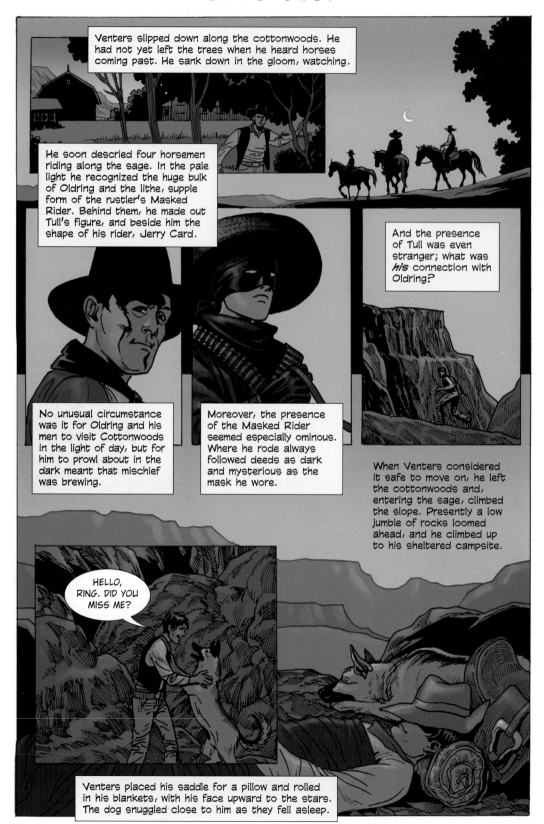

Venters slipped down along the cottonwoods. He had not yet left the trees when he heard horses coming past. He sank down in the gloom, watching.

He soon descried four horsemen riding along the sage. In the pale light he recognized the huge bulk of Oldring and the lithe, supple form of the rustler's Masked Rider. Behind them, he made out Tull's figure, and beside him the shape of his rider, Jerry Card.

And the presence of Tull was even stranger; what was *his* connection with Oldring?

No unusual circumstance was it for Oldring and his men to visit Cottonwoods in the light of day, but for him to prowl about in the dark meant that mischief was brewing.

Moreover, the presence of the Masked Rider seemed especially ominous. Where he rode always followed deeds as dark and mysterious as the mask he wore.

When Venters considered it safe to move on, he left the cottonwoods and, entering the sage, climbed the slope. Presently a low jumble of rocks loomed ahead, and he climbed up to his sheltered campsite.

HELLO, RING. DID YOU MISS ME?

Venters placed his saddle for a pillow and rolled in his blankets, with his face upward to the stars. The dog snuggled close to him as they fell asleep.

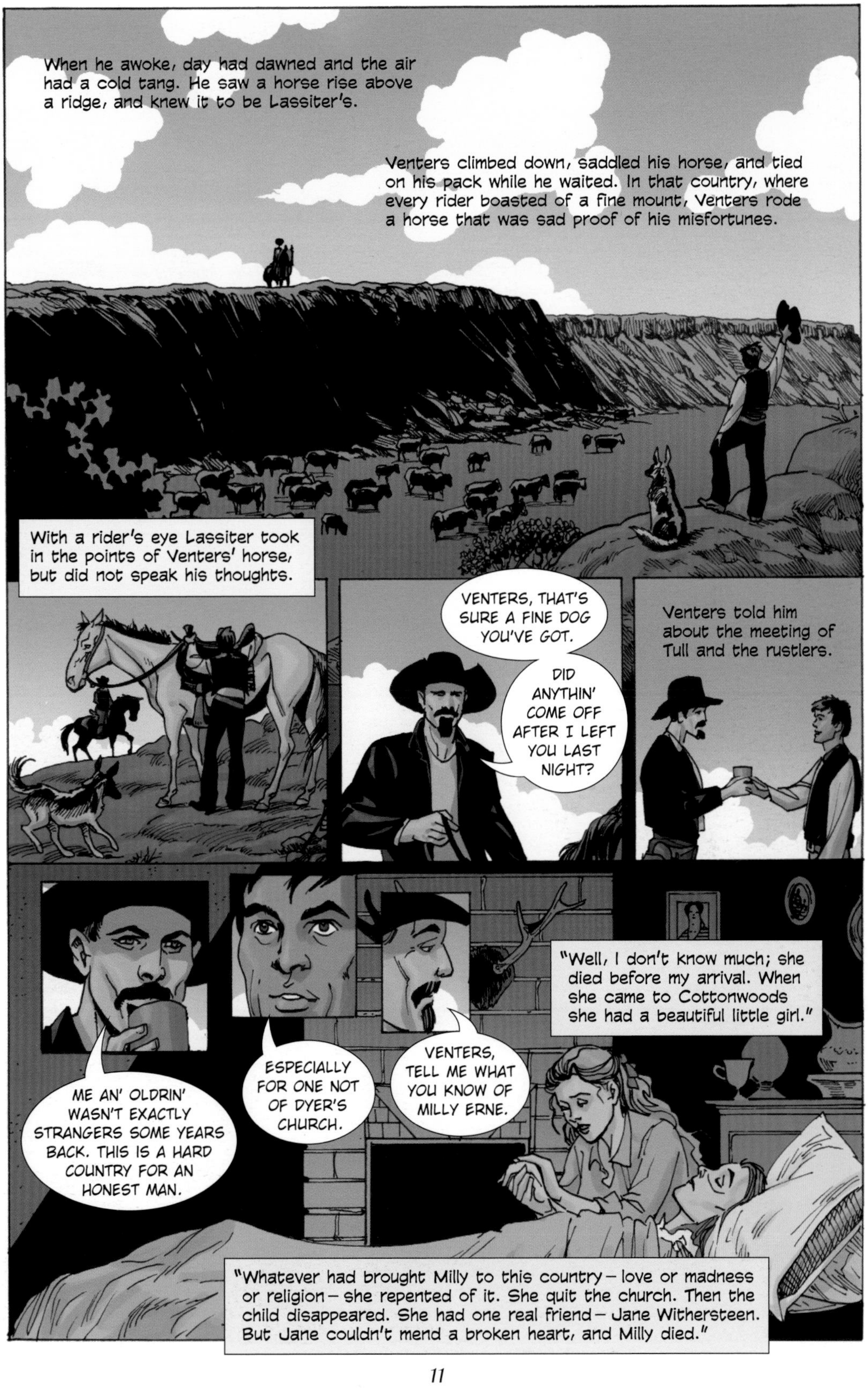

When he awoke, day had dawned and the air had a cold tang. He saw a horse rise above a ridge, and knew it to be Lassiter's.
Venters climbed down, saddled his horse, and tied on his pack while he waited. In that country, where every rider boasted of a fine mount, Venters rode a horse that was sad proof of his misfortunes.
With a rider's eye Lassiter took in the points of Venters' horse, but did not speak his thoughts.
VENTERS, THAT'S SURE A FINE DOG YOU'VE GOT.
DID ANYTHIN' COME OFF AFTER I LEFT YOU LAST NIGHT?
Venters told him about the meeting of Tull and the rustlers.
ME AN' OLDRIN' WASN'T EXACTLY STRANGERS SOME YEARS BACK. THIS IS A HARD COUNTRY FOR AN HONEST MAN.
ESPECIALLY FOR ONE NOT OF DYER'S CHURCH.
VENTERS, TELL ME WHAT YOU KNOW OF MILLY ERNE.
"Well, I don't know much; she died before my arrival. When she came to Cottonwoods she had a beautiful little girl."
"Whatever had brought Milly to this country – love or madness or religion – she repented of it. She quit the church. Then the child disappeared. She had one real friend – Jane Withersteen. But Jane couldn't mend a broken heart, and Milly died."

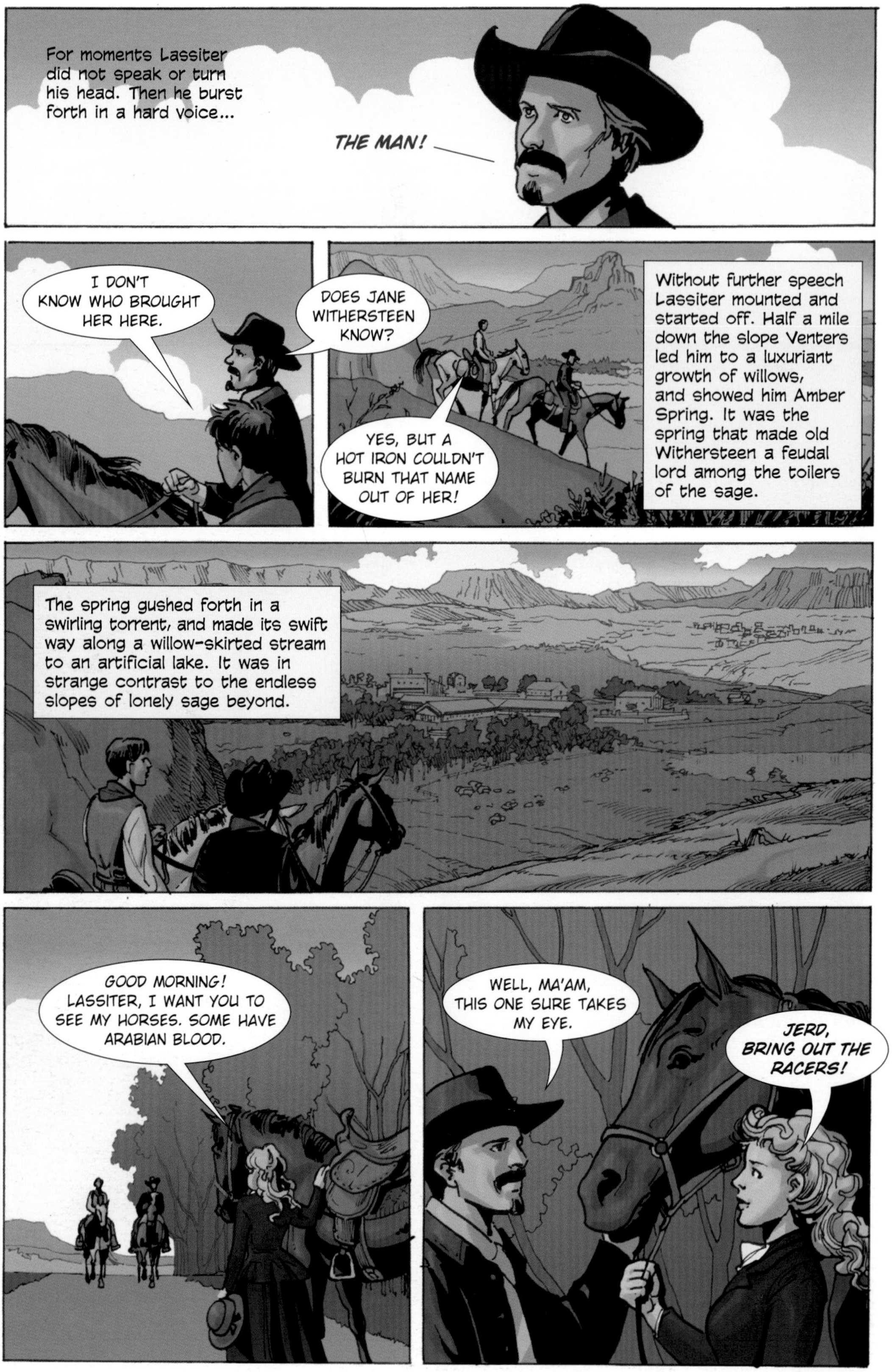
For moments Lassiter did not speak or turn his head. Then he burst forth in a hard voice...
THE MAN!
I DON'T KNOW WHO BROUGHT HER HERE.
DOES JANE WITHERSTEEN KNOW?
YES, BUT A HOT IRON COULDN'T BURN THAT NAME OUT OF HER!
Without further speech Lassiter mounted and started off. Half a mile down the slope Venters led him to a luxuriant growth of willows, and showed him Amber Spring. It was the spring that made old Withersteen a feudal lord among the toilers of the sage.
The spring gushed forth in a swirling torrent, and made its swift way along a willow-skirted stream to an artificial lake. It was in strange contrast to the endless slopes of lonely sage beyond.
GOOD MORNING! LASSITER, I WANT YOU TO SEE MY HORSES. SOME HAVE ARABIAN BLOOD.
WELL, MA'AM, THIS ONE SURE TAKES MY EYE.
JERD, BRING OUT THE RACERS!

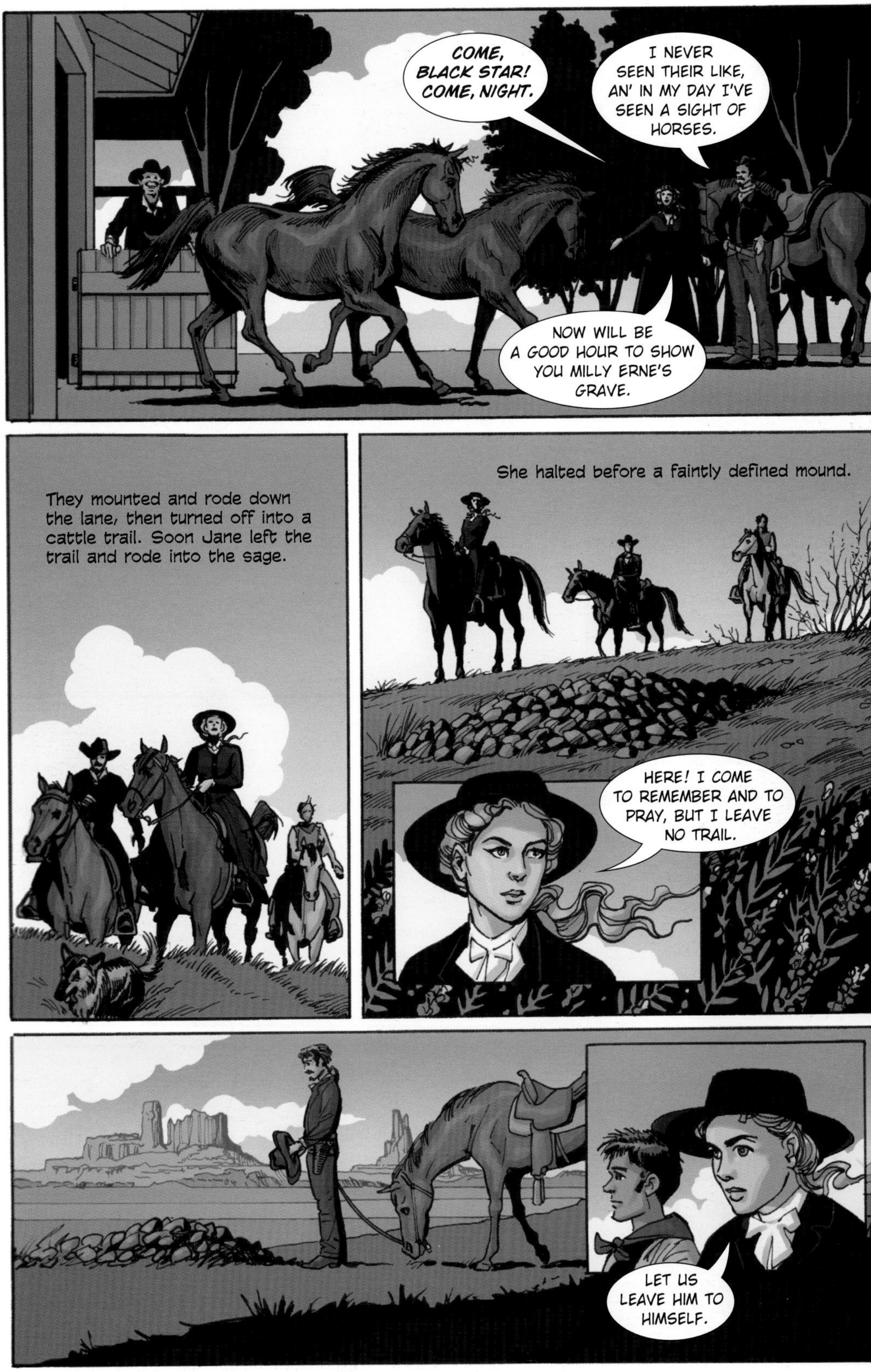
COME, BLACK STAR! COME, NIGHT.
I NEVER SEEN THEIR LIKE, AN' IN MY DAY I'VE SEEN A SIGHT OF HORSES.
NOW WILL BE A GOOD HOUR TO SHOW YOU MILLY ERNE'S GRAVE.
They mounted and rode down the lane, then turned off into a cattle trail. Soon Jane left the trail and rode into the sage.
She halted before a faintly defined mound.
HERE! I COME TO REMEMBER AND TO PRAY, BUT I LEAVE NO TRAIL.
LET US LEAVE HIM TO HIMSELF.

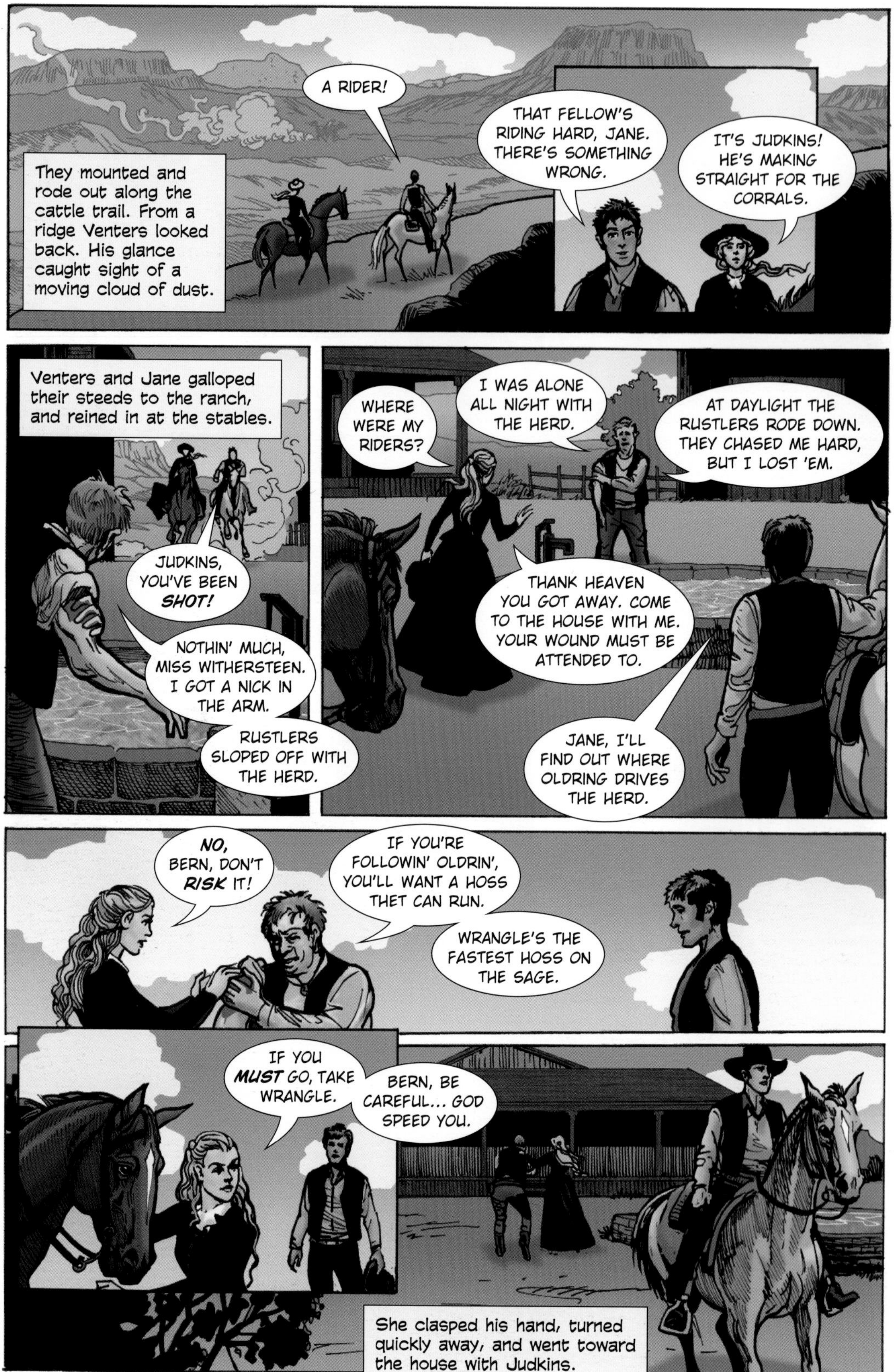

They mounted and rode out along the cattle trail. From a ridge Venters looked back. His glance caught sight of a moving cloud of dust.
A RIDER!
THAT FELLOW'S RIDING HARD, JANE. THERE'S SOMETHING WRONG.
IT'S JUDKINS! HE'S MAKING STRAIGHT FOR THE CORRALS.
Venters and Jane galloped their steeds to the ranch, and reined in at the stables.
JUDKINS, YOU'VE BEEN ***SHOT!***
NOTHIN' MUCH, MISS WITHERSTEEN. I GOT A NICK IN THE ARM.
RUSTLERS SLOPED OFF WITH THE HERD.
WHERE WERE MY RIDERS?
I WAS ALONE ALL NIGHT WITH THE HERD.
AT DAYLIGHT THE RUSTLERS RODE DOWN. THEY CHASED ME HARD, BUT I LOST 'EM.
THANK HEAVEN YOU GOT AWAY. COME TO THE HOUSE WITH ME. YOUR WOUND MUST BE ATTENDED TO.
JANE, I'LL FIND OUT WHERE OLDRING DRIVES THE HERD.
NO, BERN, DON'T ***RISK*** IT!
IF YOU'RE FOLLOWIN' OLDRIN', YOU'LL WANT A HOSS THET CAN RUN.
WRANGLE'S THE FASTEST HOSS ON THE SAGE.
IF YOU ***MUST*** GO, TAKE WRANGLE.
BERN, BE CAREFUL... GOD SPEED YOU.
She clasped his hand, turned quickly away, and went toward the house with Judkins.

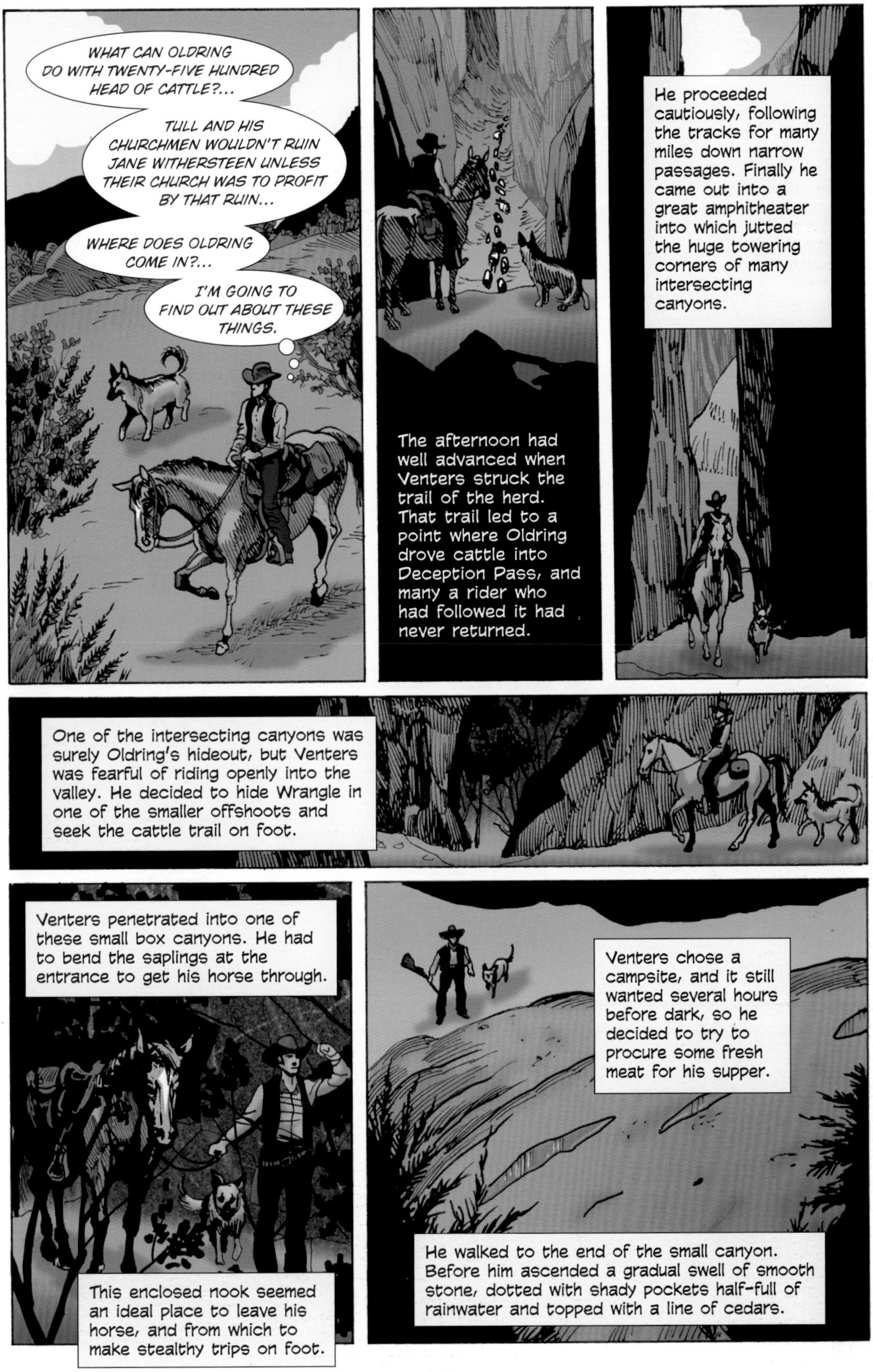
WHAT CAN OLDRING DO WITH TWENTY-FIVE HUNDRED HEAD OF CATTLE?...
TULL AND HIS CHURCHMEN WOULDN'T RUIN JANE WITHERSTEEN UNLESS THEIR CHURCH WAS TO PROFIT BY THAT RUIN...
WHERE DOES OLDRING COME IN?...
I'M GOING TO FIND OUT ABOUT THESE THINGS.
The afternoon had well advanced when Venters struck the trail of the herd. That trail led to a point where Oldring drove cattle into Deception Pass, and many a rider who had followed it had never returned.
He proceeded cautiously, following the tracks for many miles down narrow passages. Finally he came out into a great amphitheater into which jutted the huge towering corners of many intersecting canyons.
One of the intersecting canyons was surely Oldring's hideout, but Venters was fearful of riding openly into the valley. He decided to hide Wrangle in one of the smaller offshoots and seek the cattle trail on foot.
Venters penetrated into one of these small box canyons. He had to bend the saplings at the entrance to get his horse through.
This enclosed nook seemed an ideal place to leave his horse, and from which to make stealthy trips on foot.
Venters chose a campsite, and it still wanted several hours before dark, so he decided to try to procure some fresh meat for his supper.
He walked to the end of the small canyon. Before him ascended a gradual swell of smooth stone, dotted with shady pockets half-full of rainwater and topped with a line of cedars.

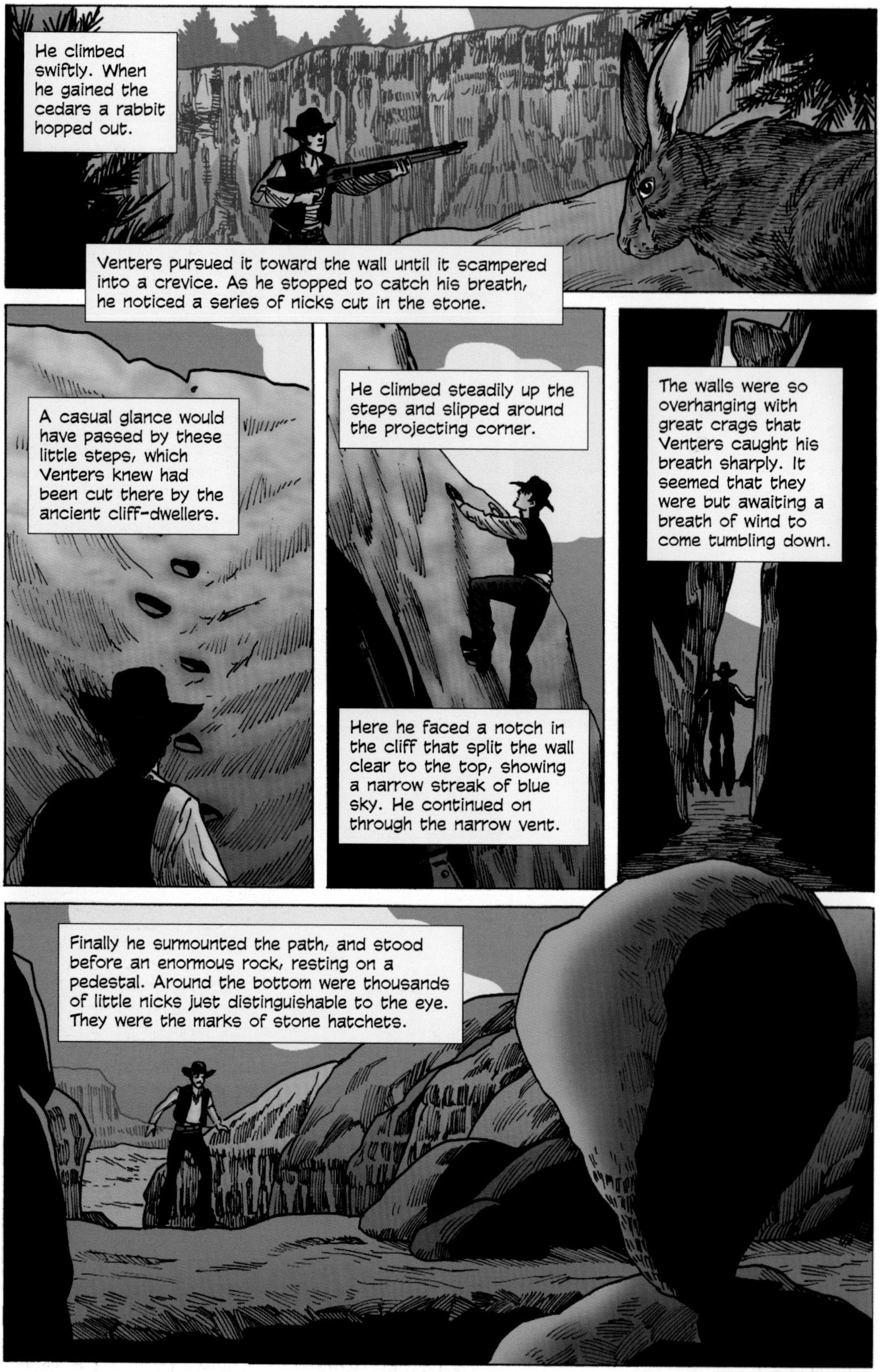
He climbed swiftly. When he gained the cedars a rabbit hopped out.
Venters pursued it toward the wall until it scampered into a crevice. As he stopped to catch his breath, he noticed a series of nicks cut in the stone.
A casual glance would have passed by these little steps, which Venters knew had been cut there by the ancient cliff-dwellers.
He climbed steadily up the steps and slipped around the projecting corner.
Here he faced a notch in the cliff that split the wall clear to the top, showing a narrow streak of blue sky. He continued on through the narrow vent.
The walls were so overhanging with great crags that Venters caught his breath sharply. It seemed that they were but awaiting a breath of wind to come tumbling down.
Finally he surmounted the path, and stood before an enormous rock, resting on a pedestal. Around the bottom were thousands of little nicks just distinguishable to the eye. They were the marks of stone hatchets.

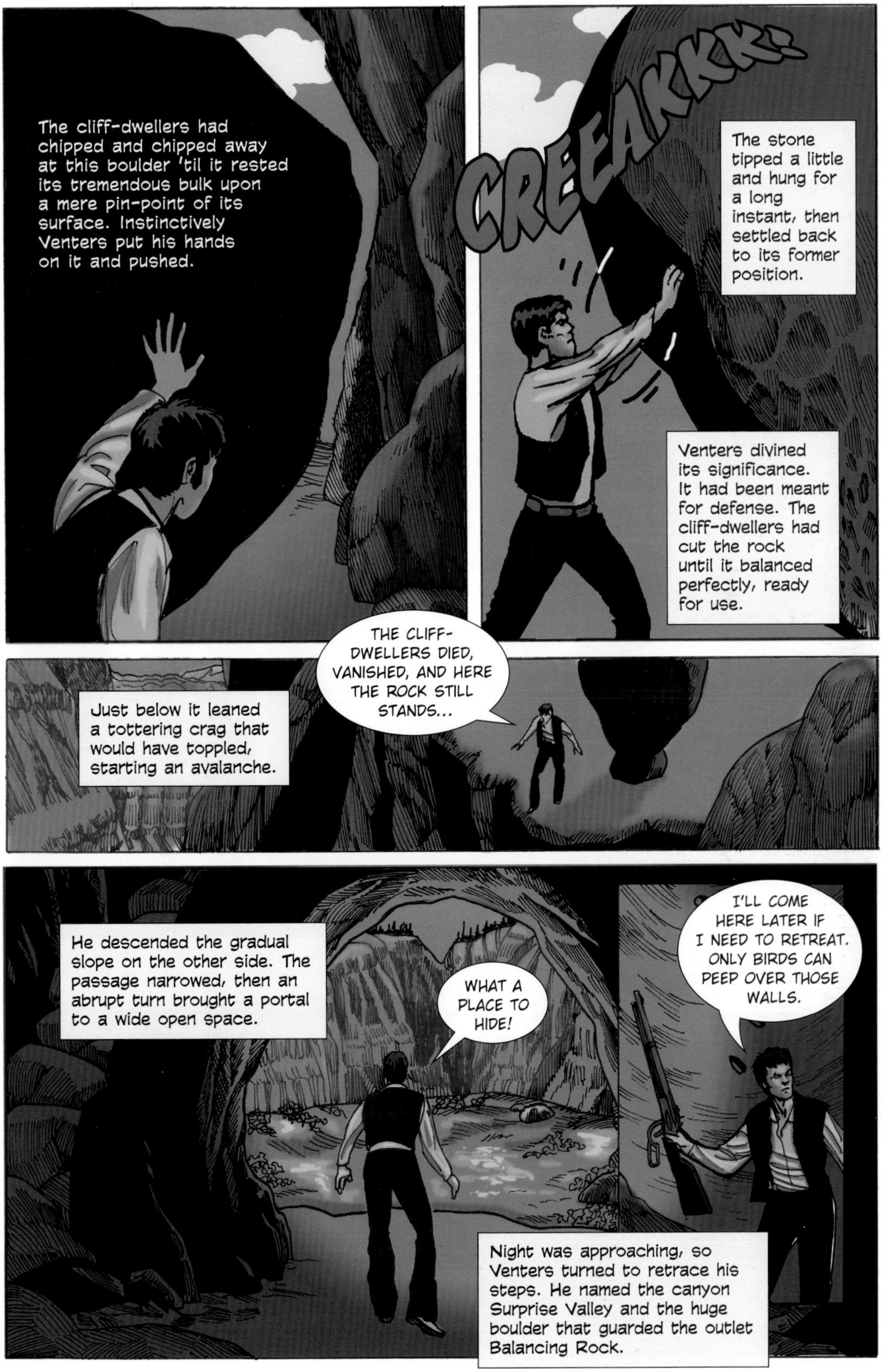
The cliff-dwellers had chipped and chipped away at this boulder 'til it rested its tremendous bulk upon a mere pin-point of its surface. Instinctively Venters put his hands on it and pushed.
CREEAKKK!
The stone tipped a little and hung for a long instant, then settled back to its former position.
Venters divined its significance. It had been meant for defense. The cliff-dwellers had cut the rock until it balanced perfectly, ready for use.
Just below it leaned a tottering crag that would have toppled, starting an avalanche.
THE CLIFF-DWELLERS DIED, VANISHED, AND HERE THE ROCK STILL STANDS...
He descended the gradual slope on the other side. The passage narrowed, then an abrupt turn brought a portal to a wide open space.
WHAT A PLACE TO HIDE!
I'LL COME HERE LATER IF I NEED TO RETREAT. ONLY BIRDS CAN PEEP OVER THOSE WALLS.
Night was approaching, so Venters turned to retrace his steps. He named the canyon Surprise Valley and the huge boulder that guarded the outlet Balancing Rock.

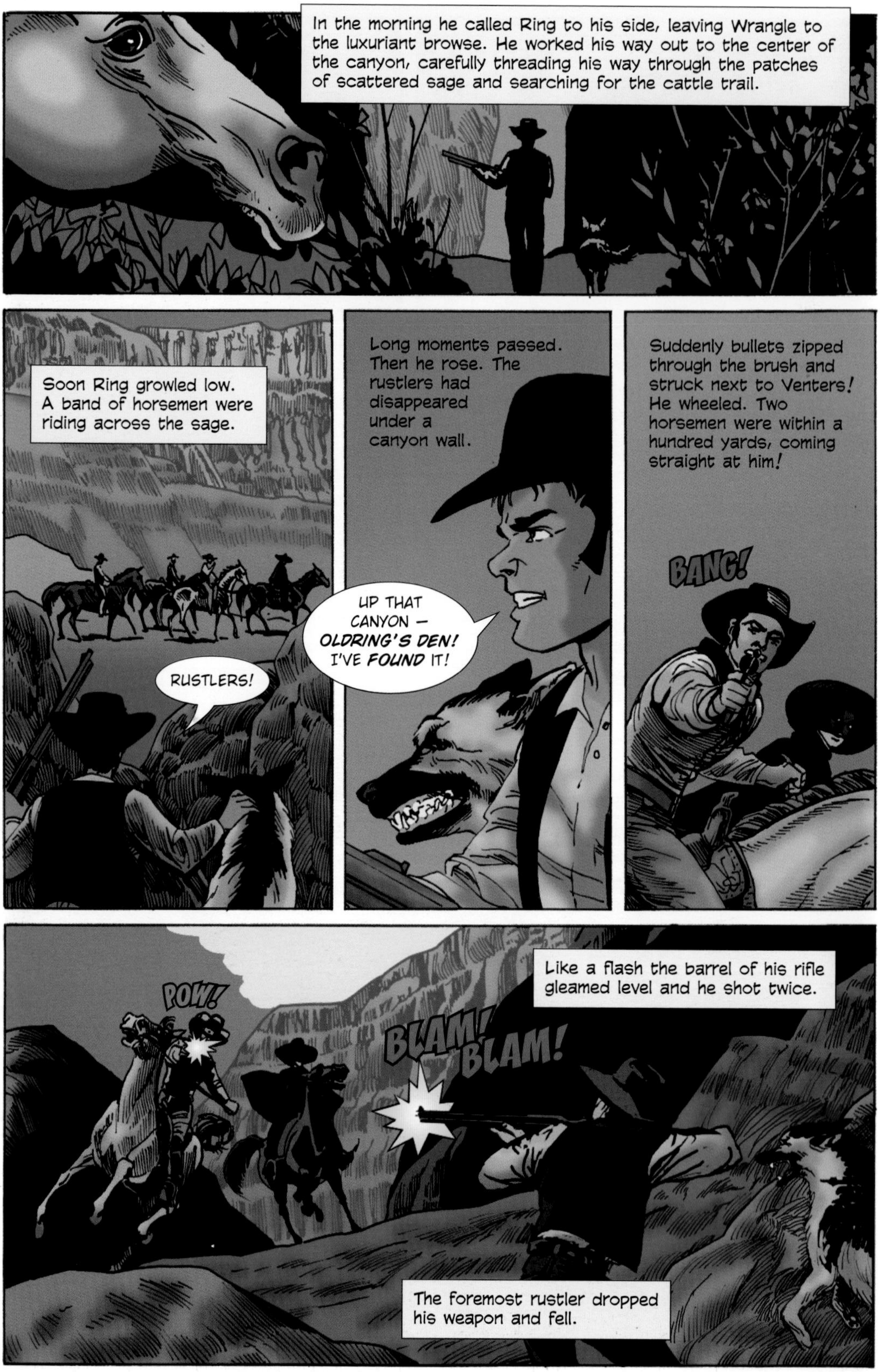
In the morning he called Ring to his side, leaving Wrangle to the luxuriant browse. He worked his way out to the center of the canyon, carefully threading his way through the patches of scattered sage and searching for the cattle trail.
Soon Ring growled low. A band of horsemen were riding across the sage.
RUSTLERS!
Long moments passed. Then he rose. The rustlers had disappeared under a canyon wall.
UP THAT CANYON — OLDRING'S DEN! I'VE FOUND IT!
Suddenly bullets zipped through the brush and struck next to Venters! He wheeled. Two horsemen were within a hundred yards, coming straight at him!
BANG!
Like a flash the barrel of his rifle gleamed level and he shot twice.
POW!
BLAM! BLAM!
The foremost rustler dropped his weapon and fell.

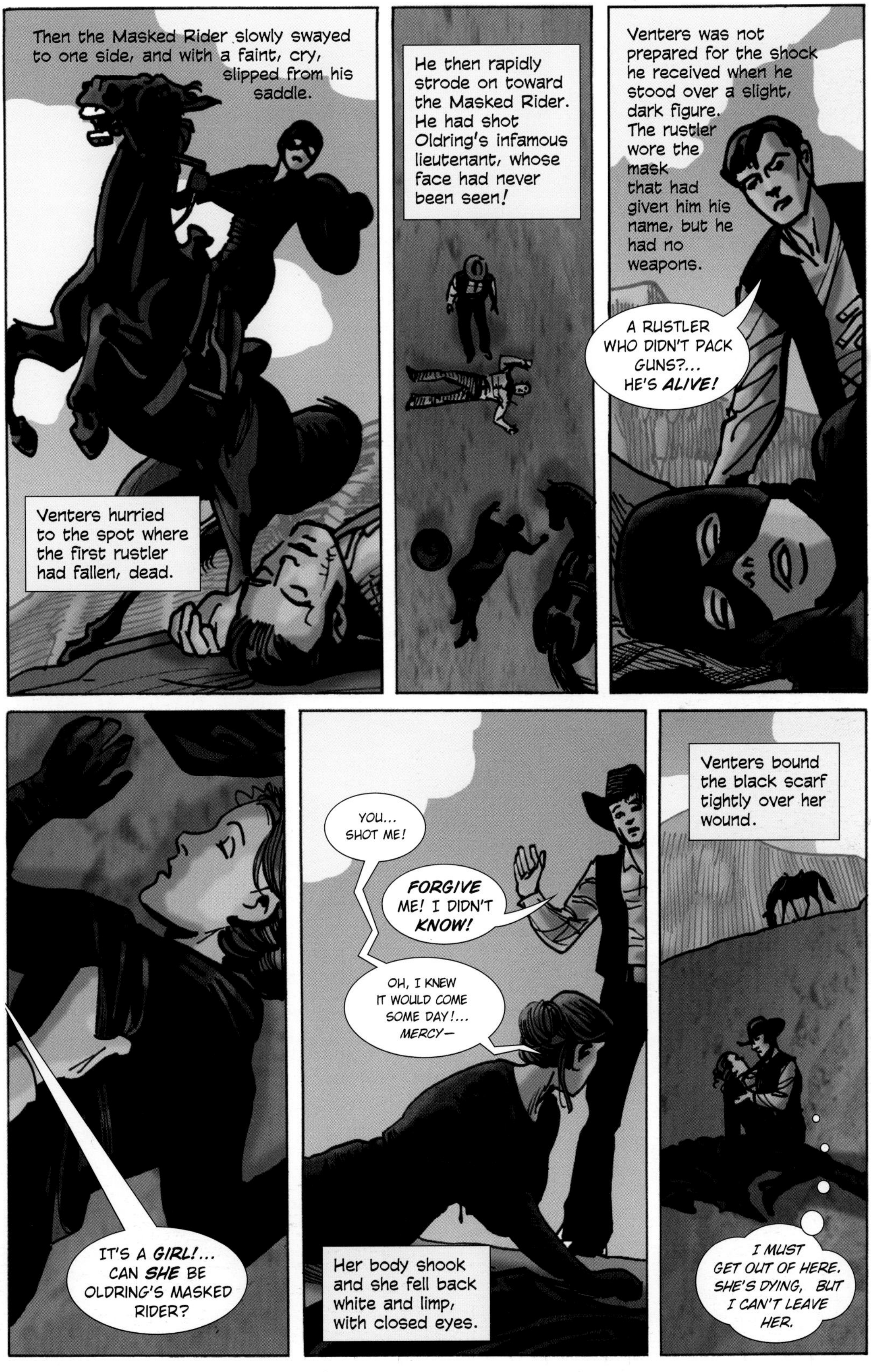
Then the Masked Rider slowly swayed to one side, and with a faint, cry, slipped from his saddle.
Venters hurried to the spot where the first rustler had fallen, dead.
He then rapidly strode on toward the Masked Rider. He had shot Oldring's infamous lieutenant, whose face had never been seen!
Venters was not prepared for the shock he received when he stood over a slight, dark figure. The rustler wore the mask that had given him his name, but he had no weapons.
A RUSTLER WHO DIDN'T PACK GUNS?... HE'S ALIVE!
IT'S A GIRL!... CAN SHE BE OLDRING'S MASKED RIDER?
YOU... SHOT ME!
FORGIVE ME! I DIDN'T KNOW!
OH, I KNEW IT WOULD COME SOME DAY!... MERCY—
Her body shook and she fell back white and limp, with closed eyes.
Venters bound the black scarf tightly over her wound.
I MUST GET OUT OF HERE. SHE'S DYING, BUT I CAN'T LEAVE HER.

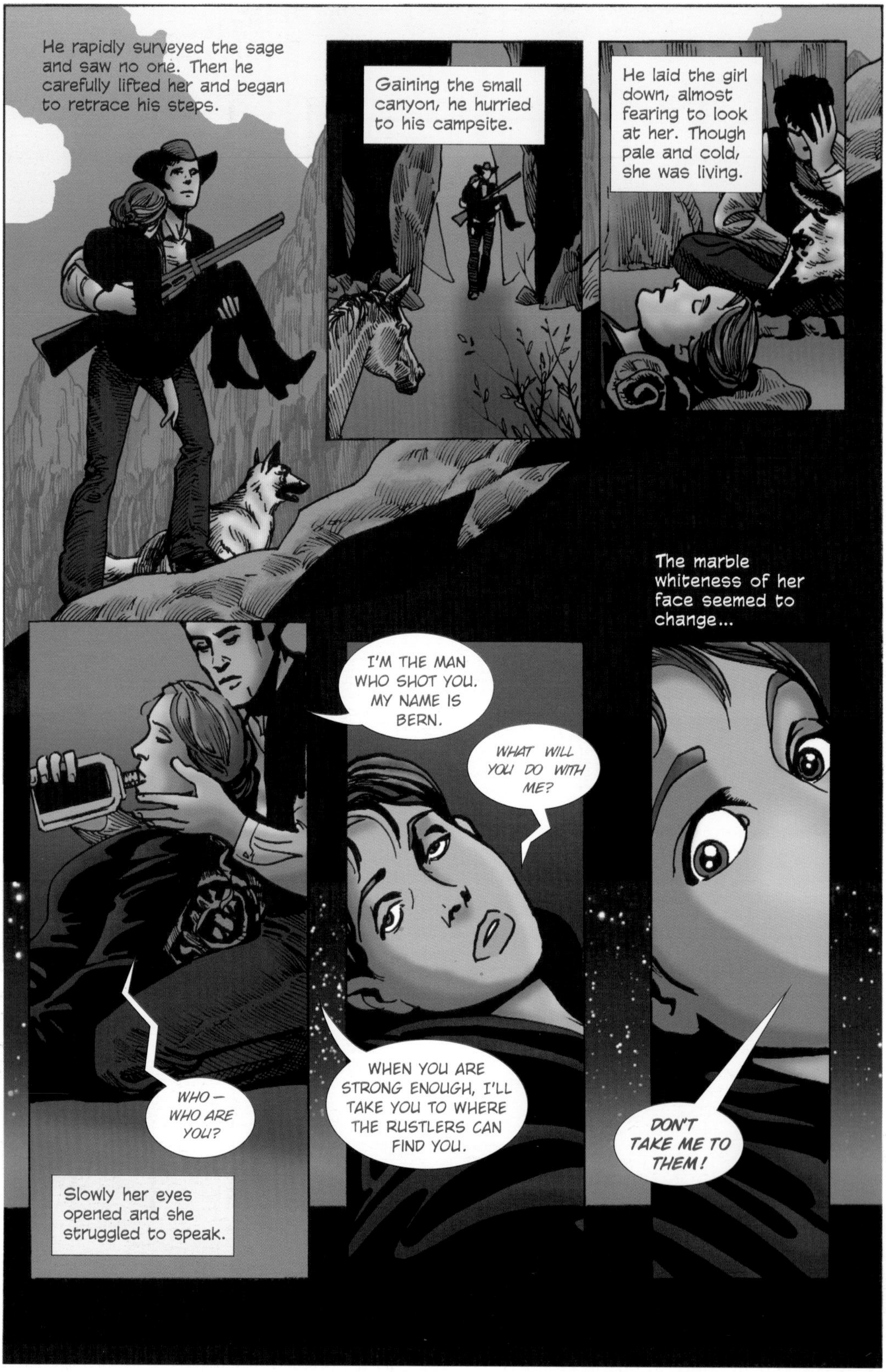
He rapidly surveyed the sage and saw no one. Then he carefully lifted her and began to retrace his steps.
Gaining the small canyon, he hurried to his campsite.
He laid the girl down, almost fearing to look at her. Though pale and cold, she was living.
The marble whiteness of her face seemed to change...
WHO— WHO ARE YOU?
Slowly her eyes opened and she struggled to speak.
I'M THE MAN WHO SHOT YOU. MY NAME IS BERN.
WHAT WILL YOU DO WITH ME?
WHEN YOU ARE STRONG ENOUGH, I'LL TAKE YOU TO WHERE THE RUSTLERS CAN FIND YOU.
DON'T TAKE ME TO THEM!

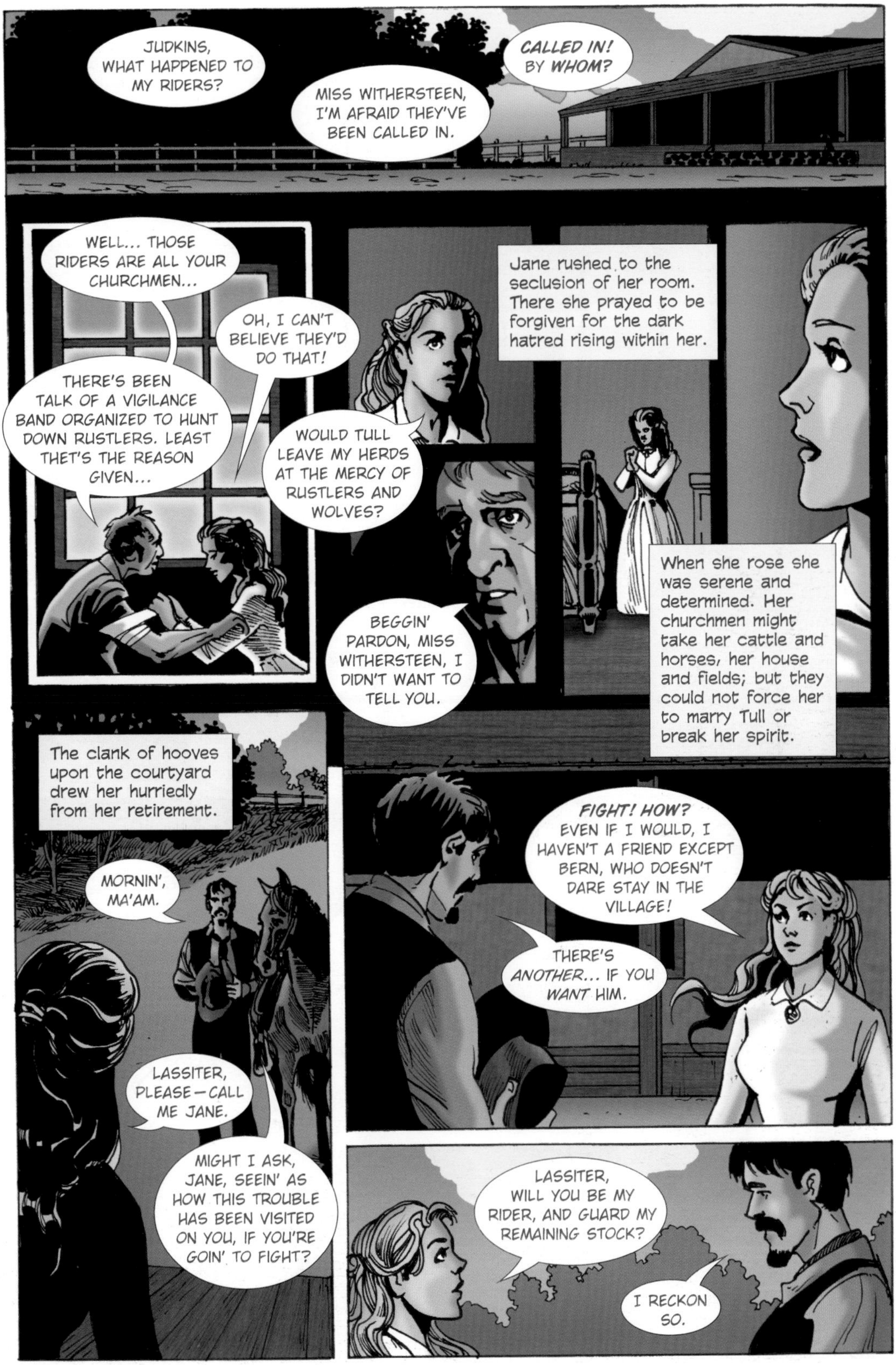
JUDKINS, WHAT HAPPENED TO MY RIDERS?
MISS WITHERSTEEN, I'M AFRAID THEY'VE BEEN CALLED IN.
CALLED IN! BY WHOM?
WELL... THOSE RIDERS ARE ALL YOUR CHURCHMEN...
THERE'S BEEN TALK OF A VIGILANCE BAND ORGANIZED TO HUNT DOWN RUSTLERS. LEAST THET'S THE REASON GIVEN...
OH, I CAN'T BELIEVE THEY'D DO THAT!
WOULD TULL LEAVE MY HERDS AT THE MERCY OF RUSTLERS AND WOLVES?
BEGGIN' PARDON, MISS WITHERSTEEN, I DIDN'T WANT TO TELL YOU.
Jane rushed to the seclusion of her room. There she prayed to be forgiven for the dark hatred rising within her.
When she rose she was serene and determined. Her churchmen might take her cattle and horses, her house and fields; but they could not force her to marry Tull or break her spirit.
The clank of hooves upon the courtyard drew her hurriedly from her retirement.
MORNIN', MA'AM.
LASSITER, PLEASE—CALL ME JANE.
MIGHT I ASK, JANE, SEEIN' AS HOW THIS TROUBLE HAS BEEN VISITED ON YOU, IF YOU'RE GOIN' TO FIGHT?
FIGHT! HOW? EVEN IF I WOULD, I HAVEN'T A FRIEND EXCEPT BERN, WHO DOESN'T DARE STAY IN THE VILLAGE!
THERE'S ANOTHER... IF YOU WANT HIM.
LASSITER, WILL YOU BE MY RIDER, AND GUARD MY REMAINING STOCK?
I RECKON SO.

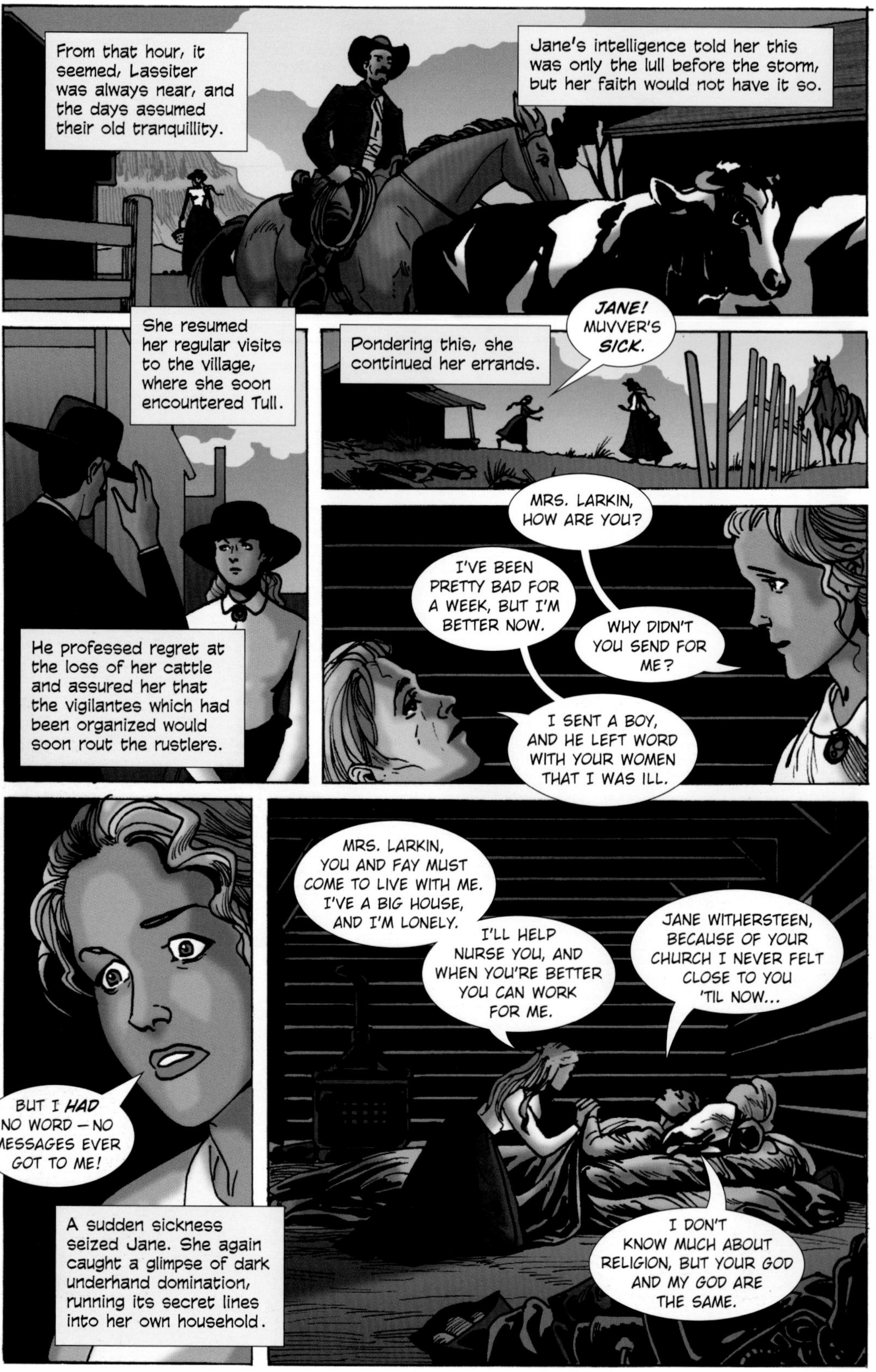
From that hour, it seemed, Lassiter was always near, and the days assumed their old tranquillity.
Jane's intelligence told her this was only the lull before the storm, but her faith would not have it so.
She resumed her regular visits to the village, where she soon encountered Tull.
He professed regret at the loss of her cattle and assured her that the vigilantes which had been organized would soon rout the rustlers.
Pondering this, she continued her errands.
JANE! MUVVER'S SICK.
MRS. LARKIN, HOW ARE YOU?
I'VE BEEN PRETTY BAD FOR A WEEK, BUT I'M BETTER NOW.
WHY DIDN'T YOU SEND FOR ME?
I SENT A BOY, AND HE LEFT WORD WITH YOUR WOMEN THAT I WAS ILL.
BUT I HAD NO WORD — NO MESSAGES EVER GOT TO ME!
A sudden sickness seized Jane. She again caught a glimpse of dark underhand domination, running its secret lines into her own household.
MRS. LARKIN, YOU AND FAY MUST COME TO LIVE WITH ME. I'VE A BIG HOUSE, AND I'M LONELY.
I'LL HELP NURSE YOU, AND WHEN YOU'RE BETTER YOU CAN WORK FOR ME.
JANE WITHERSTEEN, BECAUSE OF YOUR CHURCH I NEVER FELT CLOSE TO YOU 'TIL NOW...
I DON'T KNOW MUCH ABOUT RELIGION, BUT YOUR GOD AND MY GOD ARE THE SAME.

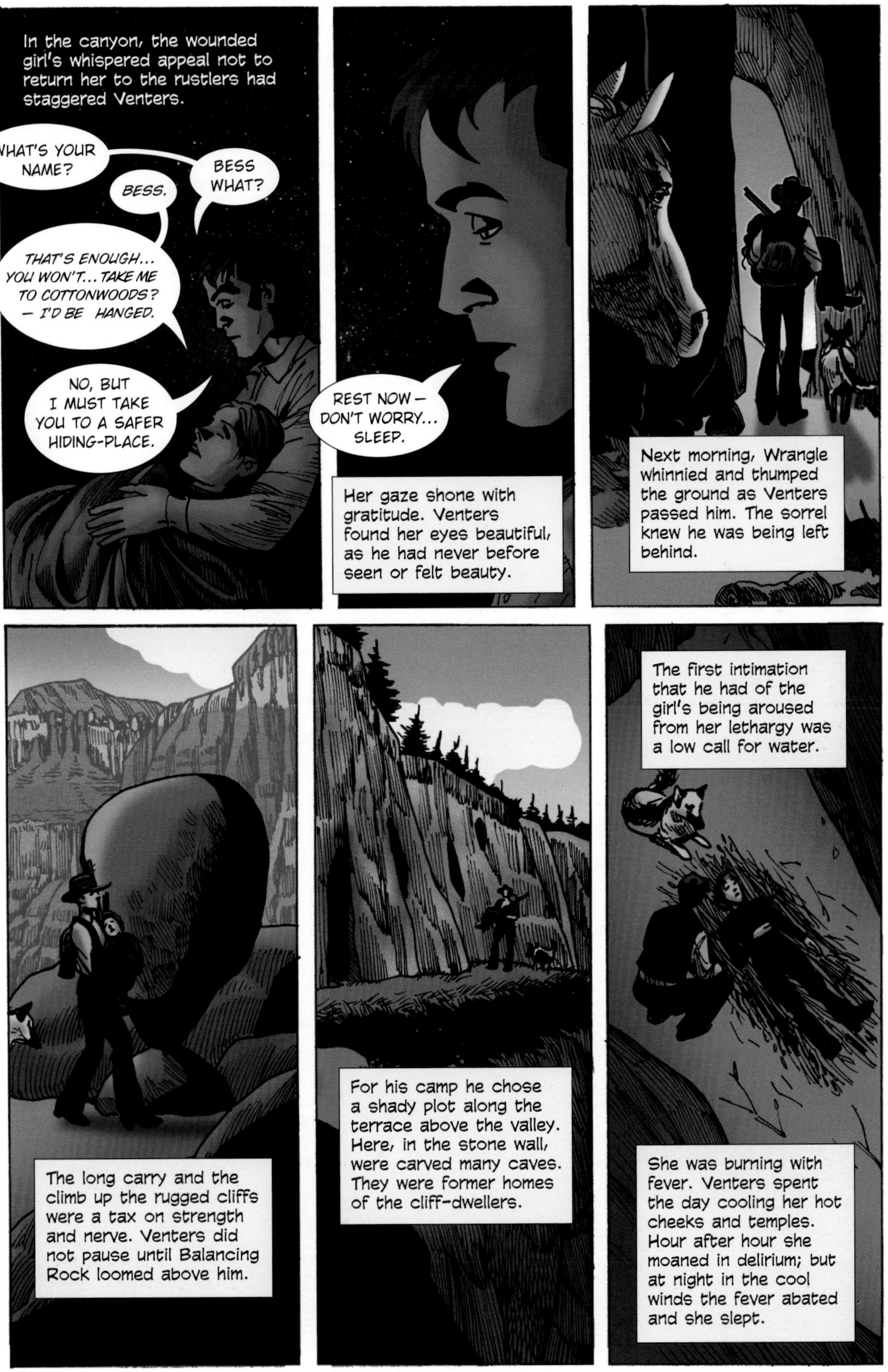
In the canyon, the wounded girl's whispered appeal not to return her to the rustlers had staggered Venters.
WHAT'S YOUR NAME?
BESS.
BESS WHAT?
THAT'S ENOUGH... YOU WON'T... TAKE ME TO COTTONWOODS? — I'D BE HANGED.
NO, BUT I MUST TAKE YOU TO A SAFER HIDING-PLACE.
REST NOW — DON'T WORRY... SLEEP.
Her gaze shone with gratitude. Venters found her eyes beautiful, as he had never before seen or felt beauty.
Next morning, Wrangle whinnied and thumped the ground as Venters passed him. The sorrel knew he was being left behind.
The long carry and the climb up the rugged cliffs were a tax on strength and nerve. Venters did not pause until Balancing Rock loomed above him.
For his camp he chose a shady plot along the terrace above the valley. Here, in the stone wall, were carved many caves. They were former homes of the cliff-dwellers.
The first intimation that he had of the girl's being aroused from her lethargy was a low call for water.
She was burning with fever. Venters spent the day cooling her hot cheeks and temples. Hour after hour she moaned in delirium; but at night in the cool winds the fever abated and she slept.

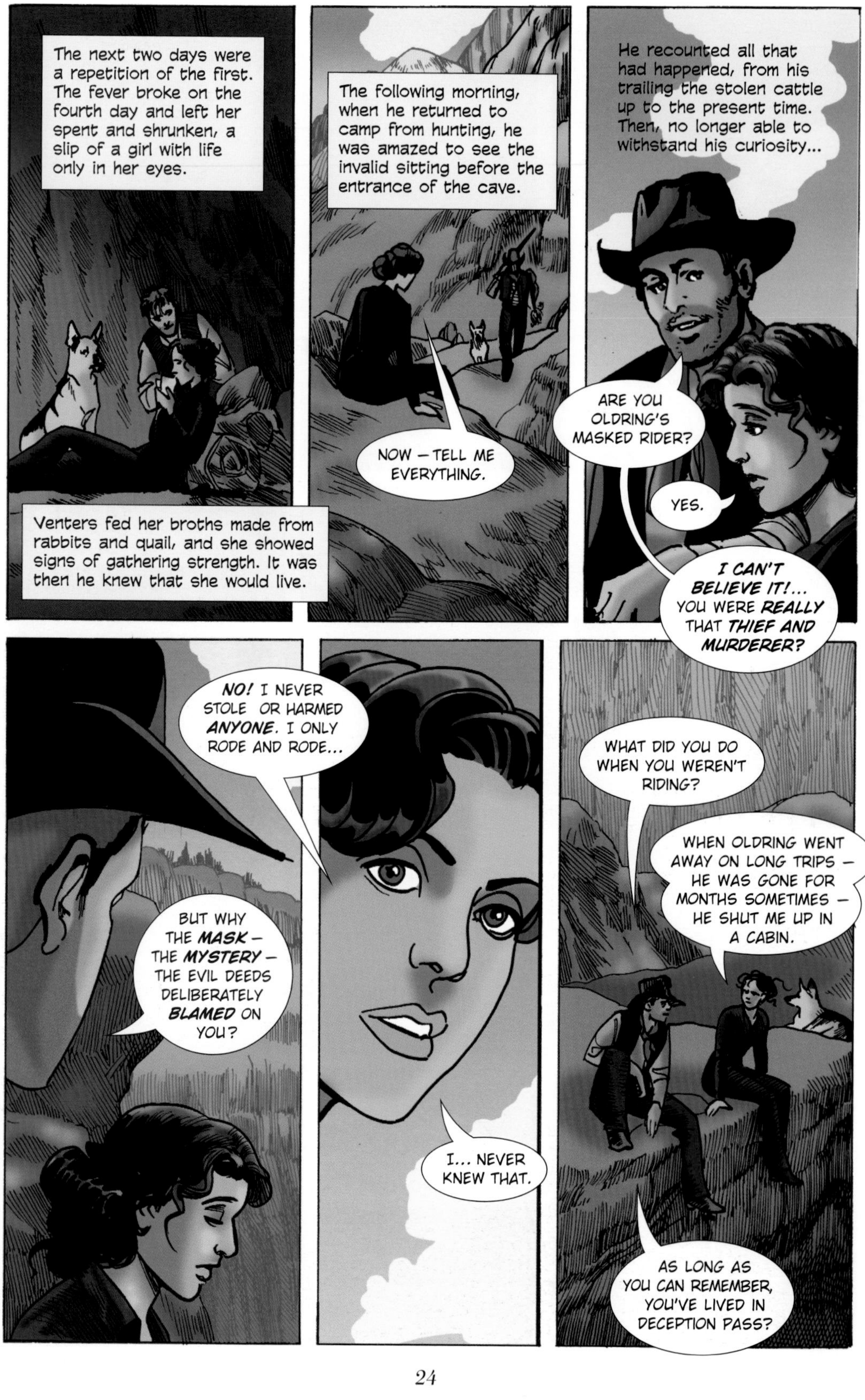

The next two days were a repetition of the first. The fever broke on the fourth day and left her spent and shrunken, a slip of a girl with life only in her eyes.
Venters fed her broths made from rabbits and quail, and she showed signs of gathering strength. It was then he knew that she would live.
The following morning, when he returned to camp from hunting, he was amazed to see the invalid sitting before the entrance of the cave.
NOW — TELL ME EVERYTHING.
He recounted all that had happened, from his trailing the stolen cattle up to the present time. Then, no longer able to withstand his curiosity...
ARE YOU OLDRING'S MASKED RIDER?
YES.
I CAN'T BELIEVE IT!... YOU WERE REALLY THAT THIEF AND MURDERER?
NO! I NEVER STOLE OR HARMED ANYONE. I ONLY RODE AND RODE...
BUT WHY THE MASK — THE MYSTERY — THE EVIL DEEDS DELIBERATELY BLAMED ON YOU?
I... NEVER KNEW THAT.
WHAT DID YOU DO WHEN YOU WEREN'T RIDING?
WHEN OLDRING WENT AWAY ON LONG TRIPS — HE WAS GONE FOR MONTHS SOMETIMES — HE SHUT ME UP IN A CABIN.
AS LONG AS YOU CAN REMEMBER, YOU'VE LIVED IN DECEPTION PASS?

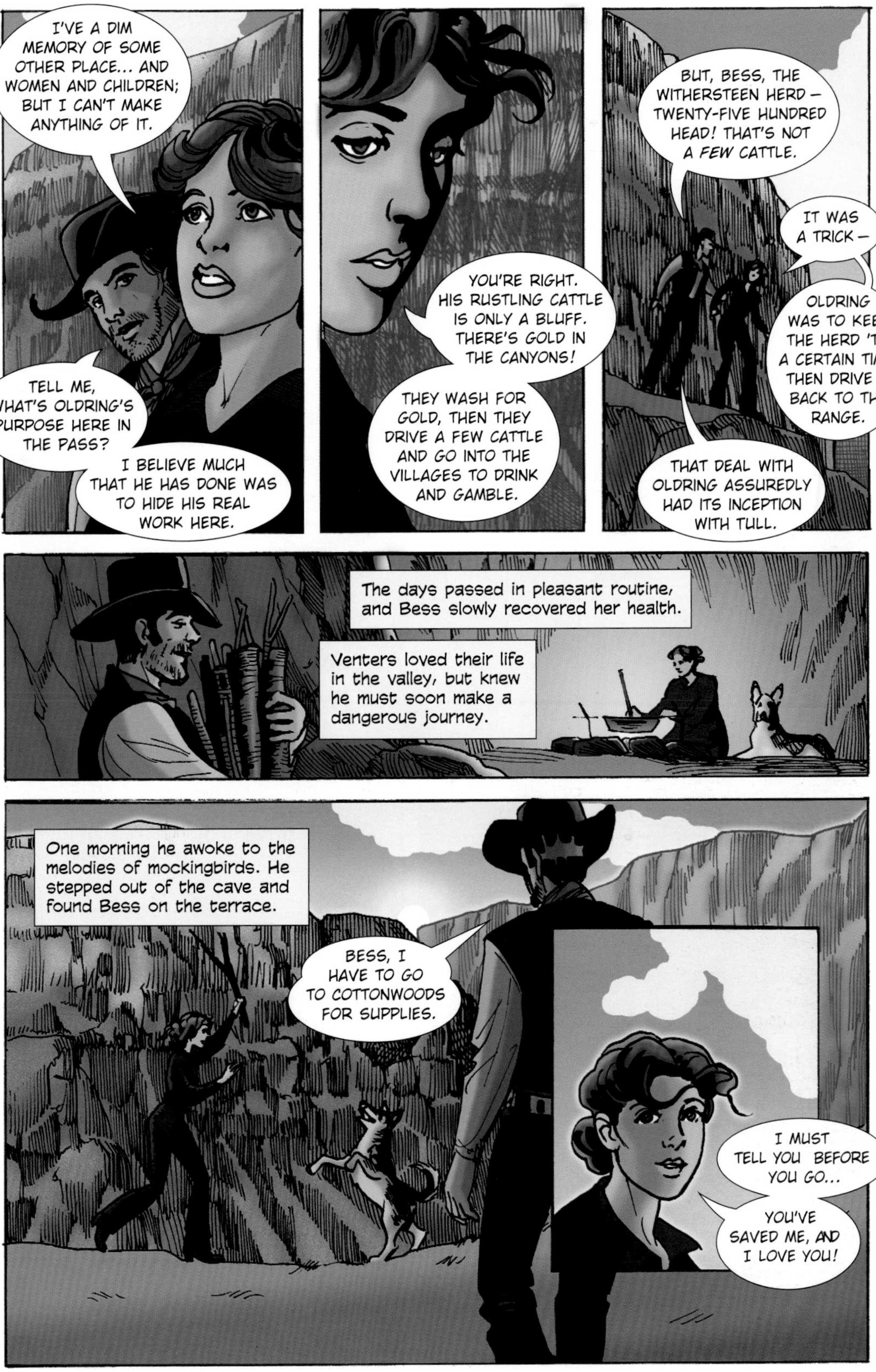
I'VE A DIM MEMORY OF SOME OTHER PLACE... AND WOMEN AND CHILDREN; BUT I CAN'T MAKE ANYTHING OF IT.
TELL ME, WHAT'S OLDRING'S PURPOSE HERE IN THE PASS?
I BELIEVE MUCH THAT HE HAS DONE WAS TO HIDE HIS REAL WORK HERE.
YOU'RE RIGHT. HIS RUSTLING CATTLE IS ONLY A BLUFF. THERE'S GOLD IN THE CANYONS!
THEY WASH FOR GOLD, THEN THEY DRIVE A FEW CATTLE AND GO INTO THE VILLAGES TO DRINK AND GAMBLE.
BUT, BESS, THE WITHERSTEEN HERD — TWENTY-FIVE HUNDRED HEAD! THAT'S NOT A *FEW* CATTLE.
IT WAS A TRICK —
OLDRING WAS TO KEEP THE HERD 'TIL A CERTAIN TIME, THEN DRIVE IT BACK TO THE RANGE.
THAT DEAL WITH OLDRING ASSUREDLY HAD ITS INCEPTION WITH TULL.
The days passed in pleasant routine, and Bess slowly recovered her health.
Venters loved their life in the valley, but knew he must soon make a dangerous journey.
One morning he awoke to the melodies of mockingbirds. He stepped out of the cave and found Bess on the terrace.
BESS, I HAVE TO GO TO COTTONWOODS FOR SUPPLIES.
I MUST TELL YOU BEFORE YOU GO...
YOU'VE SAVED ME, AND I LOVE YOU!

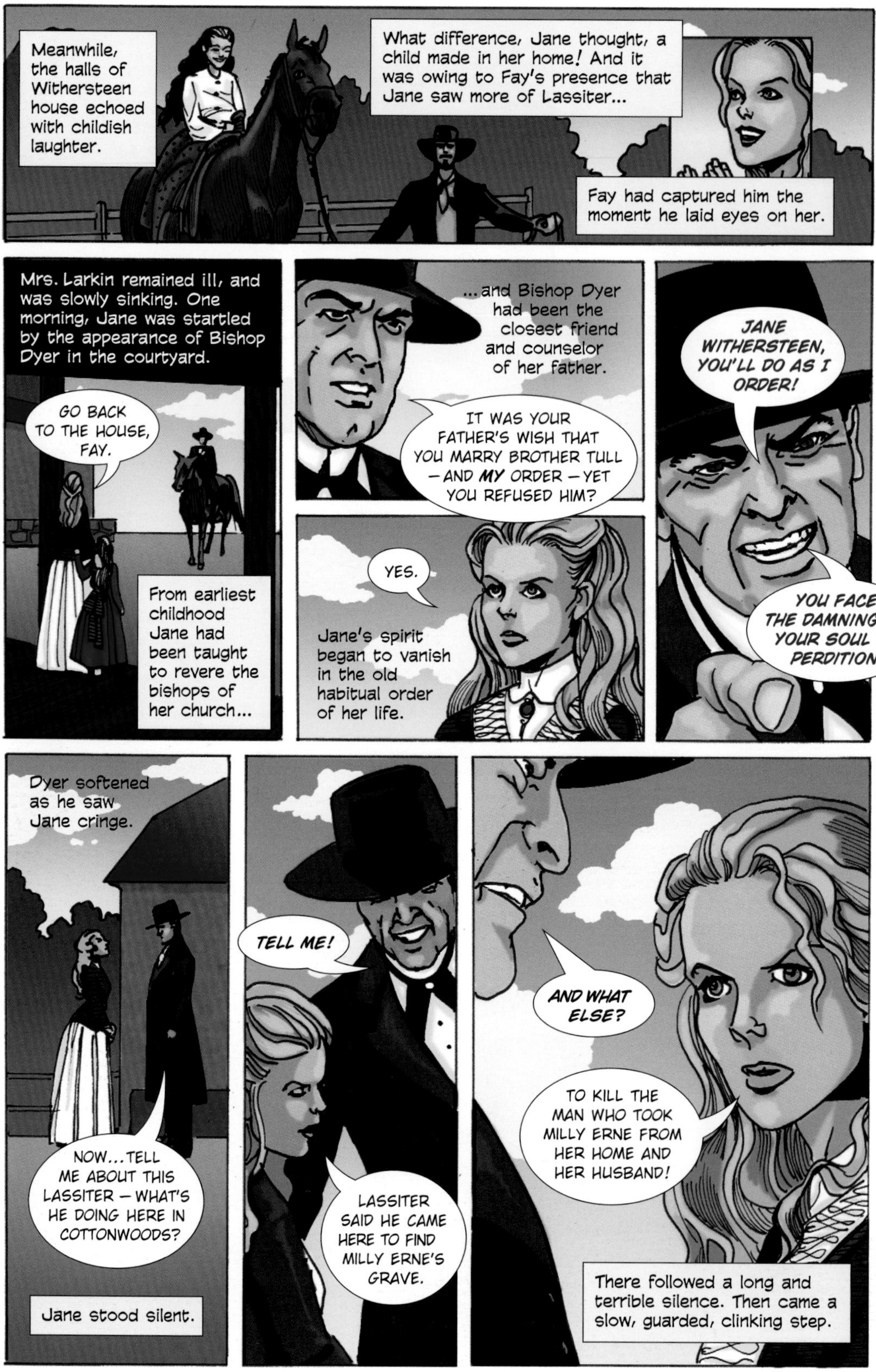
Meanwhile, the halls of Withersteen house echoed with childish laughter.
What difference, Jane thought, a child made in her home! And it was owing to Fay's presence that Jane saw more of Lassiter...
Fay had captured him the moment he laid eyes on her.
Mrs. Larkin remained ill, and was slowly sinking. One morning, Jane was startled by the appearance of Bishop Dyer in the courtyard.
GO BACK TO THE HOUSE, FAY.
From earliest childhood Jane had been taught to revere the bishops of her church...
...and Bishop Dyer had been the closest friend and counselor of her father.
IT WAS YOUR FATHER'S WISH THAT YOU MARRY BROTHER TULL — AND MY ORDER — YET YOU REFUSED HIM?
YES.
Jane's spirit began to vanish in the old habitual order of her life.
JANE WITHERSTEEN, YOU'LL DO AS I ORDER!
YOU FACE THE DAMNING OF YOUR SOUL TO PERDITION!
Dyer softened as he saw Jane cringe.
NOW...TELL ME ABOUT THIS LASSITER — WHAT'S HE DOING HERE IN COTTONWOODS?
Jane stood silent.
TELL ME!
LASSITER SAID HE CAME HERE TO FIND MILLY ERNE'S GRAVE.
AND WHAT ELSE?
TO KILL THE MAN WHO TOOK MILLY ERNE FROM HER HOME AND HER HUSBAND!
There followed a long and terrible silence. Then came a slow, guarded, clinking step.

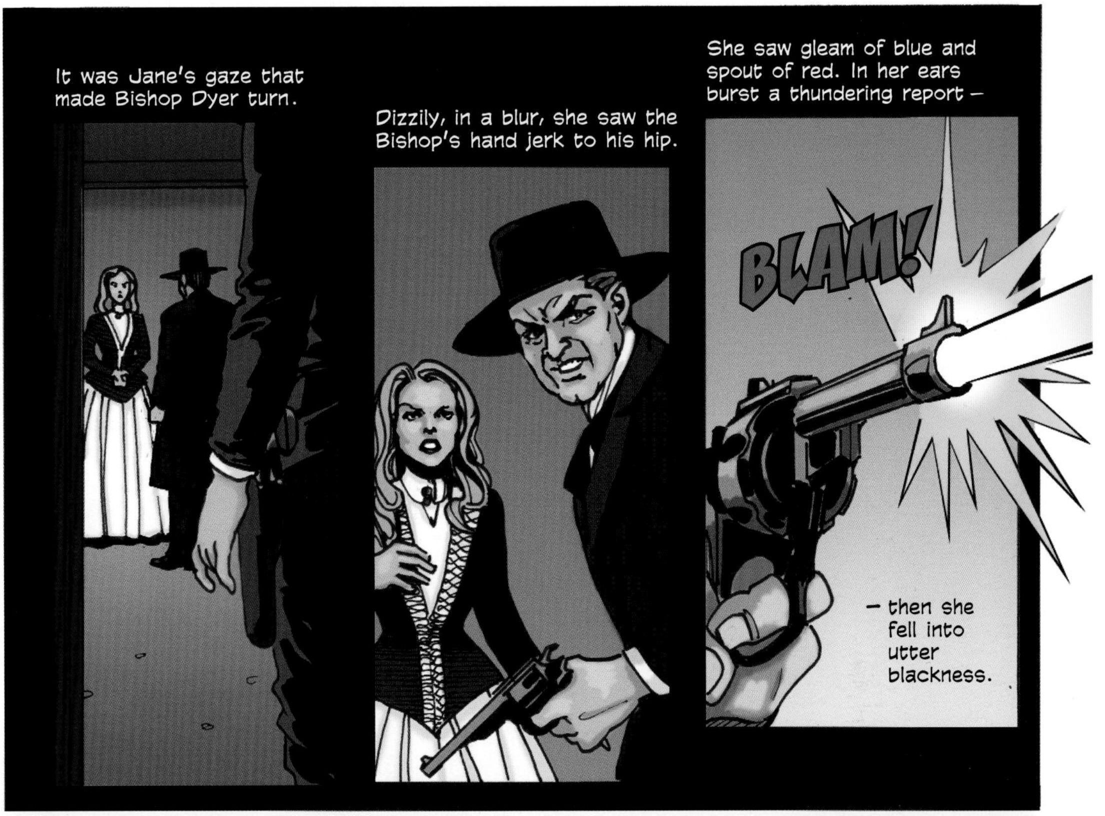
It was Jane's gaze that made Bishop Dyer turn.
Dizzily, in a blur, she saw the Bishop's hand jerk to his hip.
She saw gleam of blue and spout of red. In her ears burst a thundering report –
BLAM!
– then she fell into utter blackness.

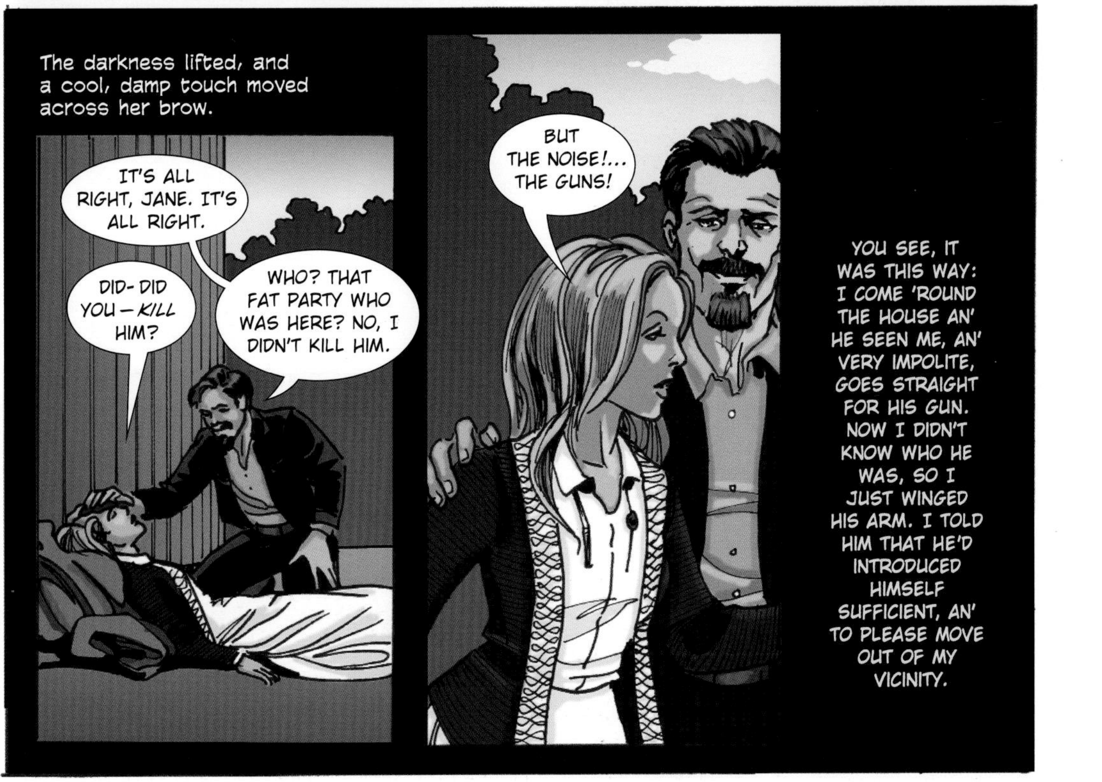
The darkness lifted, and a cool, damp touch moved across her brow.
IT'S ALL RIGHT, JANE. IT'S ALL RIGHT.
DID- DID YOU – *KILL* HIM?
WHO? THAT FAT PARTY WHO WAS HERE? NO, I DIDN'T KILL HIM.
BUT THE NOISE!... THE GUNS!
YOU SEE, IT WAS THIS WAY: I COME 'ROUND THE HOUSE AN' HE SEEN ME, AN' VERY IMPOLITE, GOES STRAIGHT FOR HIS GUN. NOW I DIDN'T KNOW WHO HE WAS, SO I JUST WINGED HIS ARM. I TOLD HIM THAT HE'D INTRODUCED HIMSELF SUFFICIENT, AN' TO PLEASE MOVE OUT OF MY VICINITY.

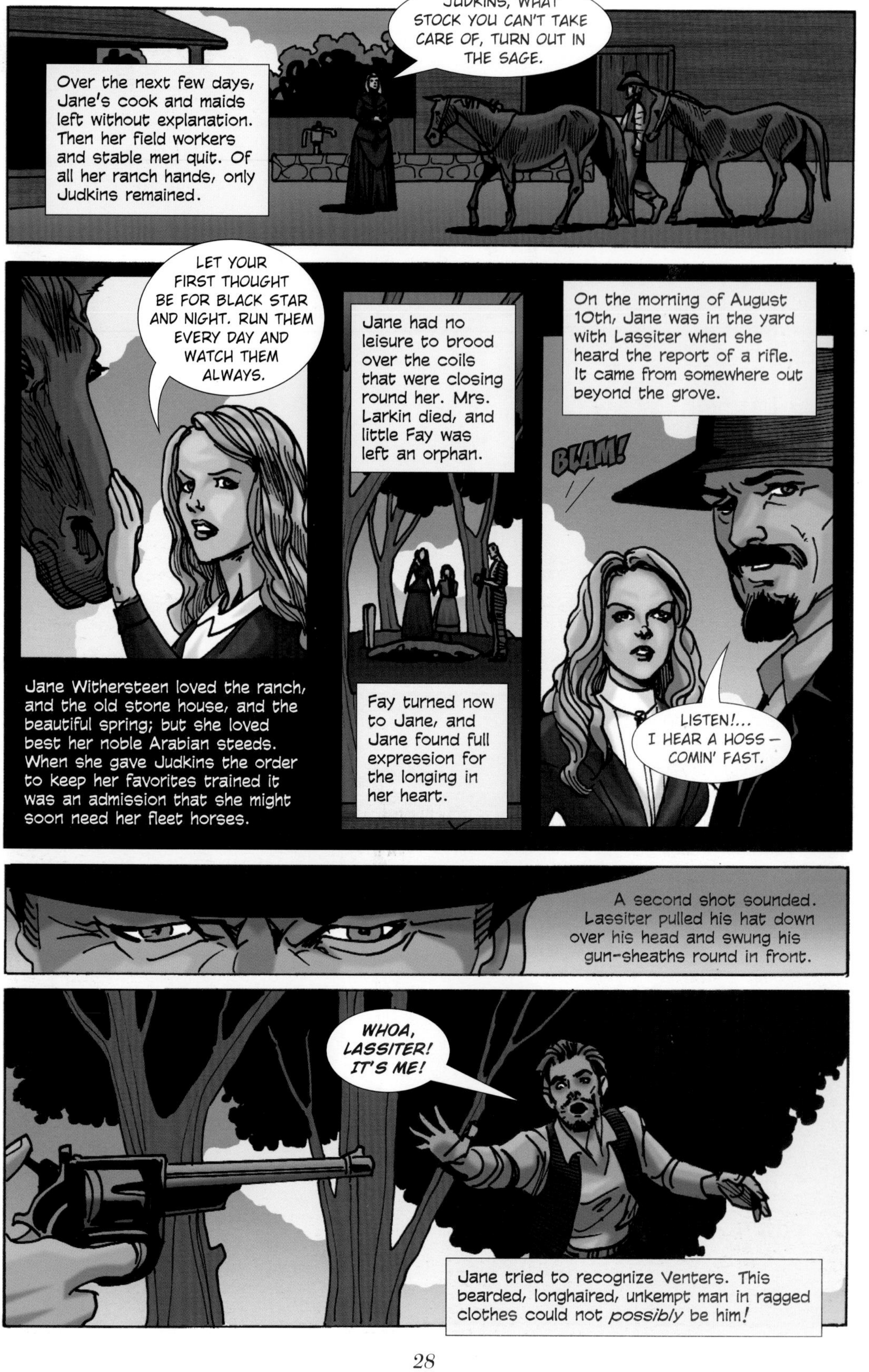
Over the next few days, Jane's cook and maids left without explanation. Then her field workers and stable men quit. Of all her ranch hands, only Judkins remained.
JUDKINS, WHAT STOCK YOU CAN'T TAKE CARE OF, TURN OUT IN THE SAGE.
LET YOUR FIRST THOUGHT BE FOR BLACK STAR AND NIGHT. RUN THEM EVERY DAY AND WATCH THEM ALWAYS.
Jane Withersteen loved the ranch, and the old stone house, and the beautiful spring; but she loved best her noble Arabian steeds. When she gave Judkins the order to keep her favorites trained it was an admission that she might soon need her fleet horses.
Jane had no leisure to brood over the coils that were closing round her. Mrs. Larkin died, and little Fay was left an orphan.
Fay turned now to Jane, and Jane found full expression for the longing in her heart.
On the morning of August 10th, Jane was in the yard with Lassiter when she heard the report of a rifle. It came from somewhere out beyond the grove.
BLAM!
LISTEN!... I HEAR A HOSS — COMIN' FAST.
A second shot sounded. Lassiter pulled his hat down over his head and swung his gun-sheaths round in front.
WHOA, LASSITER! IT'S ME!
Jane tried to recognize Venters. This bearded, longhaired, unkempt man in ragged clothes could not *possibly* be him!

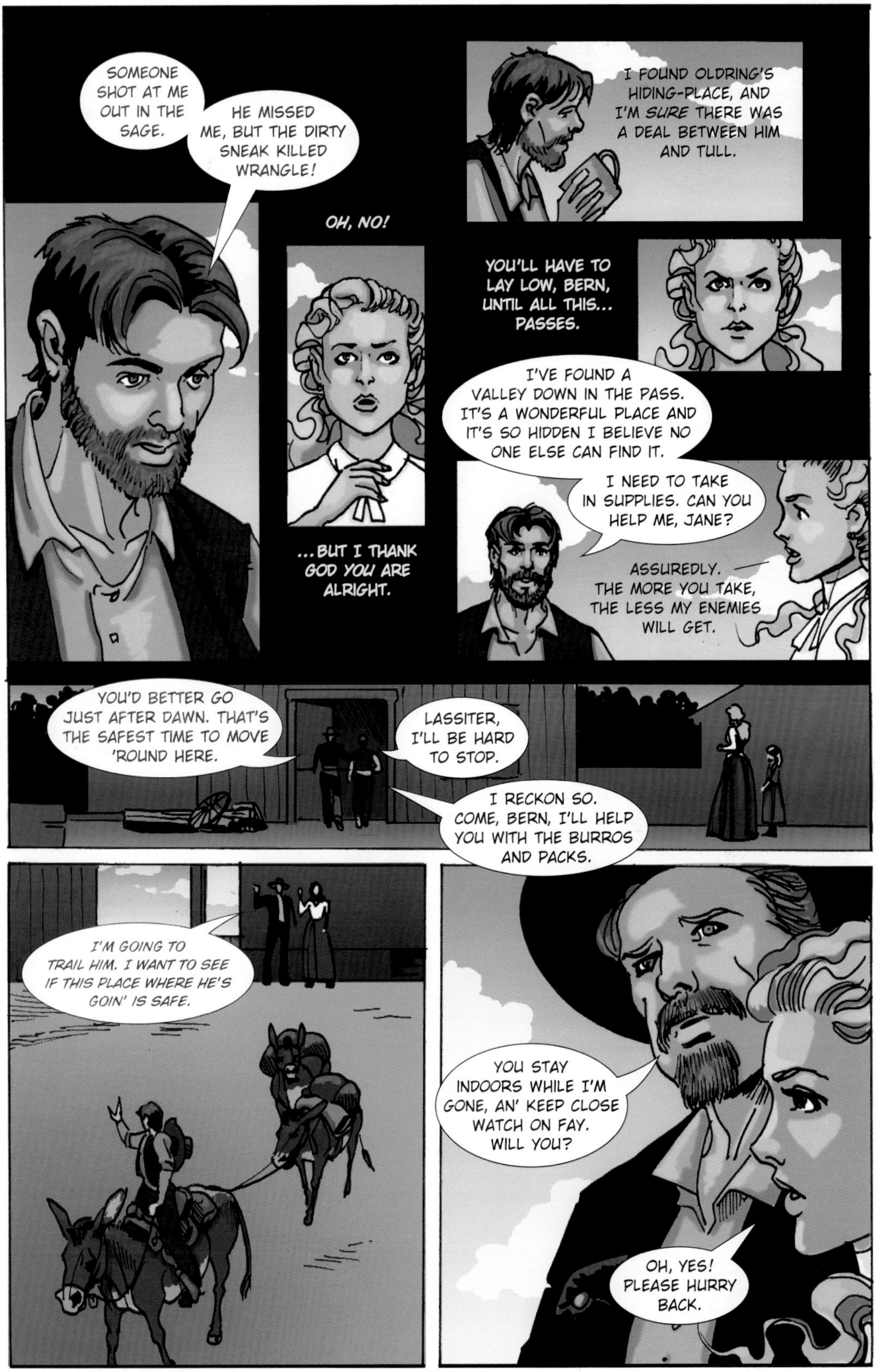
SOMEONE SHOT AT ME OUT IN THE SAGE.
HE MISSED ME, BUT THE DIRTY SNEAK KILLED WRANGLE!
I FOUND OLDRING'S HIDING-PLACE, AND I'M *SURE* THERE WAS A DEAL BETWEEN HIM AND TULL.
OH, NO!
...BUT I THANK GOD *YOU* ARE ALRIGHT.
YOU'LL HAVE TO LAY LOW, BERN, UNTIL ALL THIS... PASSES.
I'VE FOUND A VALLEY DOWN IN THE PASS. IT'S A WONDERFUL PLACE AND IT'S SO HIDDEN I BELIEVE NO ONE ELSE CAN FIND IT.
I NEED TO TAKE IN SUPPLIES. CAN YOU HELP ME, JANE?
ASSUREDLY. THE MORE YOU TAKE, THE LESS MY ENEMIES WILL GET.
YOU'D BETTER GO JUST AFTER DAWN. THAT'S THE SAFEST TIME TO MOVE 'ROUND HERE.
LASSITER, I'LL BE HARD TO STOP.
I RECKON SO. COME, BERN, I'LL HELP YOU WITH THE BURROS AND PACKS.
I'M GOING TO TRAIL HIM. I WANT TO SEE IF THIS PLACE WHERE HE'S GOIN' IS SAFE.
YOU STAY INDOORS WHILE I'M GONE, AN' KEEP CLOSE WATCH ON FAY. WILL YOU?
OH, YES! PLEASE HURRY BACK.

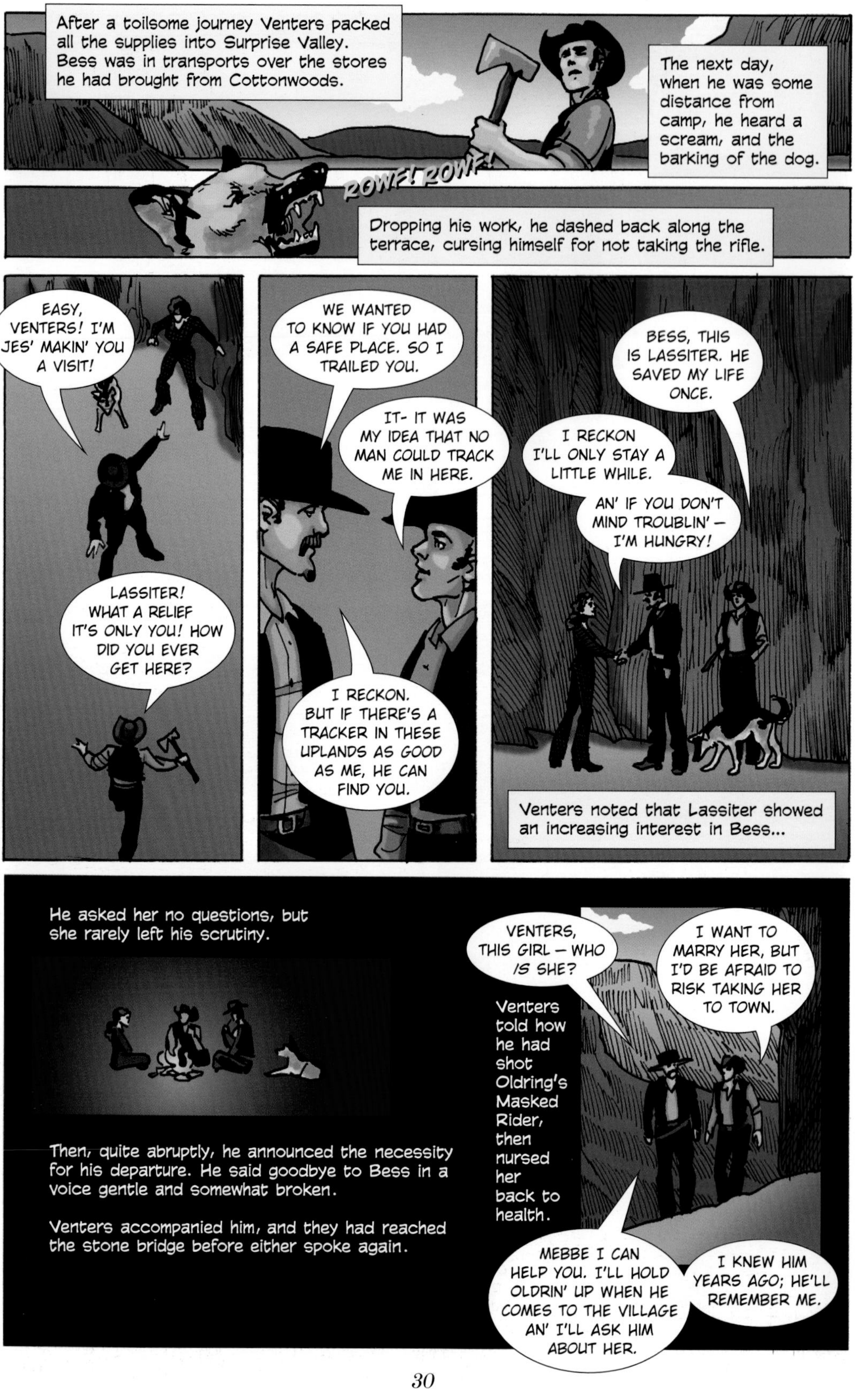
After a toilsome journey Venters packed all the supplies into Surprise Valley. Bess was in transports over the stores he had brought from Cottonwoods.
The next day, when he was some distance from camp, he heard a scream, and the barking of the dog.
ROWF! ROWF!
Dropping his work, he dashed back along the terrace, cursing himself for not taking the rifle.
EASY, VENTERS! I'M JES' MAKIN' YOU A VISIT!
LASSITER! WHAT A RELIEF IT'S ONLY YOU! HOW DID YOU EVER GET HERE?
WE WANTED TO KNOW IF YOU HAD A SAFE PLACE. SO I TRAILED YOU.
IT- IT WAS MY IDEA THAT NO MAN COULD TRACK ME IN HERE.
I RECKON. BUT IF THERE'S A TRACKER IN THESE UPLANDS AS GOOD AS ME, HE CAN FIND YOU.
BESS, THIS IS LASSITER. HE SAVED MY LIFE ONCE.
I RECKON I'LL ONLY STAY A LITTLE WHILE.
AN' IF YOU DON'T MIND TROUBLIN' — I'M HUNGRY!
Venters noted that Lassiter showed an increasing interest in Bess...
He asked her no questions, but she rarely left his scrutiny.
Then, quite abruptly, he announced the necessity for his departure. He said goodbye to Bess in a voice gentle and somewhat broken.
Venters accompanied him, and they had reached the stone bridge before either spoke again.
VENTERS, THIS GIRL — WHO IS SHE?
Venters told how he had shot Oldring's Masked Rider, then nursed her back to health.
I WANT TO MARRY HER, BUT I'D BE AFRAID TO RISK TAKING HER TO TOWN.
MEBBE I CAN HELP YOU. I'LL HOLD OLDRIN' UP WHEN HE COMES TO THE VILLAGE AN' I'LL ASK HIM ABOUT HER.
I KNEW HIM YEARS AGO; HE'LL REMEMBER ME.

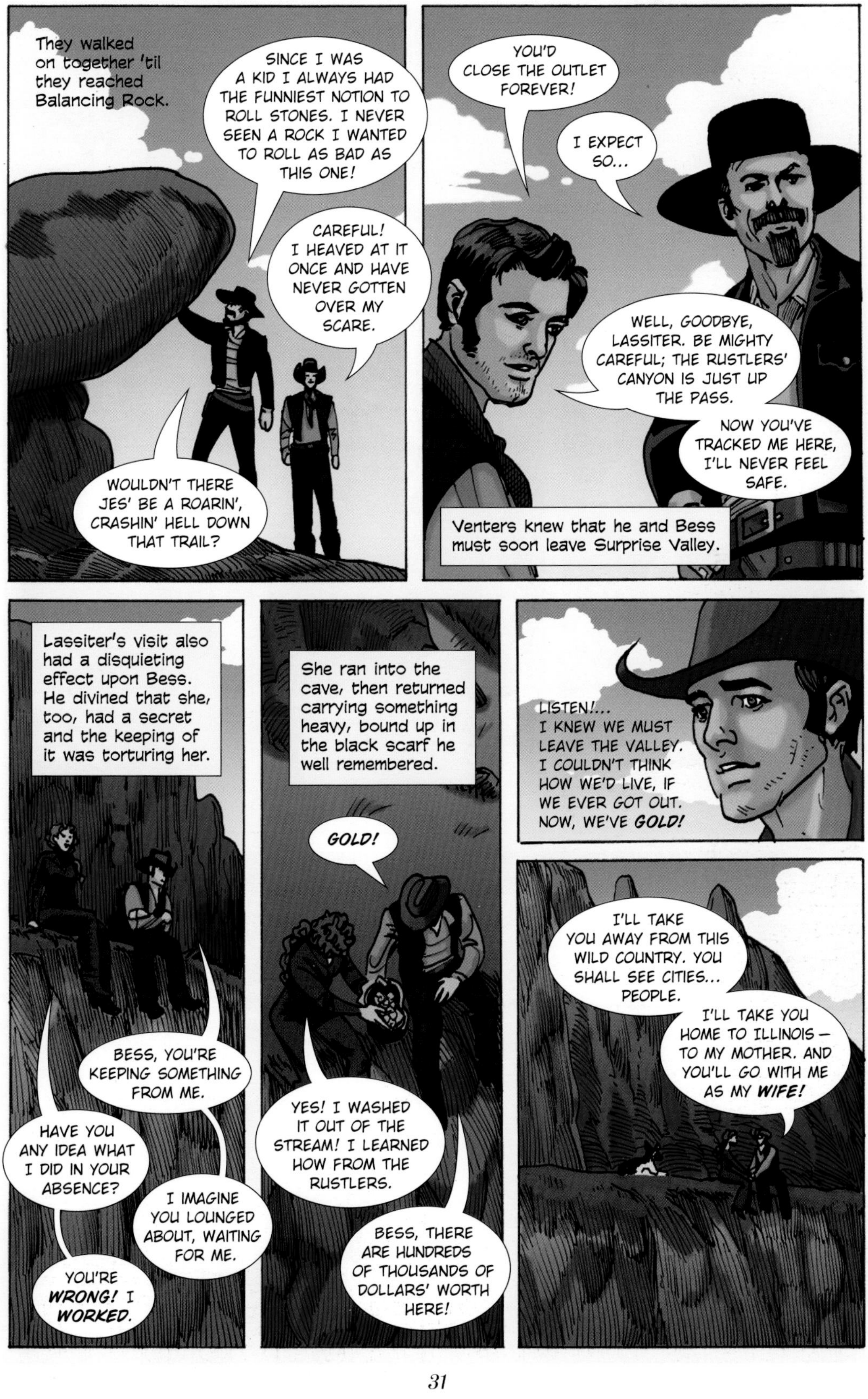
They walked on together 'til they reached Balancing Rock.
SINCE I WAS A KID I ALWAYS HAD THE FUNNIEST NOTION TO ROLL STONES. I NEVER SEEN A ROCK I WANTED TO ROLL AS BAD AS THIS ONE!
CAREFUL! I HEAVED AT IT ONCE AND HAVE NEVER GOTTEN OVER MY SCARE.
WOULDN'T THERE JES' BE A ROARIN', CRASHIN' HELL DOWN THAT TRAIL?
YOU'D CLOSE THE OUTLET FOREVER!
I EXPECT SO...
WELL, GOODBYE, LASSITER. BE MIGHTY CAREFUL; THE RUSTLERS' CANYON IS JUST UP THE PASS.
NOW YOU'VE TRACKED ME HERE, I'LL NEVER FEEL SAFE.
Venters knew that he and Bess must soon leave Surprise Valley.
Lassiter's visit also had a disquieting effect upon Bess. He divined that she, too, had a secret and the keeping of it was torturing her.
BESS, YOU'RE KEEPING SOMETHING FROM ME.
HAVE YOU ANY IDEA WHAT I DID IN YOUR ABSENCE?
I IMAGINE YOU LOUNGED ABOUT, WAITING FOR ME.
YOU'RE ***WRONG!*** I ***WORKED.***
She ran into the cave, then returned carrying something heavy, bound up in the black scarf he well remembered.
GOLD!
YES! I WASHED IT OUT OF THE STREAM! I LEARNED HOW FROM THE RUSTLERS.
BESS, THERE ARE HUNDREDS OF THOUSANDS OF DOLLARS' WORTH HERE!
LISTEN!... I KNEW WE MUST LEAVE THE VALLEY. I COULDN'T THINK HOW WE'D LIVE, IF WE EVER GOT OUT. NOW, WE'VE ***GOLD!***
I'LL TAKE YOU AWAY FROM THIS WILD COUNTRY. YOU SHALL SEE CITIES... PEOPLE.
I'LL TAKE YOU HOME TO ILLINOIS – TO MY MOTHER. AND YOU'LL GO WITH ME AS MY ***WIFE!***

It was a drowsy summer morning, and the little family was sitting in the shade of a wooded knoll. Fay's brief spell of unhappy longing for her mother had passed. For Jane Withersteen the child was a blessing; a possession infinitely more precious than all she had lost.

DOES YOU LOVE ME?

Lassiter assured Fay that he was her devoted subject.

WHY DON'T YOU MARRY MY NEW MUVVER AN' BE MY FAVVER?

FAY! RUN AND PLAY — BUT DON'T GO TOO FAR FROM THIS HILL!

Fay pranced off wildly, joyous over freedom that had not been granted her for weeks.

JANE, COME WITH ME OUT OF THIS TERRITORY! LET'S TAKE THE RACERS AN' LITTLE FAY, EN' LEAVE!

NO, LASSITER. WHAT WOULD I DO IN THE WORLD WITH MY BROKEN FORTUNES AND MY BROKEN HEART?

I ONLY WANT A CHANCE TO SHOW YOU HOW A MAN — ANY MAN — CAN BE BETTER 'N HE WAS. LISTEN TO MILLY ERNE'S STORY, AND HOW LOVE CHANGED HER... AND ME...

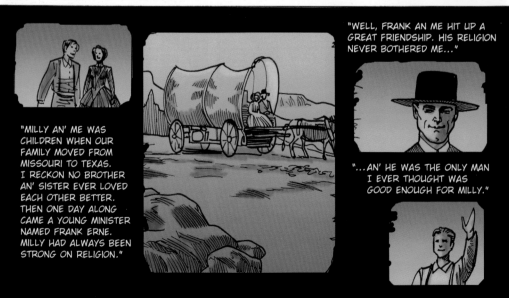

"MILLY AN' ME WAS CHILDREN WHEN OUR FAMILY MOVED FROM MISSOURI TO TEXAS. I RECKON NO BROTHER AN' SISTER EVER LOVED EACH OTHER BETTER. THEN ONE DAY ALONG CAME A YOUNG MINISTER NAMED FRANK ERNE. MILLY HAD ALWAYS BEEN STRONG ON RELIGION."

"WELL, FRANK AN ME HIT UP A GREAT FRIENDSHIP. HIS RELIGION NEVER BOTHERED ME..."

"...AN' HE WAS THE ONLY MAN I EVER THOUGHT WAS GOOD ENOUGH FOR MILLY."

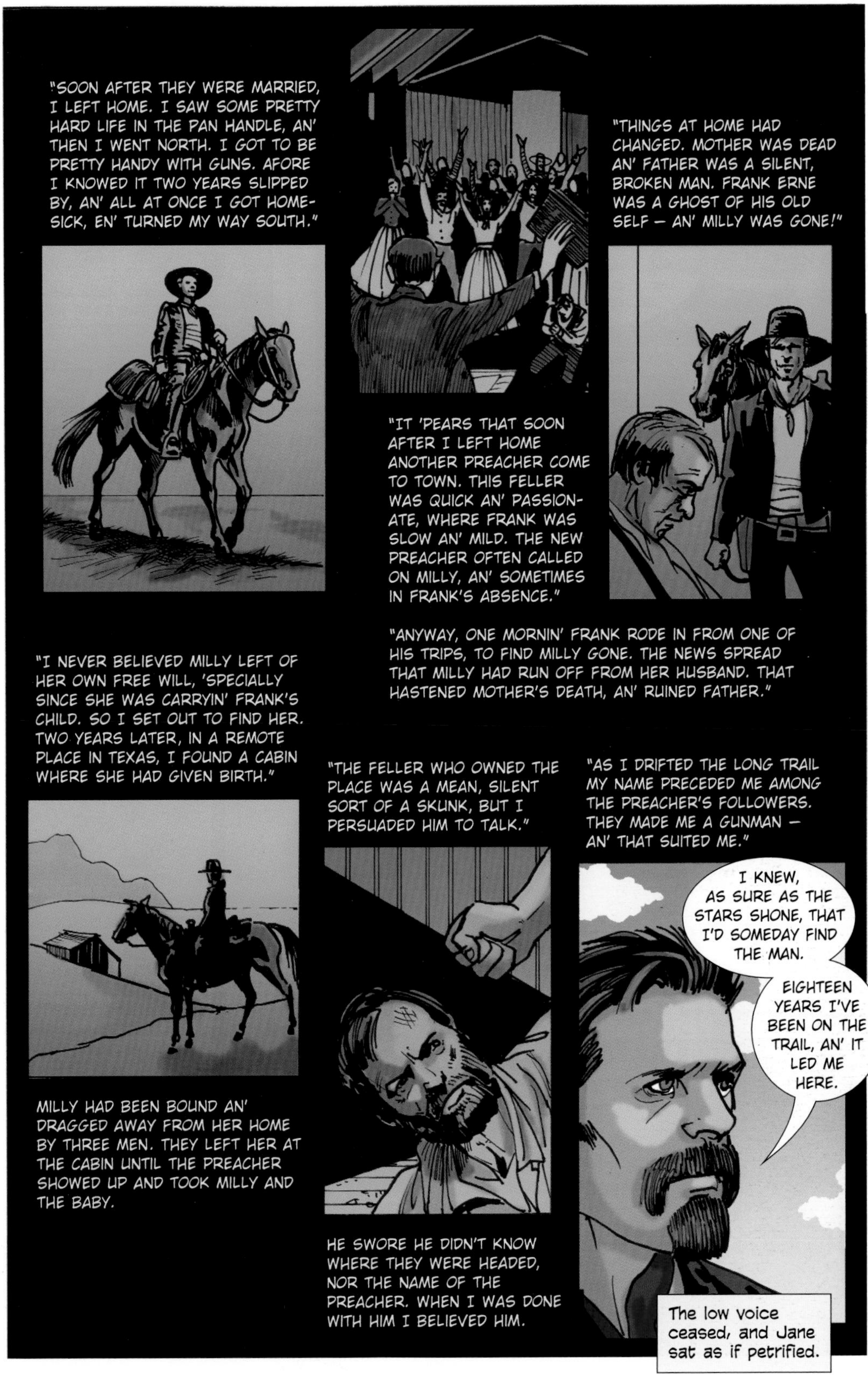
"SOON AFTER THEY WERE MARRIED, I LEFT HOME. I SAW SOME PRETTY HARD LIFE IN THE PAN HANDLE, AN' THEN I WENT NORTH. I GOT TO BE PRETTY HANDY WITH GUNS. AFORE I KNOWED IT TWO YEARS SLIPPED BY, AN' ALL AT ONCE I GOT HOME-SICK, EN' TURNED MY WAY SOUTH."
"IT 'PEARS THAT SOON AFTER I LEFT HOME ANOTHER PREACHER COME TO TOWN. THIS FELLER WAS QUICK AN' PASSION-ATE, WHERE FRANK WAS SLOW AN' MILD. THE NEW PREACHER OFTEN CALLED ON MILLY, AN' SOMETIMES IN FRANK'S ABSENCE."
"THINGS AT HOME HAD CHANGED. MOTHER WAS DEAD AN' FATHER WAS A SILENT, BROKEN MAN. FRANK ERNE WAS A GHOST OF HIS OLD SELF — AN' MILLY WAS GONE!"
"ANYWAY, ONE MORNIN' FRANK RODE IN FROM ONE OF HIS TRIPS, TO FIND MILLY GONE. THE NEWS SPREAD THAT MILLY HAD RUN OFF FROM HER HUSBAND. THAT HASTENED MOTHER'S DEATH, AN' RUINED FATHER."
"I NEVER BELIEVED MILLY LEFT OF HER OWN FREE WILL, 'SPECIALLY SINCE SHE WAS CARRYIN' FRANK'S CHILD. SO I SET OUT TO FIND HER. TWO YEARS LATER, IN A REMOTE PLACE IN TEXAS, I FOUND A CABIN WHERE SHE HAD GIVEN BIRTH."
MILLY HAD BEEN BOUND AN' DRAGGED AWAY FROM HER HOME BY THREE MEN. THEY LEFT HER AT THE CABIN UNTIL THE PREACHER SHOWED UP AND TOOK MILLY AND THE BABY.
"THE FELLER WHO OWNED THE PLACE WAS A MEAN, SILENT SORT OF A SKUNK, BUT I PERSUADED HIM TO TALK."
HE SWORE HE DIDN'T KNOW WHERE THEY WERE HEADED, NOR THE NAME OF THE PREACHER. WHEN I WAS DONE WITH HIM I BELIEVED HIM.
"AS I DRIFTED THE LONG TRAIL MY NAME PRECEDED ME AMONG THE PREACHER'S FOLLOWERS. THEY MADE ME A GUNMAN — AN' THAT SUITED ME."
I KNEW, AS SURE AS THE STARS SHONE, THAT I'D SOMEDAY FIND THE MAN.
EIGHTEEN YEARS I'VE BEEN ON THE TRAIL, AN' IT LED ME HERE.
The low voice ceased, and Jane sat as if petrified.

YOUR TEETH HAVE BEEN SHUT TIGHTER 'N THEM OF ALL THE DEAD MEN LYIN' BACK ALONG THAT TRAIL. JEST THE SAME YOU TOLD ME THE SECRET I'VE LIVED THESE EIGHTEEN YEARS TO HEAR!

OH, NO!

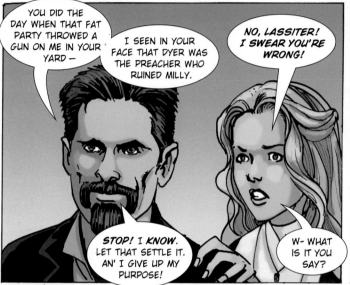

YOU DID THE DAY WHEN THAT FAT PARTY THROWED A GUN ON ME IN YOUR YARD —

I SEEN IN YOUR FACE THAT DYER WAS THE PREACHER WHO RUINED MILLY.

NO, LASSITER! I SWEAR YOU'RE WRONG!

STOP! I KNOW. LET THAT SETTLE IT. AN' I GIVE UP MY PURPOSE!

W- WHAT IS IT YOU SAY?

I GIVE UP MY PURPOSE. I CAN'T HELP POOR MILLY, AN' I'VE OUTGROWED REVENGE. HATE AIN'T THE SAME WITH ME SINCE I LOVED YOU AND LITTLE FAY.

LASSITER! YOU MEAN YOU WON'T KILL HIM?

NO. I WON'T.

FOR MY SAKE? BECAUSE YOU LOVE ME?

THAT'S IT, JANE.

OH, HOW CAN I HELP BUT LOVE YOU? MY HEART MUST BE STONE!

BUT LASSITER, GIVE ME TIME. I CAN'T HAVE FALLEN SO LOW, I CAN'T BE SO ABANDONED BY GOD, THAT I'VE NO LOVE LEFT TO GIVE YOU.

I RECKON I DON'T NEED NO MORE FER NOW.

WHERE'S FAY?

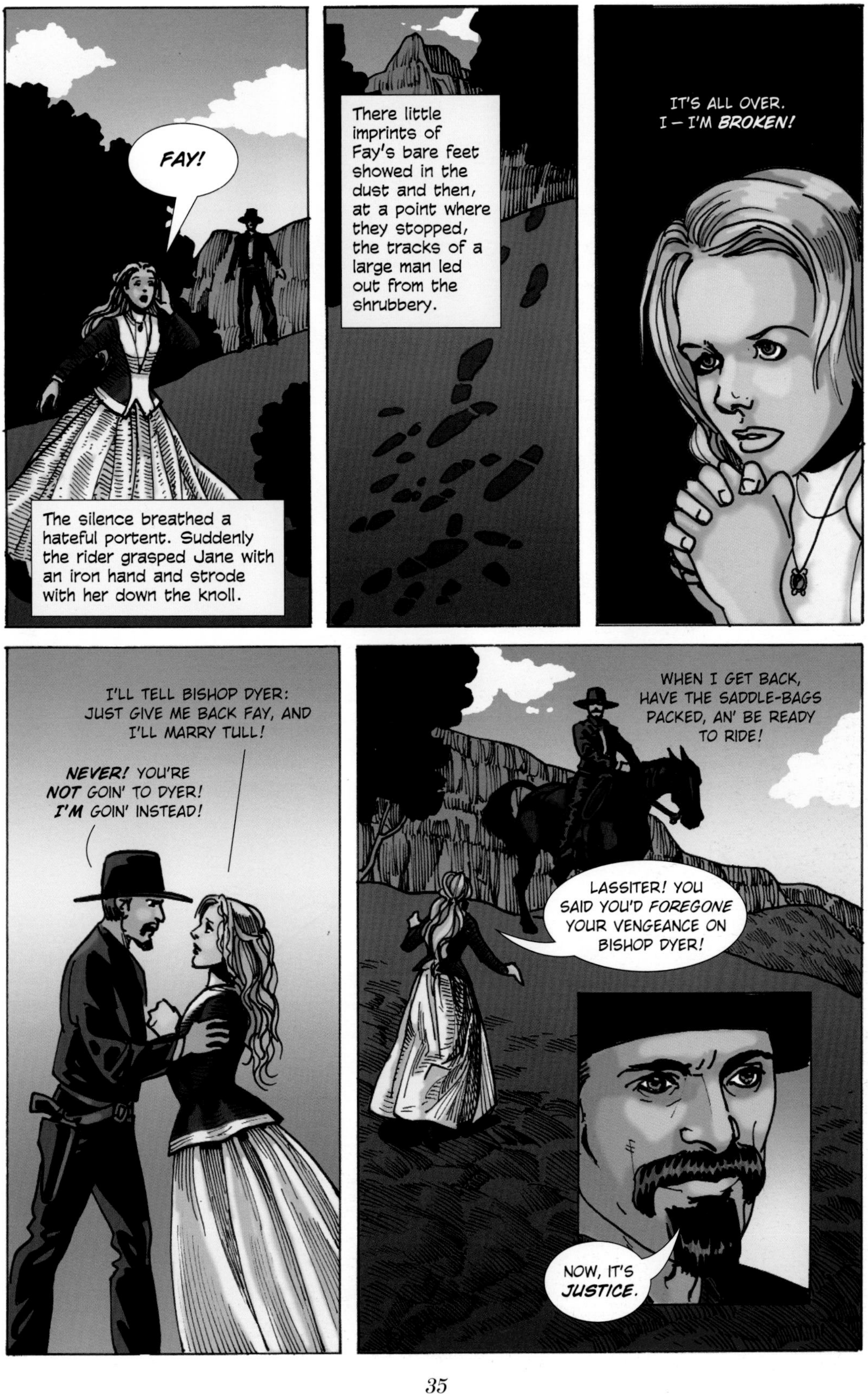
FAY!
The silence breathed a hateful portent. Suddenly the rider grasped Jane with an iron hand and strode with her down the knoll.
There little imprints of Fay's bare feet showed in the dust and then, at a point where they stopped, the tracks of a large man led out from the shrubbery.
IT'S ALL OVER. I – I'M BROKEN!
I'LL TELL BISHOP DYER: JUST GIVE ME BACK FAY, AND I'LL MARRY TULL!
NEVER! YOU'RE NOT GOIN' TO DYER! I'M GOIN' INSTEAD!
WHEN I GET BACK, HAVE THE SADDLE-BAGS PACKED, AN' BE READY TO RIDE!
LASSITER! YOU SAID YOU'D FOREGONE YOUR VENGEANCE ON BISHOP DYER!
NOW, IT'S JUSTICE.

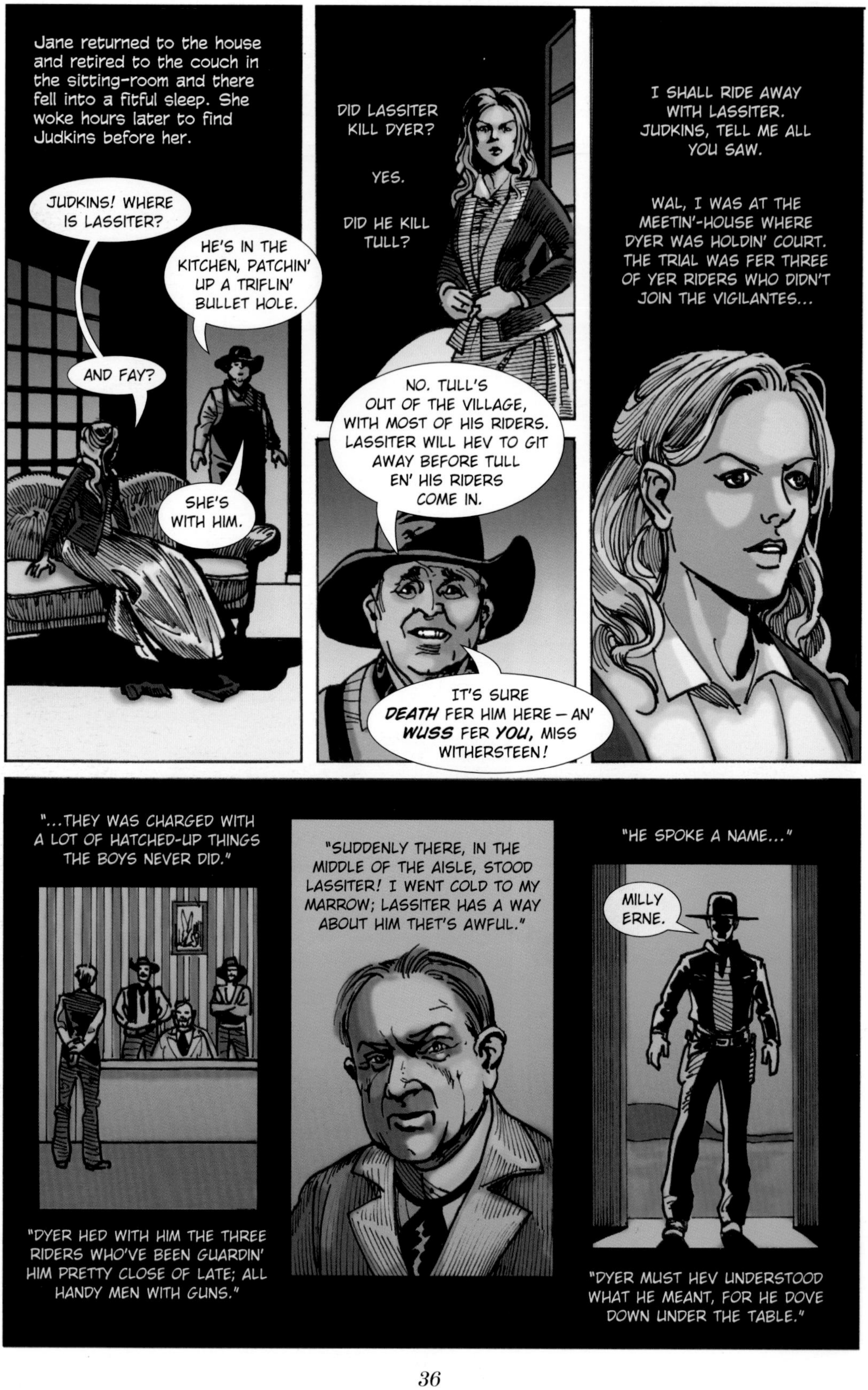
Jane returned to the house and retired to the couch in the sitting-room and there fell into a fitful sleep. She woke hours later to find Judkins before her.
JUDKINS! WHERE IS LASSITER?
HE'S IN THE KITCHEN, PATCHIN' UP A TRIFLIN' BULLET HOLE.
AND FAY?
SHE'S WITH HIM.
DID LASSITER KILL DYER?
YES.
DID HE KILL TULL?
NO. TULL'S OUT OF THE VILLAGE, WITH MOST OF HIS RIDERS. LASSITER WILL HEV TO GIT AWAY BEFORE TULL EN' HIS RIDERS COME IN.
IT'S SURE ***DEATH*** FER HIM HERE – AN' ***WUSS*** FER ***YOU***, MISS WITHERSTEEN!
I SHALL RIDE AWAY WITH LASSITER. JUDKINS, TELL ME ALL YOU SAW.
WAL, I WAS AT THE MEETIN'-HOUSE WHERE DYER WAS HOLDIN' COURT. THE TRIAL WAS FER THREE OF YER RIDERS WHO DIDN'T JOIN THE VIGILANTES...
"...THEY WAS CHARGED WITH A LOT OF HATCHED-UP THINGS THE BOYS NEVER DID."
"DYER HED WITH HIM THE THREE RIDERS WHO'VE BEEN GUARDIN' HIM PRETTY CLOSE OF LATE; ALL HANDY MEN WITH GUNS."
"SUDDENLY THERE, IN THE MIDDLE OF THE AISLE, STOOD LASSITER! I WENT COLD TO MY MARROW; LASSITER HAS A WAY ABOUT HIM THET'S AWFUL."
"HE SPOKE A NAME..."
MILLY ERNE.
"DYER MUST HEV UNDERSTOOD WHAT HE MEANT, FOR HE DOVE DOWN UNDER THE TABLE."

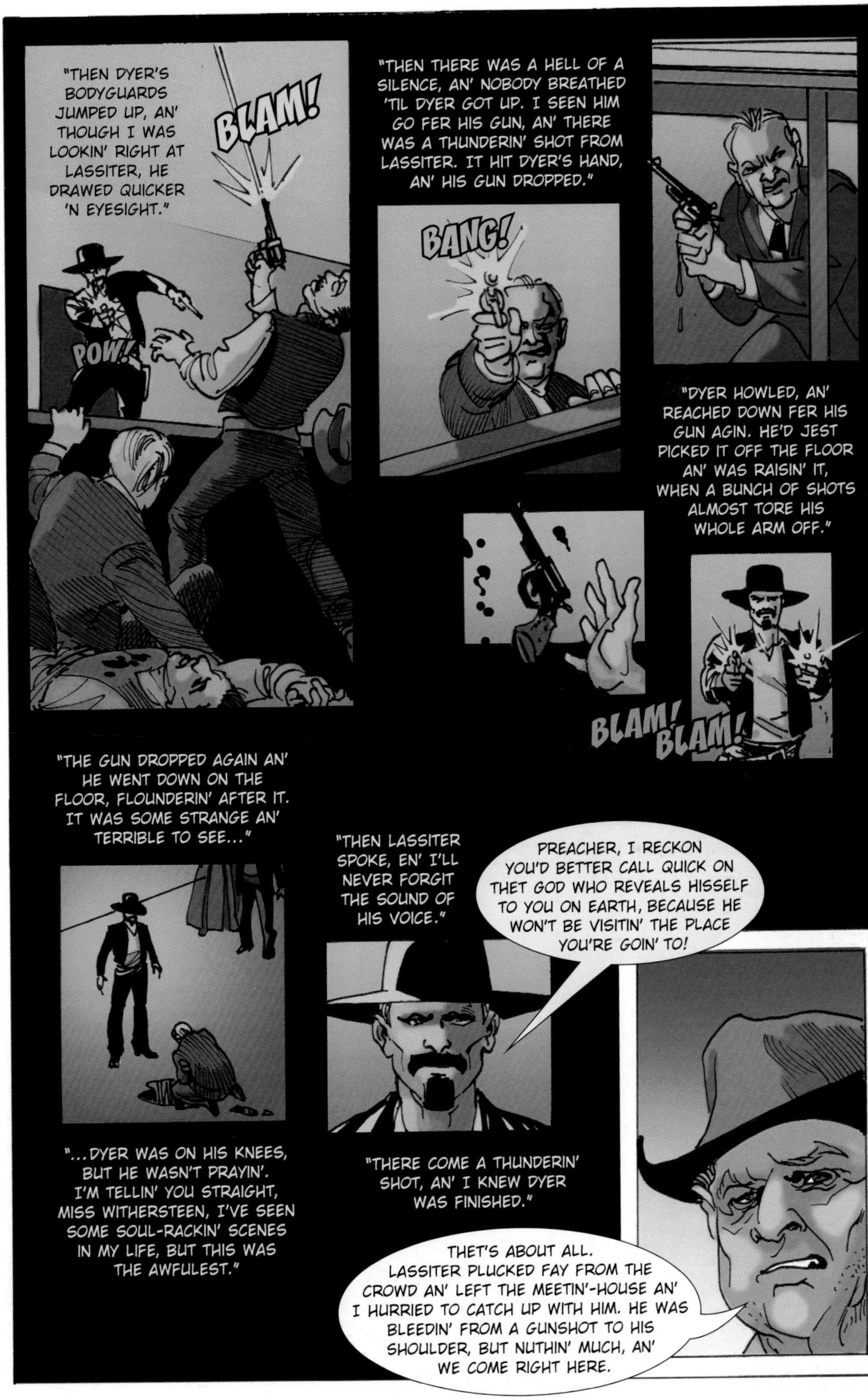
"THEN DYER'S BODYGUARDS JUMPED UP, AN' THOUGH I WAS LOOKIN' RIGHT AT LASSITER, HE DRAWED QUICKER 'N EYESIGHT."
BLAM!
POW!
"THEN THERE WAS A HELL OF A SILENCE, AN' NOBODY BREATHED 'TIL DYER GOT UP. I SEEN HIM GO FER HIS GUN, AN' THERE WAS A THUNDERIN' SHOT FROM LASSITER. IT HIT DYER'S HAND, AN' HIS GUN DROPPED."
BANG!
"DYER HOWLED, AN' REACHED DOWN FER HIS GUN AGIN. HE'D JEST PICKED IT OFF THE FLOOR AN' WAS RAISIN' IT, WHEN A BUNCH OF SHOTS ALMOST TORE HIS WHOLE ARM OFF."
BLAM! BLAM!
"THE GUN DROPPED AGAIN AN' HE WENT DOWN ON THE FLOOR, FLOUNDERIN' AFTER IT. IT WAS SOME STRANGE AN' TERRIBLE TO SEE..."
"...DYER WAS ON HIS KNEES, BUT HE WASN'T PRAYIN'. I'M TELLIN' YOU STRAIGHT, MISS WITHERSTEEN, I'VE SEEN SOME SOUL-RACKIN' SCENES IN MY LIFE, BUT THIS WAS THE AWFULEST."
"THEN LASSITER SPOKE, EN' I'LL NEVER FORGIT THE SOUND OF HIS VOICE."
PREACHER, I RECKON YOU'D BETTER CALL QUICK ON THET GOD WHO REVEALS HISSELF TO YOU ON EARTH, BECAUSE HE WON'T BE VISITIN' THE PLACE YOU'RE GOIN' TO!
"THERE COME A THUNDERIN' SHOT, AN' I KNEW DYER WAS FINISHED."
THET'S ABOUT ALL. LASSITER PLUCKED FAY FROM THE CROWD AN' LEFT THE MEETIN'-HOUSE AN' I HURRIED TO CATCH UP WITH HIM. HE WAS BLEEDIN' FROM A GUNSHOT TO HIS SHOULDER, BUT NUTHIN' MUCH, AN' WE COME RIGHT HERE.

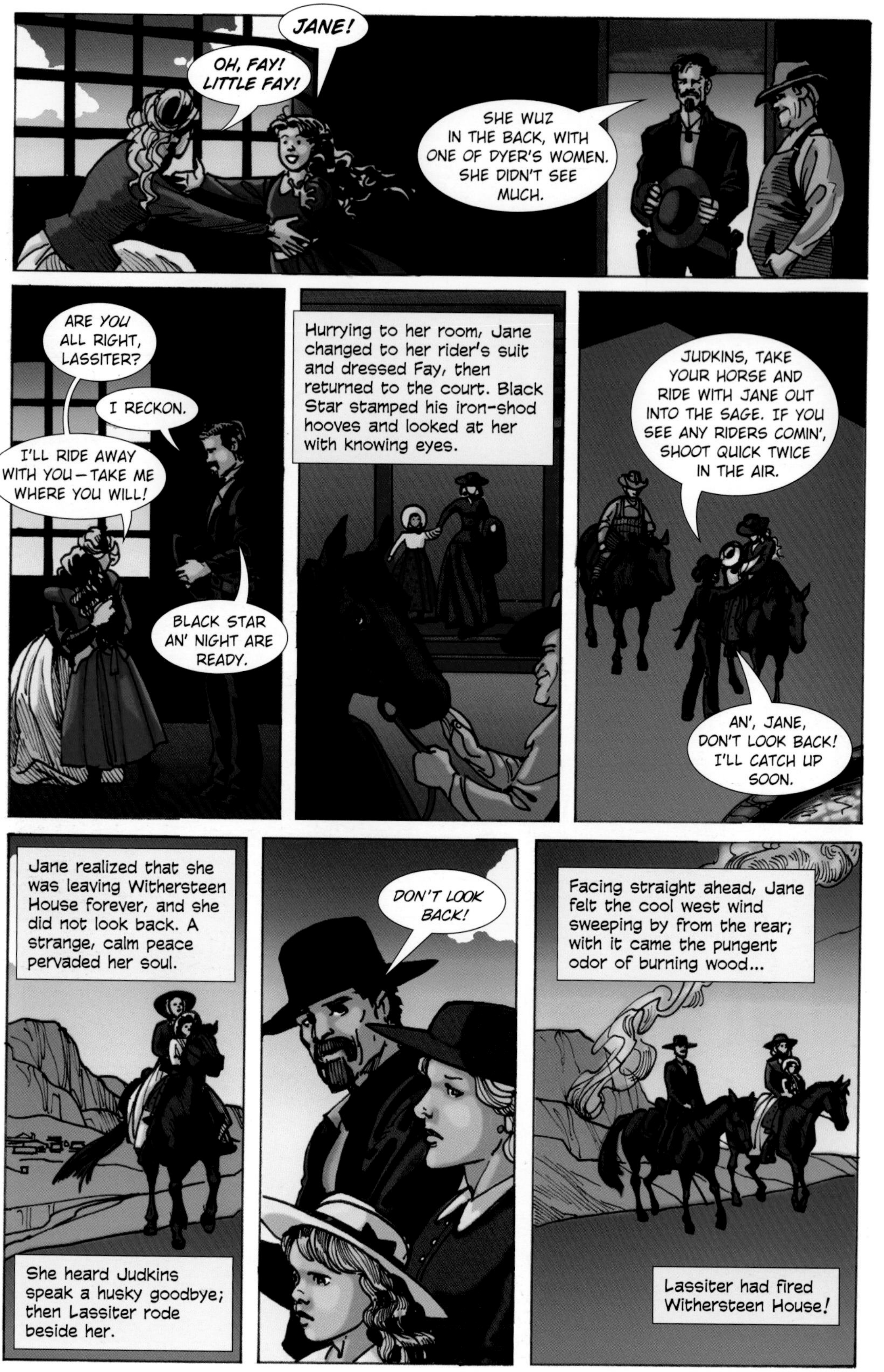
JANE!
OH, FAY! LITTLE FAY!
SHE WUZ IN THE BACK, WITH ONE OF DYER'S WOMEN. SHE DIDN'T SEE MUCH.
ARE YOU ALL RIGHT, LASSITER?
I RECKON.
I'LL RIDE AWAY WITH YOU—TAKE ME WHERE YOU WILL!
BLACK STAR AN' NIGHT ARE READY.
Hurrying to her room, Jane changed to her rider's suit and dressed Fay, then returned to the court. Black Star stamped his iron-shod hooves and looked at her with knowing eyes.
JUDKINS, TAKE YOUR HORSE AND RIDE WITH JANE OUT INTO THE SAGE. IF YOU SEE ANY RIDERS COMIN', SHOOT QUICK TWICE IN THE AIR.
AN', JANE, DON'T LOOK BACK! I'LL CATCH UP SOON.
Jane realized that she was leaving Withersteen House forever, and she did not look back. A strange, calm peace pervaded her soul.
She heard Judkins speak a husky goodbye; then Lassiter rode beside her.
DON'T LOOK BACK!
Facing straight ahead, Jane felt the cool west wind sweeping by from the rear; with it came the pungent odor of burning wood...
Lassiter had fired Withersteen House!

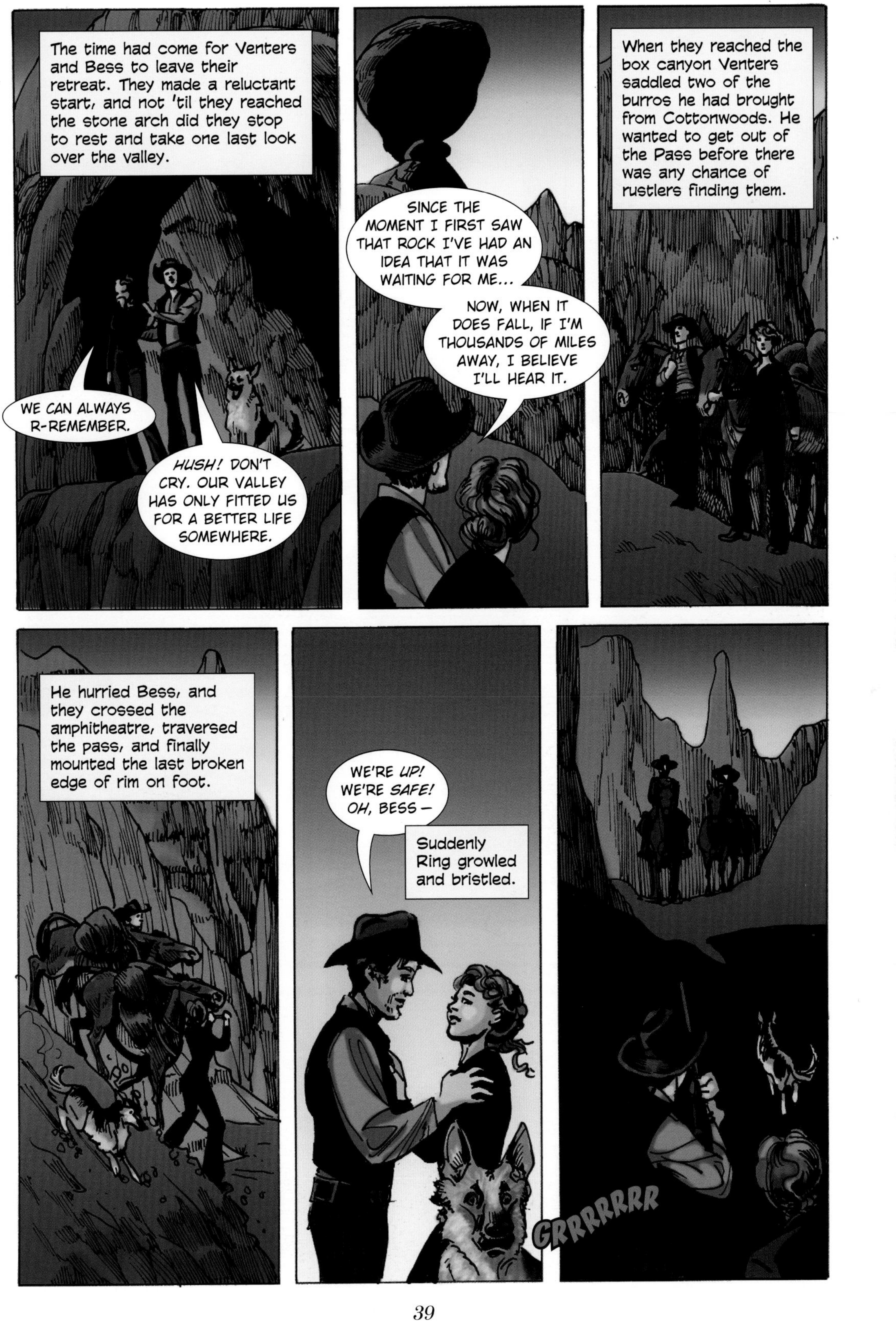
The time had come for Venters and Bess to leave their retreat. They made a reluctant start, and not 'til they reached the stone arch did they stop to rest and take one last look over the valley.
WE CAN ALWAYS R-REMEMBER.
HUSH! DON'T CRY. OUR VALLEY HAS ONLY FITTED US FOR A BETTER LIFE SOMEWHERE.
SINCE THE MOMENT I FIRST SAW THAT ROCK I'VE HAD AN IDEA THAT IT WAS WAITING FOR ME...
NOW, WHEN IT DOES FALL, IF I'M THOUSANDS OF MILES AWAY, I BELIEVE I'LL HEAR IT.
When they reached the box canyon Venters saddled two of the burros he had brought from Cottonwoods. He wanted to get out of the Pass before there was any chance of rustlers finding them.
He hurried Bess, and they crossed the amphitheatre, traversed the pass, and finally mounted the last broken edge of rim on foot.
WE'RE UP! WE'RE SAFE! OH, BESS —
Suddenly Ring growled and bristled.
GRRRRRRR

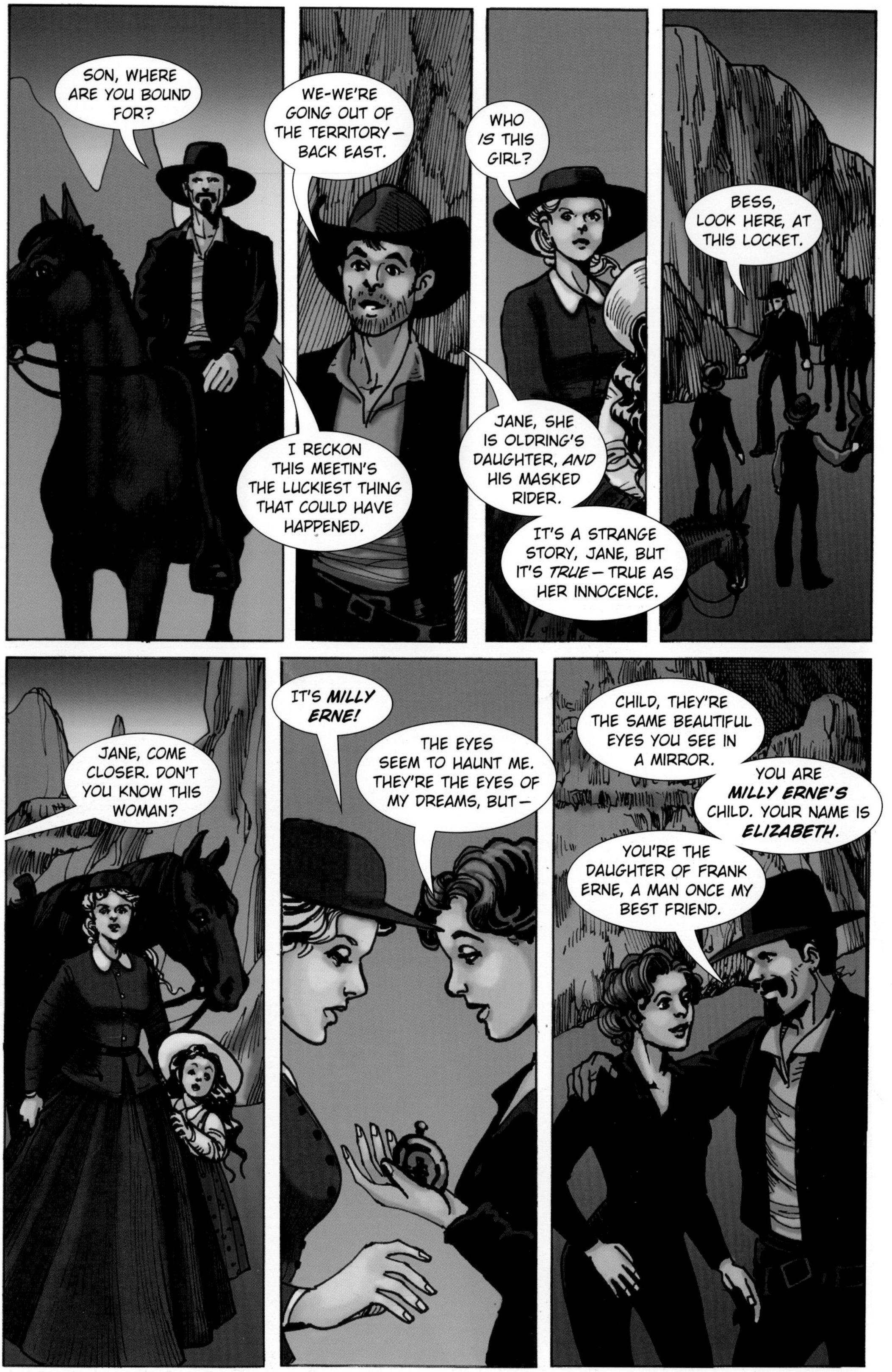
SON, WHERE ARE YOU BOUND FOR?
WE-WE'RE GOING OUT OF THE TERRITORY— BACK EAST.
I RECKON THIS MEETIN'S THE LUCKIEST THING THAT COULD HAVE HAPPENED.
WHO *IS* THIS GIRL?
JANE, SHE IS OLDRING'S DAUGHTER, *AND* HIS MASKED RIDER.
IT'S A STRANGE STORY, JANE, BUT IT'S *TRUE*— TRUE AS HER INNOCENCE.
BESS, LOOK HERE, AT THIS LOCKET.
JANE, COME CLOSER. DON'T YOU KNOW THIS WOMAN?
IT'S **MILLY ERNE!**
THE EYES SEEM TO HAUNT ME. THEY'RE THE EYES OF MY DREAMS, BUT—
CHILD, THEY'RE THE SAME BEAUTIFUL EYES YOU SEE IN A MIRROR.
YOU ARE **MILLY ERNE'S** CHILD. YOUR NAME IS **ELIZABETH**.
YOU'RE THE DAUGHTER OF FRANK ERNE, A MAN ONCE MY BEST FRIEND.

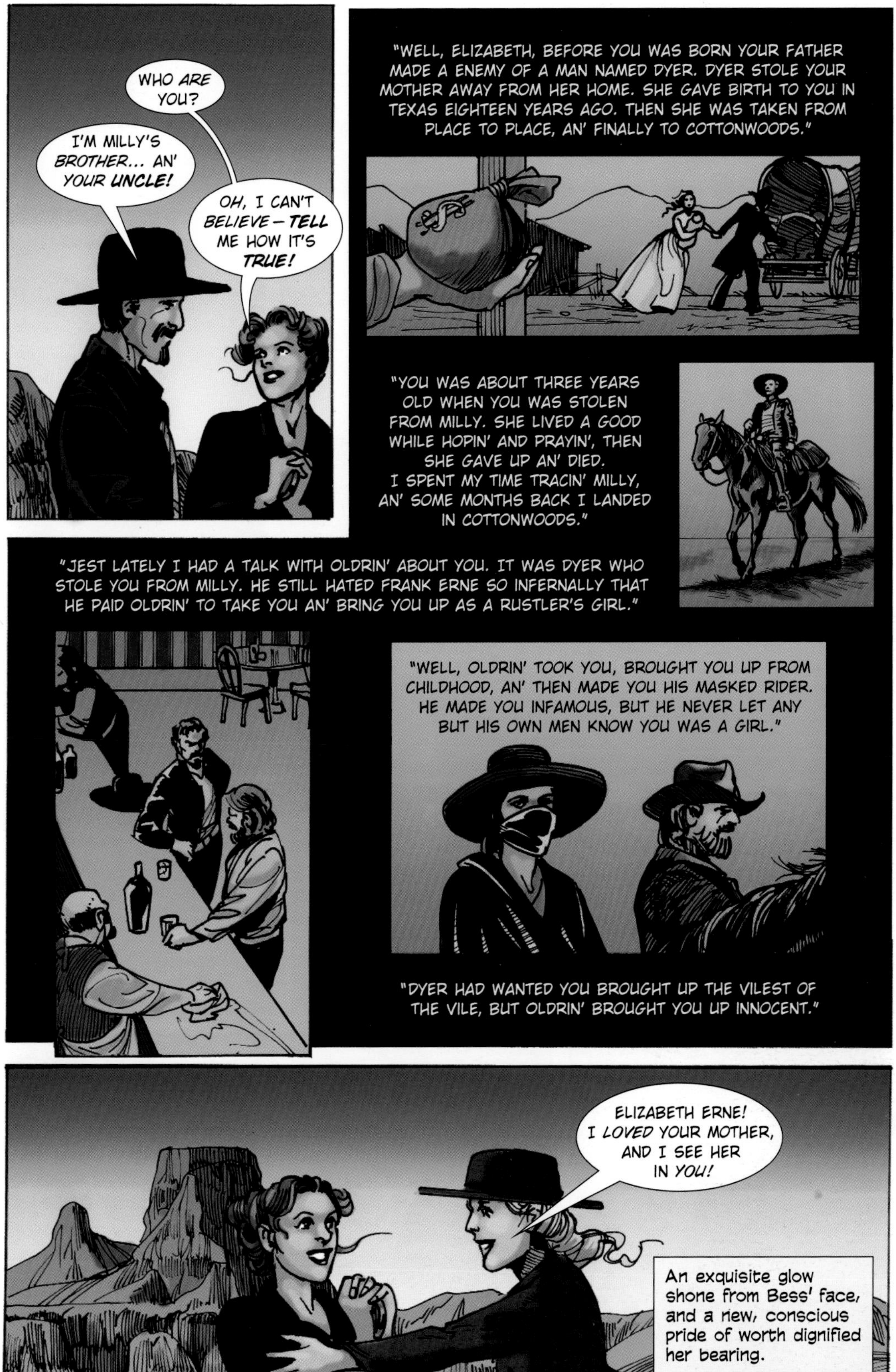
WHO ARE YOU?
I'M MILLY'S BROTHER... AN' YOUR UNCLE!
OH, I CAN'T BELIEVE—TELL ME HOW IT'S TRUE!
"WELL, ELIZABETH, BEFORE YOU WAS BORN YOUR FATHER MADE A ENEMY OF A MAN NAMED DYER. DYER STOLE YOUR MOTHER AWAY FROM HER HOME. SHE GAVE BIRTH TO YOU IN TEXAS EIGHTEEN YEARS AGO. THEN SHE WAS TAKEN FROM PLACE TO PLACE, AN' FINALLY TO COTTONWOODS."
"YOU WAS ABOUT THREE YEARS OLD WHEN YOU WAS STOLEN FROM MILLY. SHE LIVED A GOOD WHILE HOPIN' AND PRAYIN', THEN SHE GAVE UP AN' DIED.
I SPENT MY TIME TRACIN' MILLY, AN' SOME MONTHS BACK I LANDED IN COTTONWOODS."
"JEST LATELY I HAD A TALK WITH OLDRIN' ABOUT YOU. IT WAS DYER WHO STOLE YOU FROM MILLY. HE STILL HATED FRANK ERNE SO INFERNALLY THAT HE PAID OLDRIN' TO TAKE YOU AN' BRING YOU UP AS A RUSTLER'S GIRL."
"WELL, OLDRIN' TOOK YOU, BROUGHT YOU UP FROM CHILDHOOD, AN' THEN MADE YOU HIS MASKED RIDER. HE MADE YOU INFAMOUS, BUT HE NEVER LET ANY BUT HIS OWN MEN KNOW YOU WAS A GIRL."
"DYER HAD WANTED YOU BROUGHT UP THE VILEST OF THE VILE, BUT OLDRIN' BROUGHT YOU UP INNOCENT."
ELIZABETH ERNE! I LOVED YOUR MOTHER, AND I SEE HER IN YOU!
An exquisite glow shone from Bess' face, and a new, conscious pride of worth dignified her bearing.

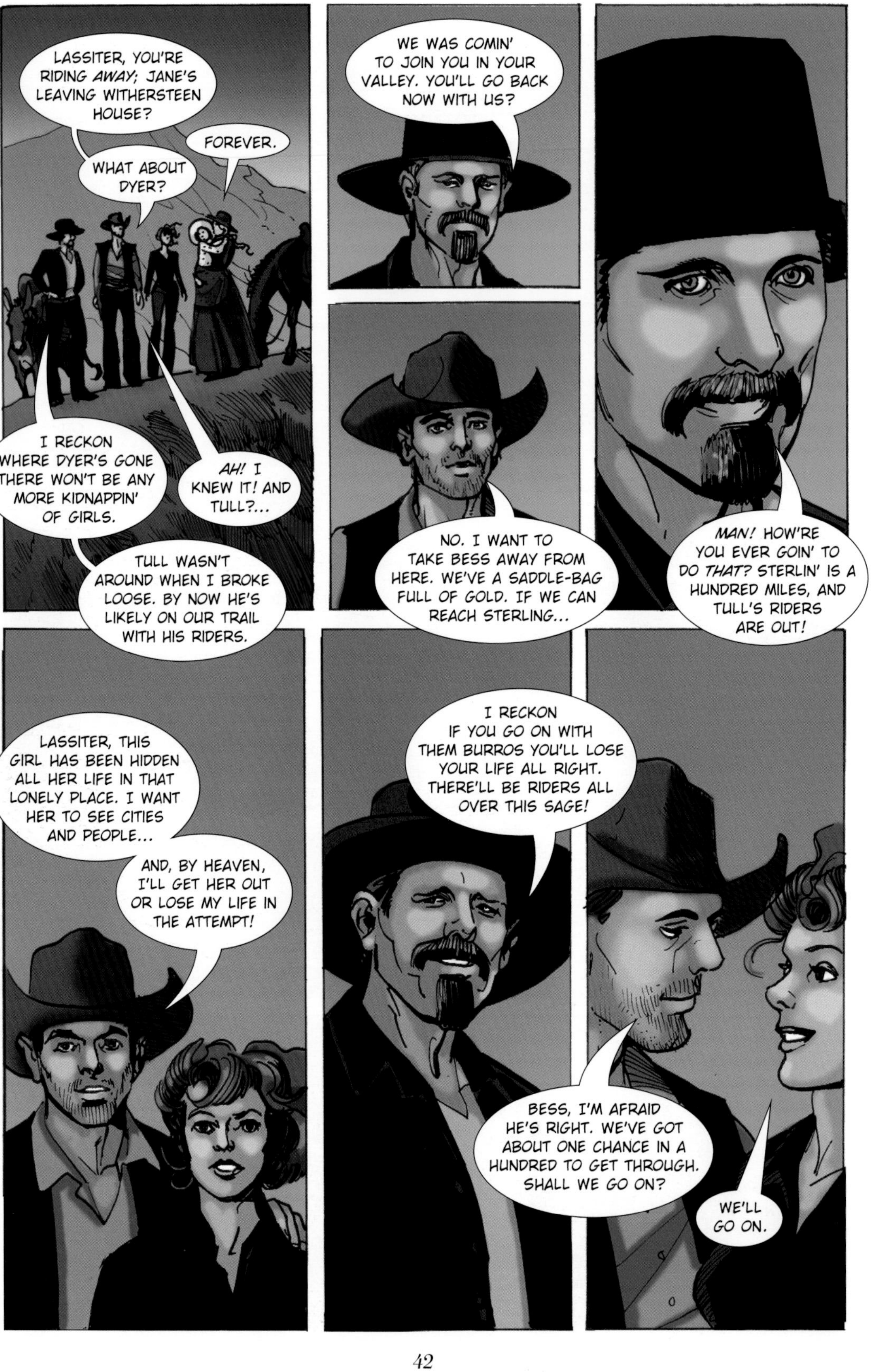
LASSITER, YOU'RE RIDING *AWAY*; JANE'S LEAVING WITHERSTEEN HOUSE?
FOREVER.
WHAT ABOUT DYER?
I RECKON WHERE DYER'S GONE THERE WON'T BE ANY MORE KIDNAPPIN' OF GIRLS.
AH! I KNEW IT! AND TULL?...
TULL WASN'T AROUND WHEN I BROKE LOOSE. BY NOW HE'S LIKELY ON OUR TRAIL WITH HIS RIDERS.
WE WAS *COMIN'* TO JOIN YOU IN YOUR VALLEY. YOU'LL GO BACK NOW WITH US?
NO. I WANT TO TAKE BESS AWAY FROM HERE. WE'VE A SADDLE-BAG FULL OF GOLD. IF WE CAN REACH STERLING...
MAN! HOW'RE YOU EVER GOIN' TO DO *THAT*? STERLIN' IS A HUNDRED MILES, AND TULL'S RIDERS ARE OUT!
LASSITER, THIS GIRL HAS BEEN HIDDEN ALL HER LIFE IN THAT LONELY PLACE. I WANT HER TO SEE CITIES AND PEOPLE...
AND, BY HEAVEN, I'LL GET HER OUT OR LOSE MY LIFE IN THE ATTEMPT!
I RECKON IF YOU GO ON WITH THEM BURROS YOU'LL LOSE YOUR LIFE ALL RIGHT. THERE'LL BE RIDERS ALL OVER THIS SAGE!
BESS, I'M AFRAID HE'S RIGHT. WE'VE GOT ABOUT ONE CHANCE IN A HUNDRED TO GET THROUGH. SHALL WE GO ON?
WE'LL GO ON.

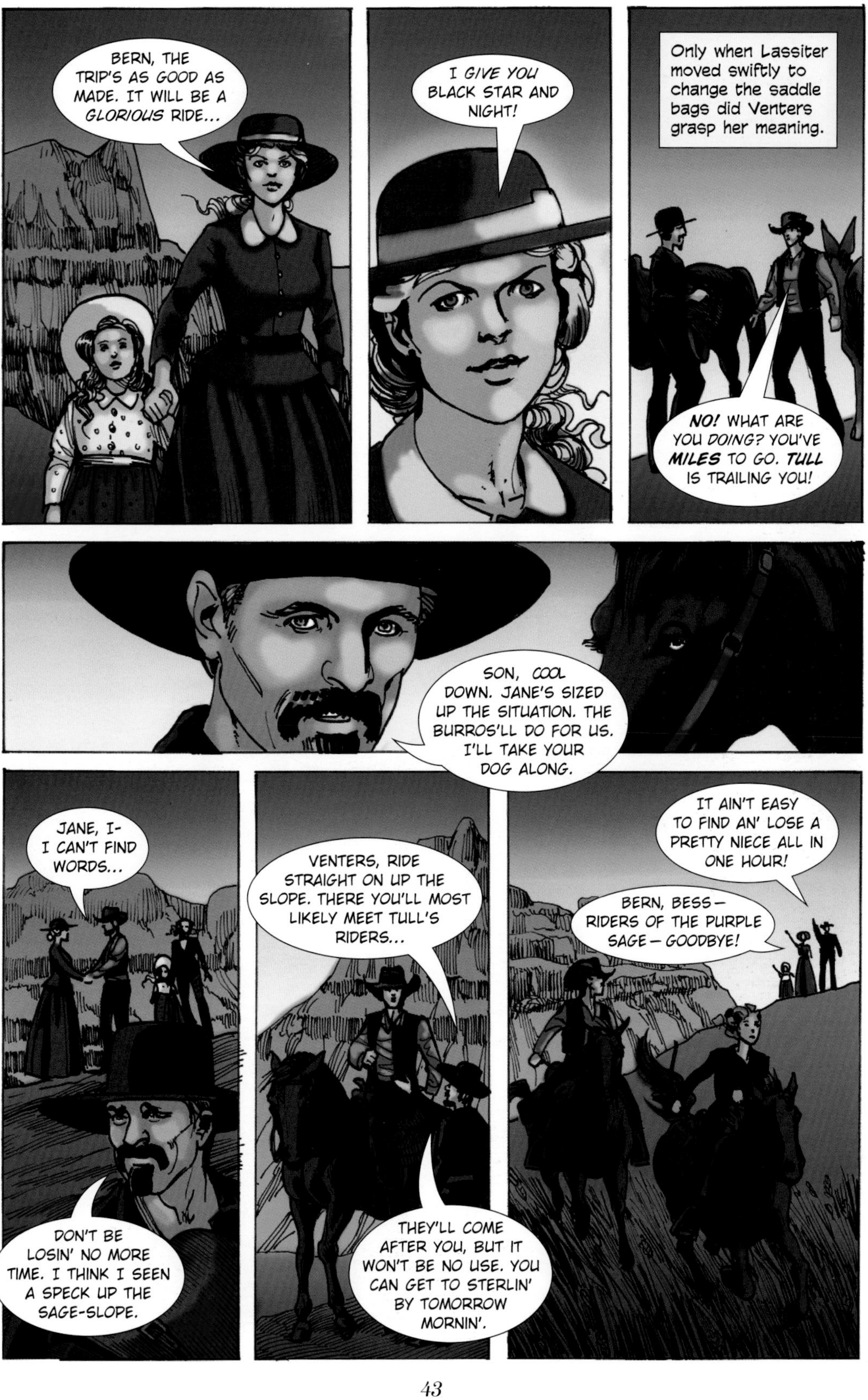
BERN, THE TRIP'S AS GOOD AS MADE. IT WILL BE A *GLORIOUS* RIDE...
I *GIVE YOU* BLACK STAR AND NIGHT!
Only when Lassiter moved swiftly to change the saddle bags did Venters grasp her meaning.
NO! WHAT ARE YOU *DOING?* YOU'VE ***MILES*** TO GO. ***TULL*** IS TRAILING YOU!
SON, COOL DOWN. JANE'S SIZED UP THE SITUATION. THE BURROS'LL DO FOR US. I'LL TAKE YOUR DOG ALONG.
JANE, I- I CAN'T FIND WORDS...
DON'T BE LOSIN' NO MORE TIME. I THINK I SEEN A SPECK UP THE SAGE-SLOPE.
VENTERS, RIDE STRAIGHT ON UP THE SLOPE. THERE YOU'LL MOST LIKELY MEET TULL'S RIDERS...
THEY'LL COME AFTER YOU, BUT IT WON'T BE NO USE. YOU CAN GET TO STERLIN' BY TOMORROW MORNIN'.
IT AIN'T EASY TO FIND AN' LOSE A PRETTY NIECE ALL IN ONE HOUR!
BERN, BESS— RIDERS OF THE PURPLE SAGE—GOODBYE!

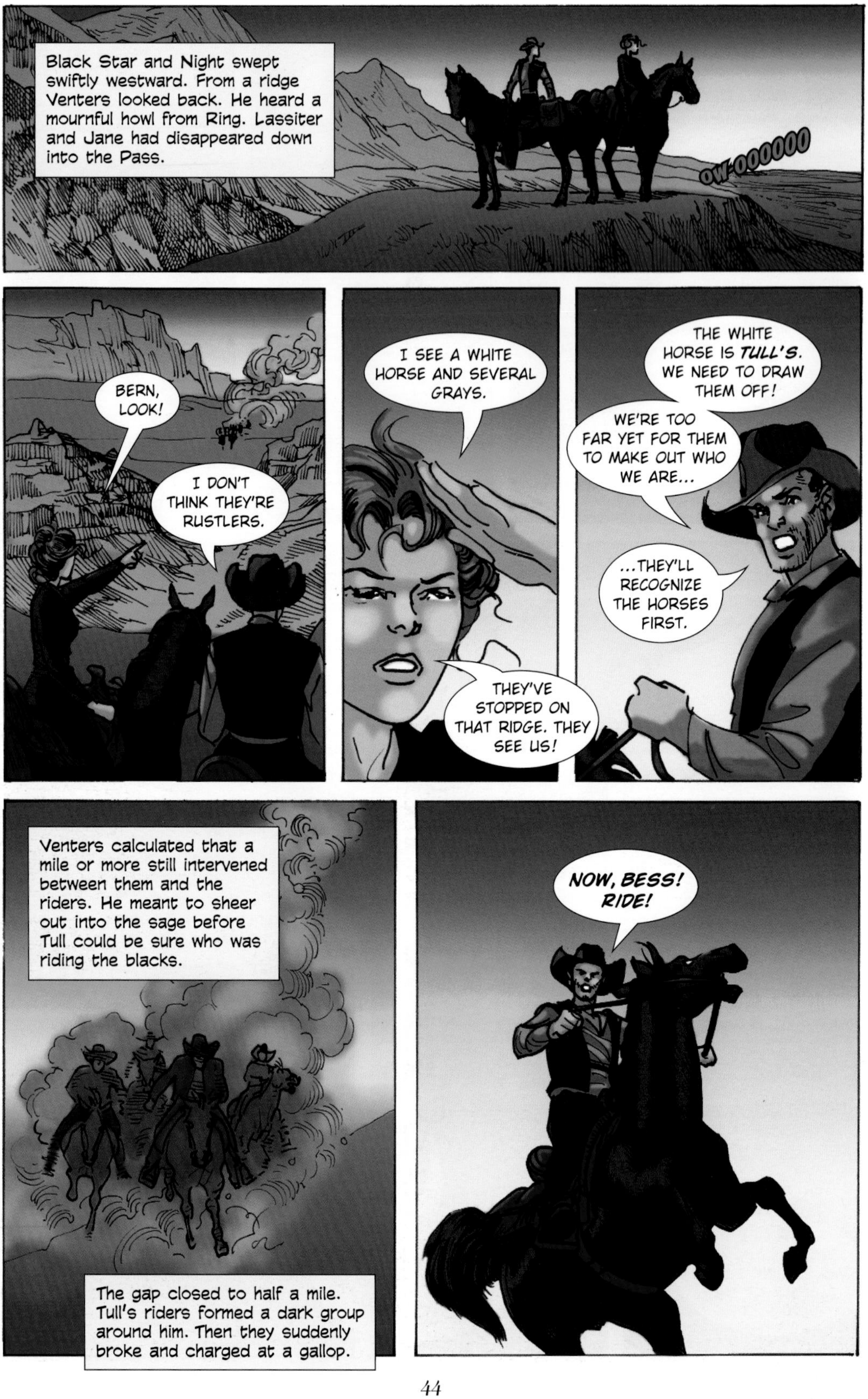
Black Star and Night swept swiftly westward. From a ridge Venters looked back. He heard a mournful howl from Ring. Lassiter and Jane had disappeared down into the Pass.
OW-OOOOOO
BERN, LOOK!
I DON'T THINK THEY'RE RUSTLERS.
I SEE A WHITE HORSE AND SEVERAL GRAYS.
THEY'VE STOPPED ON THAT RIDGE. THEY SEE US!
THE WHITE HORSE IS TULL'S. WE NEED TO DRAW THEM OFF!
WE'RE TOO FAR YET FOR THEM TO MAKE OUT WHO WE ARE...
...THEY'LL RECOGNIZE THE HORSES FIRST.
Venters calculated that a mile or more still intervened between them and the riders. He meant to sheer out into the sage before Tull could be sure who was riding the blacks.
The gap closed to half a mile. Tull's riders formed a dark group around him. Then they suddenly broke and charged at a gallop.
NOW, BESS! RIDE!

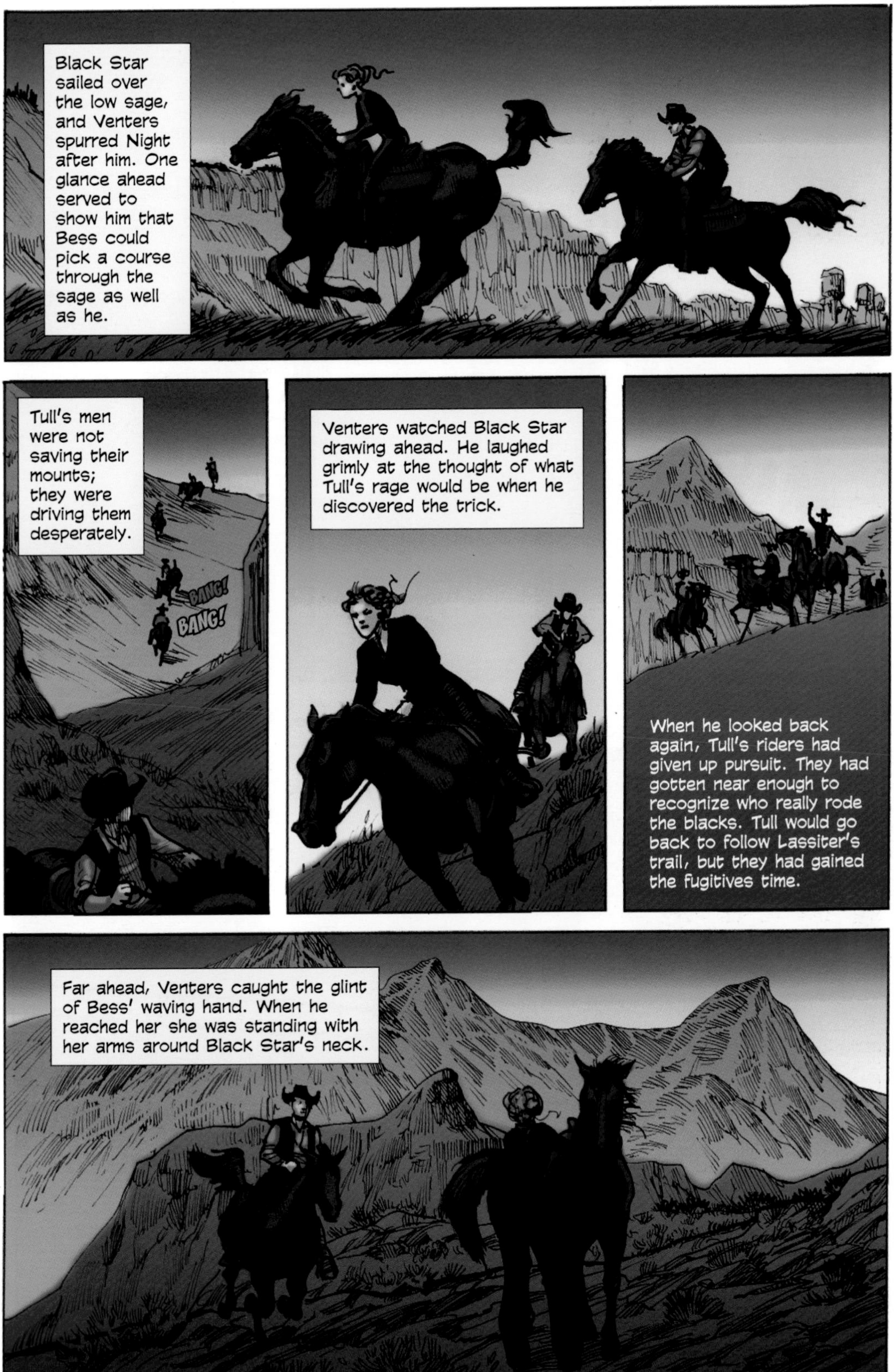
Black Star sailed over the low sage, and Venters spurred Night after him. One glance ahead served to show him that Bess could pick a course through the sage as well as he.
Tull's men were not saving their mounts; they were driving them desperately.
BANG!
BANG!
Venters watched Black Star drawing ahead. He laughed grimly at the thought of what Tull's rage would be when he discovered the trick.
When he looked back again, Tull's riders had given up pursuit. They had gotten near enough to recognize who really rode the blacks. Tull would go back to follow Lassiter's trail, but they had gained the fugitives time.
Far ahead, Venters caught the glint of Bess' waving hand. When he reached her she was standing with her arms around Black Star's neck.

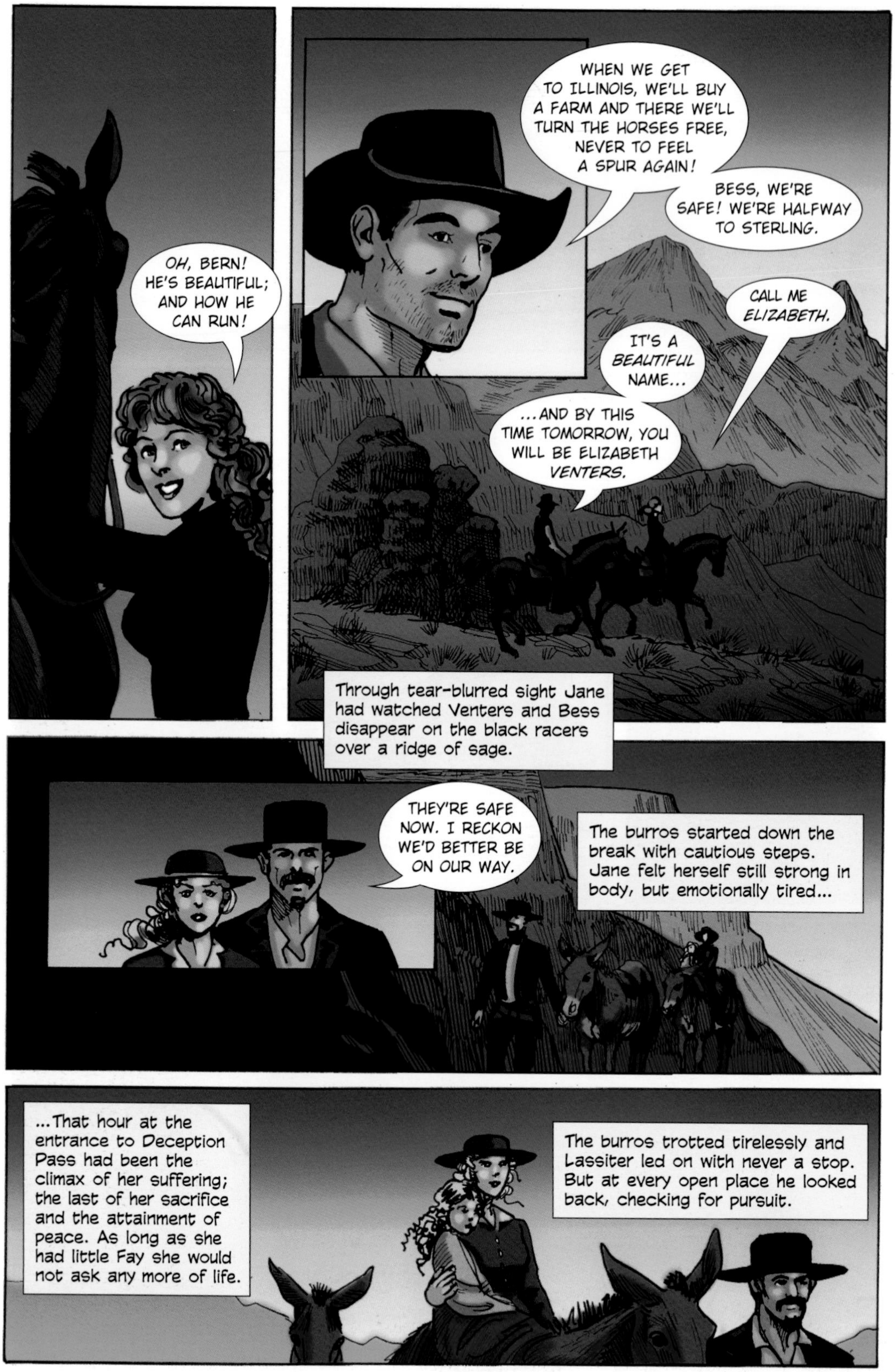
OH, BERN! HE'S BEAUTIFUL; AND HOW HE CAN RUN!
WHEN WE GET TO ILLINOIS, WE'LL BUY A FARM AND THERE WE'LL TURN THE HORSES FREE, NEVER TO FEEL A SPUR AGAIN!
BESS, WE'RE SAFE! WE'RE HALFWAY TO STERLING.
CALL ME ELIZABETH.
IT'S A BEAUTIFUL NAME...
...AND BY THIS TIME TOMORROW, YOU WILL BE ELIZABETH VENTERS.
Through tear-blurred sight Jane had watched Venters and Bess disappear on the black racers over a ridge of sage.
THEY'RE SAFE NOW. I RECKON WE'D BETTER BE ON OUR WAY.
The burros started down the break with cautious steps. Jane felt herself still strong in body, but emotionally tired...
...That hour at the entrance to Deception Pass had been the climax of her suffering; the last of her sacrifice and the attainment of peace. As long as she had little Fay she would not ask any more of life.
The burros trotted tirelessly and Lassiter led on with never a stop. But at every open place he looked back, checking for pursuit.

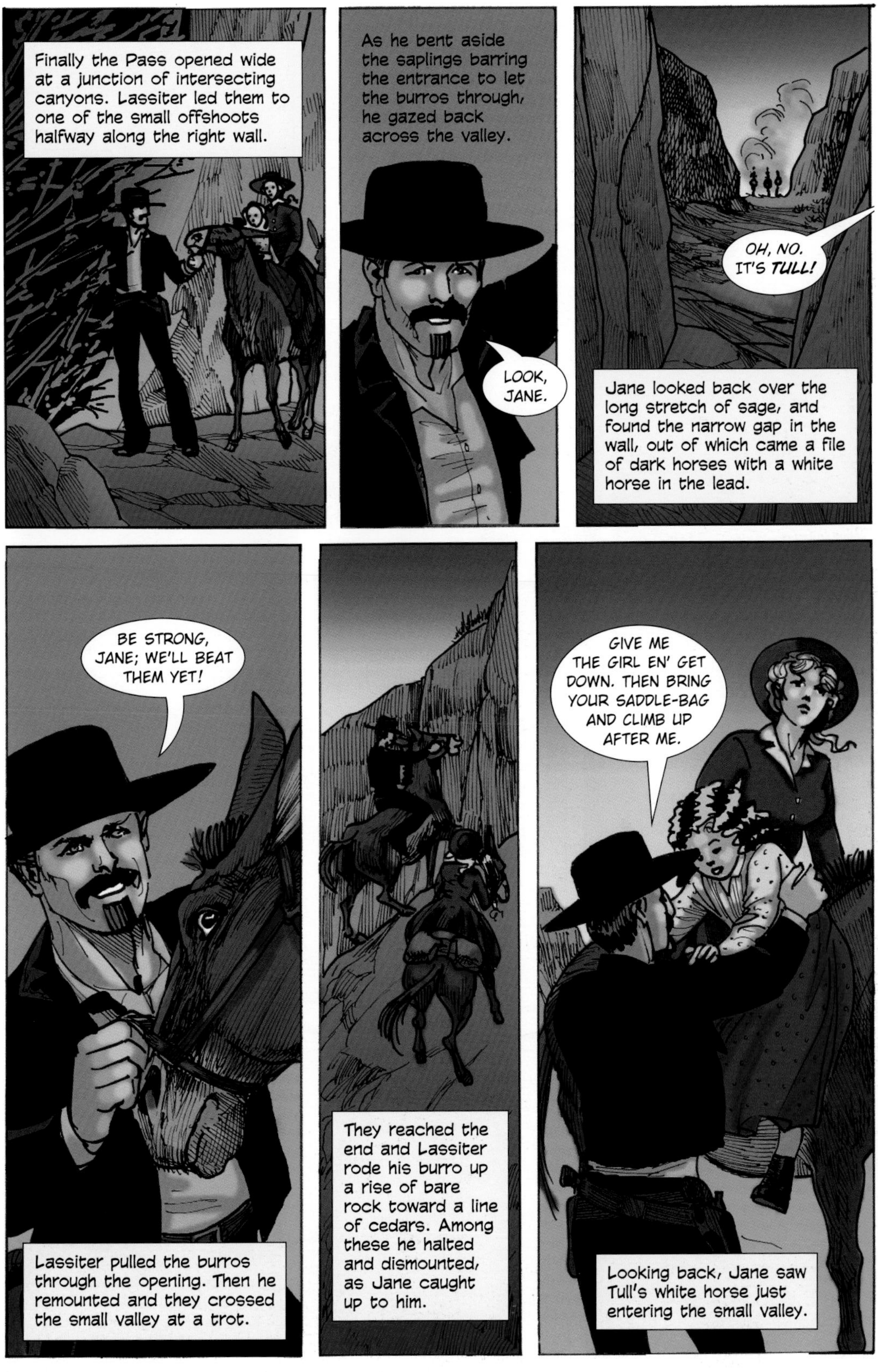
Finally the Pass opened wide at a junction of intersecting canyons. Lassiter led them to one of the small offshoots halfway along the right wall.
As he bent aside the saplings barring the entrance to let the burros through, he gazed back across the valley.
LOOK, JANE.
OH, NO. IT'S TULL!
Jane looked back over the long stretch of sage, and found the narrow gap in the wall, out of which came a file of dark horses with a white horse in the lead.
BE STRONG, JANE; WE'LL BEAT THEM YET!
Lassiter pulled the burros through the opening. Then he remounted and they crossed the small valley at a trot.
They reached the end and Lassiter rode his burro up a rise of bare rock toward a line of cedars. Among these he halted and dismounted, as Jane caught up to him.
GIVE ME THE GIRL EN' GET DOWN. THEN BRING YOUR SADDLE-BAG AND CLIMB UP AFTER ME.
Looking back, Jane saw Tull's white horse just entering the small valley.

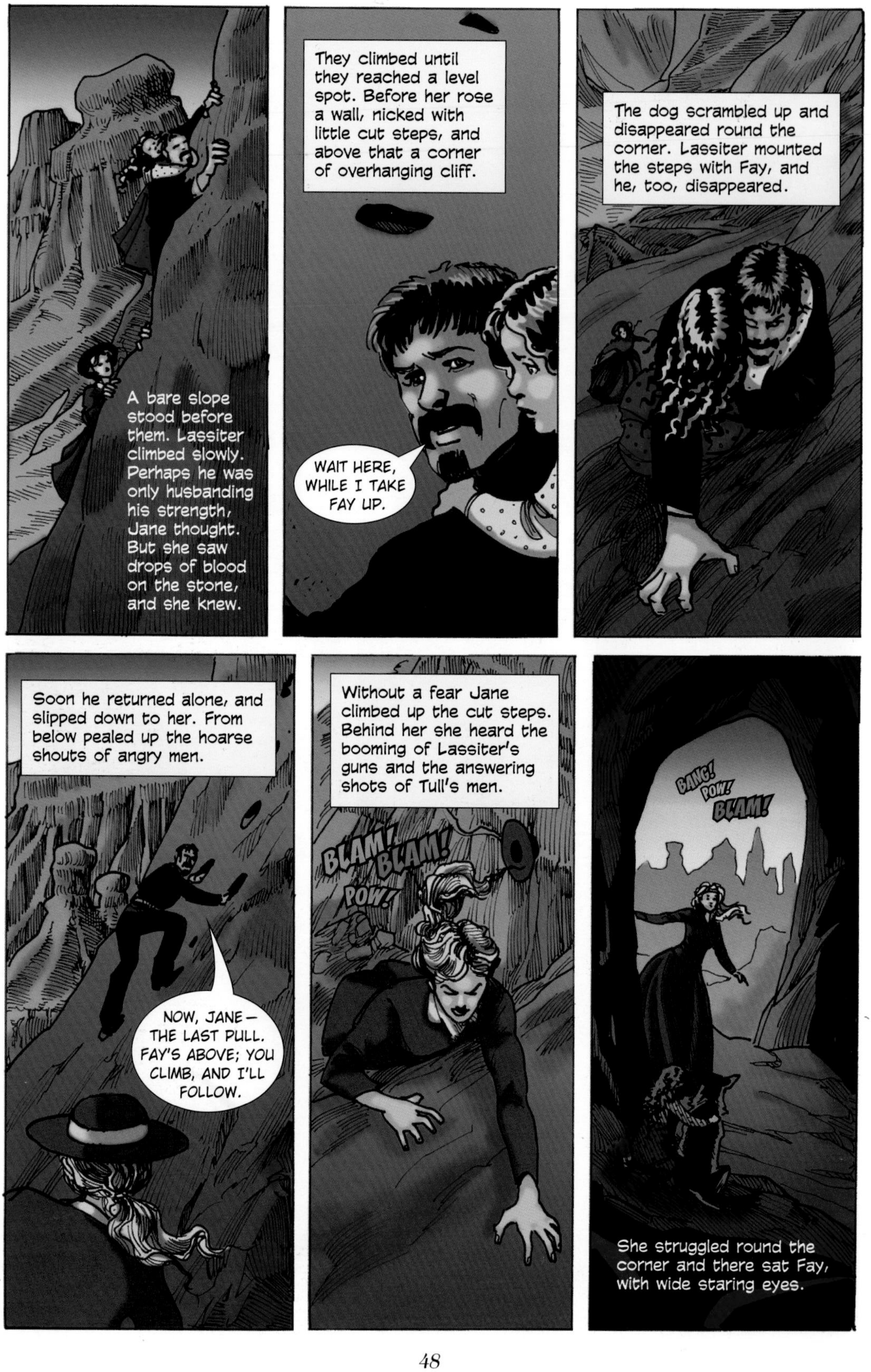
A bare slope stood before them. Lassiter climbed slowly. Perhaps he was only husbanding his strength, Jane thought. But she saw drops of blood on the stone, and she knew.
They climbed until they reached a level spot. Before her rose a wall, nicked with little cut steps, and above that a corner of overhanging cliff.
WAIT HERE, WHILE I TAKE FAY UP.
The dog scrambled up and disappeared round the corner. Lassiter mounted the steps with Fay, and he, too, disappeared.
Soon he returned alone, and slipped down to her. From below pealed up the hoarse shouts of angry men.
NOW, JANE— THE LAST PULL. FAY'S ABOVE; YOU CLIMB, AND I'LL FOLLOW.
Without a fear Jane climbed up the cut steps. Behind her she heard the booming of Lassiter's guns and the answering shots of Tull's men.
BLAM! BLAM!
POW!
BANG! POW! BLAM!
She struggled round the corner and there sat Fay, with wide staring eyes.

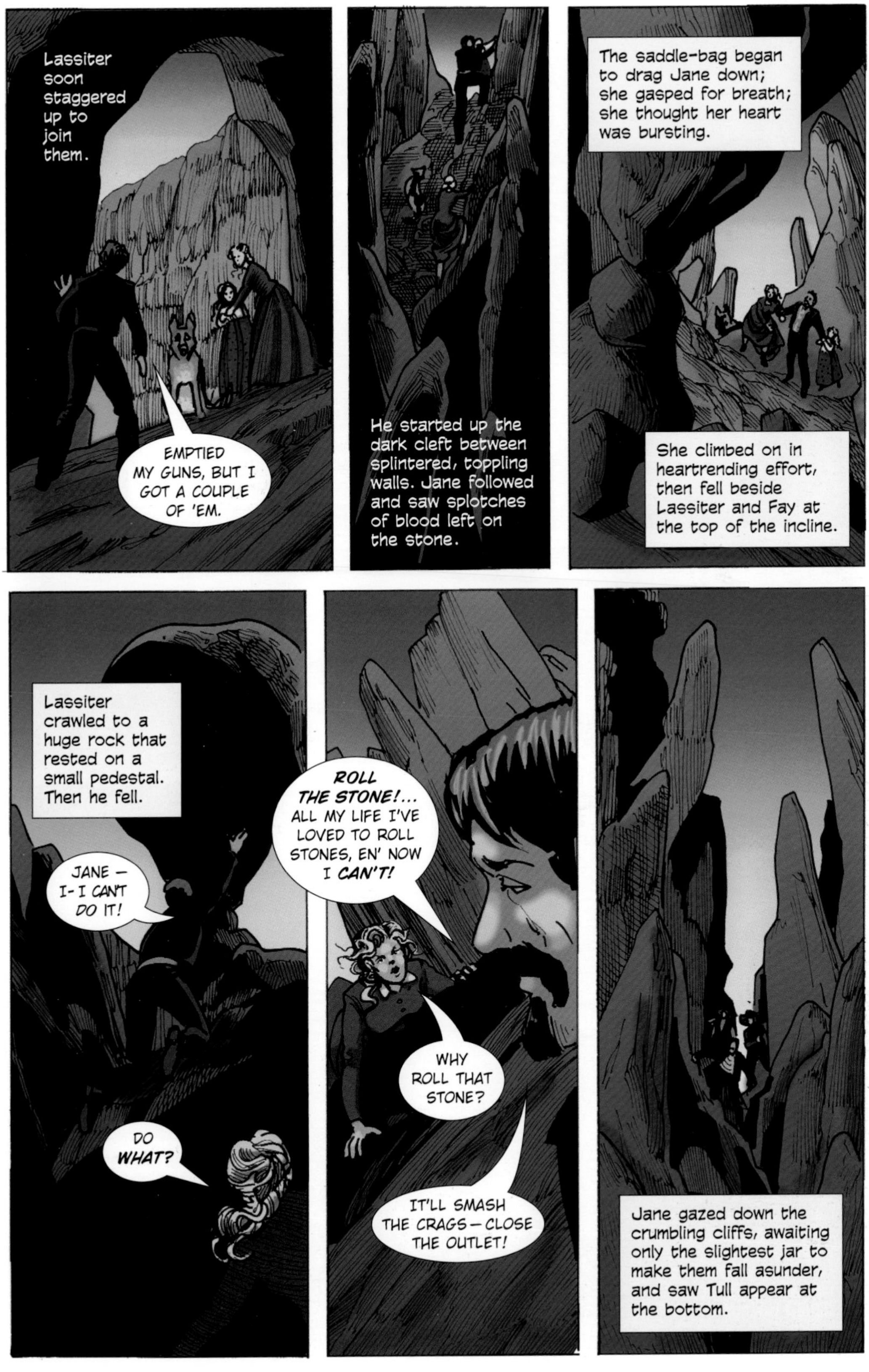
Lassiter soon staggered up to join them.
EMPTIED MY GUNS, BUT I GOT A COUPLE OF 'EM.
He started up the dark cleft between splintered, toppling walls. Jane followed and saw splotches of blood left on the stone.
The saddle-bag began to drag Jane down; she gasped for breath; she thought her heart was bursting.
She climbed on in heartrending effort, then fell beside Lassiter and Fay at the top of the incline.
Lassiter crawled to a huge rock that rested on a small pedestal. Then he fell.
JANE — I- I CAN'T DO IT!
DO WHAT?
ROLL THE STONE!... ALL MY LIFE I'VE LOVED TO ROLL STONES, EN' NOW I CAN'T!
WHY ROLL THAT STONE?
IT'LL SMASH THE CRAGS—CLOSE THE OUTLET!
Jane gazed down the crumbling cliffs, awaiting only the slightest jar to make them fall asunder, and saw Tull appear at the bottom.

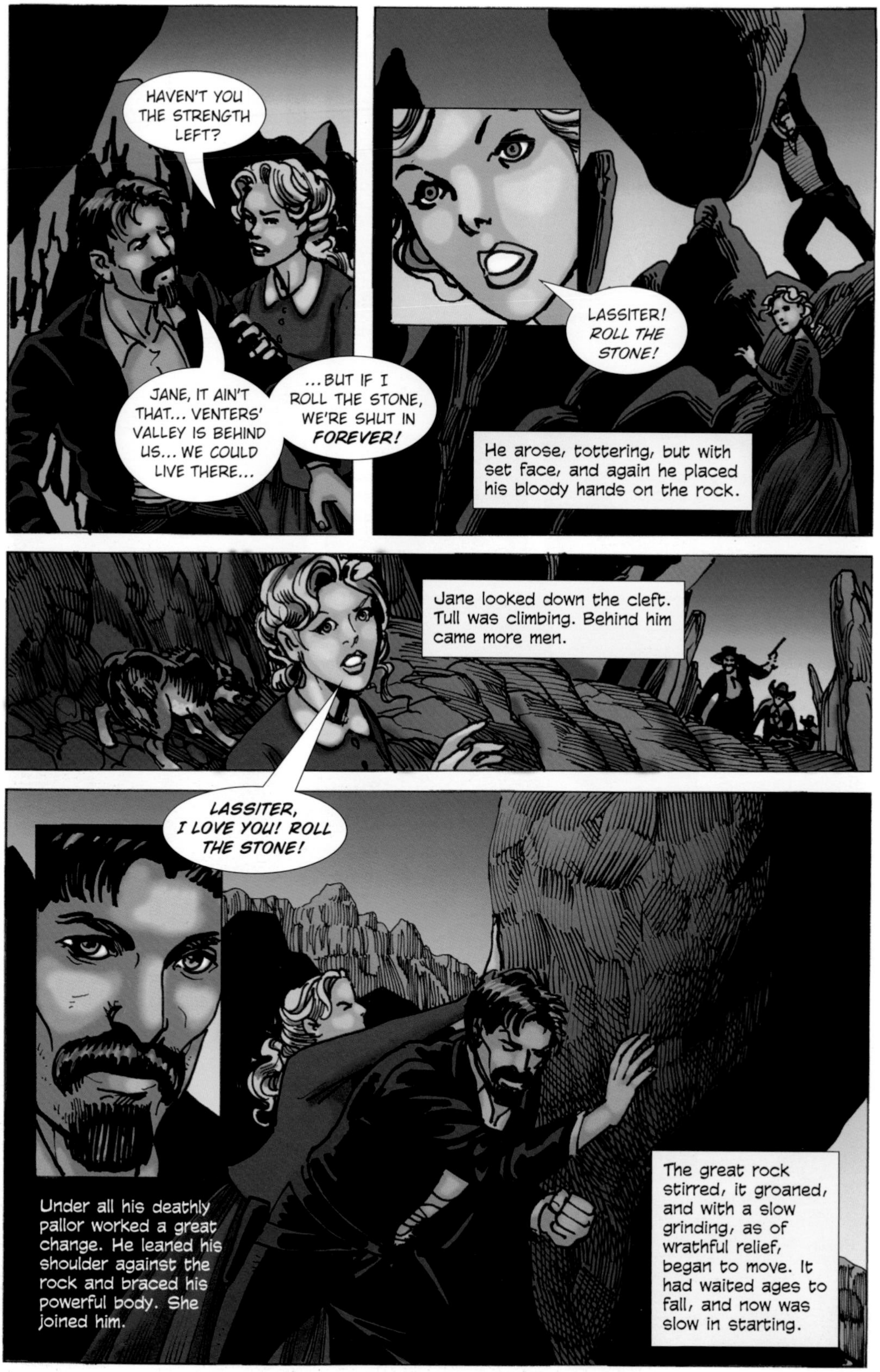
HAVEN'T YOU THE STRENGTH LEFT?
JANE, IT AIN'T THAT... VENTERS' VALLEY IS BEHIND US... WE COULD LIVE THERE...
...BUT IF I ROLL THE STONE, WE'RE SHUT IN FOREVER!
LASSITER! ROLL THE STONE!
He arose, tottering, but with set face, and again he placed his bloody hands on the rock.
Jane looked down the cleft. Tull was climbing. Behind him came more men.
LASSITER, I LOVE YOU! ROLL THE STONE!
Under all his deathly pallor worked a great change. He leaned his shoulder against the rock and braced his powerful body. She joined him.
The great rock stirred, it groaned, and with a slow grinding, as of wrathful relief, began to move. It had waited ages to fall, and now was slow in starting.

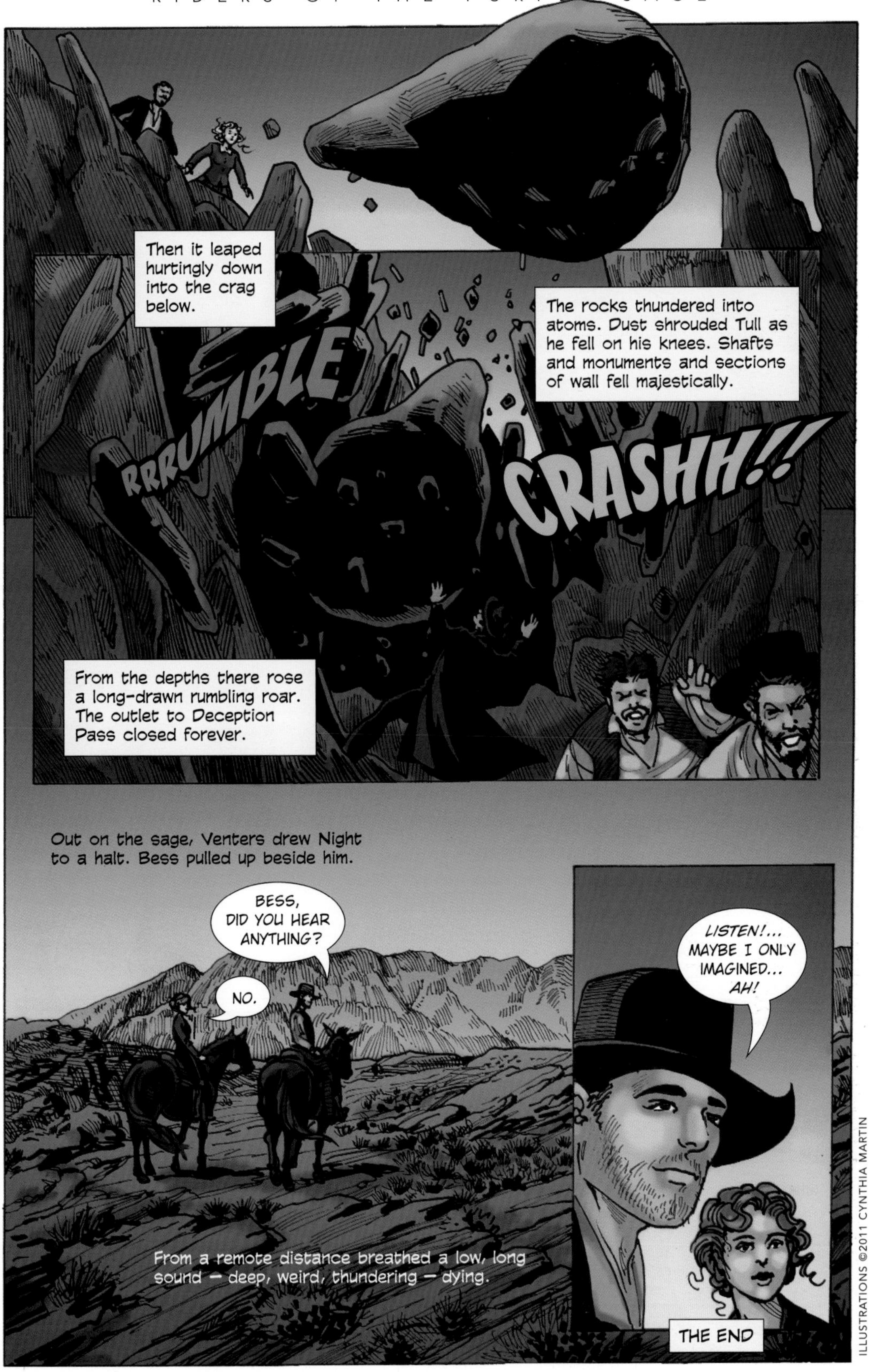
Then it leaped hurtingly down into the crag below.
The rocks thundered into atoms. Dust shrouded Tull as he fell on his knees. Shafts and monuments and sections of wall fell majestically.
RRRUMBLE
CRASHH!!
From the depths there rose a long-drawn rumbling roar. The outlet to Deception Pass closed forever.
Out on the sage, Venters drew Night to a halt. Bess pulled up beside him.
BESS, DID YOU HEAR ANYTHING?
NO.
From a remote distance breathed a low, long sound — deep, weird, thundering — dying.
LISTEN!... MAYBE I ONLY IMAGINED... AH!
THE END

ADAPTED BY BEN AVERY~ART BY GEORGE SELLAS WITH SCOTT LINCOLN & RICHARD DOAK

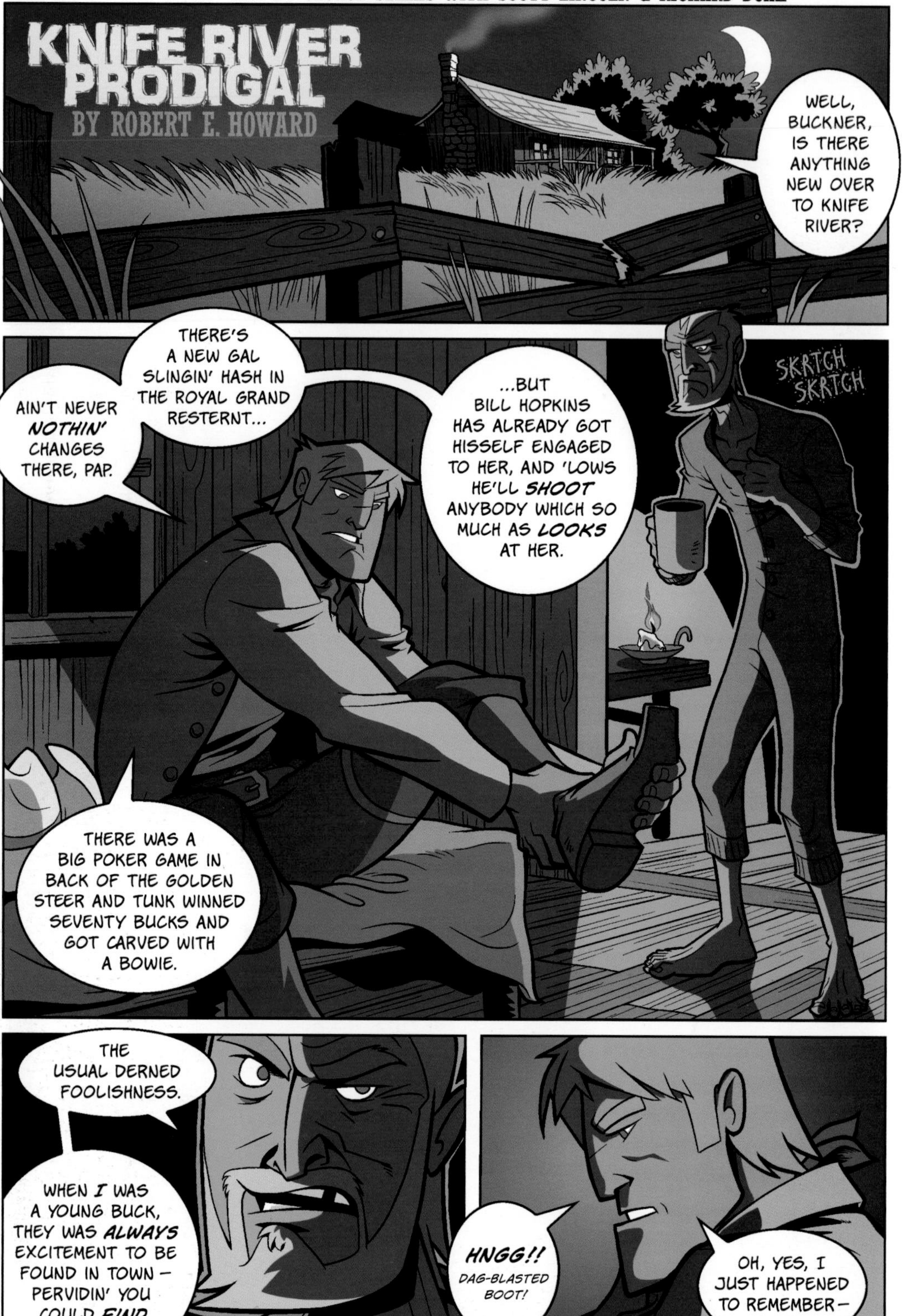
KNIFE RIVER PRODIGAL
BY ROBERT E. HOWARD
WELL, BUCKNER, IS THERE ANYTHING NEW OVER TO KNIFE RIVER?
AIN'T NEVER NOTHIN' CHANGES THERE, PAP.
THERE'S A NEW GAL SLINGIN' HASH IN THE ROYAL GRAND RESTERNT...
...BUT BILL HOPKINS HAS ALREADY GOT HISSELF ENGAGED TO HER, AND 'LOWS HE'LL SHOOT ANYBODY WHICH SO MUCH AS LOOKS AT HER.
SKRTCH SKRTCH
THERE WAS A BIG POKER GAME IN BACK OF THE GOLDEN STEER AND TUNK WINNED SEVENTY BUCKS AND GOT CARVED WITH A BOWIE.
THE USUAL DERNED FOOLISHNESS.
WHEN I WAS A YOUNG BUCK, THEY WAS ALWAYS EXCITEMENT TO BE FOUND IN TOWN— PERVIDIN' YOU COULD FIND A TOWN.
HNGG!! DAG-BLASTED BOOT!
OH, YES, I JUST HAPPENED TO REMEMBER—

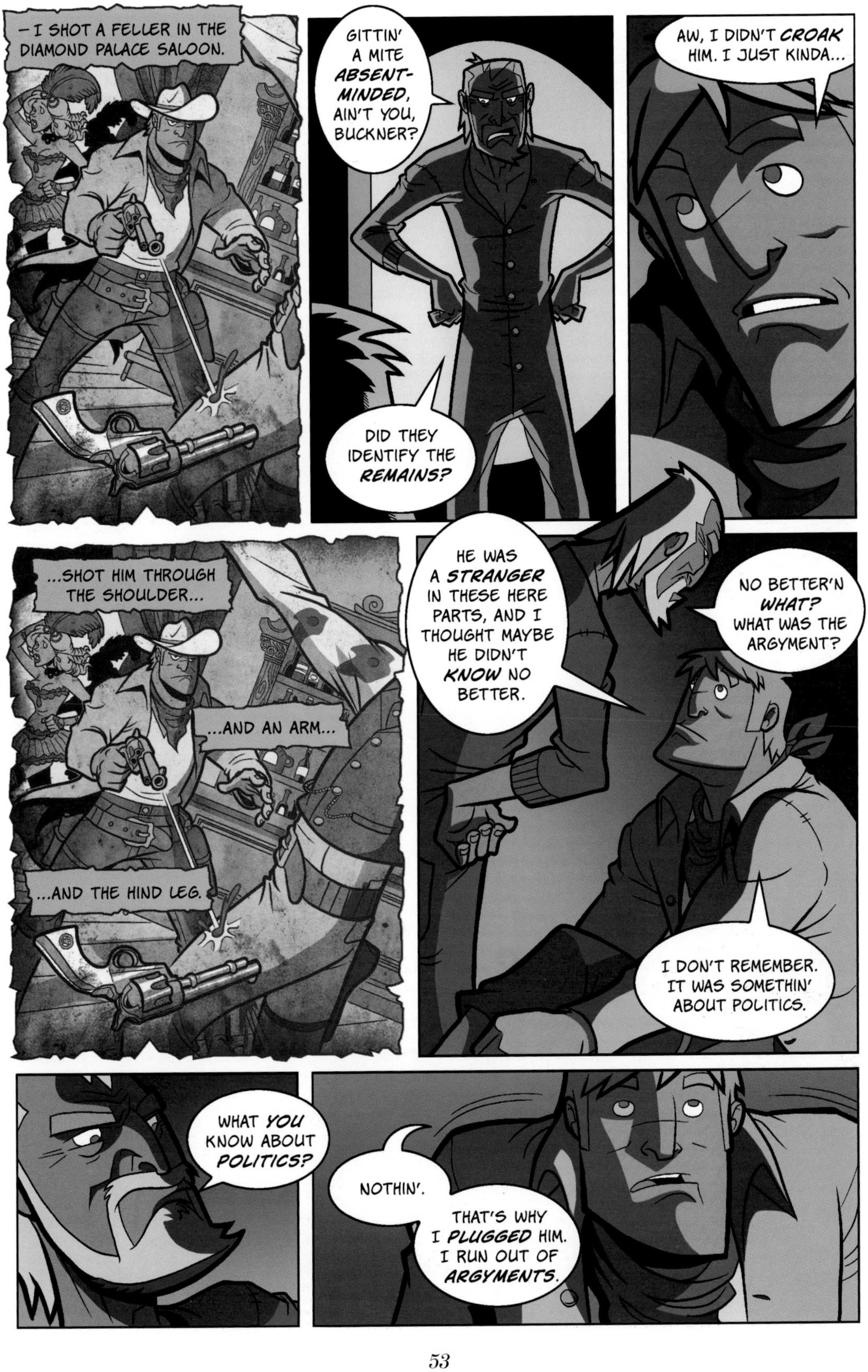
—I SHOT A FELLER IN THE DIAMOND PALACE SALOON.
GITTIN' A MITE ABSENT-MINDED, AIN'T YOU, BUCKNER?
DID THEY IDENTIFY THE REMAINS?
AW, I DIDN'T CROAK HIM. I JUST KINDA...
...SHOT HIM THROUGH THE SHOULDER...
...AND AN ARM...
...AND THE HIND LEG.
HE WAS A STRANGER IN THESE HERE PARTS, AND I THOUGHT MAYBE HE DIDN'T KNOW NO BETTER.
NO BETTER'N WHAT? WHAT WAS THE ARGYMENT?
I DON'T REMEMBER. IT WAS SOMETHIN' ABOUT POLITICS.
WHAT YOU KNOW ABOUT POLITICS?
NOTHIN'.
THAT'S WHY I PLUGGED HIM. I RUN OUT OF ARGYMENTS.

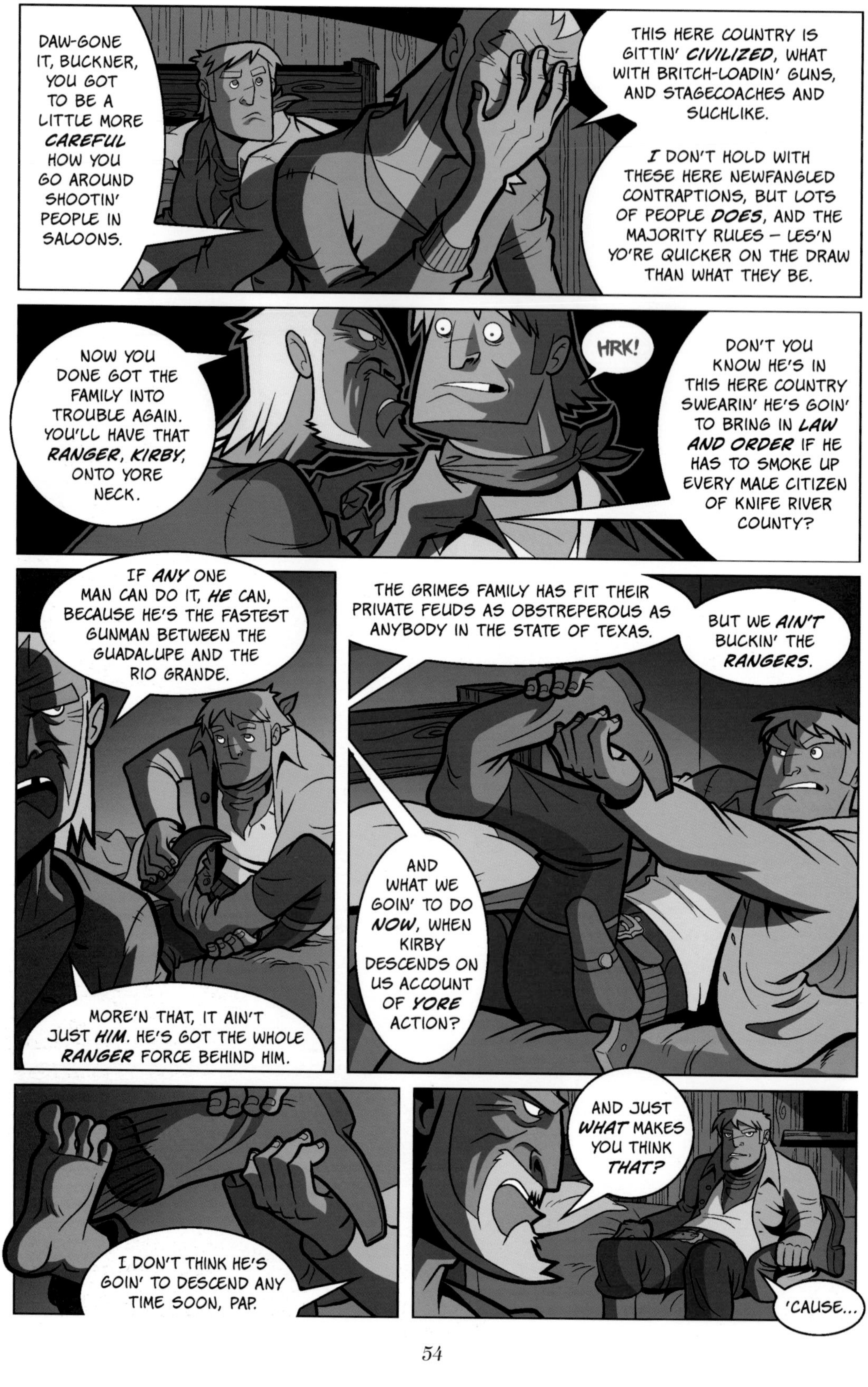
DAW-GONE IT, BUCKNER, YOU GOT TO BE A LITTLE MORE CAREFUL HOW YOU GO AROUND SHOOTIN' PEOPLE IN SALOONS.
THIS HERE COUNTRY IS GITTIN' CIVILIZED, WHAT WITH BRITCH-LOADIN' GUNS, AND STAGECOACHES AND SUCHLIKE.
I DON'T HOLD WITH THESE HERE NEWFANGLED CONTRAPTIONS, BUT LOTS OF PEOPLE DOES, AND THE MAJORITY RULES – LES'N YO'RE QUICKER ON THE DRAW THAN WHAT THEY BE.
NOW YOU DONE GOT THE FAMILY INTO TROUBLE AGAIN. YOU'LL HAVE THAT RANGER, KIRBY, ONTO YORE NECK.
HRK!
DON'T YOU KNOW HE'S IN THIS HERE COUNTRY SWEARIN' HE'S GOIN' TO BRING IN LAW AND ORDER IF HE HAS TO SMOKE UP EVERY MALE CITIZEN OF KNIFE RIVER COUNTY?
IF ANY ONE MAN CAN DO IT, HE CAN, BECAUSE HE'S THE FASTEST GUNMAN BETWEEN THE GUADALUPE AND THE RIO GRANDE.
MORE'N THAT, IT AIN'T JUST HIM. HE'S GOT THE WHOLE RANGER FORCE BEHIND HIM.
THE GRIMES FAMILY HAS FIT THEIR PRIVATE FEUDS AS OBSTREPEROUS AS ANYBODY IN THE STATE OF TEXAS.
BUT WE AIN'T BUCKIN' THE RANGERS.
AND WHAT WE GOIN' TO DO NOW, WHEN KIRBY DESCENDS ON US ACCOUNT OF YORE ACTION?
I DON'T THINK HE'S GOIN' TO DESCEND ANY TIME SOON, PAP.
AND JUST WHAT MAKES YOU THINK THAT?
'CAUSE...

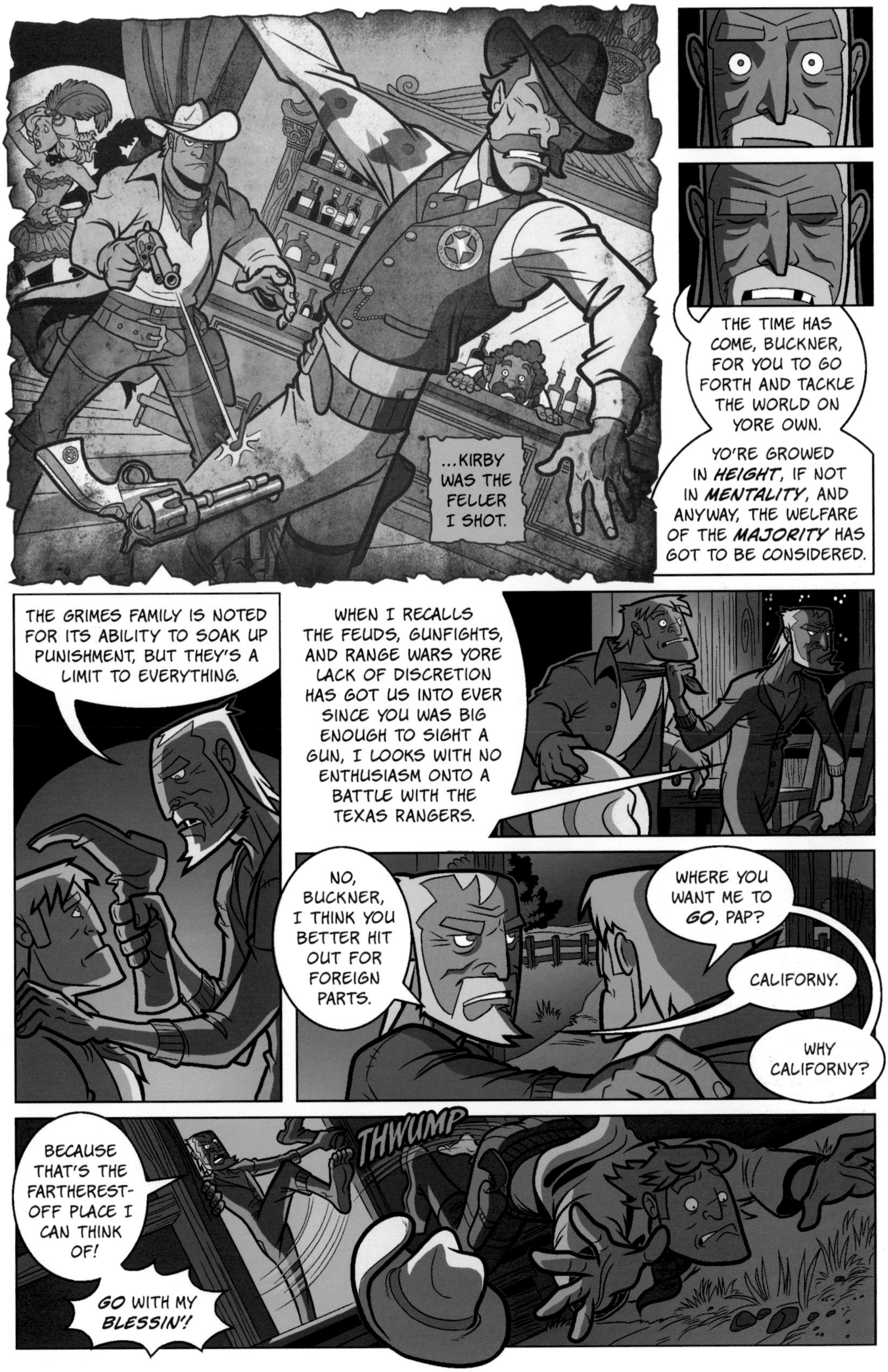
...KIRBY WAS THE FELLER I SHOT.
THE TIME HAS COME, BUCKNER, FOR YOU TO GO FORTH AND TACKLE THE WORLD ON YORE OWN.
YO'RE GROWED IN *HEIGHT*, IF NOT IN *MENTALITY*, AND ANYWAY, THE WELFARE OF THE *MAJORITY* HAS GOT TO BE CONSIDERED.
THE GRIMES FAMILY IS NOTED FOR ITS ABILITY TO SOAK UP PUNISHMENT, BUT THEY'S A LIMIT TO EVERYTHING.
WHEN I RECALLS THE FEUDS, GUNFIGHTS, AND RANGE WARS YORE LACK OF DISCRETION HAS GOT US INTO EVER SINCE YOU WAS BIG ENOUGH TO SIGHT A GUN, I LOOKS WITH NO ENTHUSIASM ONTO A BATTLE WITH THE TEXAS RANGERS.
NO, BUCKNER, I THINK YOU BETTER HIT OUT FOR FOREIGN PARTS.
WHERE YOU WANT ME TO *GO*, PAP?
CALIFORNY.
WHY CALIFORNY?
BECAUSE THAT'S THE FARTHEREST-OFF PLACE I CAN THINK OF!
THWUMP
GO WITH MY *BLESSIN'*!

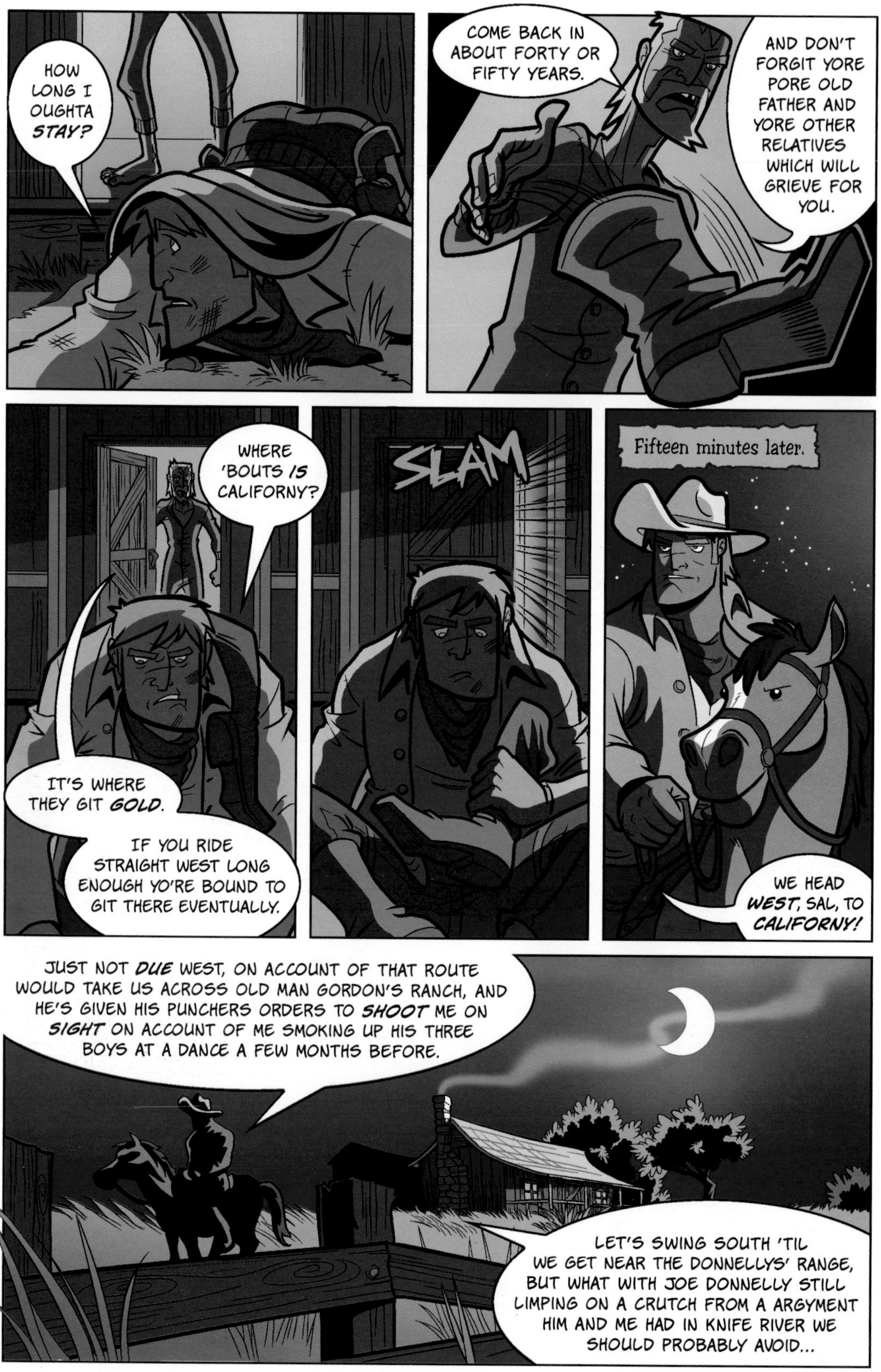
HOW LONG I OUGHTA *STAY?*
COME BACK IN ABOUT FORTY OR FIFTY YEARS.
AND DON'T FORGIT YORE PORE OLD FATHER AND YORE OTHER RELATIVES WHICH WILL GRIEVE FOR YOU.
WHERE 'BOUTS *IS* CALIFORNY?
IT'S WHERE THEY GIT *GOLD*.
IF YOU RIDE STRAIGHT WEST LONG ENOUGH YO'RE BOUND TO GIT THERE EVENTUALLY.
SLAM
Fifteen minutes later.
WE HEAD *WEST*, SAL, TO *CALIFORNY!*
JUST NOT *DUE* WEST, ON ACCOUNT OF THAT ROUTE WOULD TAKE US ACROSS OLD MAN GORDON'S RANCH, AND HE'S GIVEN HIS PUNCHERS ORDERS TO *SHOOT* ME ON *SIGHT* ON ACCOUNT OF ME SMOKING UP HIS THREE BOYS AT A DANCE A FEW MONTHS BEFORE.
LET'S SWING SOUTH 'TIL WE GET NEAR THE DONNELLYS' RANGE, BUT WHAT WITH JOE DONNELLY STILL LIMPING ON A CRUTCH FROM A ARGYMENT HIM AND ME HAD IN KNIFE RIVER WE SHOULD PROBABLY AVOID...

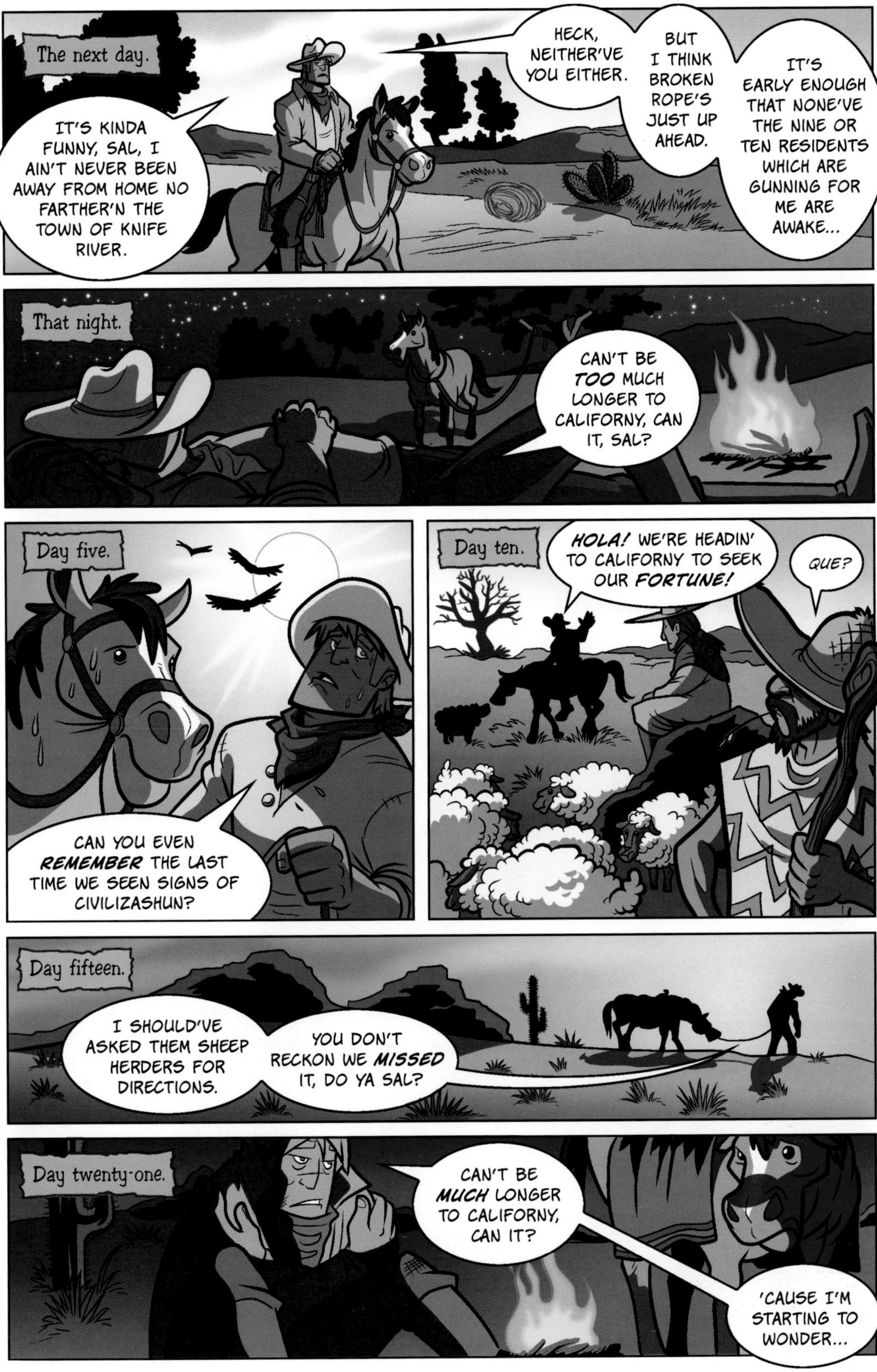
The next day.
IT'S KINDA FUNNY, SAL, I AIN'T NEVER BEEN AWAY FROM HOME NO FARTHER'N THE TOWN OF KNIFE RIVER.
HECK, NEITHER'VE YOU EITHER.
BUT I THINK BROKEN ROPE'S JUST UP AHEAD.
IT'S EARLY ENOUGH THAT NONE'VE THE NINE OR TEN RESIDENTS WHICH ARE GUNNING FOR ME ARE AWAKE...
That night.
CAN'T BE TOO MUCH LONGER TO CALIFORNY, CAN IT, SAL?
Day five.
CAN YOU EVEN REMEMBER THE LAST TIME WE SEEN SIGNS OF CIVILIZASHUN?
Day ten.
HOLA! WE'RE HEADIN' TO CALIFORNY TO SEEK OUR FORTUNE!
QUE?
Day fifteen.
I SHOULD'VE ASKED THEM SHEEP HERDERS FOR DIRECTIONS.
YOU DON'T RECKON WE MISSED IT, DO YA SAL?
Day twenty-one.
CAN'T BE MUCH LONGER TO CALIFORNY, CAN IT?
'CAUSE I'M STARTING TO WONDER...

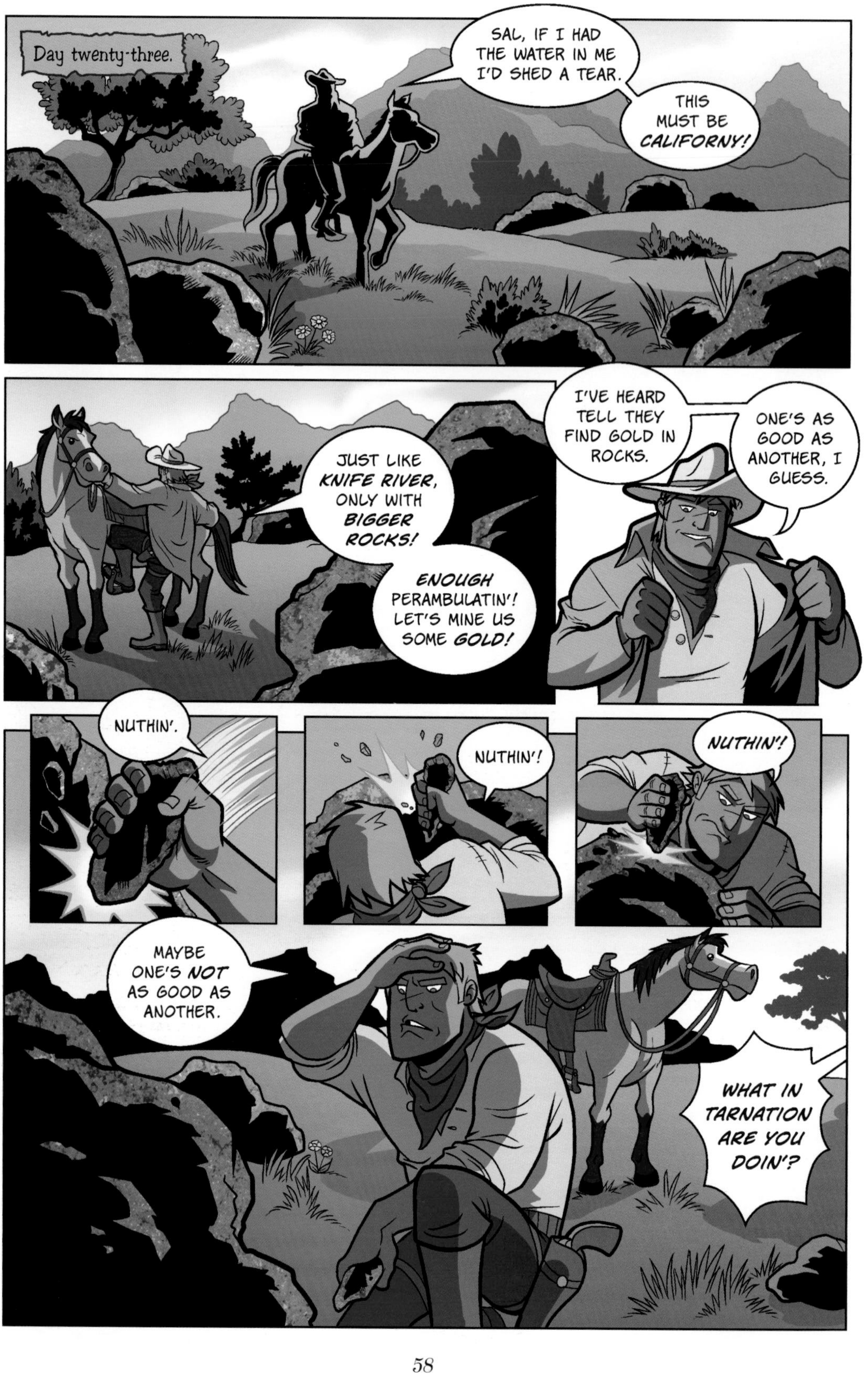
Day twenty-three.
SAL, IF I HAD THE WATER IN ME I'D SHED A TEAR.
THIS MUST BE CALIFORNY!
JUST LIKE KNIFE RIVER, ONLY WITH BIGGER ROCKS!
ENOUGH PERAMBULATIN'! LET'S MINE US SOME GOLD!
I'VE HEARD TELL THEY FIND GOLD IN ROCKS.
ONE'S AS GOOD AS ANOTHER, I GUESS.
NUTHIN'.
NUTHIN'!
NUTHIN'!
MAYBE ONE'S NOT AS GOOD AS ANOTHER.
WHAT IN TARNATION ARE YOU DOIN'?

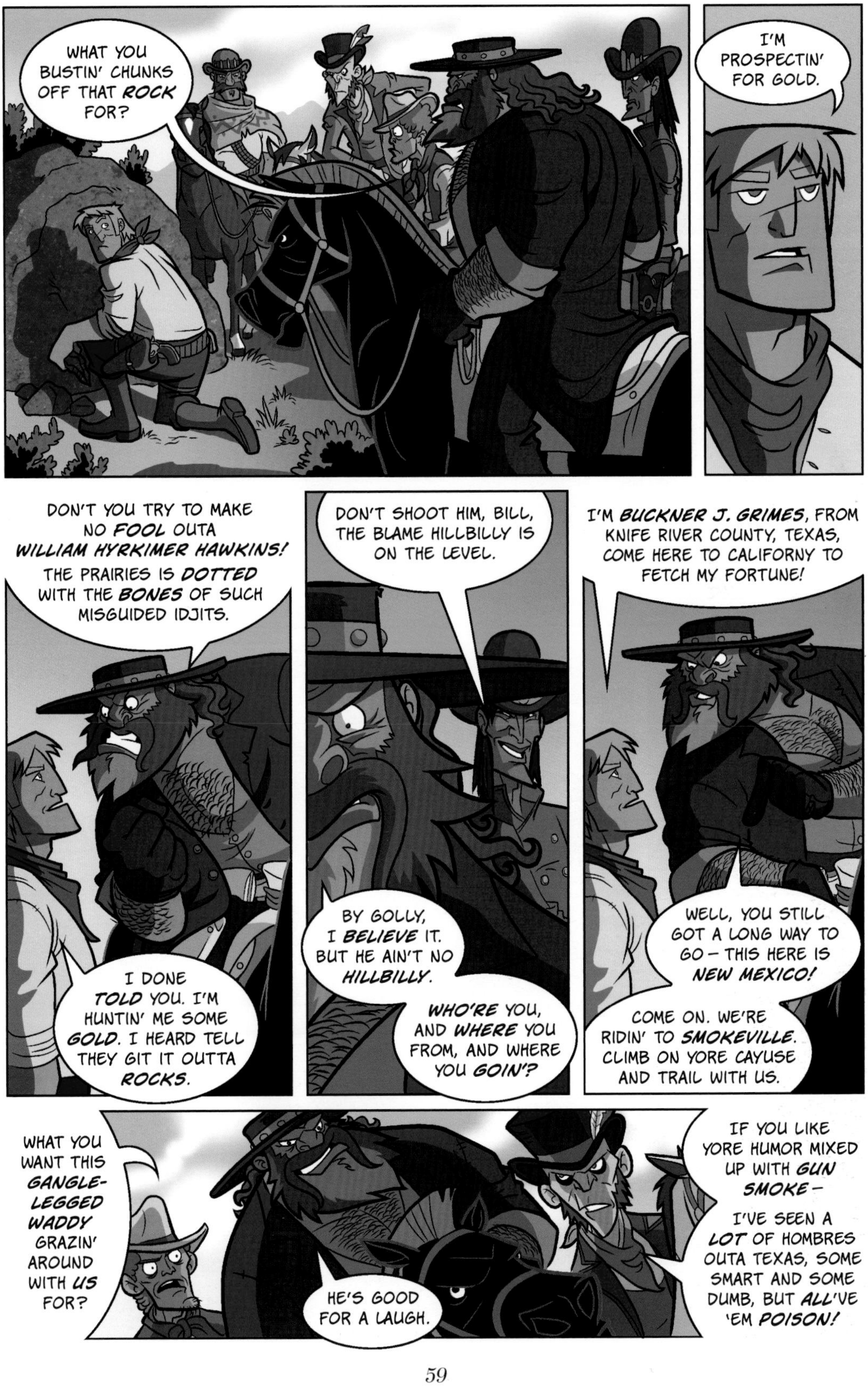
WHAT YOU BUSTIN' CHUNKS OFF THAT *ROCK* FOR?
I'M PROSPECTIN' FOR GOLD.
DON'T YOU TRY TO MAKE NO *FOOL* OUTA *WILLIAM HYRKIMER HAWKINS!* THE PRAIRIES IS *DOTTED* WITH THE *BONES* OF SUCH MISGUIDED IDJITS.
I DONE *TOLD* YOU. I'M HUNTIN' ME SOME *GOLD*. I HEARD TELL THEY GIT IT OUTTA *ROCKS*.
DON'T SHOOT HIM, BILL, THE BLAME HILLBILLY IS ON THE LEVEL.
BY GOLLY, I *BELIEVE* IT. BUT HE AIN'T NO *HILLBILLY*.
WHO'RE YOU, AND *WHERE* YOU FROM, AND WHERE YOU *GOIN'?*
I'M *BUCKNER J. GRIMES*, FROM KNIFE RIVER COUNTY, TEXAS, COME HERE TO CALIFORNY TO FETCH MY FORTUNE!
WELL, YOU STILL GOT A LONG WAY TO GO – THIS HERE IS *NEW MEXICO!*
COME ON. WE'RE RIDIN' TO *SMOKEVILLE*. CLIMB ON YORE CAYUSE AND TRAIL WITH US.
WHAT YOU WANT THIS *GANGLE-LEGGED WADDY* GRAZIN' AROUND WITH *US* FOR?
HE'S GOOD FOR A LAUGH.
IF YOU LIKE YORE HUMOR MIXED UP WITH *GUN SMOKE* –
I'VE SEEN A *LOT* OF HOMBRES OUTA TEXAS, SOME SMART AND SOME DUMB, BUT *ALL*'VE 'EM *POISON!*

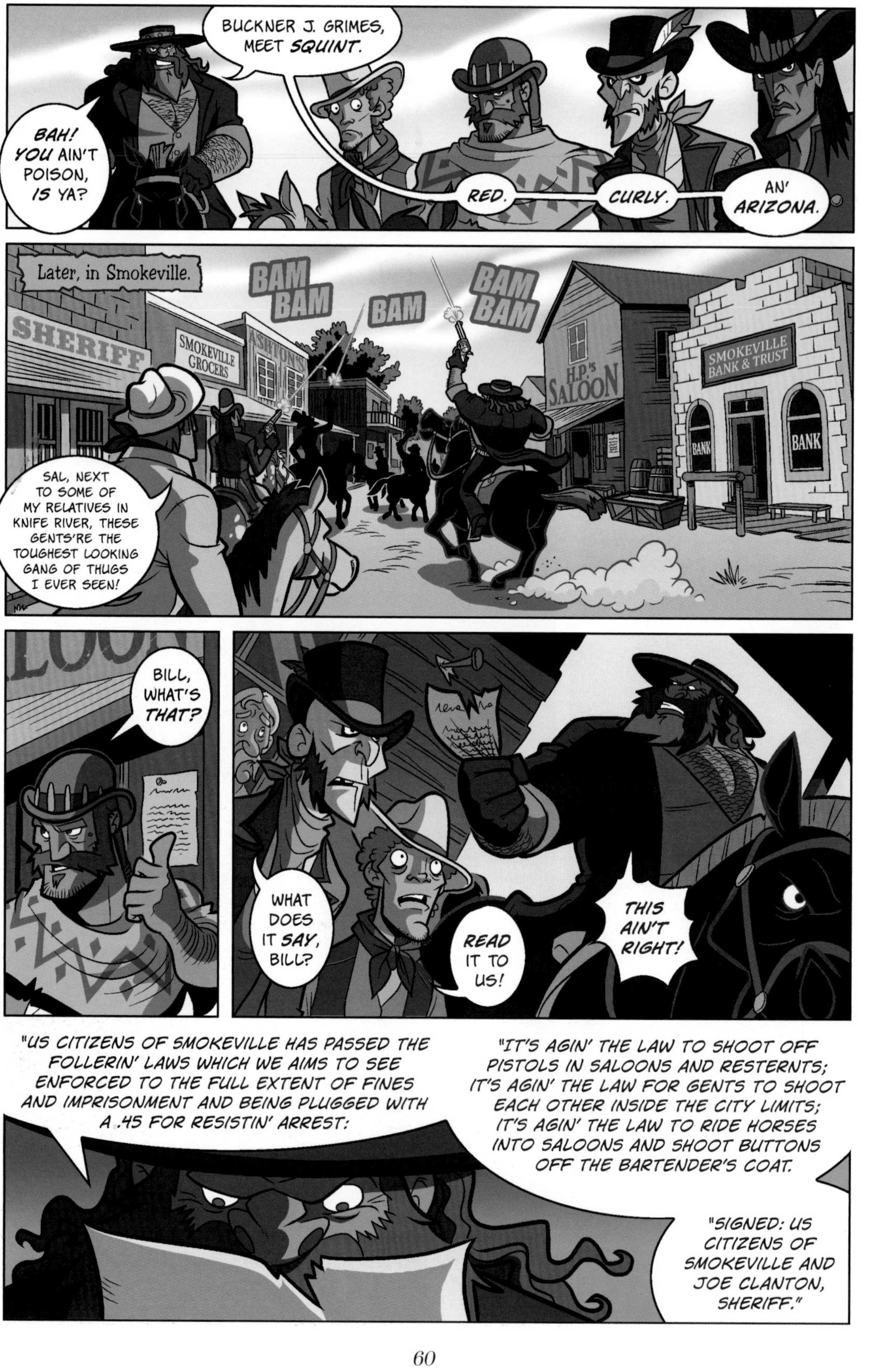
BUCKNER J. GRIMES, MEET SQUINT.
RED.
CURLY.
AN' ARIZONA.
BAH! YOU AIN'T POISON, IS YA?
Later, in Smokeville.
BAM BAM
BAM
BAM BAM
SHERIFF
SMOKEVILLE GROCERS
ASHTON'S
H.P.'s SALOON
SMOKEVILLE BANK & TRUST
BANK
BANK
SAL, NEXT TO SOME OF MY RELATIVES IN KNIFE RIVER, THESE GENTS'RE THE TOUGHEST LOOKING GANG OF THUGS I EVER SEEN!
BILL, WHAT'S THAT?
WHAT DOES IT SAY, BILL?
READ IT TO US!
THIS AIN'T RIGHT!
"US CITIZENS OF SMOKEVILLE HAS PASSED THE FOLLERIN' LAWS WHICH WE AIMS TO SEE ENFORCED TO THE FULL EXTENT OF FINES AND IMPRISONMENT AND BEING PLUGGED WITH A .45 FOR RESISTIN' ARREST:
"IT'S AGIN' THE LAW TO SHOOT OFF PISTOLS IN SALOONS AND RESTERNTS; IT'S AGIN' THE LAW FOR GENTS TO SHOOT EACH OTHER INSIDE THE CITY LIMITS; IT'S AGIN' THE LAW TO RIDE HORSES INTO SALOONS AND SHOOT BUTTONS OFF THE BARTENDER'S COAT.
"SIGNED: US CITIZENS OF SMOKEVILLE AND JOE CLANTON, SHERIFF."

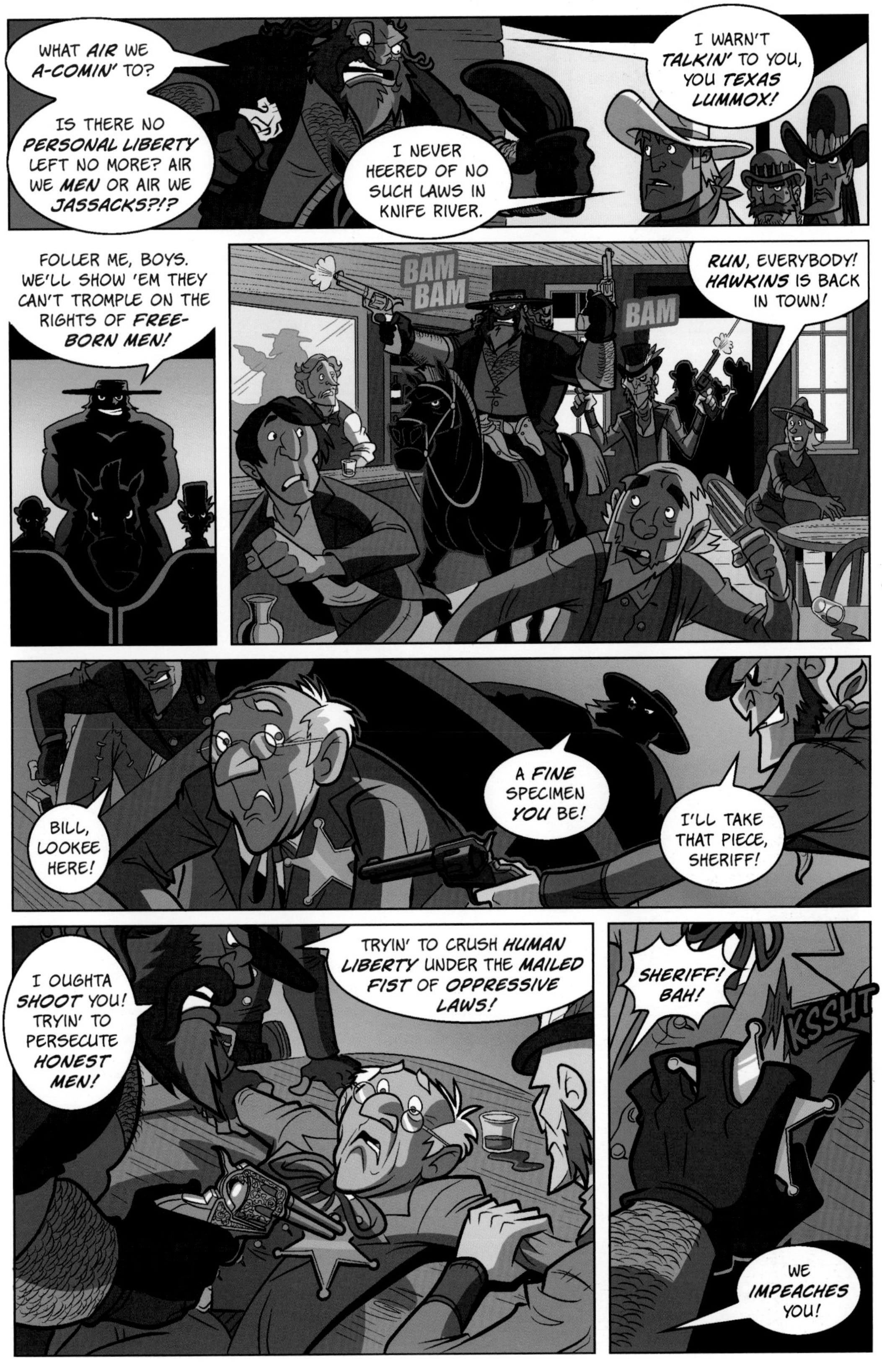
WHAT AIR WE A-COMIN' TO?
IS THERE NO PERSONAL LIBERTY LEFT NO MORE? AIR WE MEN OR AIR WE JASSACKS?!?
I NEVER HEERED OF NO SUCH LAWS IN KNIFE RIVER.
I WARN'T TALKIN' TO YOU, YOU TEXAS LUMMOX!
FOLLER ME, BOYS. WE'LL SHOW 'EM THEY CAN'T TROMPLE ON THE RIGHTS OF FREE-BORN MEN!
BAM BAM
BAM
RUN, EVERYBODY! HAWKINS IS BACK IN TOWN!
BILL, LOOKEE HERE!
A FINE SPECIMEN YOU BE!
I'LL TAKE THAT PIECE, SHERIFF!
I OUGHTA SHOOT YOU! TRYIN' TO PERSECUTE HONEST MEN!
TRYIN' TO CRUSH HUMAN LIBERTY UNDER THE MAILED FIST OF OPPRESSIVE LAWS!
SHERIFF! BAH!
KSSHT
WE IMPEACHES YOU!

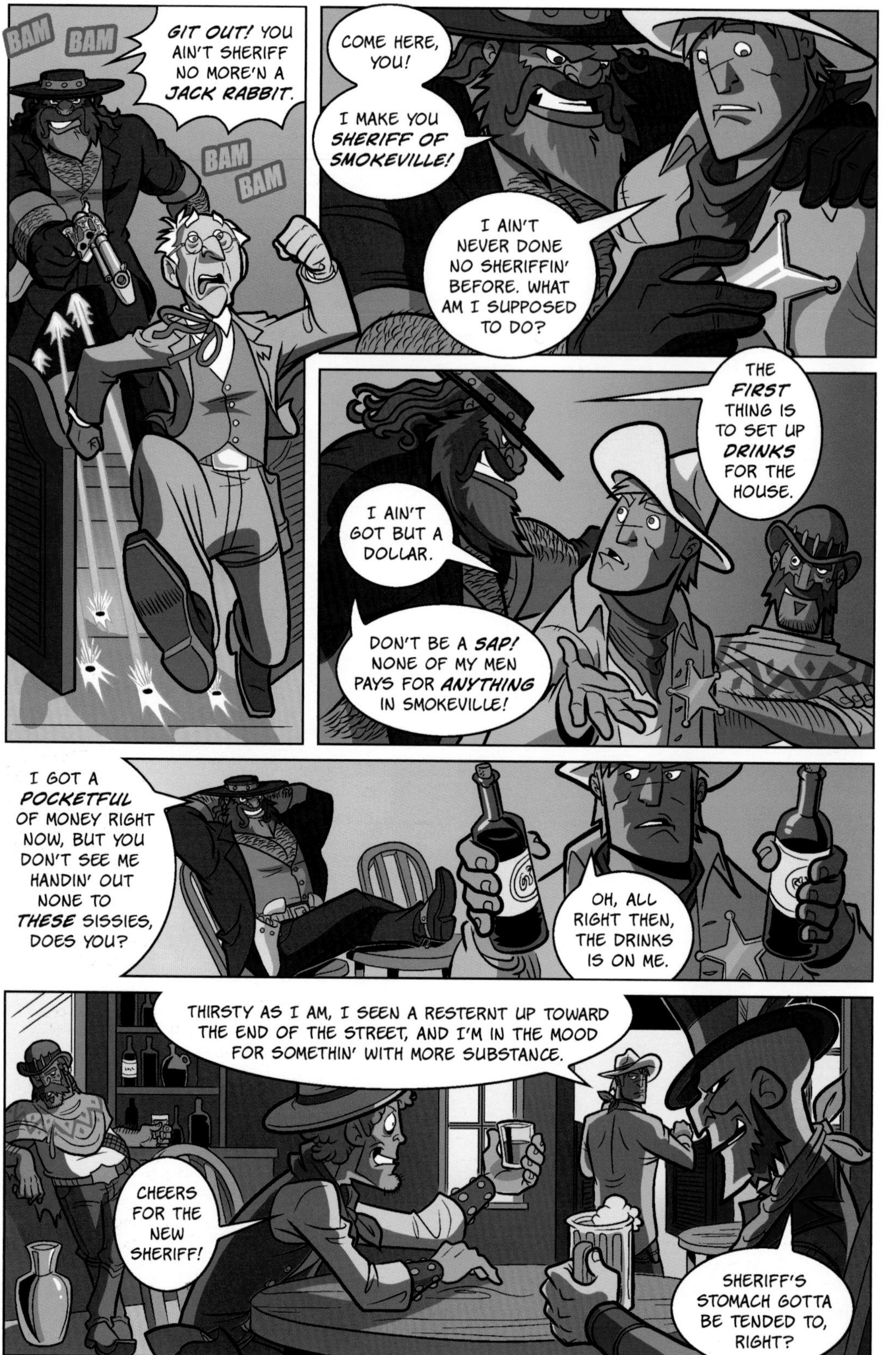
BAM BAM
GIT OUT! YOU AIN'T SHERIFF NO MORE'N A JACK RABBIT.
BAM BAM
COME HERE, YOU!
I MAKE YOU SHERIFF OF SMOKEVILLE!
I AIN'T NEVER DONE NO SHERIFFIN' BEFORE. WHAT AM I SUPPOSED TO DO?
THE FIRST THING IS TO SET UP DRINKS FOR THE HOUSE.
I AIN'T GOT BUT A DOLLAR.
DON'T BE A SAP! NONE OF MY MEN PAYS FOR ANYTHING IN SMOKEVILLE!
I GOT A POCKETFUL OF MONEY RIGHT NOW, BUT YOU DON'T SEE ME HANDIN' OUT NONE TO THESE SISSIES, DOES YOU?
OH, ALL RIGHT THEN, THE DRINKS IS ON ME.
THIRSTY AS I AM, I SEEN A RESTERNT UP TOWARD THE END OF THE STREET, AND I'M IN THE MOOD FOR SOMETHIN' WITH MORE SUBSTANCE.
CHEERS FOR THE NEW SHERIFF!
SHERIFF'S STOMACH GOTTA BE TENDED TO, RIGHT?

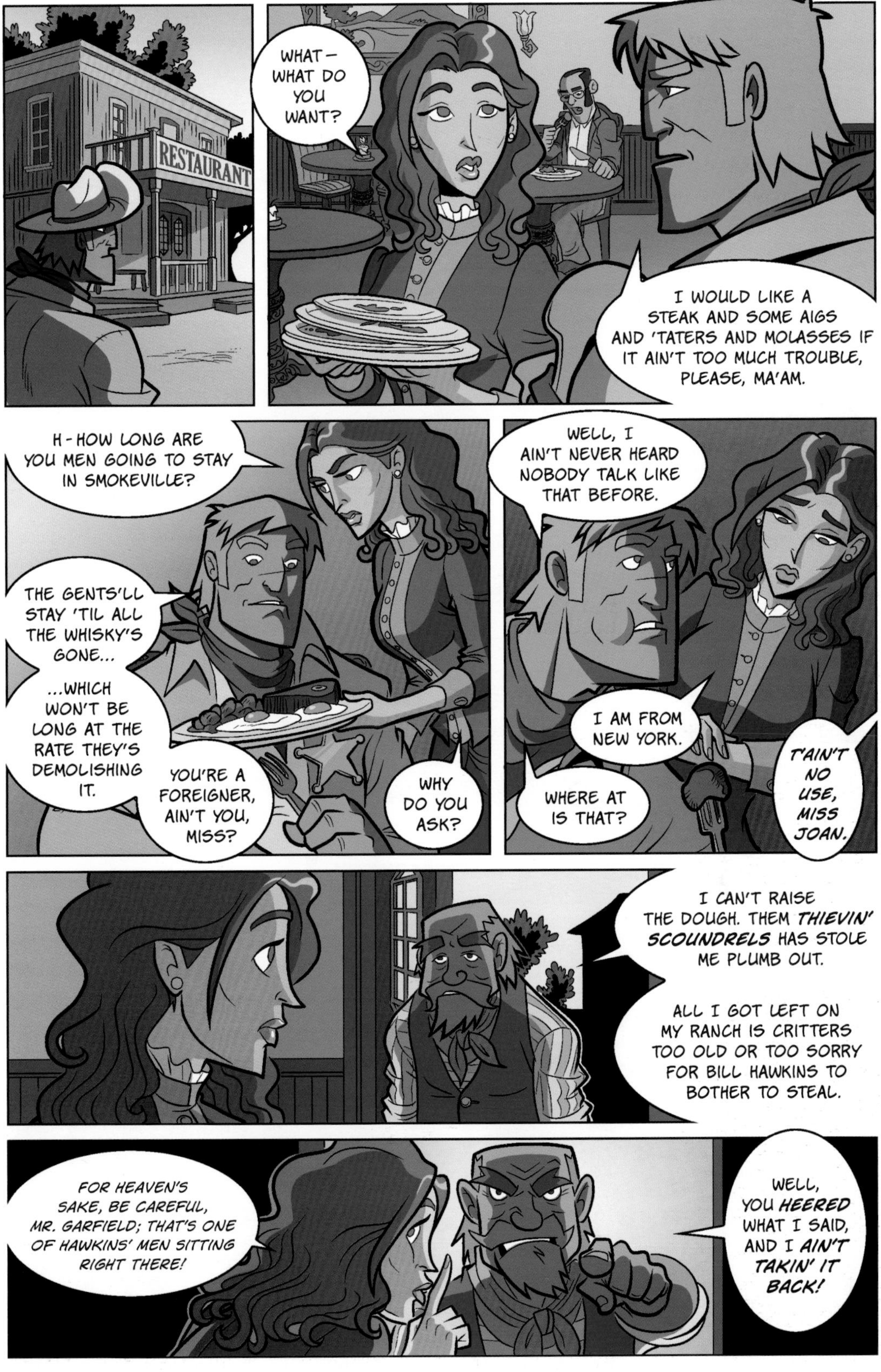
RESTAURANT
WHAT— WHAT DO YOU WANT?
I WOULD LIKE A STEAK AND SOME AIGS AND 'TATERS AND MOLASSES IF IT AIN'T TOO MUCH TROUBLE, PLEASE, MA'AM.
H-HOW LONG ARE YOU MEN GOING TO STAY IN SMOKEVILLE?
THE GENTS'LL STAY 'TIL ALL THE WHISKY'S GONE...
...WHICH WON'T BE LONG AT THE RATE THEY'S DEMOLISHING IT.
YOU'RE A FOREIGNER, AIN'T YOU, MISS?
WHY DO YOU ASK?
WELL, I AIN'T NEVER HEARD NOBODY TALK LIKE THAT BEFORE.
I AM FROM NEW YORK.
WHERE AT IS THAT?
T'AIN'T NO USE, MISS JOAN.
I CAN'T RAISE THE DOUGH. THEM THIEVIN' SCOUNDRELS HAS STOLE ME PLUMB OUT.
ALL I GOT LEFT ON MY RANCH IS CRITTERS TOO OLD OR TOO SORRY FOR BILL HAWKINS TO BOTHER TO STEAL.
FOR HEAVEN'S SAKE, BE CAREFUL, MR. GARFIELD; THAT'S ONE OF HAWKINS' MEN SITTING RIGHT THERE!
WELL, YOU HEERED WHAT I SAID, AND I AIN'T TAKIN' IT BACK!

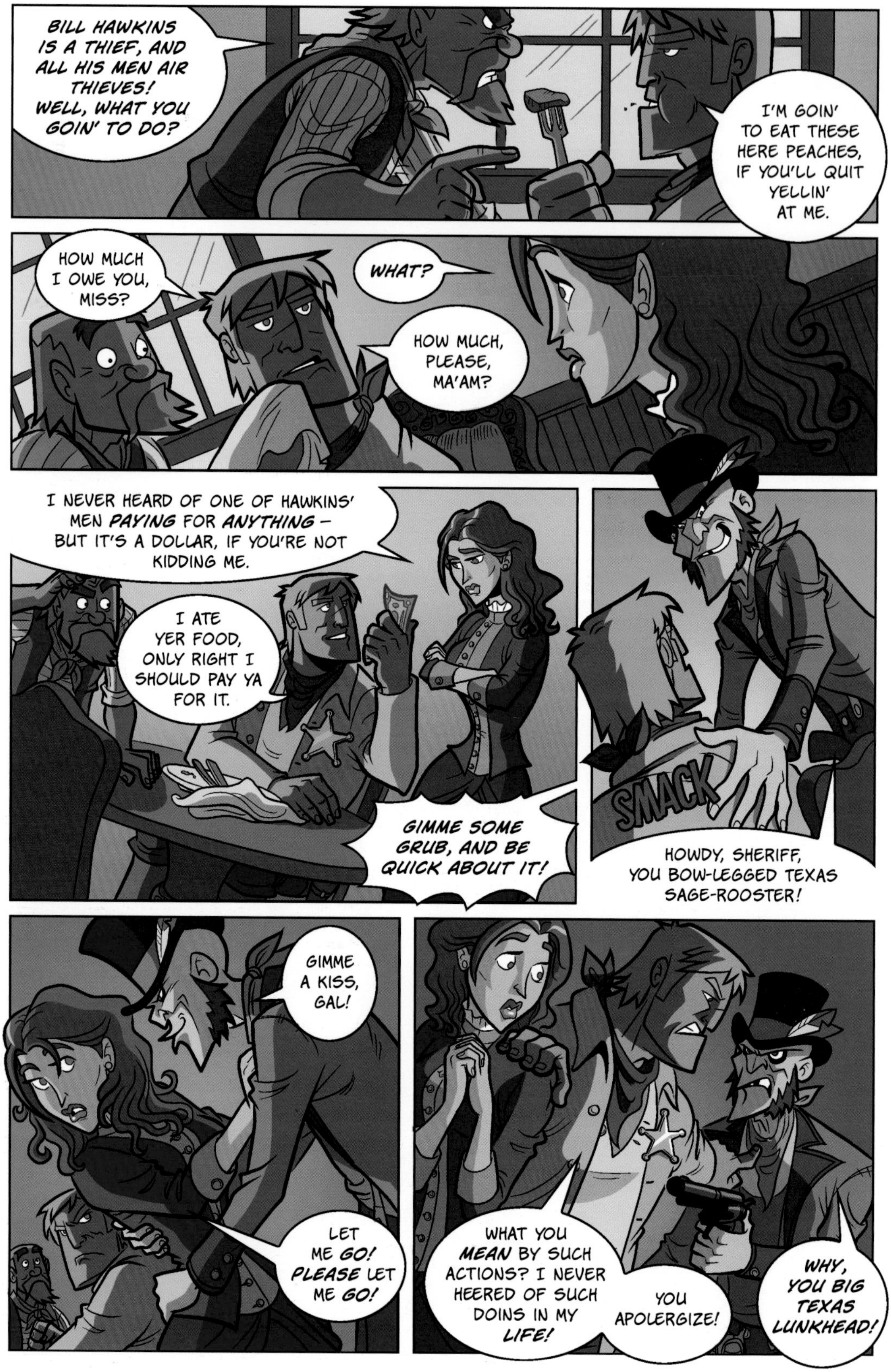
BILL HAWKINS IS A THIEF, AND ALL HIS MEN AIR THIEVES! WELL, WHAT YOU GOIN' TO DO?
I'M GOIN' TO EAT THESE HERE PEACHES, IF YOU'LL QUIT YELLIN' AT ME.
HOW MUCH I OWE YOU, MISS?
WHAT?
HOW MUCH, PLEASE, MA'AM?
I NEVER HEARD OF ONE OF HAWKINS' MEN PAYING FOR ANYTHING – BUT IT'S A DOLLAR, IF YOU'RE NOT KIDDING ME.
I ATE YER FOOD, ONLY RIGHT I SHOULD PAY YA FOR IT.
GIMME SOME GRUB, AND BE QUICK ABOUT IT!
SMACK
HOWDY, SHERIFF, YOU BOW-LEGGED TEXAS SAGE-ROOSTER!
GIMME A KISS, GAL!
LET ME GO! PLEASE LET ME GO!
WHAT YOU MEAN BY SUCH ACTIONS? I NEVER HEERED OF SUCH DOINS IN MY LIFE!
YOU APOLERGIZE!
WHY, YOU BIG TEXAS LUNKHEAD!

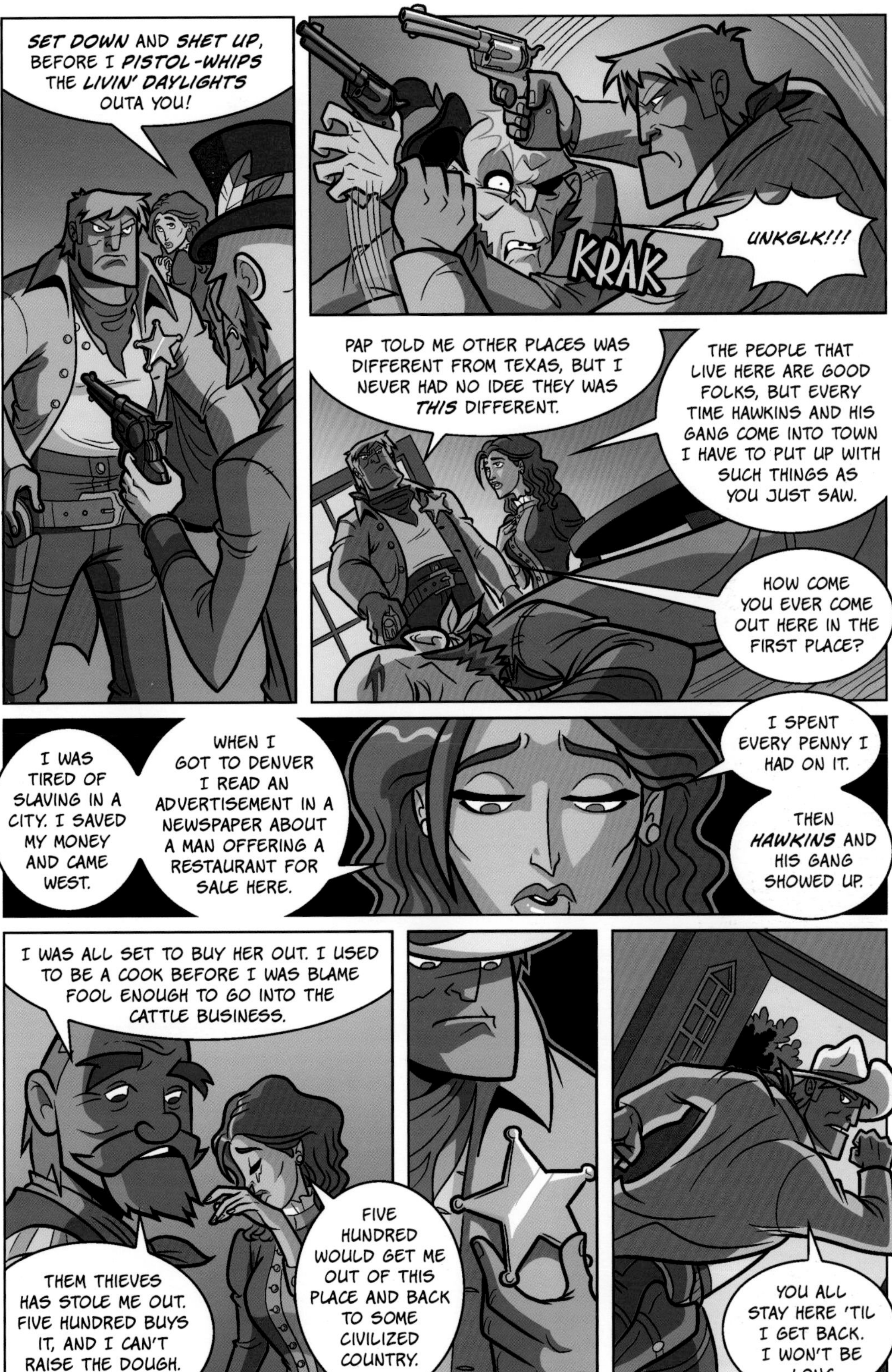
SET DOWN AND SHET UP, BEFORE I PISTOL-WHIPS THE LIVIN' DAYLIGHTS OUTA YOU!
KRAK
UNKGLK!!!
PAP TOLD ME OTHER PLACES WAS DIFFERENT FROM TEXAS, BUT I NEVER HAD NO IDEE THEY WAS THIS DIFFERENT.
THE PEOPLE THAT LIVE HERE ARE GOOD FOLKS, BUT EVERY TIME HAWKINS AND HIS GANG COME INTO TOWN I HAVE TO PUT UP WITH SUCH THINGS AS YOU JUST SAW.
HOW COME YOU EVER COME OUT HERE IN THE FIRST PLACE?
I WAS TIRED OF SLAVING IN A CITY. I SAVED MY MONEY AND CAME WEST.
WHEN I GOT TO DENVER I READ AN ADVERTISEMENT IN A NEWSPAPER ABOUT A MAN OFFERING A RESTAURANT FOR SALE HERE.
I SPENT EVERY PENNY I HAD ON IT.
THEN HAWKINS AND HIS GANG SHOWED UP.
I WAS ALL SET TO BUY HER OUT. I USED TO BE A COOK BEFORE I WAS BLAME FOOL ENOUGH TO GO INTO THE CATTLE BUSINESS.
THEM THIEVES HAS STOLE ME OUT. FIVE HUNDRED BUYS IT, AND I CAN'T RAISE THE DOUGH.
FIVE HUNDRED WOULD GET ME OUT OF THIS PLACE AND BACK TO SOME CIVILIZED COUNTRY.
YOU ALL STAY HERE 'TIL I GET BACK. I WON'T BE LONG.

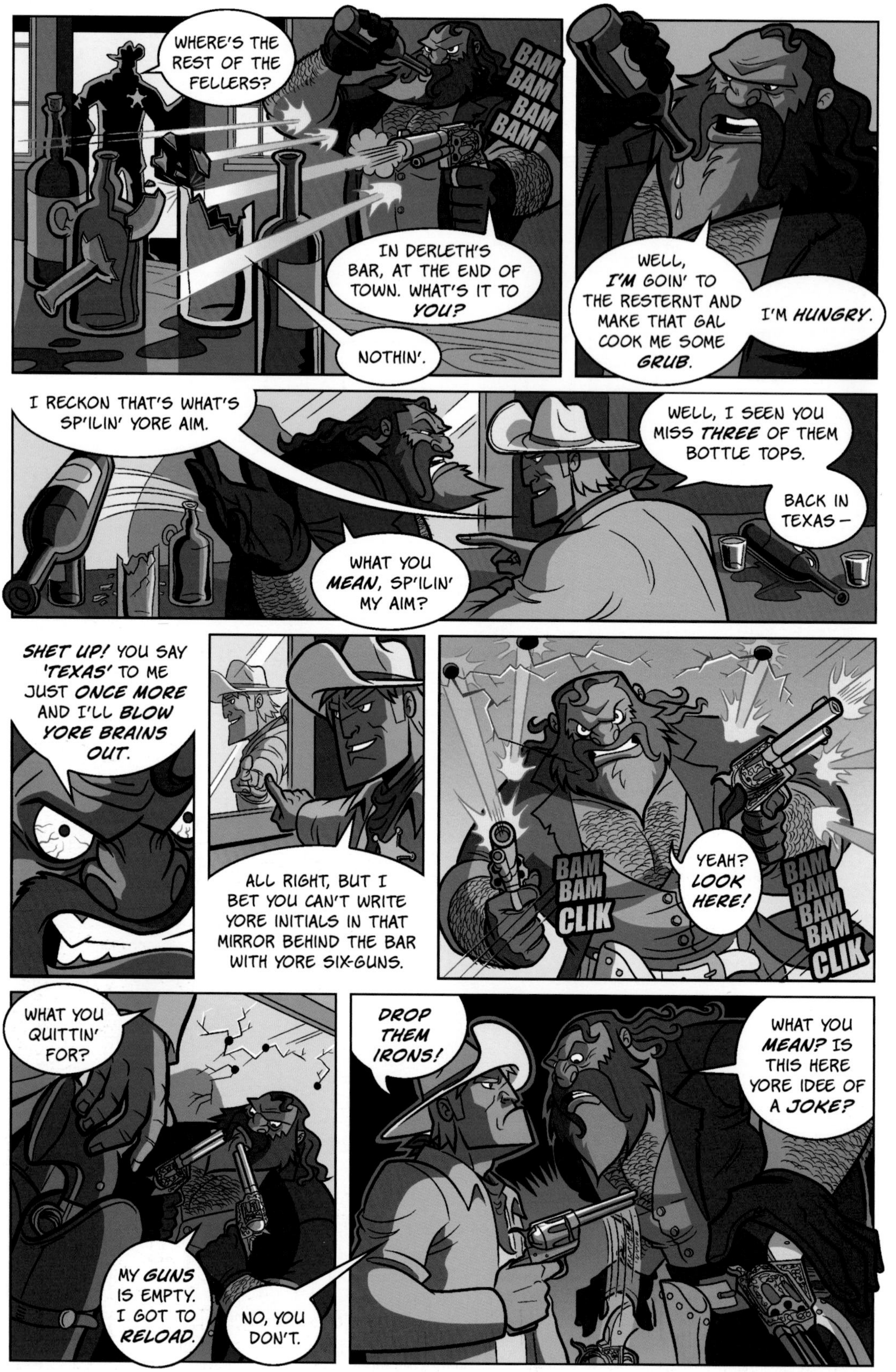
WHERE'S THE REST OF THE FELLERS?
BAM BAM BAM BAM
IN DERLETH'S BAR, AT THE END OF TOWN. WHAT'S IT TO YOU?
NOTHIN'.
WELL, I'M GOIN' TO THE RESTERNT AND MAKE THAT GAL COOK ME SOME GRUB.
I'M HUNGRY.
I RECKON THAT'S WHAT'S SP'ILIN' YORE AIM.
WHAT YOU MEAN, SP'ILIN' MY AIM?
WELL, I SEEN YOU MISS THREE OF THEM BOTTLE TOPS.
BACK IN TEXAS —
SHET UP! YOU SAY 'TEXAS' TO ME JUST ONCE MORE AND I'LL BLOW YORE BRAINS OUT.
ALL RIGHT, BUT I BET YOU CAN'T WRITE YORE INITIALS IN THAT MIRROR BEHIND THE BAR WITH YORE SIX-GUNS.
BAM BAM CLIK
YEAH? LOOK HERE!
BAM BAM BAM BAM CLIK
WHAT YOU QUITTIN' FOR?
MY GUNS IS EMPTY. I GOT TO RELOAD.
NO, YOU DON'T.
DROP THEM IRONS!
WHAT YOU MEAN? IS THIS HERE YORE IDEE OF A JOKE?

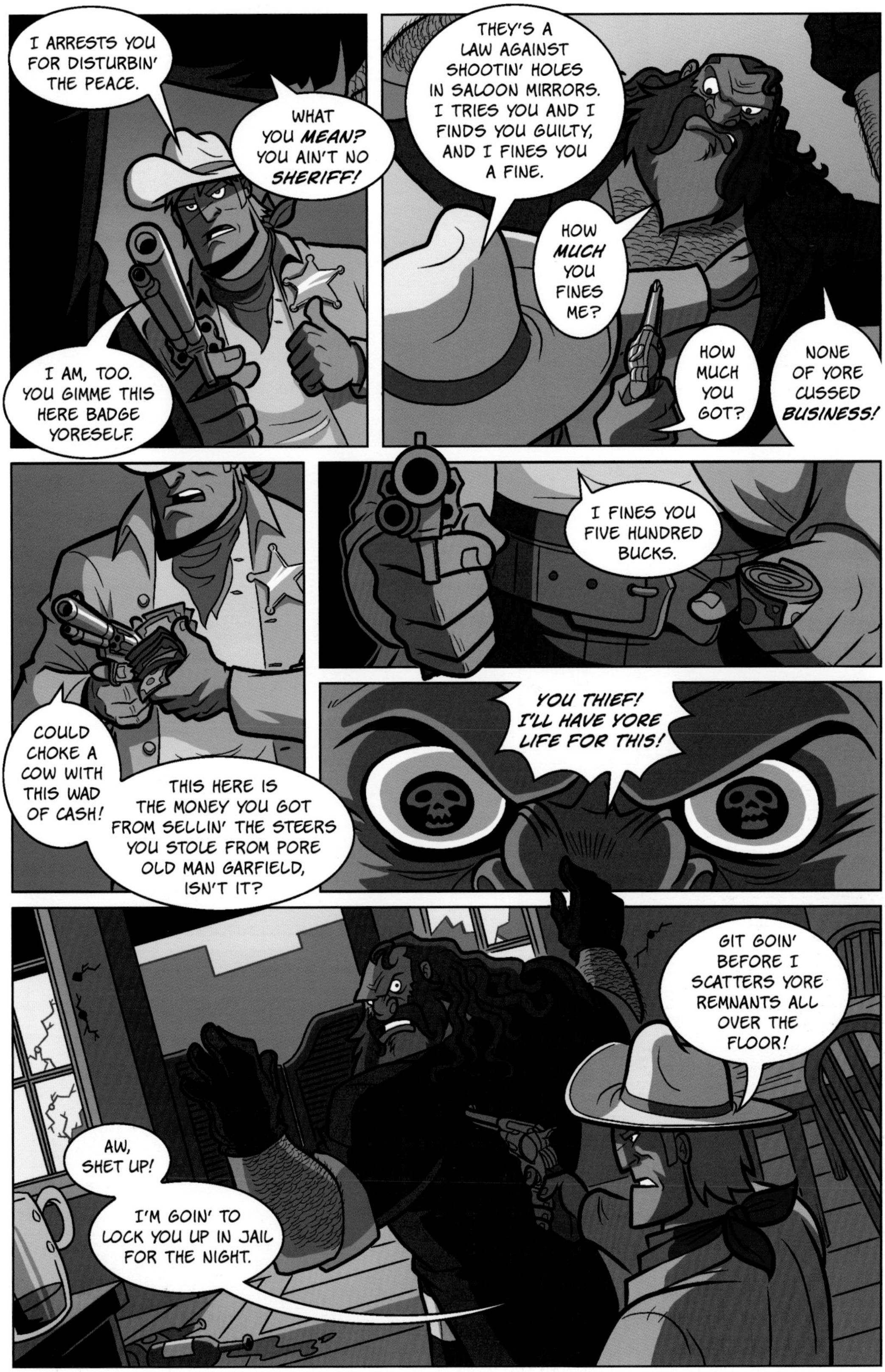
I ARRESTS YOU FOR DISTURBIN' THE PEACE.
WHAT YOU ***MEAN?*** YOU AIN'T NO ***SHERIFF!***
I AM, TOO. YOU GIMME THIS HERE BADGE YORESELF.
THEY'S A LAW AGAINST SHOOTIN' HOLES IN SALOON MIRRORS. I TRIES YOU AND I FINDS YOU GUILTY, AND I FINES YOU A FINE.
HOW ***MUCH*** YOU FINES ME?
HOW MUCH YOU GOT?
NONE OF YORE CUSSED ***BUSINESS!***
I FINES YOU FIVE HUNDRED BUCKS.
COULD CHOKE A COW WITH THIS WAD OF CASH!
THIS HERE IS THE MONEY YOU GOT FROM SELLIN' THE STEERS YOU STOLE FROM PORE OLD MAN GARFIELD, ISN'T IT?
YOU THIEF! I'LL HAVE YORE LIFE FOR THIS!
GIT GOIN' BEFORE I SCATTERS YORE REMNANTS ALL OVER THE FLOOR!
AW, SHET UP!
I'M GOIN' TO LOCK YOU UP IN JAIL FOR THE NIGHT.

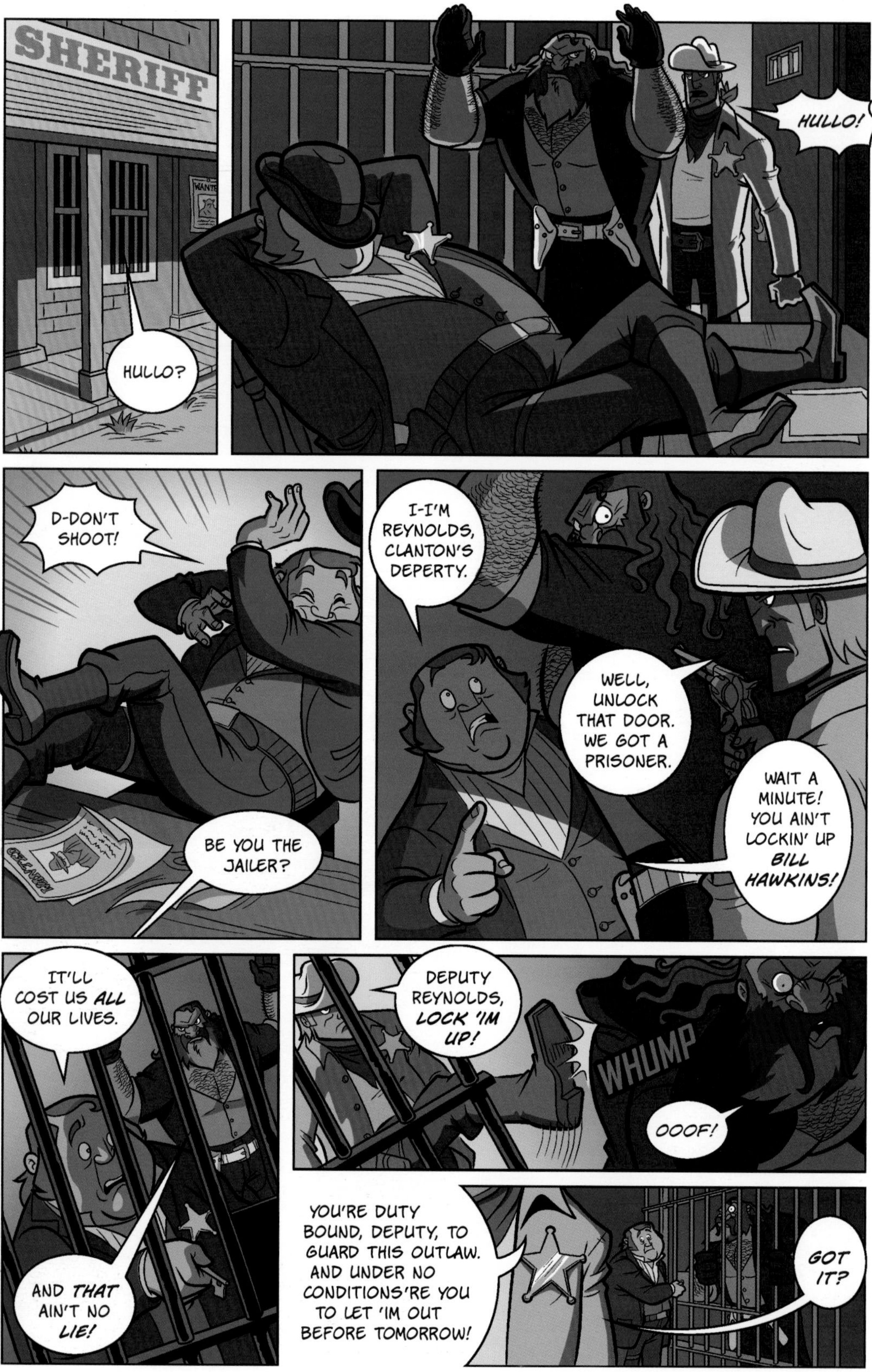
SHERIFF
HULLO?
HULLO!
D-DON'T SHOOT!
BE YOU THE JAILER?
I-I'M REYNOLDS, CLANTON'S DEPERTY.
WELL, UNLOCK THAT DOOR. WE GOT A PRISONER.
WAIT A MINUTE! YOU AIN'T LOCKIN' UP BILL HAWKINS!
IT'LL COST US ALL OUR LIVES.
AND THAT AIN'T NO LIE!
DEPUTY REYNOLDS, LOCK 'IM UP!
WHUMP
OOOF!
YOU'RE DUTY BOUND, DEPUTY, TO GUARD THIS OUTLAW. AND UNDER NO CONDITIONS'RE YOU TO LET 'IM OUT BEFORE TOMORROW!
GOT IT?

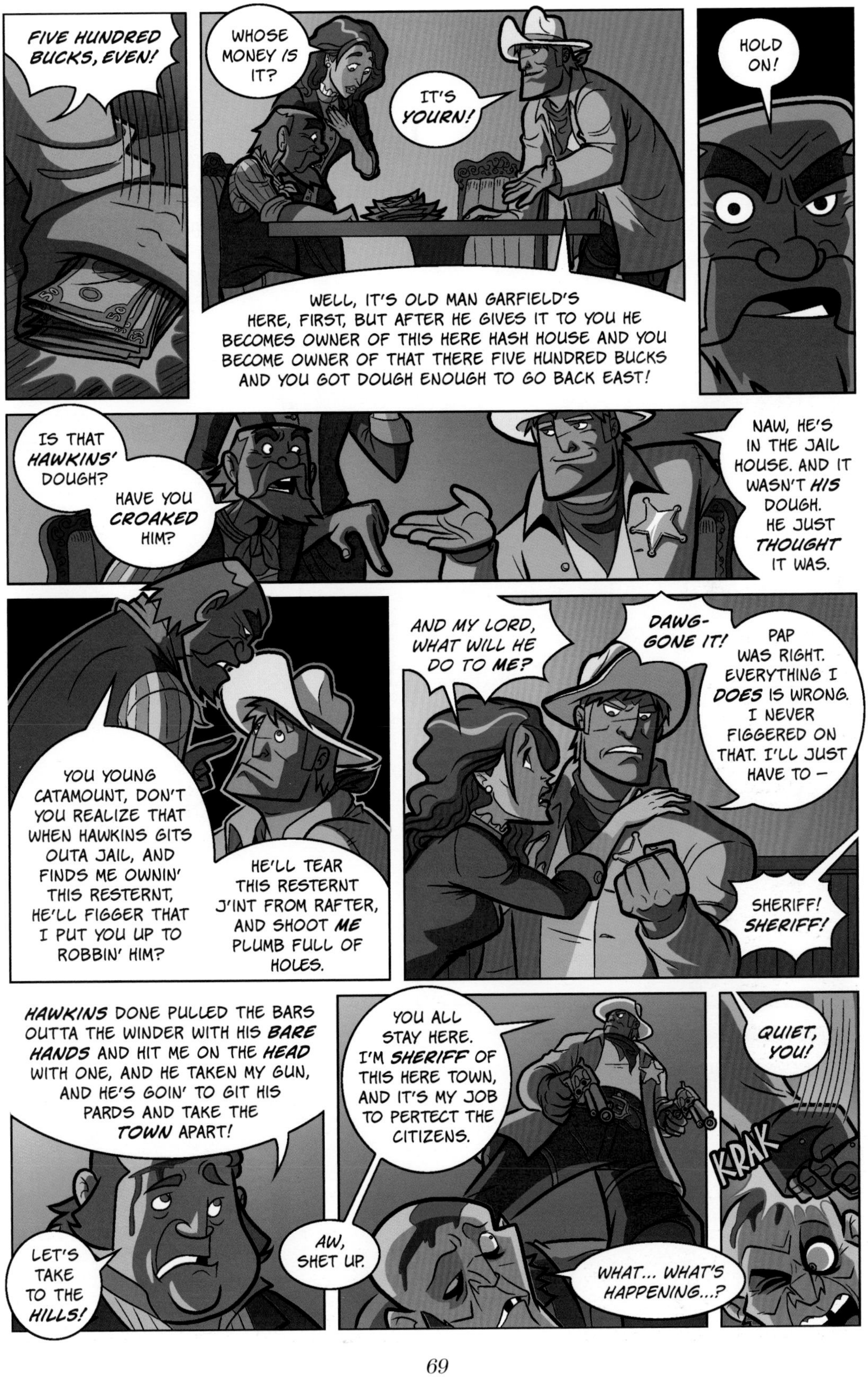
FIVE HUNDRED BUCKS, EVEN!
WHOSE MONEY IS IT?
IT'S YOURN!
WELL, IT'S OLD MAN GARFIELD'S HERE, FIRST, BUT AFTER HE GIVES IT TO YOU HE BECOMES OWNER OF THIS HERE HASH HOUSE AND YOU BECOME OWNER OF THAT THERE FIVE HUNDRED BUCKS AND YOU GOT DOUGH ENOUGH TO GO BACK EAST!
HOLD ON!
IS THAT HAWKINS' DOUGH?
HAVE YOU CROAKED HIM?
NAW, HE'S IN THE JAIL HOUSE. AND IT WASN'T HIS DOUGH. HE JUST THOUGHT IT WAS.
YOU YOUNG CATAMOUNT, DON'T YOU REALIZE THAT WHEN HAWKINS GITS OUTA JAIL, AND FINDS ME OWNIN' THIS RESTERNT, HE'LL FIGGER THAT I PUT YOU UP TO ROBBIN' HIM?
HE'LL TEAR THIS RESTERNT J'INT FROM RAFTER, AND SHOOT ME PLUMB FULL OF HOLES.
AND MY LORD, WHAT WILL HE DO TO ME?
DAWG-GONE IT!
PAP WAS RIGHT. EVERYTHING I DOES IS WRONG. I NEVER FIGGERED ON THAT. I'LL JUST HAVE TO —
SHERIFF! SHERIFF!
HAWKINS DONE PULLED THE BARS OUTTA THE WINDER WITH HIS BARE HANDS AND HIT ME ON THE HEAD WITH ONE, AND HE TAKEN MY GUN, AND HE'S GOIN' TO GIT HIS PARDS AND TAKE THE TOWN APART!
LET'S TAKE TO THE HILLS!
YOU ALL STAY HERE. I'M SHERIFF OF THIS HERE TOWN, AND IT'S MY JOB TO PERTECT THE CITIZENS.
AW, SHET UP.
WHAT... WHAT'S HAPPENING...?
QUIET, YOU!
KRAK

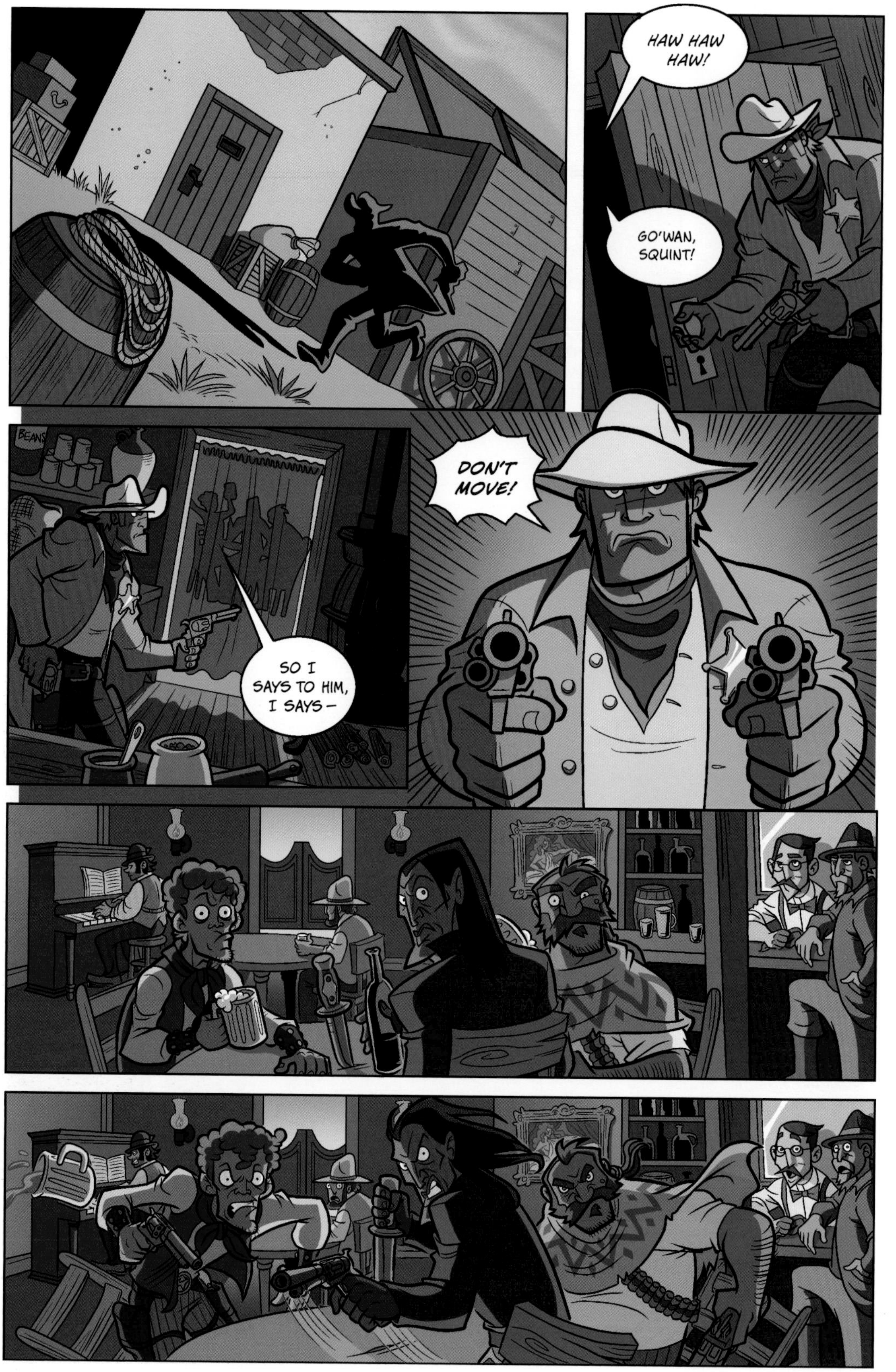
HAW HAW HAW!
GO'WAN, SQUINT!
BEANS
SO I SAYS TO HIM, I SAYS—
DON'T MOVE!

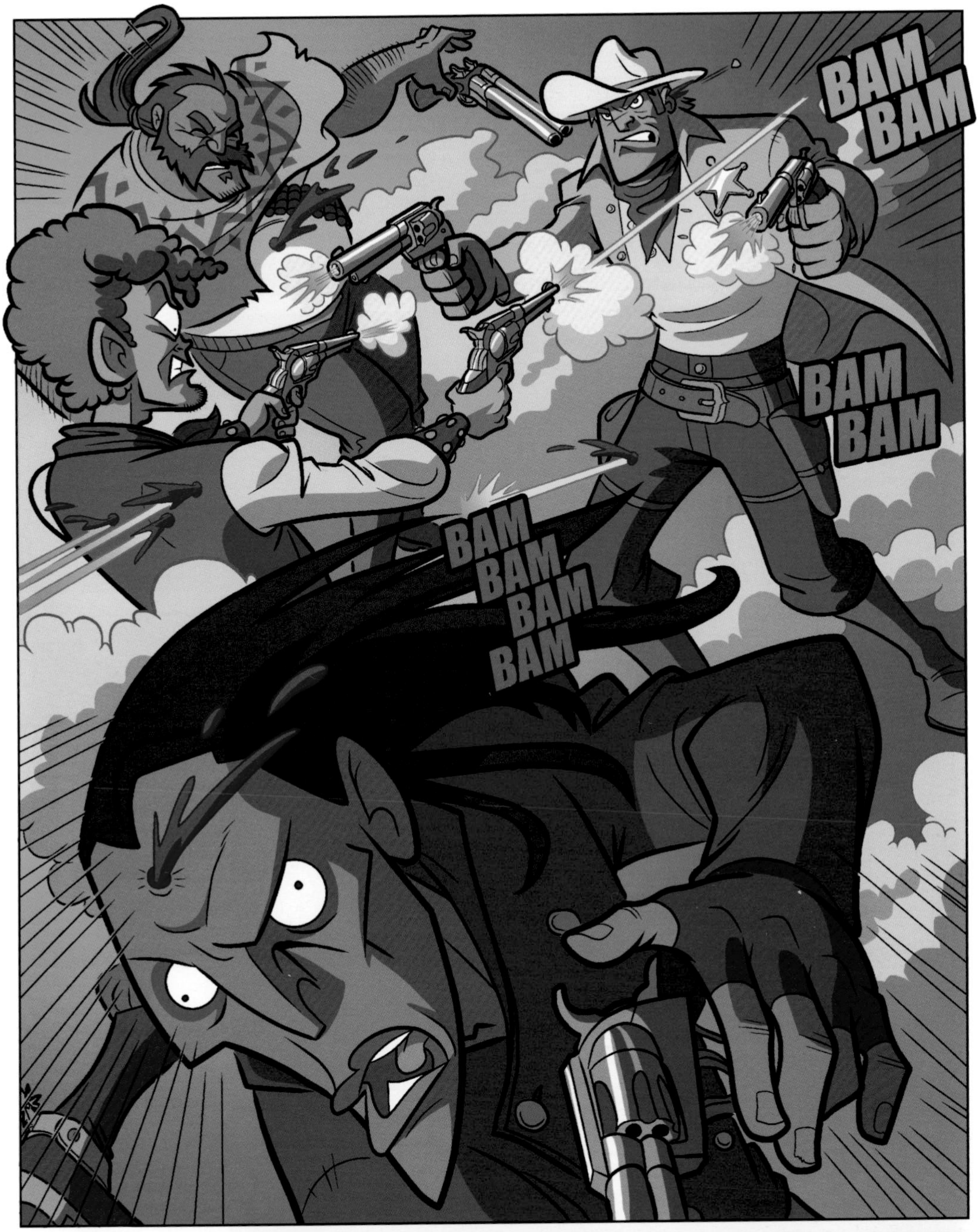
BAM
BAM
BAM
BAM
BAM
BAM
BAM
BAM

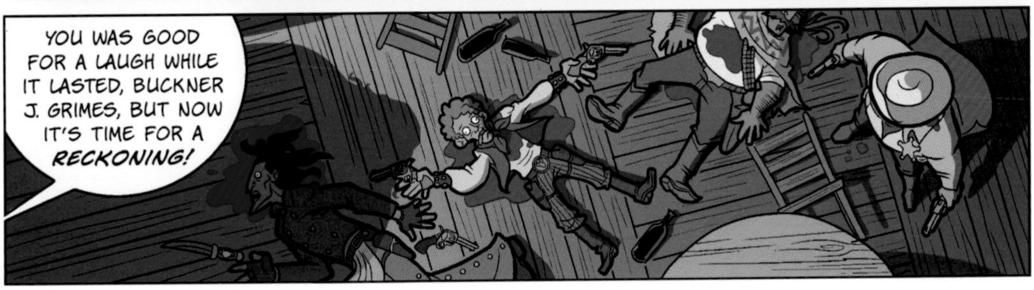
YOU WAS GOOD FOR A LAUGH WHILE IT LASTED, BUCKNER J. GRIMES, BUT NOW IT'S TIME FOR A *RECKONING!*

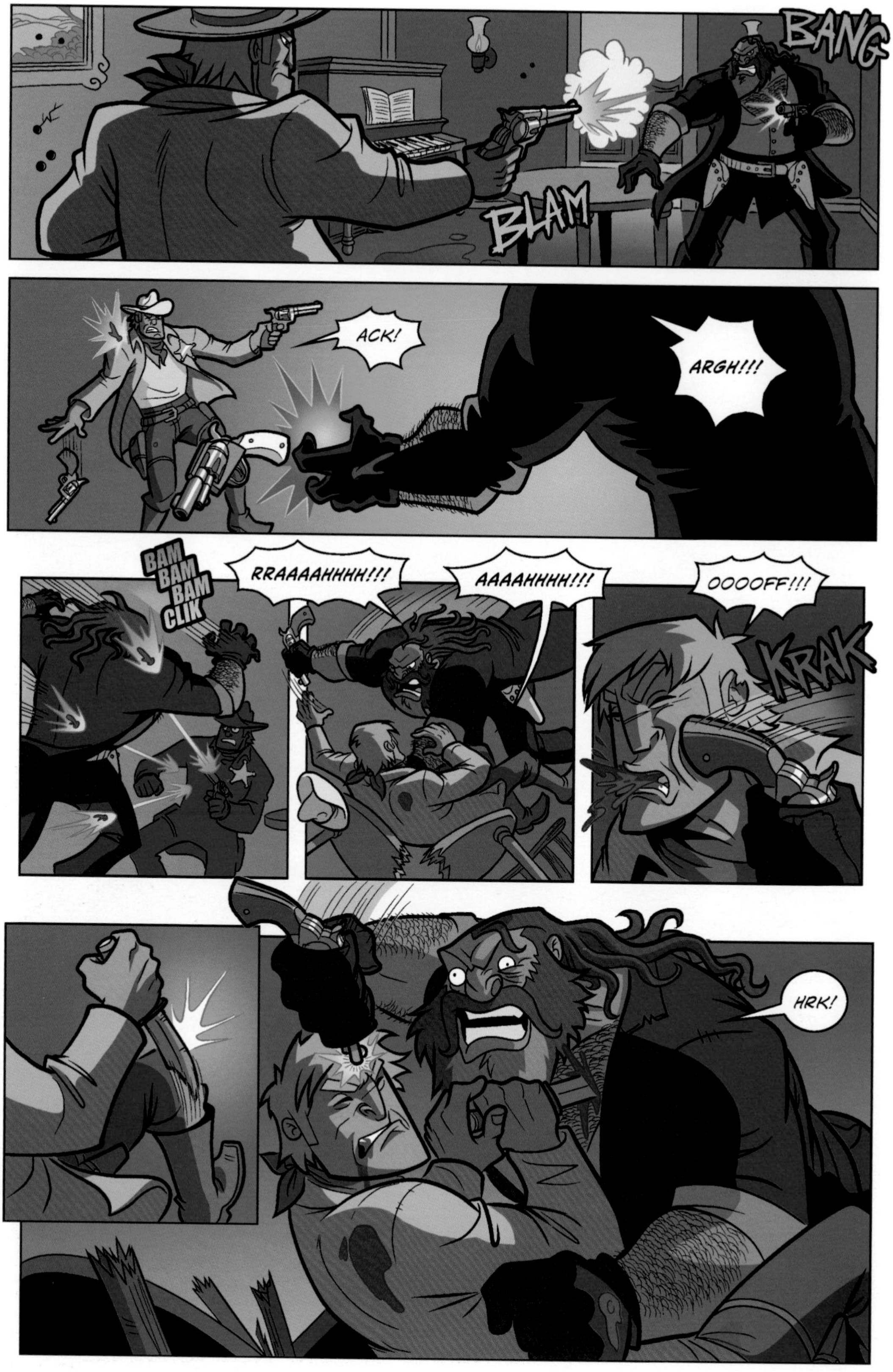
BANG
BLAM
ACK!
ARGH!!!
BAM BAM BAM CLIK
RRAAAAAHHHH!!!
AAAAHHHH!!!
OOOOFF!!!
KRAK
HRK!

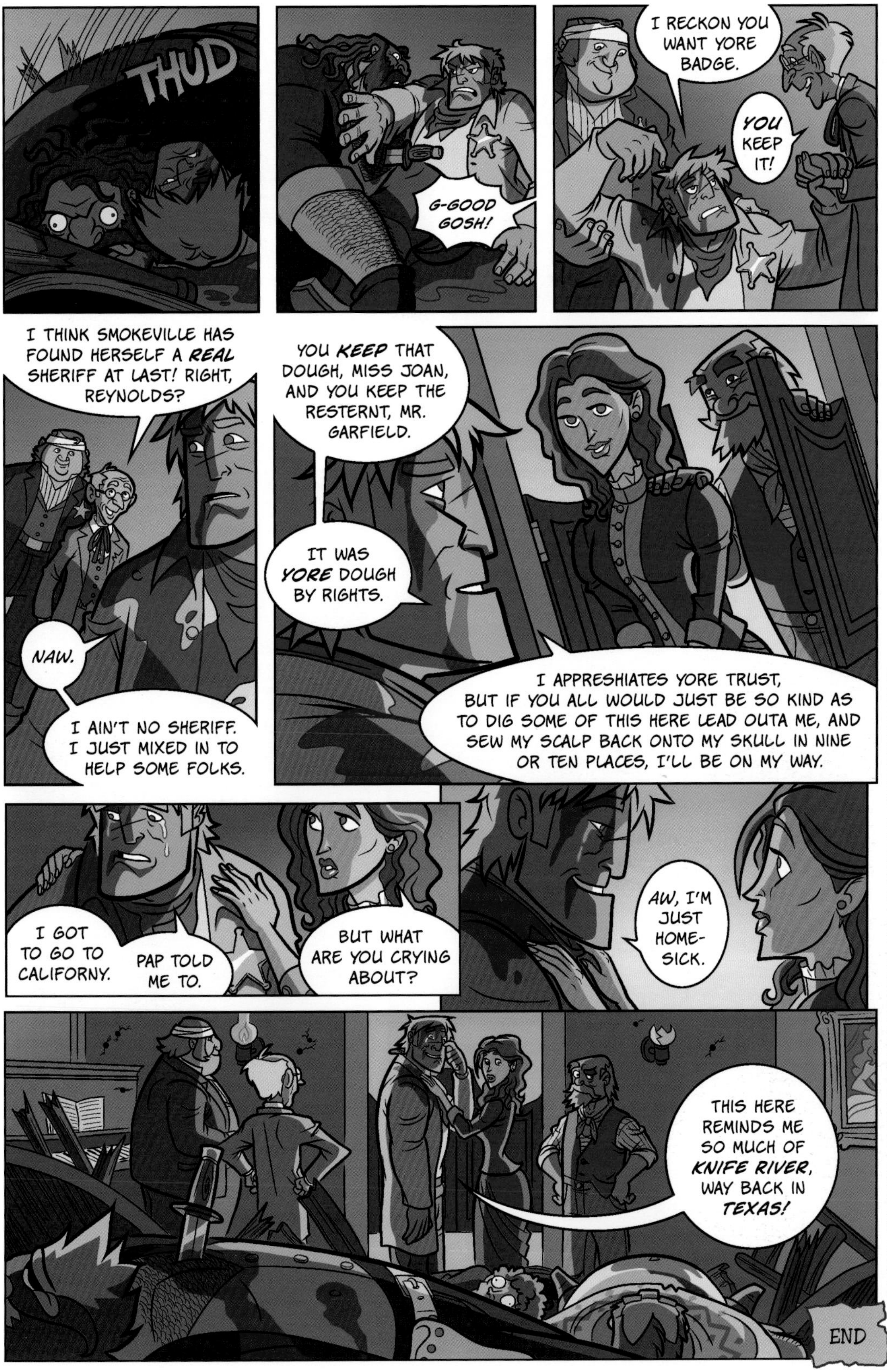
THUD
G-GOOD GOSH!
I RECKON YOU WANT YORE BADGE.
YOU KEEP IT!
I THINK SMOKEVILLE HAS FOUND HERSELF A REAL SHERIFF AT LAST! RIGHT, REYNOLDS?
NAW.
I AIN'T NO SHERIFF. I JUST MIXED IN TO HELP SOME FOLKS.
YOU KEEP THAT DOUGH, MISS JOAN, AND YOU KEEP THE RESTERNT, MR. GARFIELD.
IT WAS YORE DOUGH BY RIGHTS.
I APPRESHIATES YORE TRUST, BUT IF YOU ALL WOULD JUST BE SO KIND AS TO DIG SOME OF THIS HERE LEAD OUTA ME, AND SEW MY SCALP BACK ONTO MY SKULL IN NINE OR TEN PLACES, I'LL BE ON MY WAY.
I GOT TO GO TO CALIFORNY.
PAP TOLD ME TO.
BUT WHAT ARE YOU CRYING ABOUT?
AW, I'M JUST HOME-SICK.
THIS HERE REMINDS ME SO MUCH OF KNIFE RIVER, WAY BACK IN TEXAS!
END

The year of grace 1797 was on its last breaths, even as a southwesterly gale whipped the coast of California into a frenzy of sand and spume.

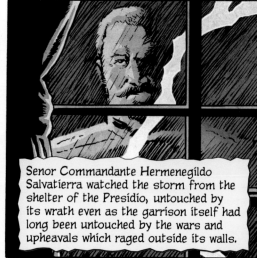

Senor Commandante Hermenegildo Salvatierra watched the storm from the shelter of the Presidio, untouched by its wrath even as the garrison itself had long been untouched by the wars and upheavals which raged outside its walls.

Abandoning the window, the Commander turned to admiring the copybooks of the pupils of San Carlos — particularly that of little Paquita — a film of honest pride dimming his lone left eye.

The right, alas, twenty years before had been sealed by an Indian arrow.

THE RIGHT EYE OF THE COMMANDER

BY BRET HARTE · Adapted by David Hontiveros · Illustrated by Reno Maniquis

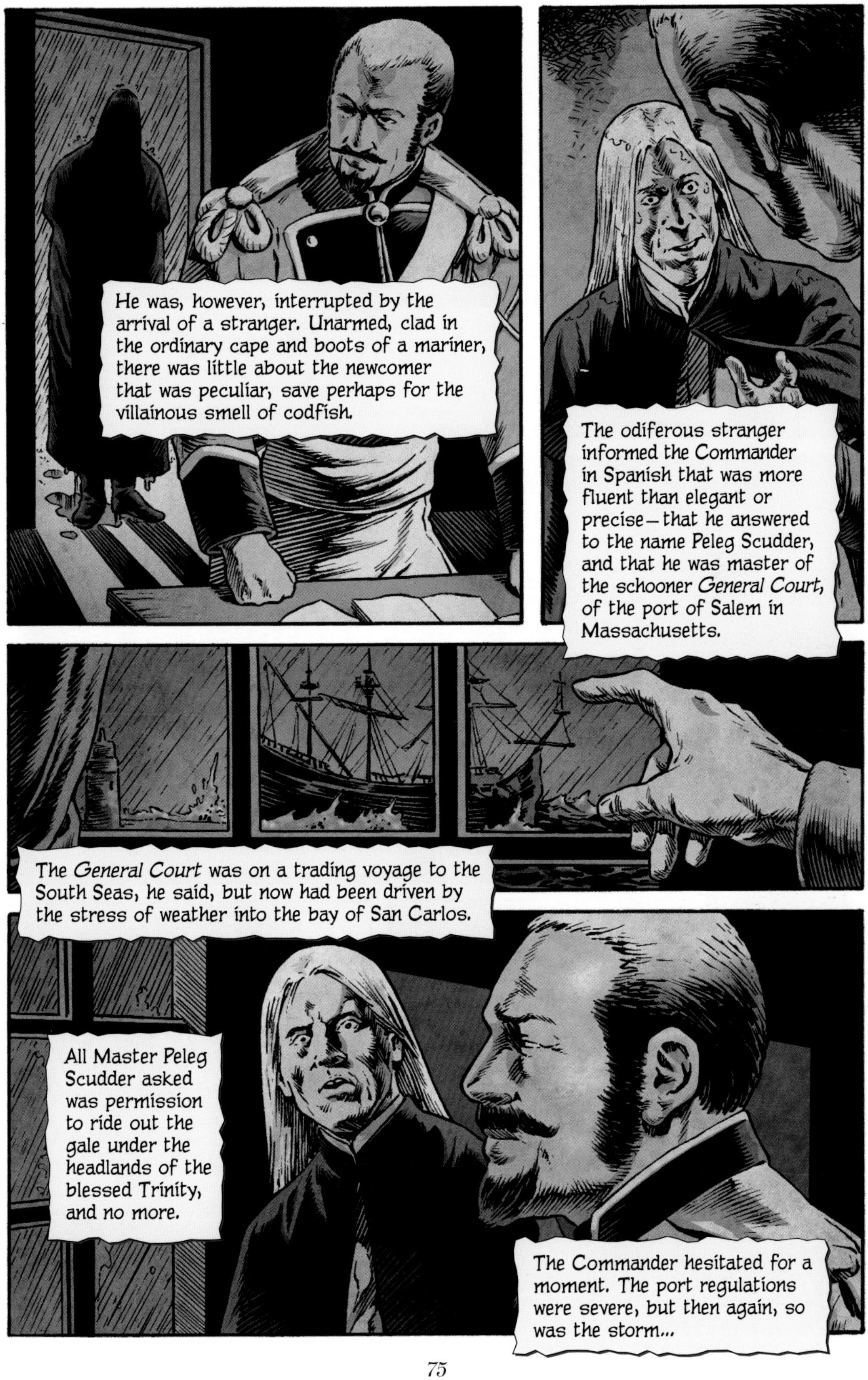
He was, however, interrupted by the arrival of a stranger. Unarmed, clad in the ordinary cape and boots of a mariner, there was little about the newcomer that was peculiar, save perhaps for the villainous smell of codfish.
The odiferous stranger informed the Commander in Spanish that was more fluent than elegant or precise—that he answered to the name Peleg Scudder, and that he was master of the schooner *General Court*, of the port of Salem in Massachusetts.
The *General Court* was on a trading voyage to the South Seas, he said, but now had been driven by the stress of weather into the bay of San Carlos.
All Master Peleg Scudder asked was permission to ride out the gale under the headlands of the blessed Trinity, and no more.
The Commander hesitated for a moment. The port regulations were severe, but then again, so was the storm...

FOR YOURSELF, SENOR CAPTAIN, ACCEPT MY HOSPITALITY. THE FORT IS YOURS AS LONG AS YOU SHALL GRACE IT WITH YOUR DISTINGUISHED PRESENCE.

In the end, the Commander acceded to the request, his only stipulation that there be no communication between the ship and the shore.

Over many glasses of aguardiente, much was subsequently shared between the Commander and the Captain, both matters of the world beyond the garrison, and gossip of the Mission and Presidio.

Circuitously, the conversation turned to the circumstances surrounding the Commander's missing eye.

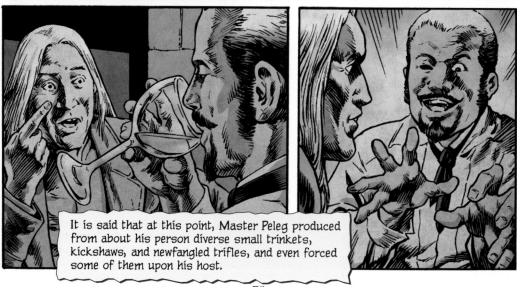

It is said that at this point, Master Peleg produced from about his person diverse small trinkets, kickshaws, and newfangled trifles, and even forced some of them upon his host.

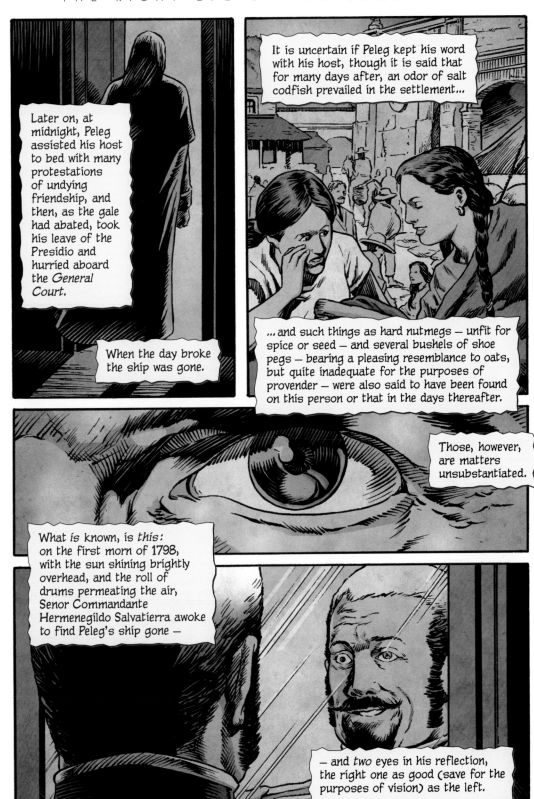

Later on, at midnight, Peleg assisted his host to bed with many protestations of undying friendship, and then, as the gale had abated, took his leave of the Presidio and hurried aboard the *General Court*.

When the day broke the ship was gone.

It is uncertain if Peleg kept his word with his host, though it is said that for many days after, an odor of salt codfish prevailed in the settlement...

...and such things as hard nutmegs — unfit for spice or seed — and several bushels of shoe pegs — bearing a pleasing resemblance to oats, but quite inadequate for the purposes of provender — were also said to have been found on this person or that in the days thereafter.

Those, however, are matters unsubstantiated.

What *is* known, is *this*: on the first morn of 1798, with the sun shining brightly overhead, and the roll of drums permeating the air, Senor Commandante Hermenegildo Salvatierra awoke to find Peleg's ship gone —

— and *two* eyes in his reflection, the right one as good (save for the purposes of vision) as the left.

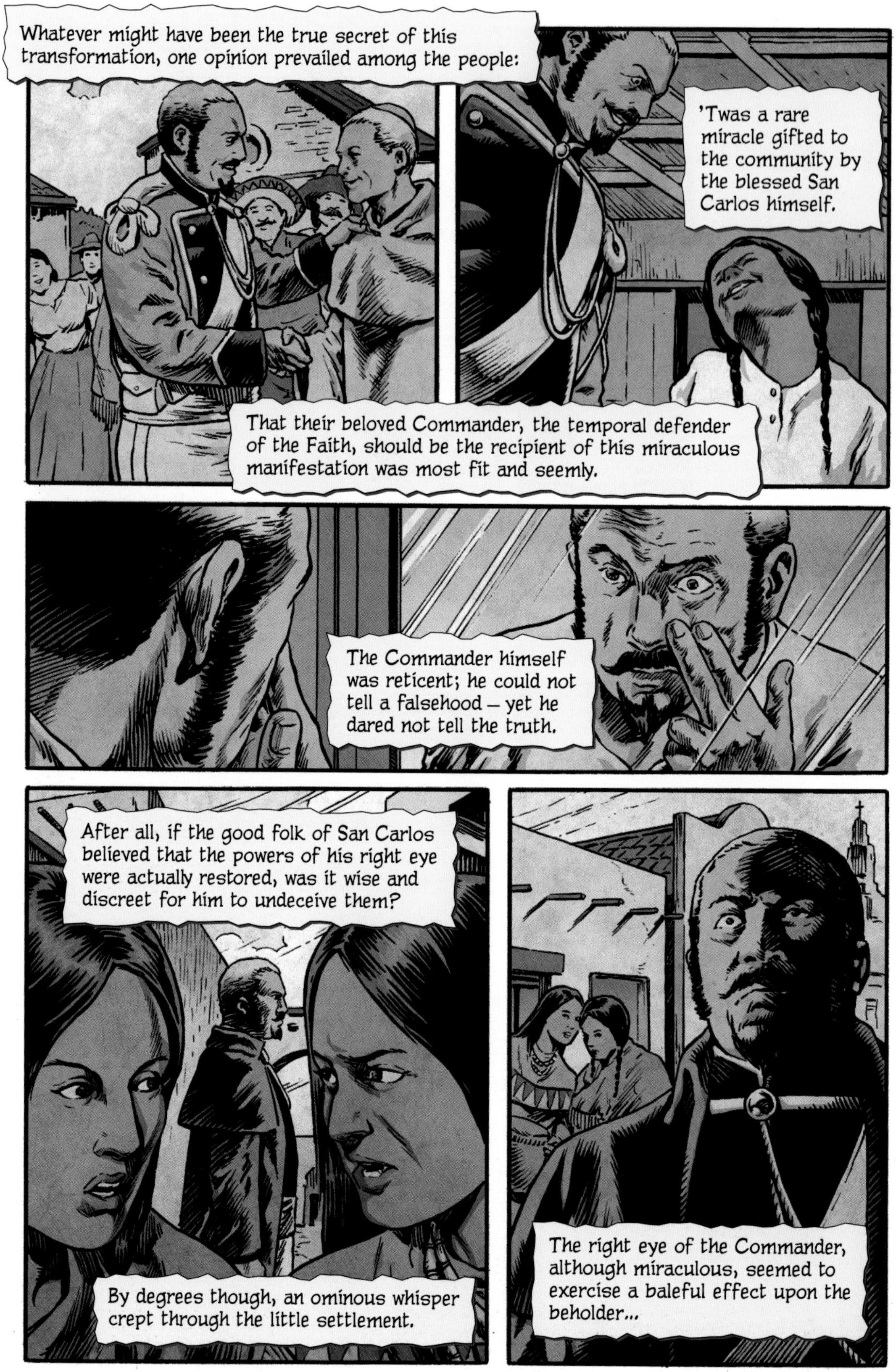
Whatever might have been the true secret of this transformation, one opinion prevailed among the people:
'Twas a rare miracle gifted to the community by the blessed San Carlos himself.
That their beloved Commander, the temporal defender of the Faith, should be the recipient of this miraculous manifestation was most fit and seemly.
The Commander himself was reticent; he could not tell a falsehood – yet he dared not tell the truth.
After all, if the good folk of San Carlos believed that the powers of his right eye were actually restored, was it wise and discreet for him to undeceive them?
By degrees though, an ominous whisper crept through the little settlement.
The right eye of the Commander, although miraculous, seemed to exercise a baleful effect upon the beholder...

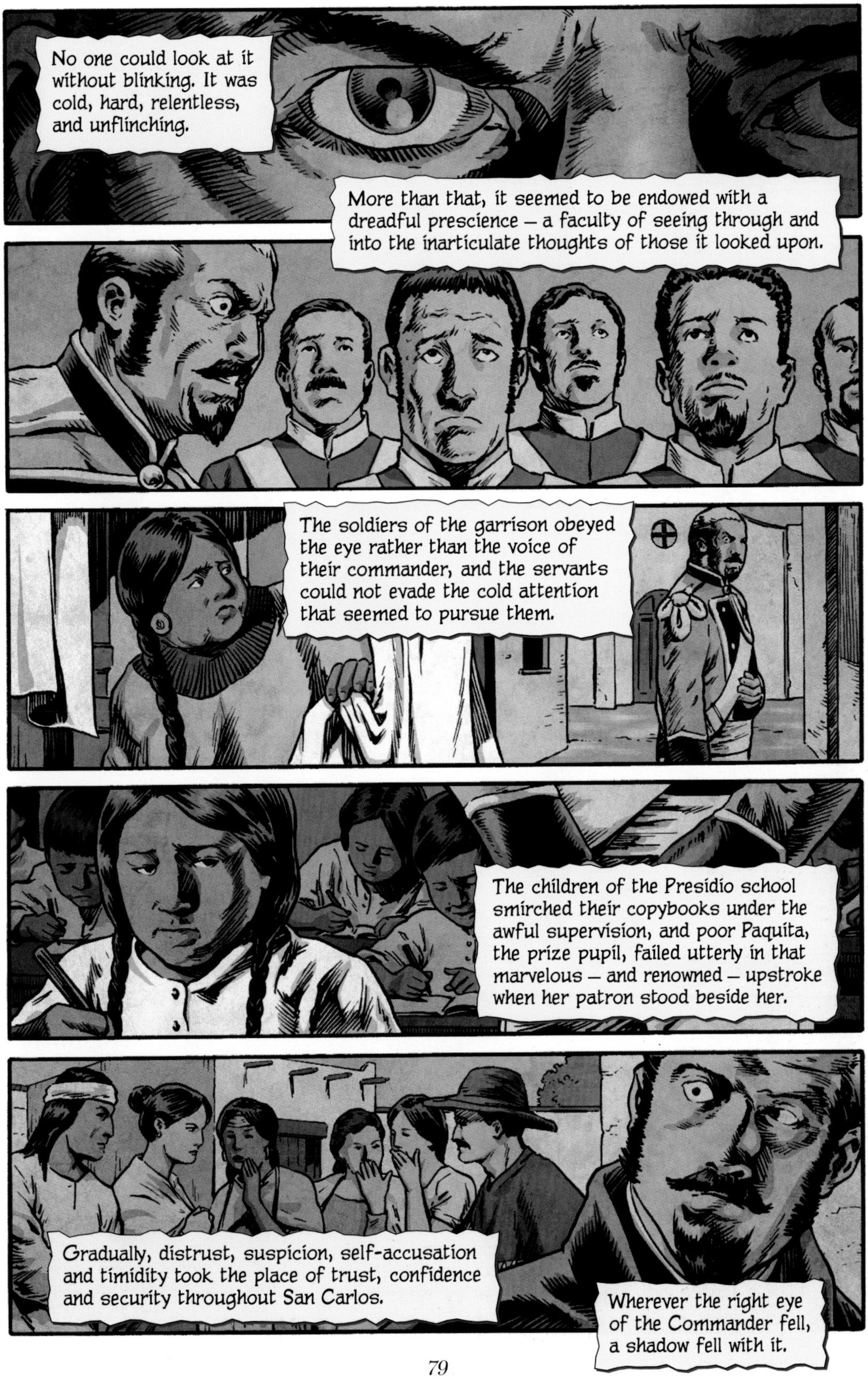
No one could look at it without blinking. It was cold, hard, relentless, and unflinching.
More than that, it seemed to be endowed with a dreadful prescience – a faculty of seeing through and into the inarticulate thoughts of those it looked upon.
The soldiers of the garrison obeyed the eye rather than the voice of their commander, and the servants could not evade the cold attention that seemed to pursue them.
The children of the Presidio school smirched their copybooks under the awful supervision, and poor Paquita, the prize pupil, failed utterly in that marvelous – and renowned – upstroke when her patron stood beside her.
Gradually, distrust, suspicion, self-accusation and timidity took the place of trust, confidence and security throughout San Carlos.
Wherever the right eye of the Commander fell, a shadow fell with it.

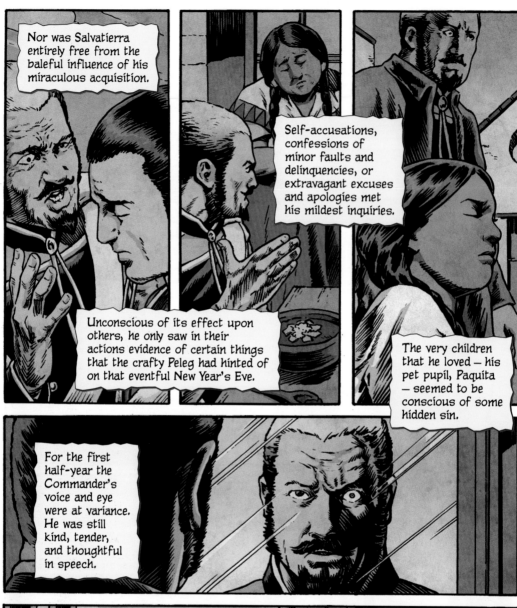

Nor was Salvatierra entirely free from the baleful influence of his miraculous acquisition.

Self-accusations, confessions of minor faults and delinquencies, or extravagant excuses and apologies met his mildest inquiries.

Unconscious of its effect upon others, he only saw in their actions evidence of certain things that the crafty Peleg had hinted of on that eventful New Year's Eve.

The very children that he loved — his pet pupil, Paquita — seemed to be conscious of some hidden sin.

For the first half-year the Commander's voice and eye were at variance. He was still kind, tender, and thoughtful in speech.

Gradually, however, his voice took upon itself the hardness of his glance and its skeptical, impassive quality, and as the year again neared its close it was plain that the Commander had fitted himself to the eye, and not the eye to the Commander.

It may be surmised that these changes did not escape the watchful solicitude of the Fathers.

Indeed, the few who were first to ascribe the right eye of Salvatierra to the special grace of the blessed San Carlos, now talked openly of witchcraft and the agency of Luzbel, the evil one.

It would have fared ill with Hermenegildo Salvatierra had he been aught but Commander or amenable to local authority.

But the reverend father, Friar Manuel de Cortes, had no power over the political executive, and all attempts at spiritual advice failed signally.

He retired baffled and confused from his first interview with the Commander, who seemed now to take a grim satisfaction in the fateful power of his glance.

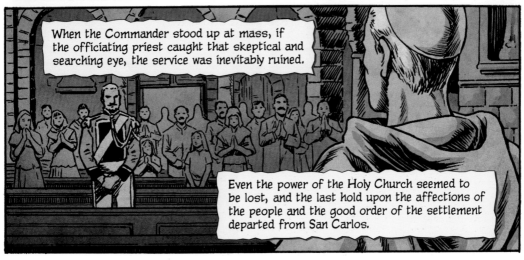

When the Commander stood up at mass, if the officiating priest caught that skeptical and searching eye, the service was inevitably ruined.

Even the power of the Holy Church seemed to be lost, and the last hold upon the affections of the people and the good order of the settlement departed from San Carlos.

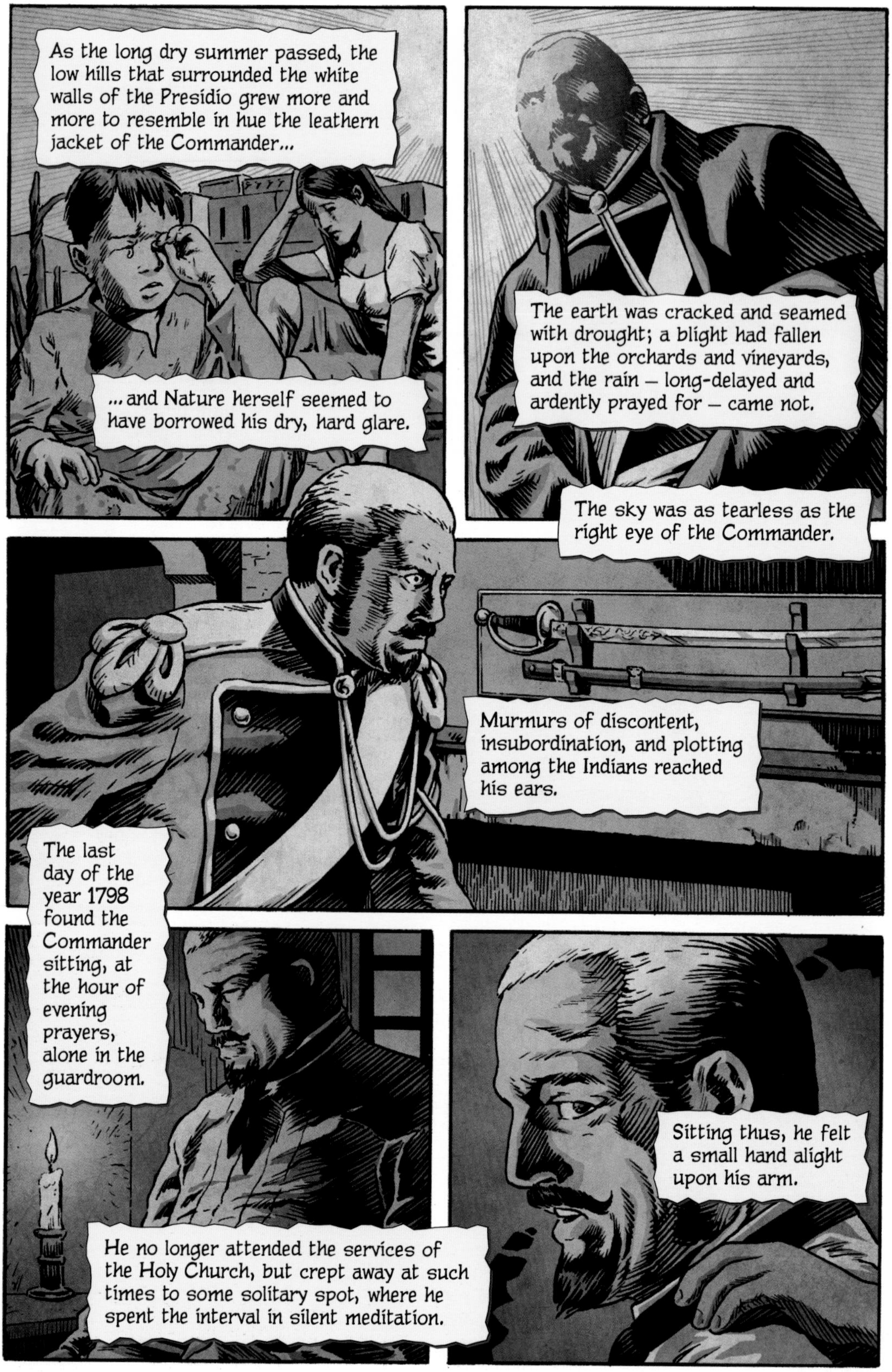
As the long dry summer passed, the low hills that surrounded the white walls of the Presidio grew more and more to resemble in hue the leathern jacket of the Commander...
...and Nature herself seemed to have borrowed his dry, hard glare.
The earth was cracked and seamed with drought; a blight had fallen upon the orchards and vineyards, and the rain – long-delayed and ardently prayed for – came not.
The sky was as tearless as the right eye of the Commander.
Murmurs of discontent, insubordination, and plotting among the Indians reached his ears.
The last day of the year 1798 found the Commander sitting, at the hour of evening prayers, alone in the guardroom.
He no longer attended the services of the Holy Church, but crept away at such times to some solitary spot, where he spent the interval in silent meditation.
Sitting thus, he felt a small hand alight upon his arm.

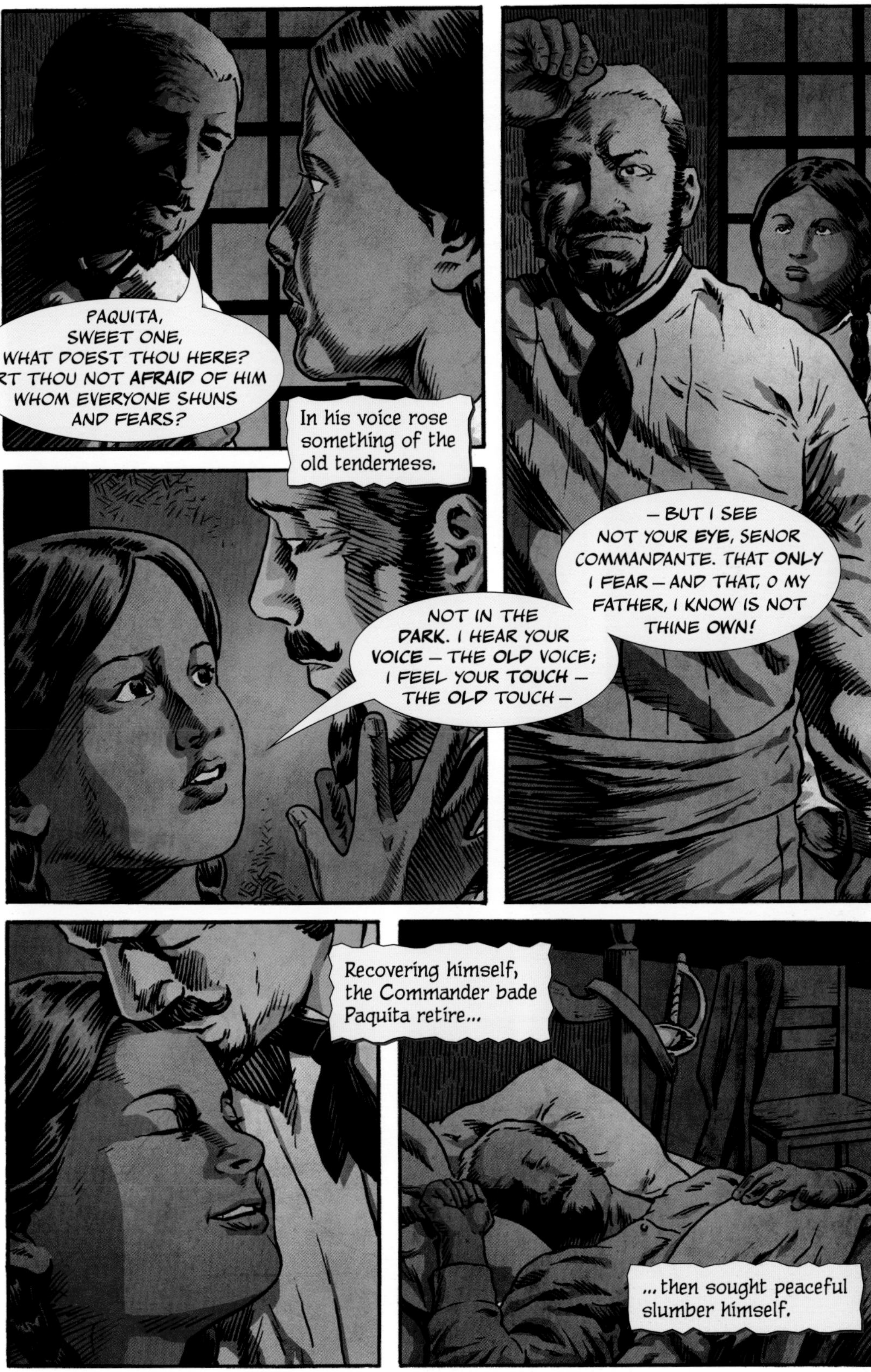
PAQUITA, SWEET ONE, WHAT DOEST THOU HERE? ART THOU NOT AFRAID OF HIM WHOM EVERYONE SHUNS AND FEARS?
In his voice rose something of the old tenderness.
NOT IN THE DARK. I HEAR YOUR VOICE — THE OLD VOICE; I FEEL YOUR TOUCH — THE OLD TOUCH —
— BUT I SEE NOT YOUR EYE, SENOR COMMANDANTE. THAT ONLY I FEAR — AND THAT, O MY FATHER, I KNOW IS NOT THINE OWN!
Recovering himself, the Commander bade Paquita retire...
...then sought peaceful slumber himself.

Come the middle watch of the night, stealthy figures flitted through the garrison —

— figures the Commander might have seen had he not slept so quietly.

One such figure crept noiselessly up to the Commander's reclined form...

Another moment and the sore perplexities of Hermenegildo Salvatierra would have been over, had his attacker not seen —

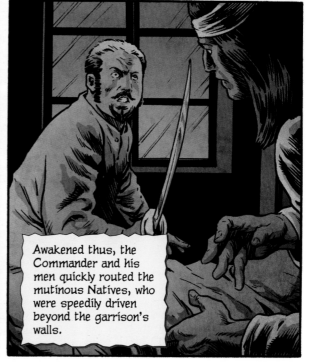

Awakened thus, the Commander and his men quickly routed the mutinous Natives, who were speedily driven beyond the garrison's walls.

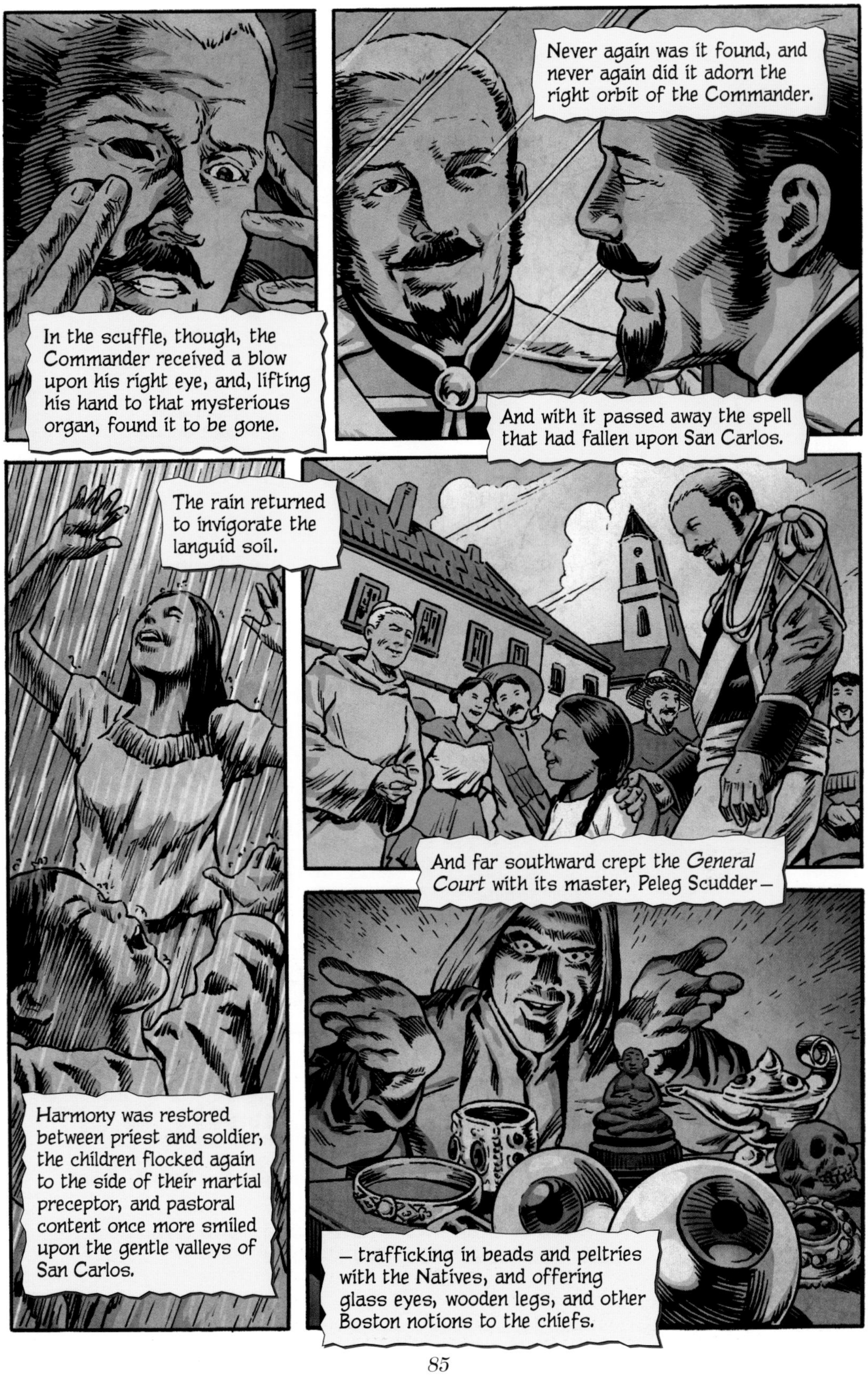
In the scuffle, though, the Commander received a blow upon his right eye, and, lifting his hand to that mysterious organ, found it to be gone.
Never again was it found, and never again did it adorn the right orbit of the Commander.
And with it passed away the spell that had fallen upon San Carlos.
The rain returned to invigorate the languid soil.
Harmony was restored between priest and soldier, the children flocked again to the side of their martial preceptor, and pastoral content once more smiled upon the gentle valleys of San Carlos.
And far southward crept the *General Court* with its master, Peleg Scudder—
—trafficking in beads and peltries with the Natives, and offering glass eyes, wooden legs, and other Boston notions to the chiefs.

HOPALONG CASSIDY IN

THE HOLDUP

STORY BY CLARENCE E. MULFORD · ADAPTED BY TIM LASIUTA
ART AND COLOR BY DAN SPIEGLE

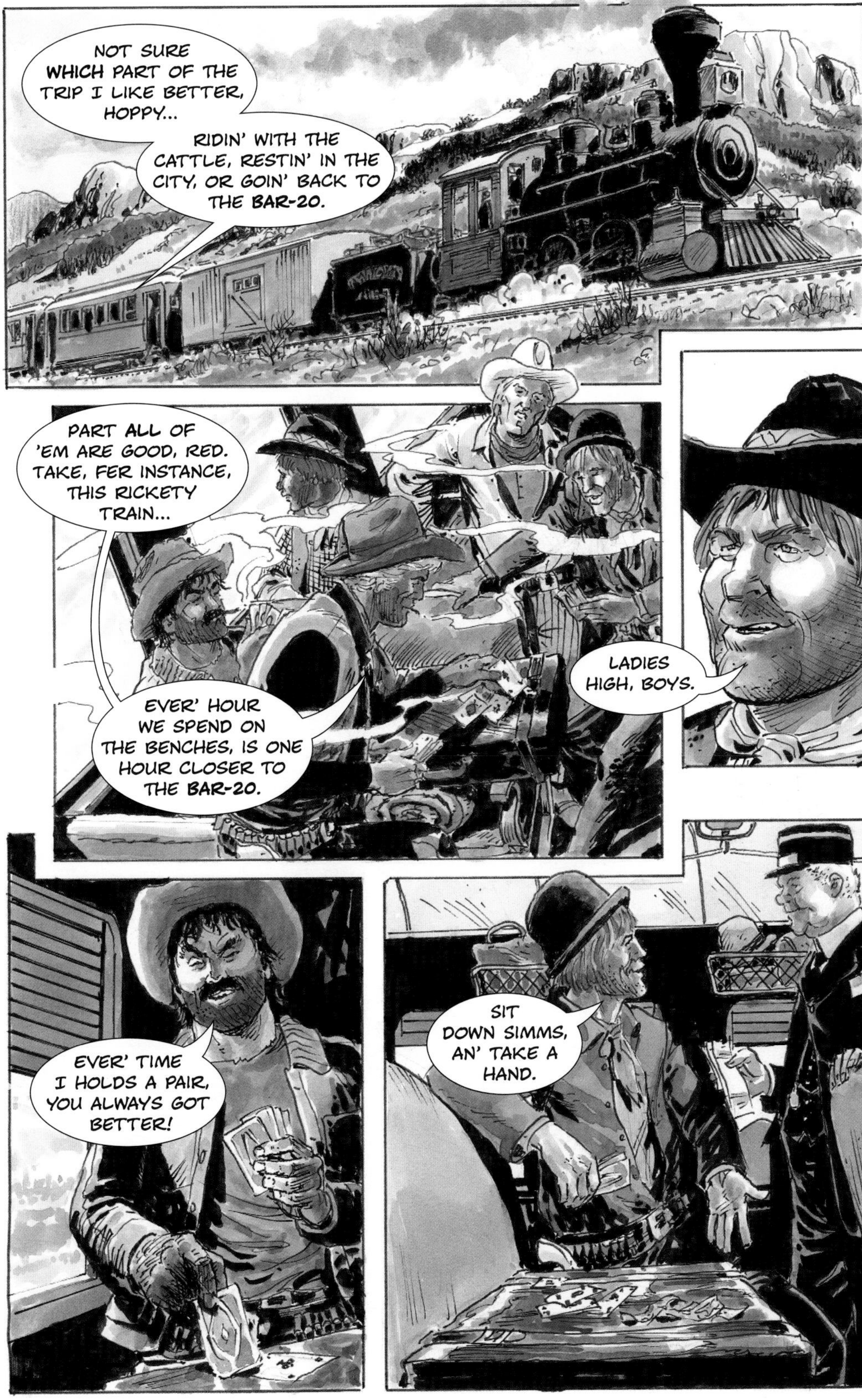
NOT SURE WHICH PART OF THE TRIP I LIKE BETTER, HOPPY...
RIDIN' WITH THE CATTLE, RESTIN' IN THE CITY, OR GOIN' BACK TO THE BAR-20.
PART ALL OF 'EM ARE GOOD, RED. TAKE, FER INSTANCE, THIS RICKETY TRAIN...
EVER' HOUR WE SPEND ON THE BENCHES, IS ONE HOUR CLOSER TO THE BAR-20.
LADIES HIGH, BOYS.
EVER' TIME I HOLDS A PAIR, YOU ALWAYS GOT BETTER!
SIT DOWN SIMMS, AN' TAKE A HAND.

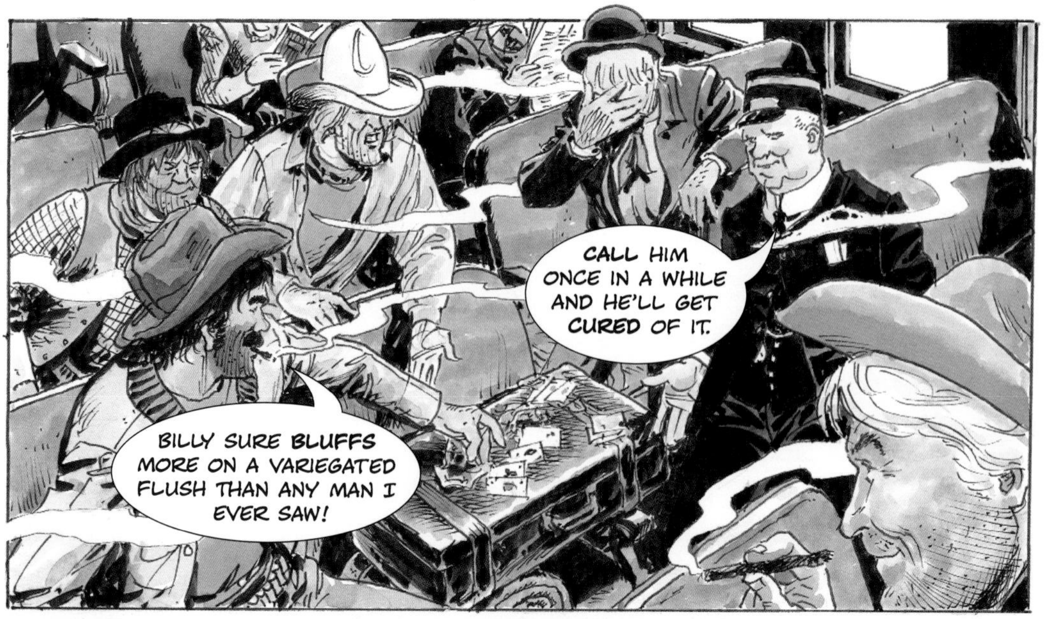
CALL HIM ONCE IN A WHILE AND HE'LL GET CURED OF IT.
BILLY SURE BLUFFS MORE ON A VARIEGATED FLUSH THAN ANY MAN I EVER SAW!

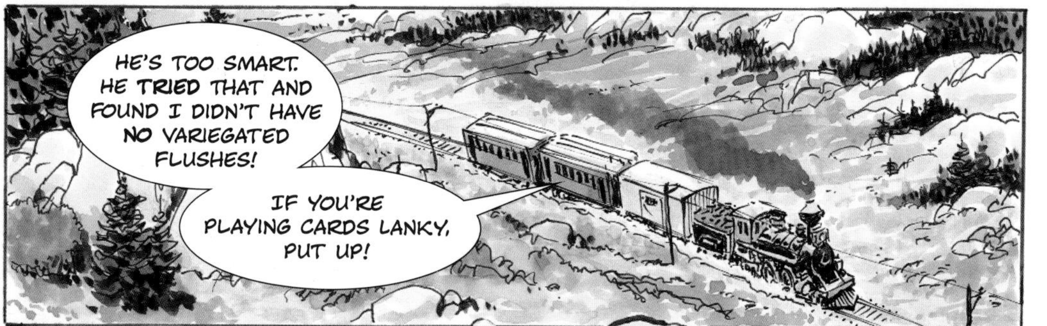
HE'S TOO SMART. HE TRIED THAT AND FOUND I DIDN'T HAVE NO VARIEGATED FLUSHES!
IF YOU'RE PLAYING CARDS LANKY, PUT UP!

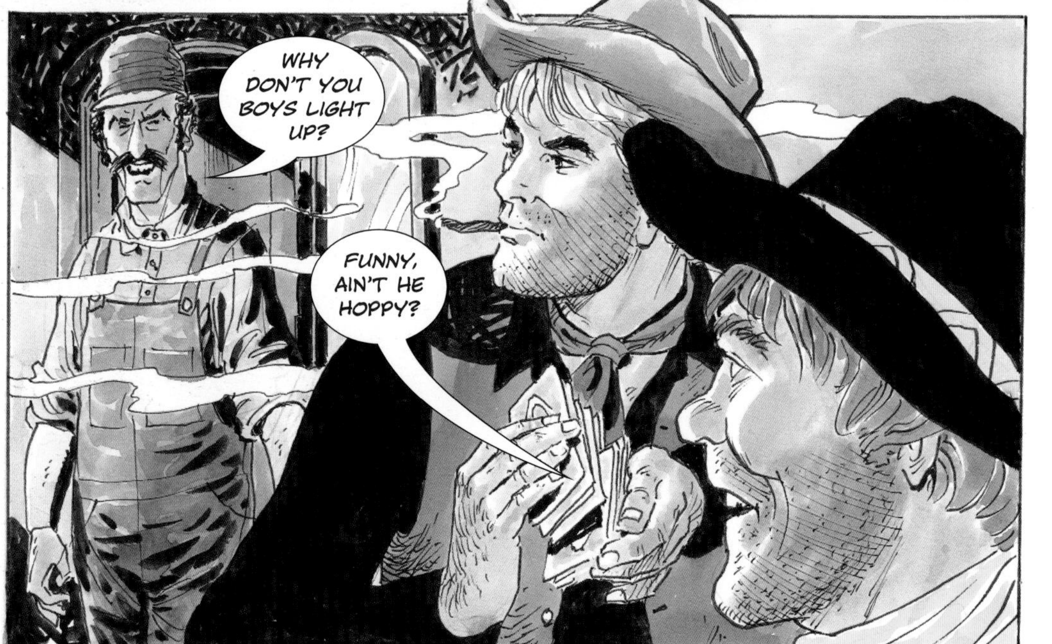
WHY DON'T YOU BOYS LIGHT UP?
FUNNY, AIN'T HE HOPPY?

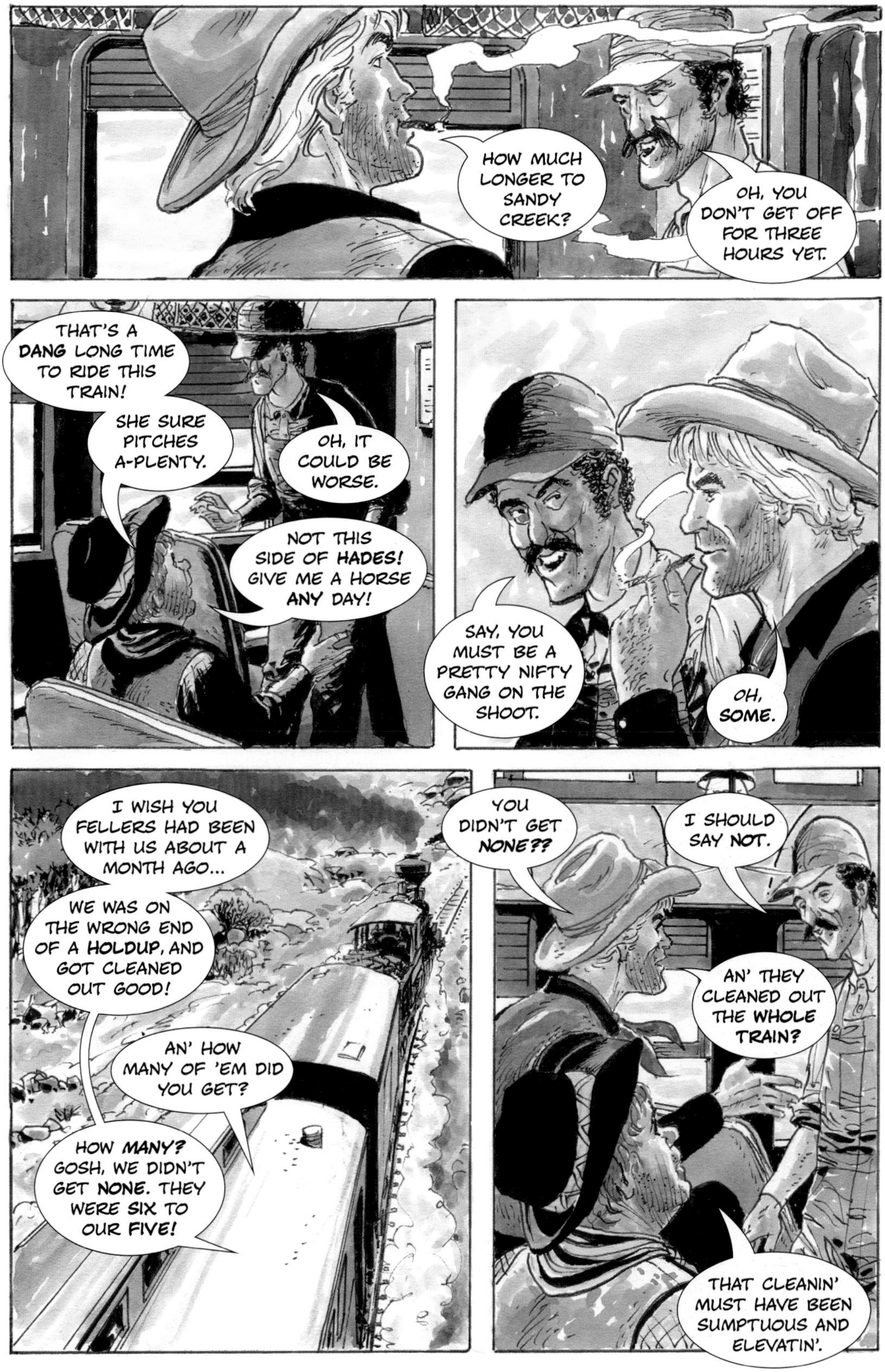
HOW MUCH LONGER TO SANDY CREEK?
OH, YOU DON'T GET OFF FOR THREE HOURS YET.
THAT'S A DANG LONG TIME TO RIDE THIS TRAIN!
SHE SURE PITCHES A-PLENTY.
OH, IT COULD BE WORSE.
NOT THIS SIDE OF HADES! GIVE ME A HORSE ANY DAY!
SAY, YOU MUST BE A PRETTY NIFTY GANG ON THE SHOOT.
OH, SOME.
I WISH YOU FELLERS HAD BEEN WITH US ABOUT A MONTH AGO...
WE WAS ON THE WRONG END OF A HOLDUP, AND GOT CLEANED OUT GOOD!
AN' HOW MANY OF 'EM DID YOU GET?
HOW MANY? GOSH, WE DIDN'T GET NONE. THEY WERE SIX TO OUR FIVE!
YOU DIDN'T GET NONE??
I SHOULD SAY NOT.
AN' THEY CLEANED OUT THE WHOLE TRAIN?
THAT CLEANIN' MUST HAVE BEEN SUMPTUOUS AND ELEVATIN'.

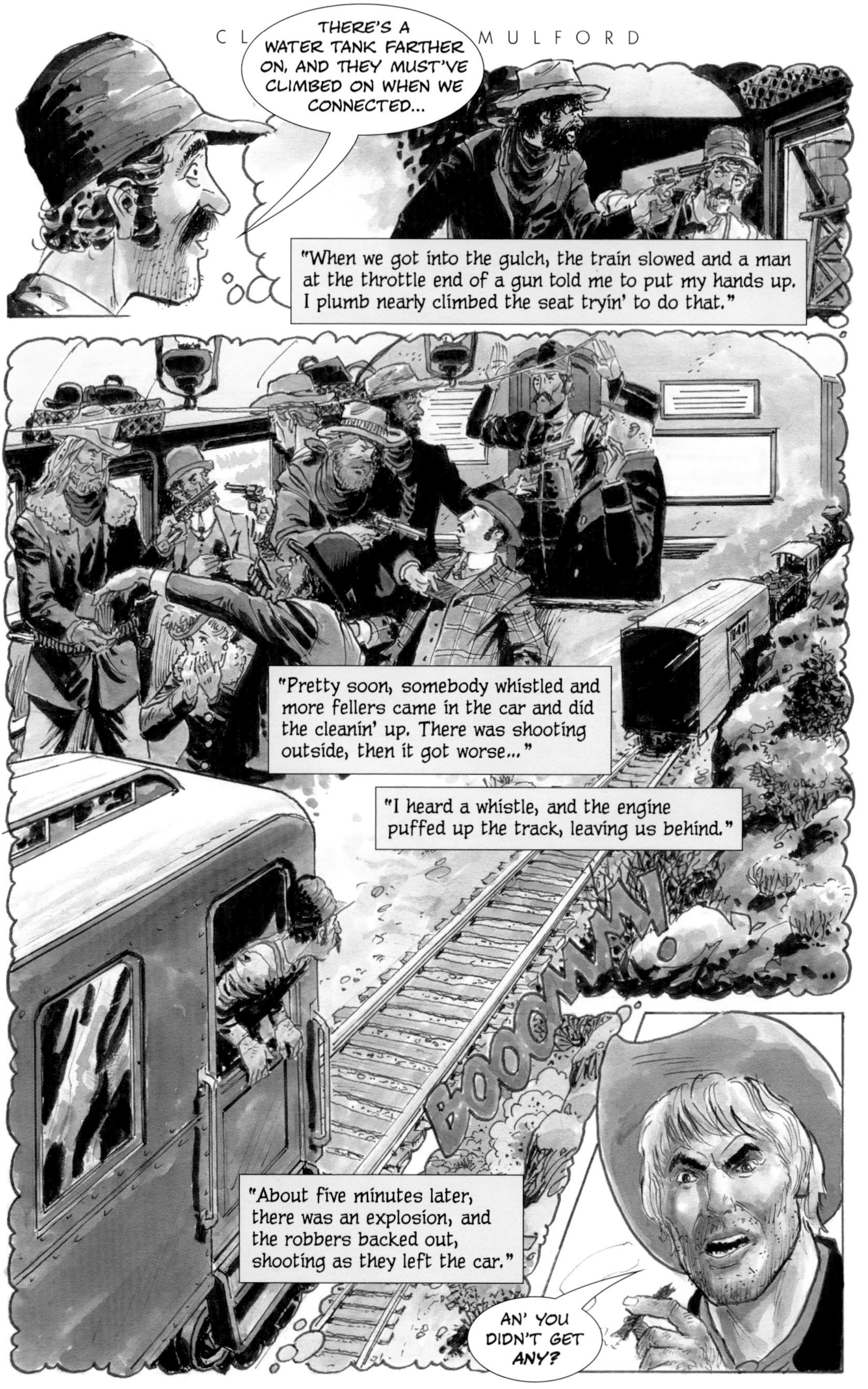
THERE'S A WATER TANK FARTHER ON, AND THEY MUST'VE CLIMBED ON WHEN WE CONNECTED...
"When we got into the gulch, the train slowed and a man at the throttle end of a gun told me to put my hands up. I plumb nearly climbed the seat tryin' to do that."
"Pretty soon, somebody whistled and more fellers came in the car and did the cleanin' up. There was shooting outside, then it got worse..."
"I heard a whistle, and the engine puffed up the track, leaving us behind."
BOOOMMM!
"About five minutes later, there was an explosion, and the robbers backed out, shooting as they left the car."
AN' YOU DIDN'T GET ANY?

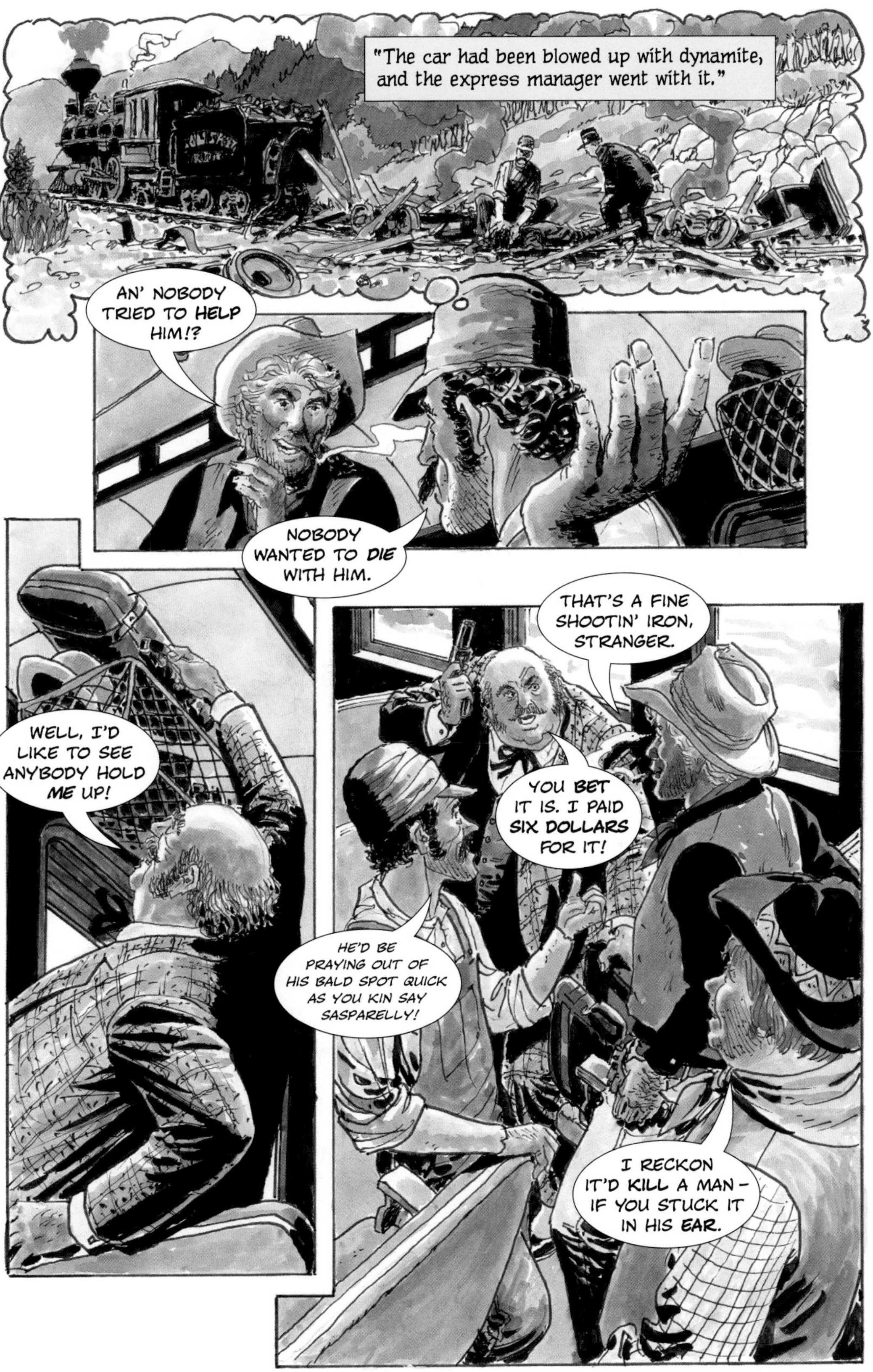
"The car had been blowed up with dynamite, and the express manager went with it."
AN' NOBODY TRIED TO HELP HIM!?
NOBODY WANTED TO DIE WITH HIM.
WELL, I'D LIKE TO SEE ANYBODY HOLD ME UP!
HE'D BE PRAYING OUT OF HIS BALD SPOT QUICK AS YOU KIN SAY SASPARELLY!
THAT'S A FINE SHOOTIN' IRON, STRANGER.
YOU BET IT IS. I PAID SIX DOLLARS FOR IT!
I RECKON IT'D KILL A MAN - IF YOU STUCK IT IN HIS EAR.

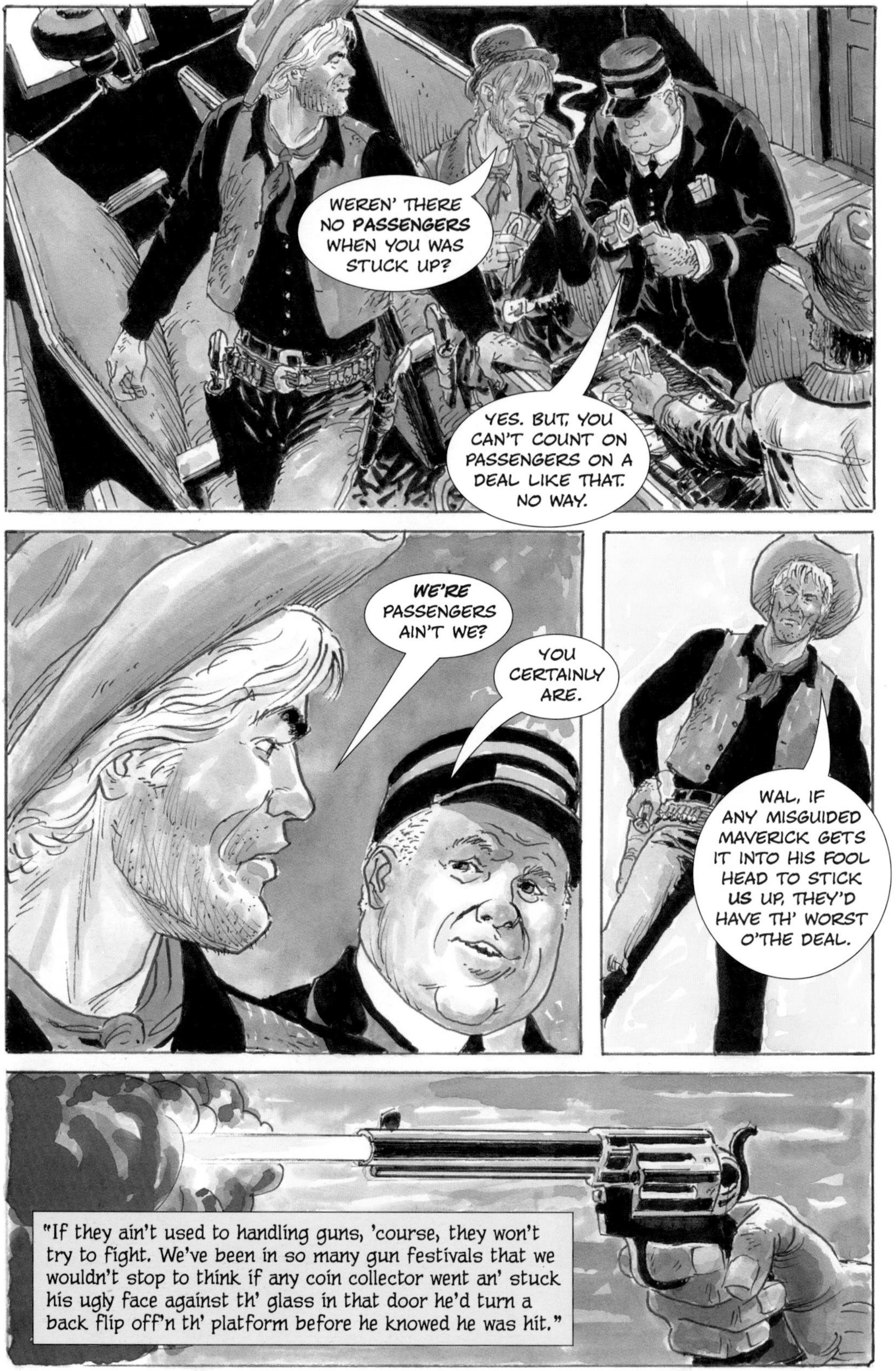
WEREN' THERE NO PASSENGERS WHEN YOU WAS STUCK UP?
YES. BUT, YOU CAN'T COUNT ON PASSENGERS ON A DEAL LIKE THAT. NO WAY.
WE'RE PASSENGERS AIN'T WE?
YOU CERTAINLY ARE.
WAL, IF ANY MISGUIDED MAVERICK GETS IT INTO HIS FOOL HEAD TO STICK US UP, THEY'D HAVE TH' WORST O'THE DEAL.
"If they ain't used to handling guns, 'course, they won't try to fight. We've been in so many gun festivals that we wouldn't stop to think if any coin collector went an' stuck his ugly face against th' glass in that door he'd turn a back flip off'n th' platform before he knowed he was hit."

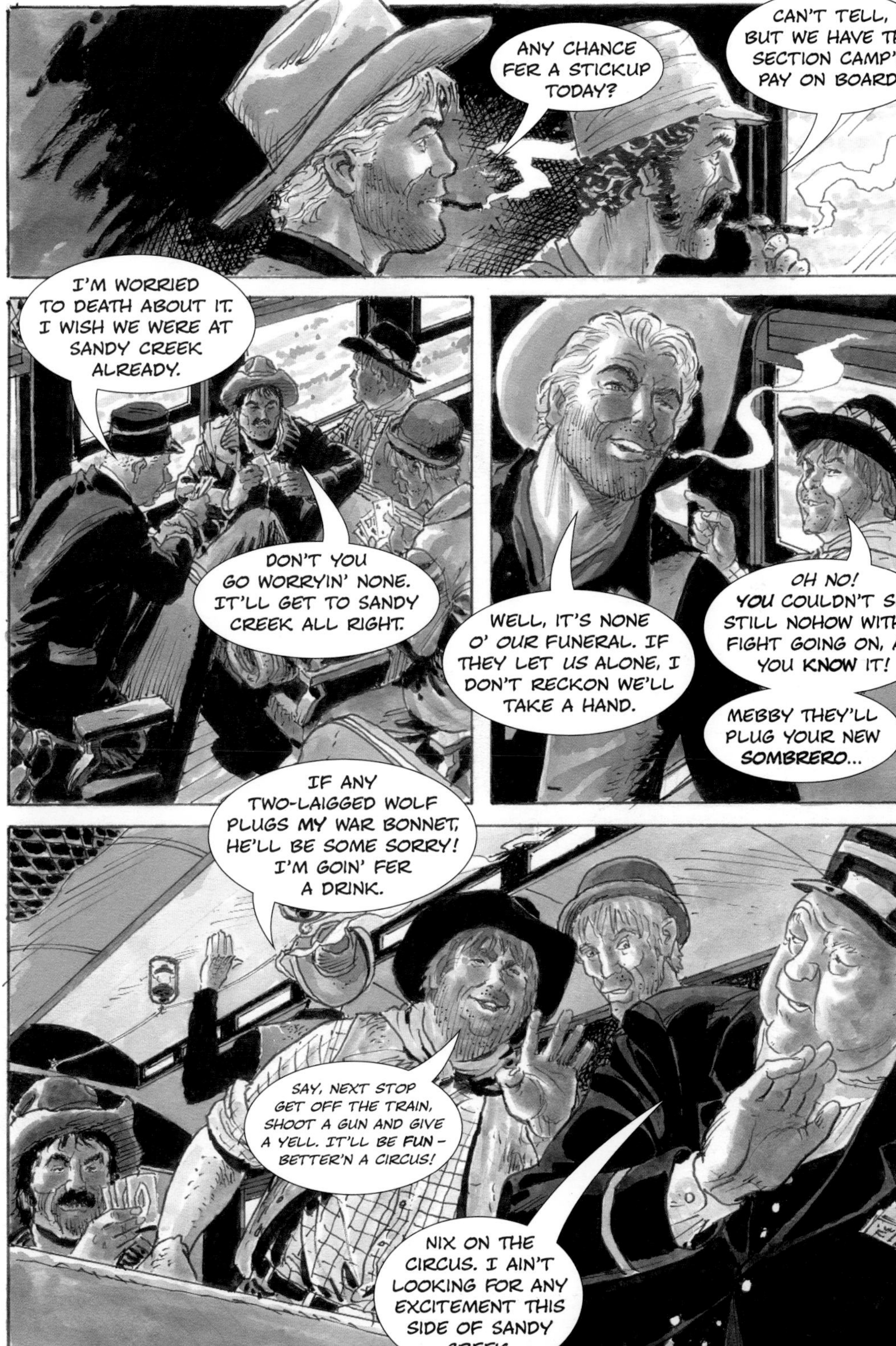
ANY CHANCE FER A STICKUP TODAY?
CAN'T TELL, BUT WE HAVE THE SECTION CAMP'S PAY ON BOARD.
I'M WORRIED TO DEATH ABOUT IT. I WISH WE WERE AT SANDY CREEK ALREADY.
DON'T YOU GO WORRYIN' NONE. IT'LL GET TO SANDY CREEK ALL RIGHT.
WELL, IT'S NONE O' OUR FUNERAL. IF THEY LET US ALONE, I DON'T RECKON WE'LL TAKE A HAND.
OH NO! YOU COULDN'T SIT STILL NOHOW WITH A FIGHT GOING ON, AN' YOU KNOW IT!
MEBBY THEY'LL PLUG YOUR NEW SOMBRERO...
IF ANY TWO-LAIGGED WOLF PLUGS MY WAR BONNET, HE'LL BE SOME SORRY! I'M GOIN' FER A DRINK.
SAY, NEXT STOP GET OFF THE TRAIN, SHOOT A GUN AND GIVE A YELL. IT'LL BE FUN – BETTER'N A CIRCUS!
NIX ON THE CIRCUS. I AIN'T LOOKING FOR ANY EXCITEMENT THIS SIDE OF SANDY CREEK.

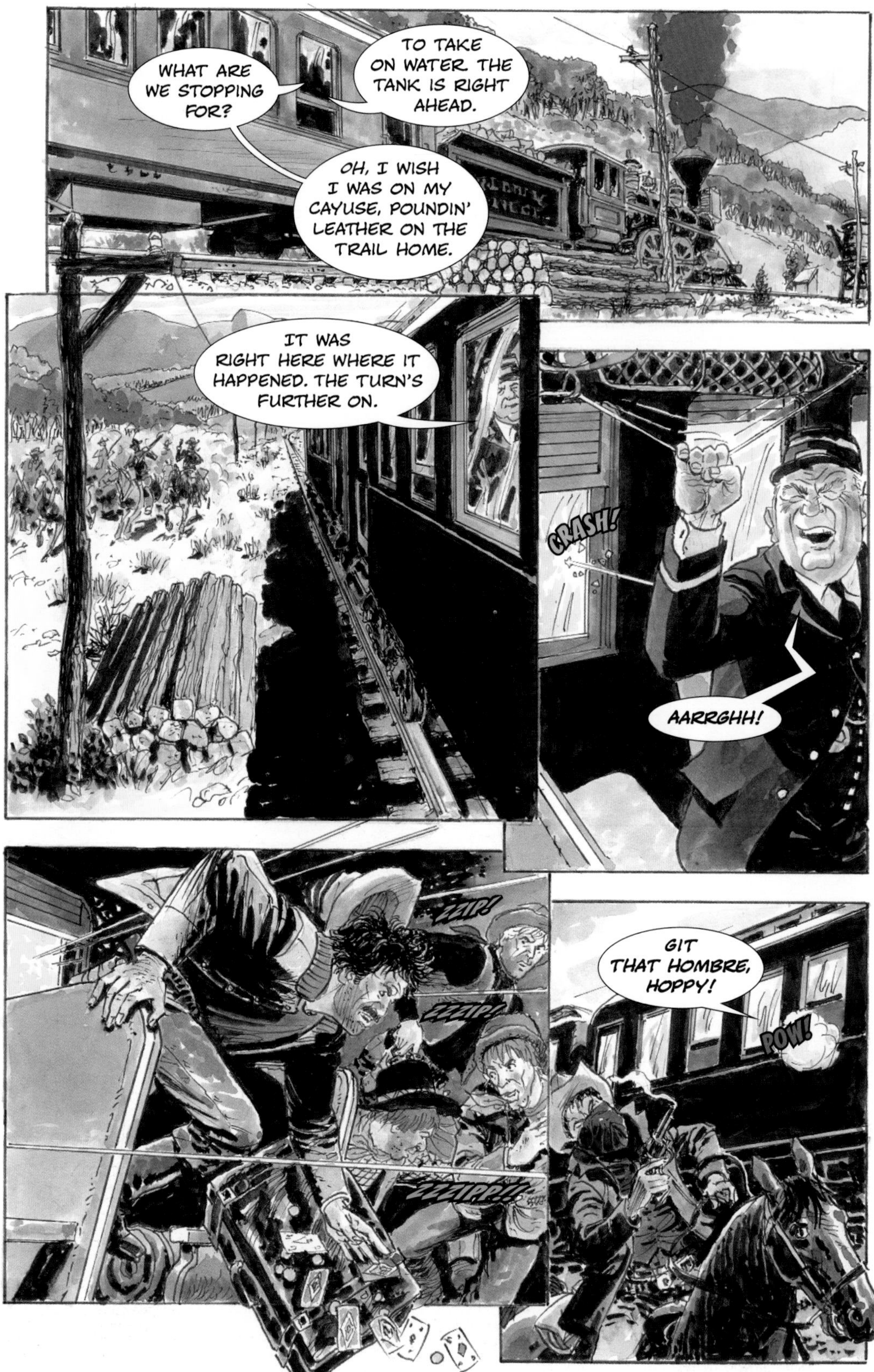
WHAT ARE WE STOPPING FOR?
TO TAKE ON WATER. THE TANK IS RIGHT AHEAD.
OH, I WISH I WAS ON MY CAYUSE, POUNDIN' LEATHER ON THE TRAIL HOME.
IT WAS RIGHT HERE WHERE IT HAPPENED. THE TURN'S FURTHER ON.
CRASH!
AARRGHH!
ZZIP!
ZZZIP!
ZZZIPP!!
GIT THAT HOMBRE, HOPPY!
POW!

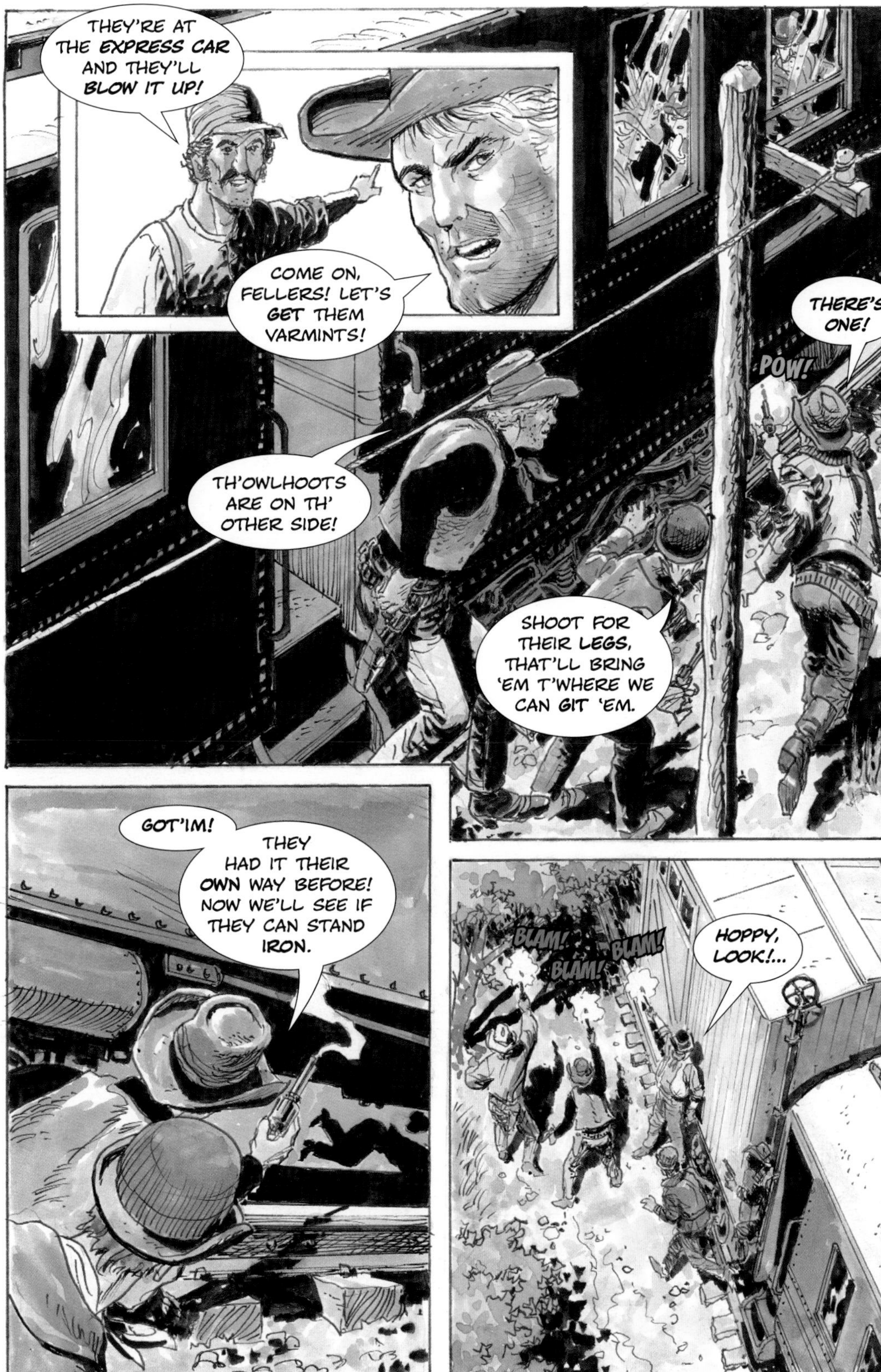
THEY'RE AT THE EXPRESS CAR AND THEY'LL BLOW IT UP!
COME ON, FELLERS! LET'S GET THEM VARMINTS!
TH'OWLHOOTS ARE ON TH' OTHER SIDE!
THERE'S ONE!
POW!
SHOOT FOR THEIR LEGS, THAT'LL BRING 'EM T'WHERE WE CAN GIT 'EM.
GOT'IM!
THEY HAD IT THEIR OWN WAY BEFORE! NOW WE'LL SEE IF THEY CAN STAND IRON.
BLAM!
BLAM!
BLAM!
HOPPY, LOOK!...

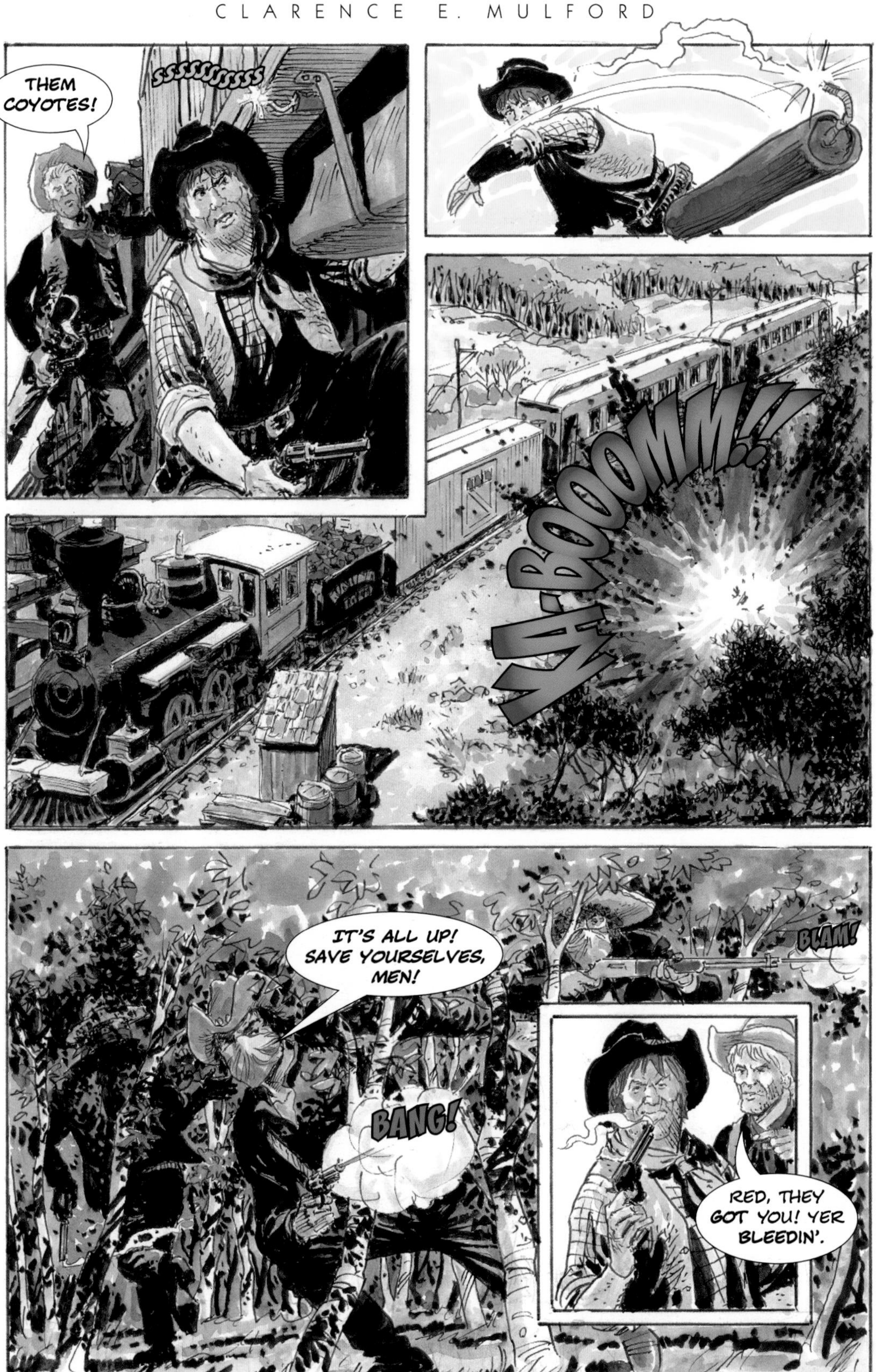
THEM COYOTES!
SSSSSSSSSSS
KA-BOOOMM!!!
IT'S ALL UP! SAVE YOURSELVES, MEN!
BLAM!
BANG!
RED, THEY GOT YOU! YER BLEEDIN'.

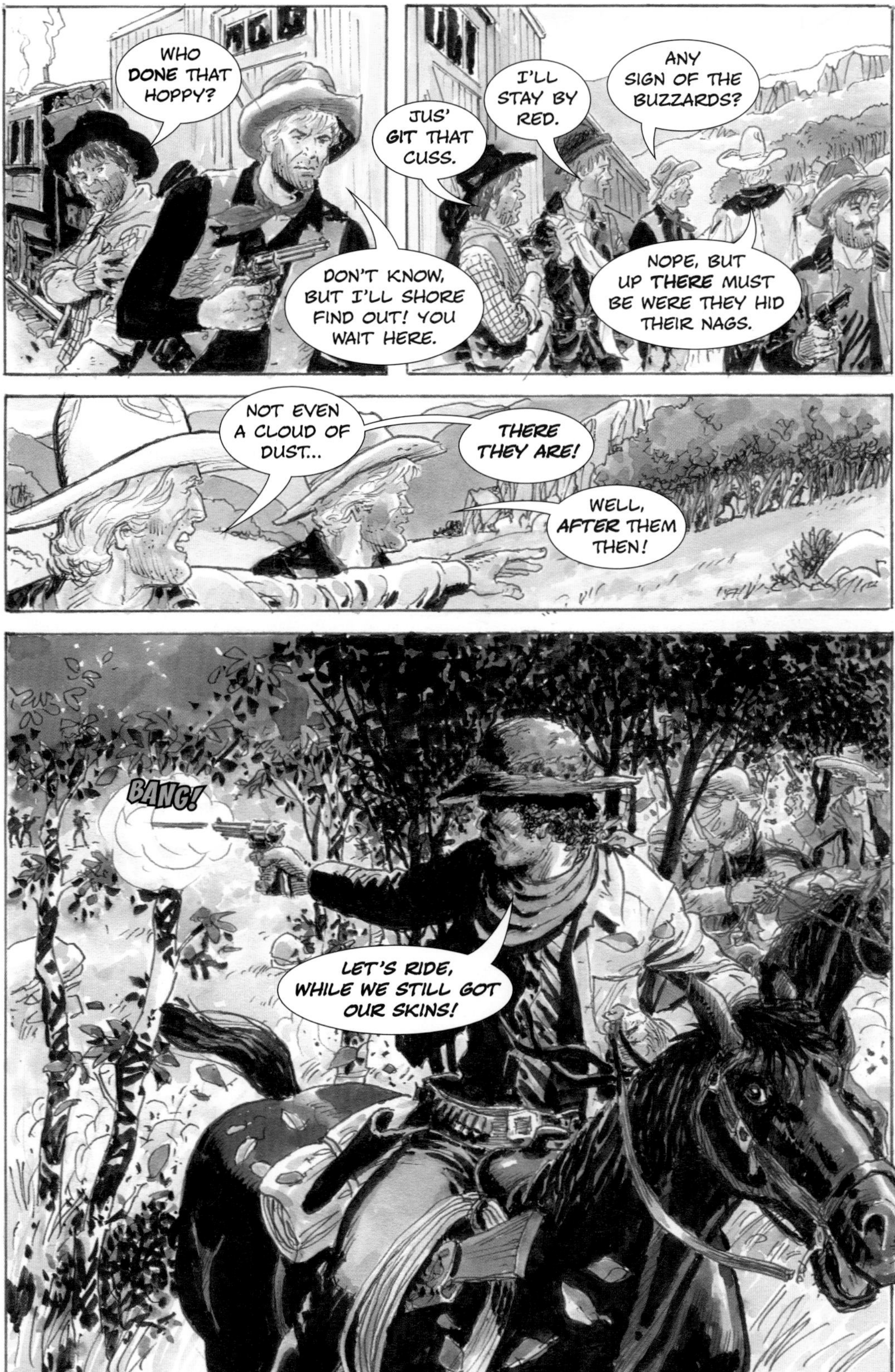
WHO DONE THAT HOPPY?
DON'T KNOW, BUT I'LL SHORE FIND OUT! YOU WAIT HERE.
JUS' GIT THAT CUSS.
I'LL STAY BY RED.
ANY SIGN OF THE BUZZARDS?
NOPE, BUT UP THERE MUST BE WERE THEY HID THEIR NAGS.
NOT EVEN A CLOUD OF DUST...
THERE THEY ARE!
WELL, AFTER THEM THEN!
BANG!
LET'S RIDE, WHILE WE STILL GOT OUR SKINS!

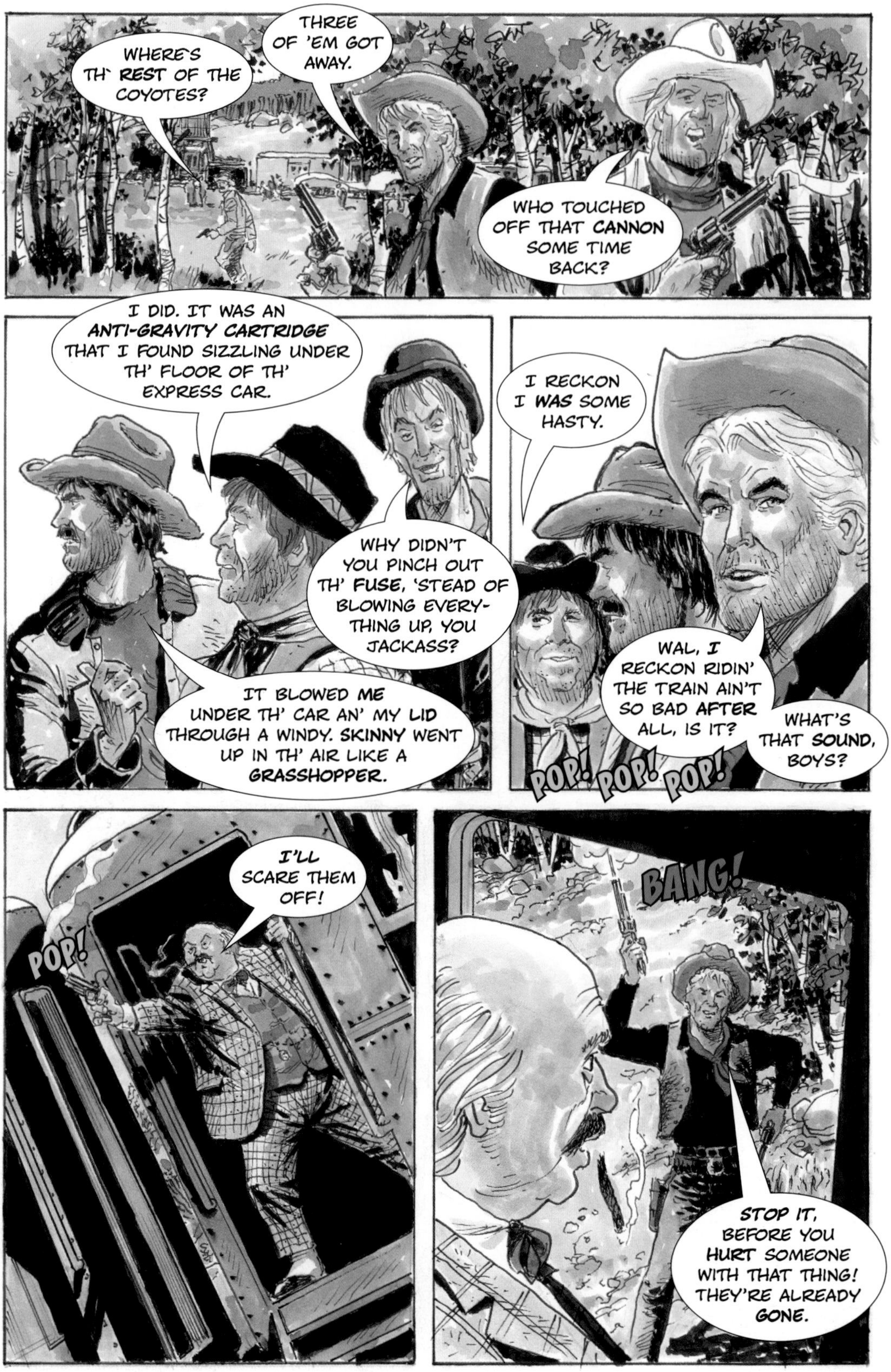
WHERE'S TH' REST OF THE COYOTES?
THREE OF 'EM GOT AWAY.
WHO TOUCHED OFF THAT CANNON SOME TIME BACK?
I DID. IT WAS AN ANTI-GRAVITY CARTRIDGE THAT I FOUND SIZZLING UNDER TH' FLOOR OF TH' EXPRESS CAR.
WHY DIDN'T YOU PINCH OUT TH' FUSE, 'STEAD OF BLOWING EVERY-THING UP, YOU JACKASS?
IT BLOWED ME UNDER TH' CAR AN' MY LID THROUGH A WINDY. SKINNY WENT UP IN TH' AIR LIKE A GRASSHOPPER.
I RECKON I WAS SOME HASTY.
WAL, I RECKON RIDIN' THE TRAIN AIN'T SO BAD AFTER ALL, IS IT?
WHAT'S THAT SOUND, BOYS?
POP! POP! POP!
POP!
I'LL SCARE THEM OFF!
BANG!
STOP IT, BEFORE YOU HURT SOMEONE WITH THAT THING! THEY'RE ALREADY GONE.

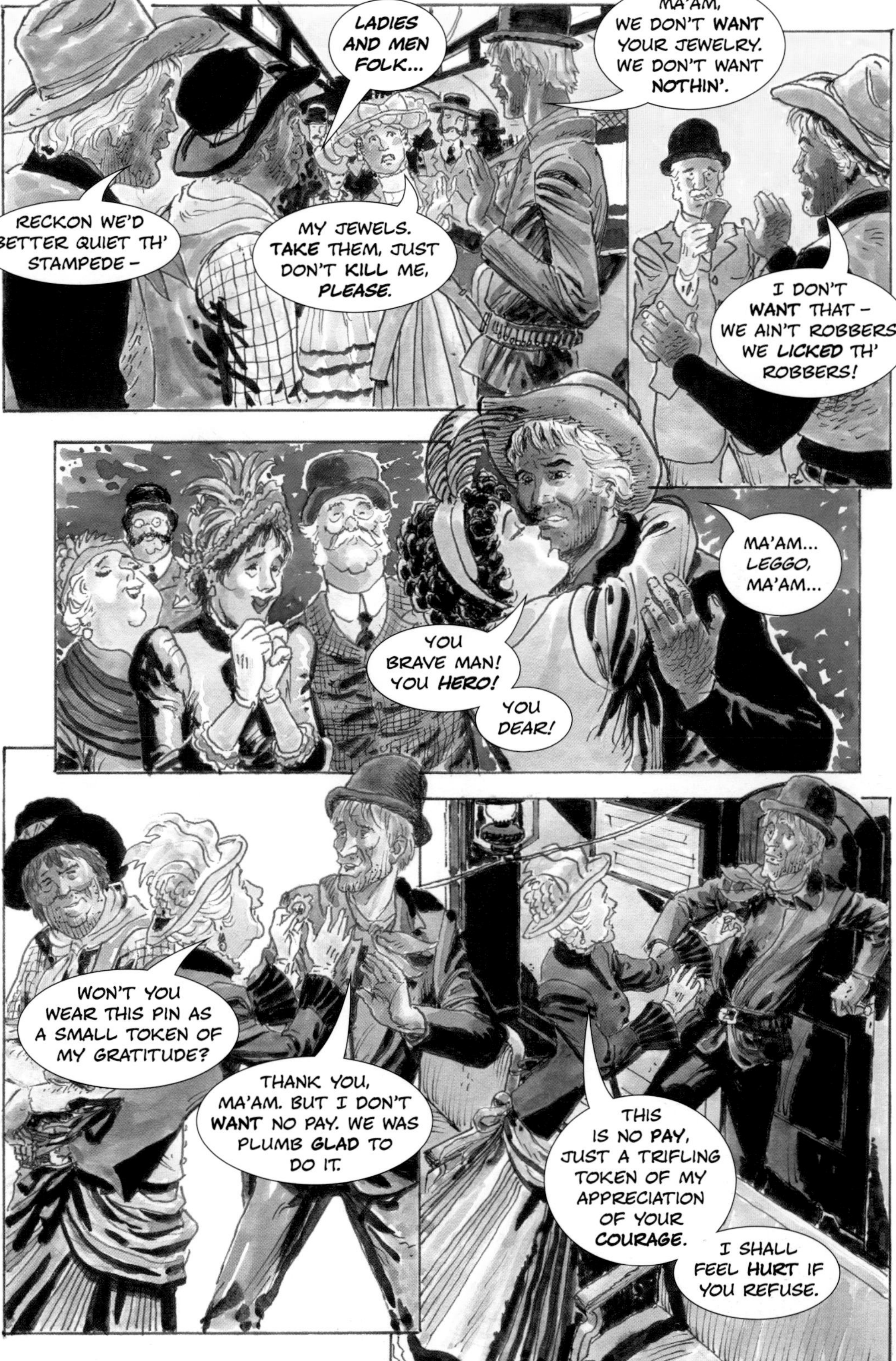
LADIES AND MEN FOLK...
MA'AM, WE DON'T WANT YOUR JEWELRY. WE DON'T WANT NOTHIN'.
RECKON WE'D BETTER QUIET TH' STAMPEDE –
MY JEWELS. TAKE THEM, JUST DON'T KILL ME, PLEASE.
I DON'T WANT THAT – WE AIN'T ROBBERS, WE LICKED TH' ROBBERS!
MA'AM... LEGGO, MA'AM...
YOU BRAVE MAN! YOU HERO!
YOU DEAR!
WON'T YOU WEAR THIS PIN AS A SMALL TOKEN OF MY GRATITUDE?
THANK YOU, MA'AM. BUT I DON'T WANT NO PAY. WE WAS PLUMB GLAD TO DO IT.
THIS IS NO PAY, JUST A TRIFLING TOKEN OF MY APPRECIATION OF YOUR COURAGE.
I SHALL FEEL HURT IF YOU REFUSE.

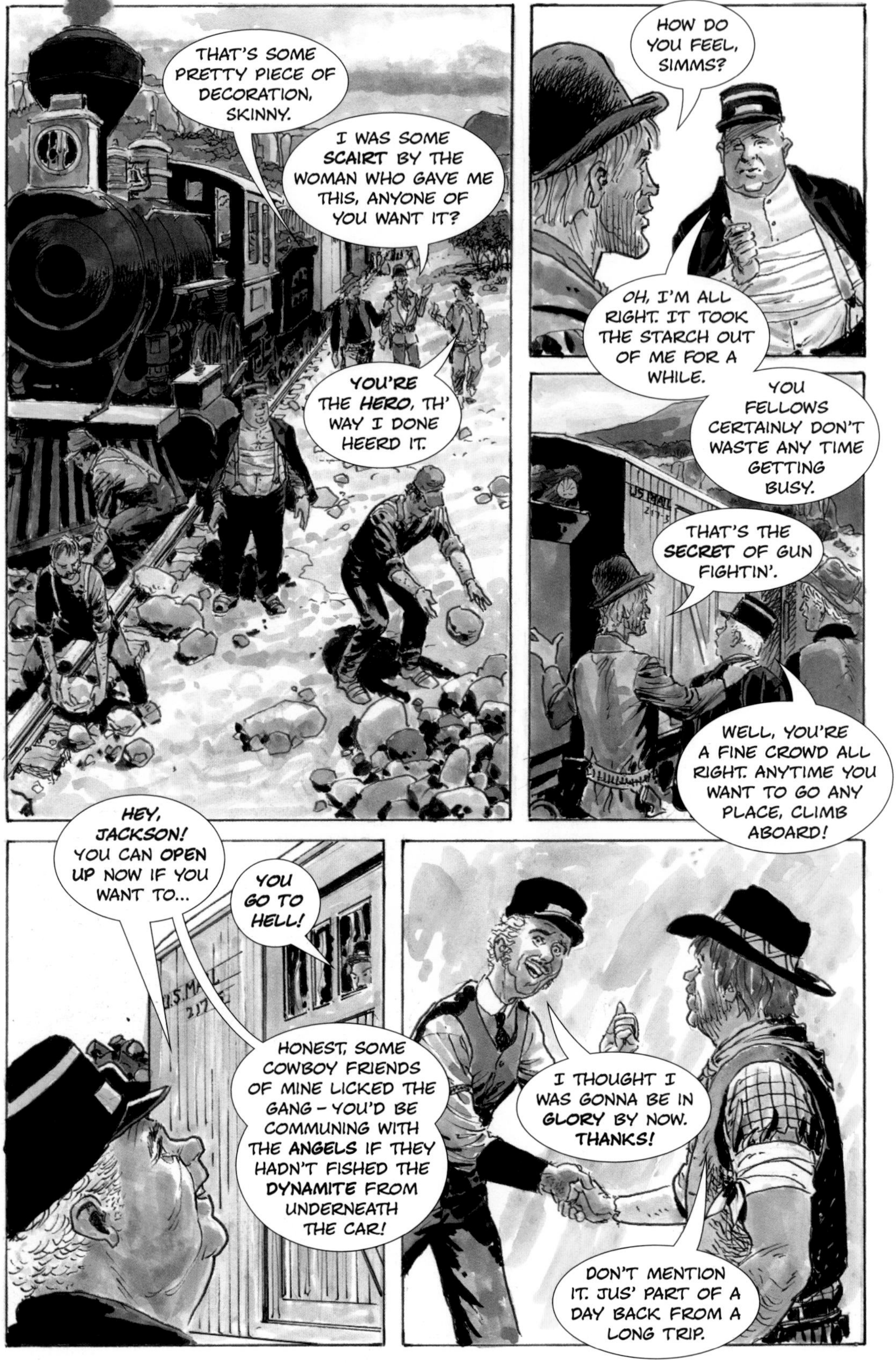
THAT'S SOME PRETTY PIECE OF DECORATION, SKINNY.
I WAS SOME SCAIRT BY THE WOMAN WHO GAVE ME THIS, ANYONE OF YOU WANT IT?
YOU'RE THE HERO, TH' WAY I DONE HEERD IT.
HOW DO YOU FEEL, SIMMS?
OH, I'M ALL RIGHT. IT TOOK THE STARCH OUT OF ME FOR A WHILE.
YOU FELLOWS CERTAINLY DON'T WASTE ANY TIME GETTING BUSY.
THAT'S THE SECRET OF GUN FIGHTIN'.
WELL, YOU'RE A FINE CROWD ALL RIGHT. ANYTIME YOU WANT TO GO ANY PLACE, CLIMB ABOARD!
HEY, JACKSON! YOU CAN OPEN UP NOW IF YOU WANT TO...
YOU GO TO HELL!
HONEST, SOME COWBOY FRIENDS OF MINE LICKED THE GANG – YOU'D BE COMMUNING WITH THE ANGELS IF THEY HADN'T FISHED THE DYNAMITE FROM UNDERNEATH THE CAR!
I THOUGHT I WAS GONNA BE IN GLORY BY NOW. THANKS!
DON'T MENTION IT. JUS' PART OF A DAY BACK FROM A LONG TRIP.

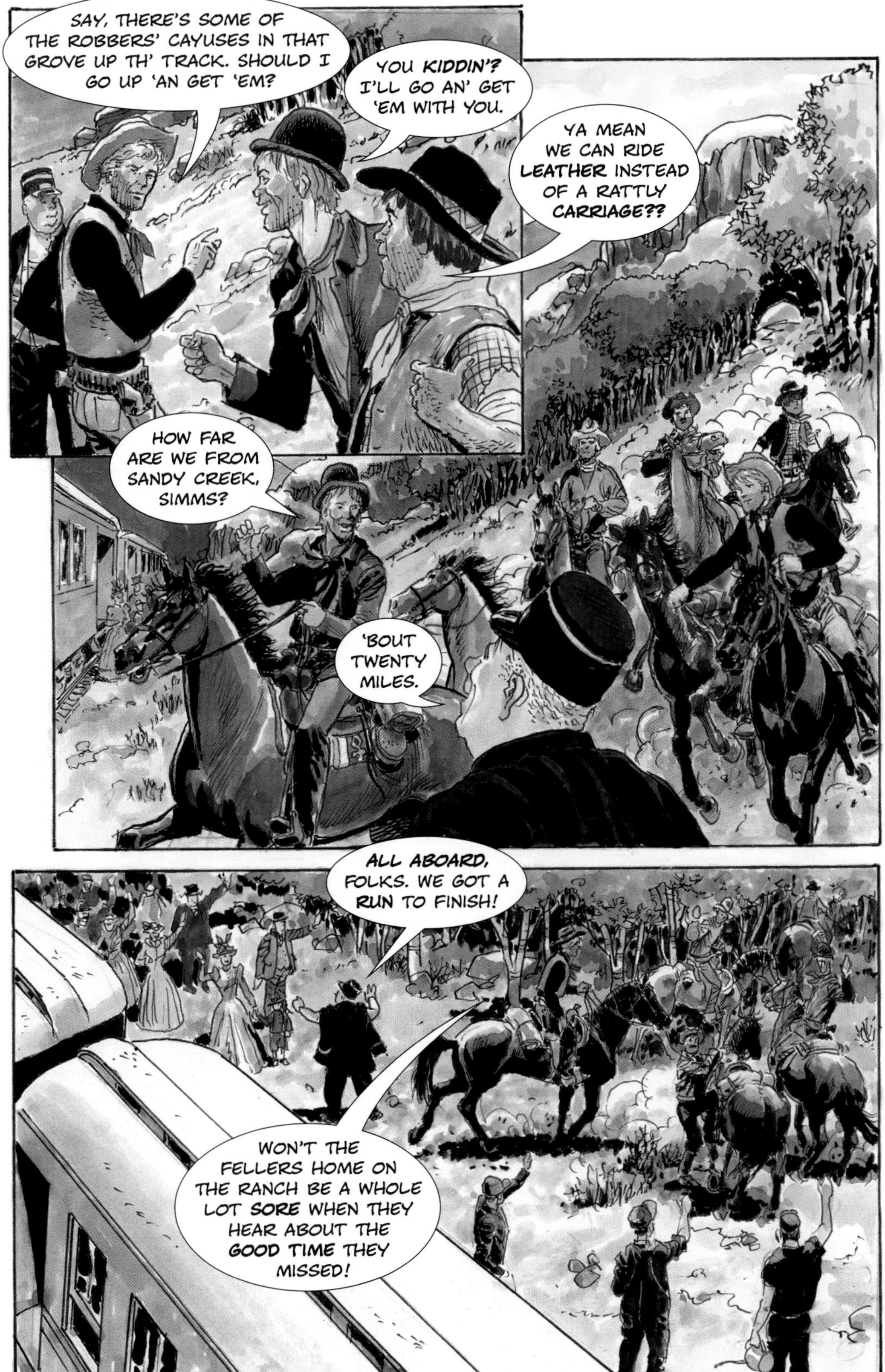
SAY, THERE'S SOME OF THE ROBBERS' CAYUSES IN THAT GROVE UP TH' TRACK. SHOULD I GO UP 'AN GET 'EM?
YOU **KIDDIN'?** I'LL GO AN' GET 'EM WITH YOU.
YA MEAN WE CAN RIDE **LEATHER** INSTEAD OF A RATTLY **CARRIAGE??**
HOW FAR ARE WE FROM SANDY CREEK, SIMMS?
'BOUT TWENTY MILES.
ALL ABOARD, FOLKS. WE GOT A **RUN** TO FINISH!
WON'T THE FELLERS HOME ON THE RANCH BE A WHOLE LOT **SORE** WHEN THEY HEAR ABOUT THE **GOOD TIME** THEY MISSED!

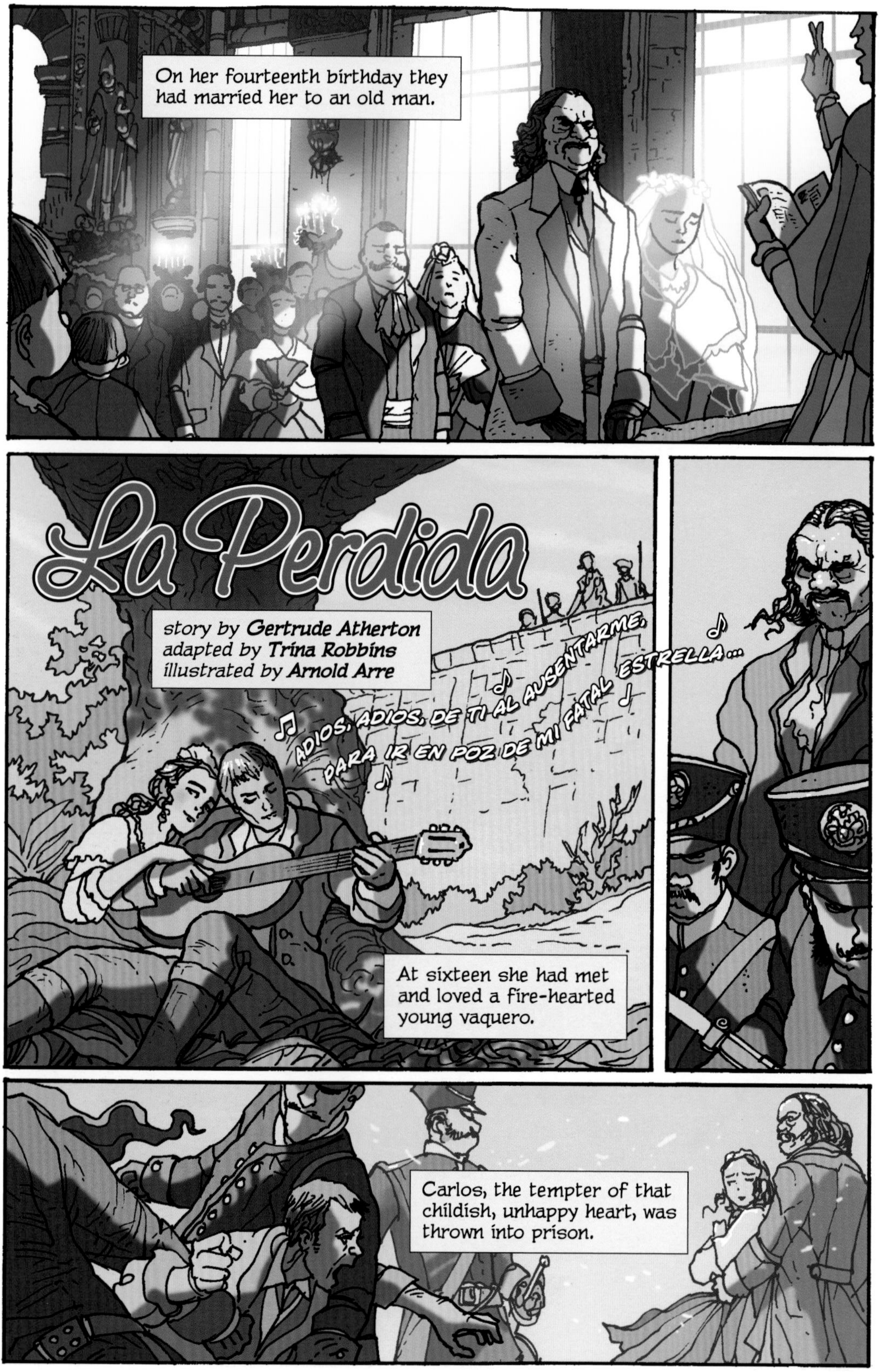
On her fourteenth birthday they had married her to an old man.
La Perdida
story by Gertrude Atherton
adapted by Trina Robbins
illustrated by Arnold Arre
ADIOS, ADIOS, DE TI AL AUSENTARME,
PARA IR EN POZ DE MI FATAL ESTRELLA...
At sixteen she had met and loved a fire-hearted young vaquero.
Carlos, the tempter of that childish, unhappy heart, was thrown into prison.

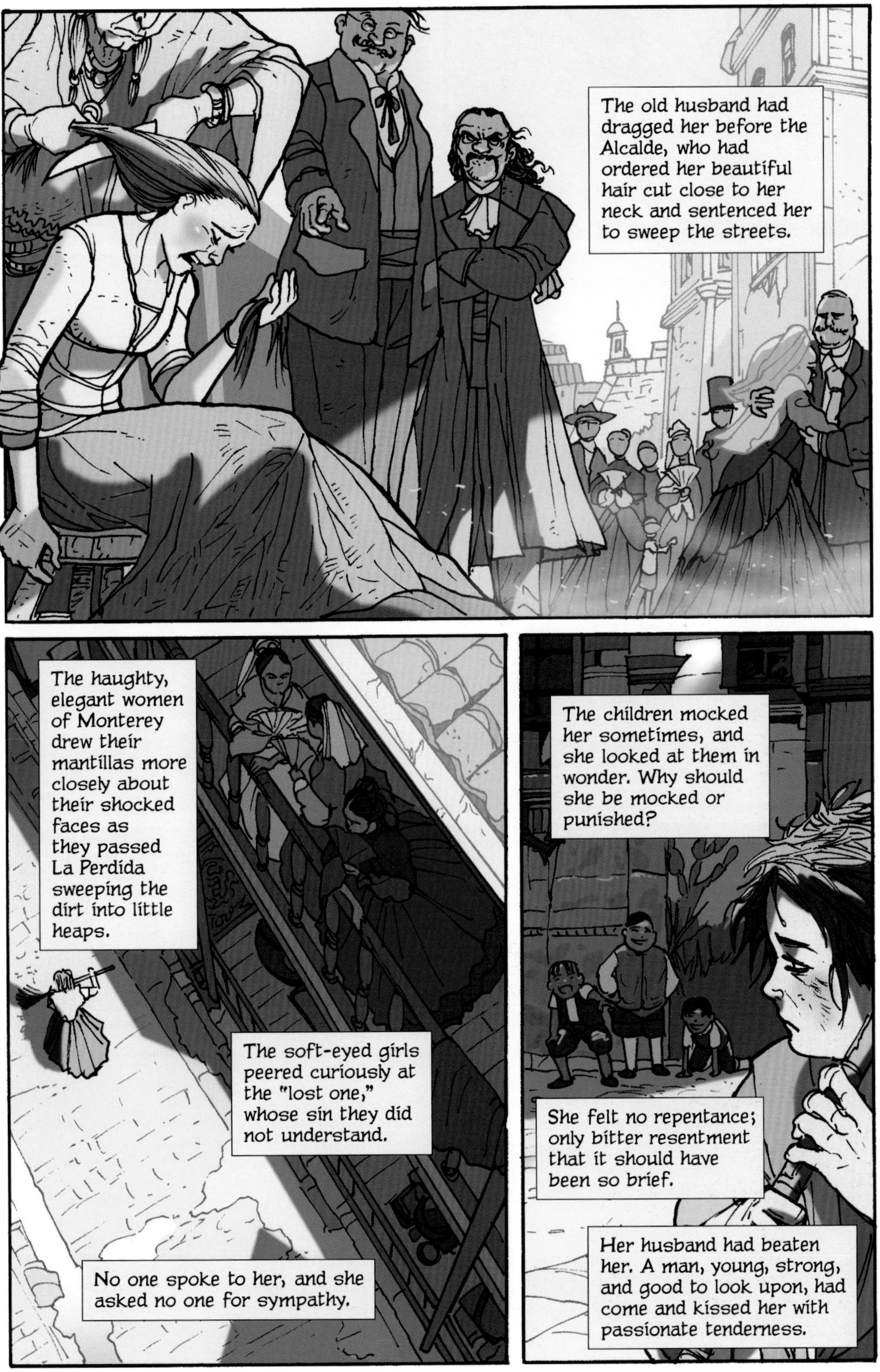
The old husband had dragged her before the Alcalde, who had ordered her beautiful hair cut close to her neck and sentenced her to sweep the streets.
The haughty, elegant women of Monterey drew their mantillas more closely about their shocked faces as they passed La Perdida sweeping the dirt into little heaps.
The soft-eyed girls peered curiously at the "lost one," whose sin they did not understand.
No one spoke to her, and she asked no one for sympathy.
The children mocked her sometimes, and she looked at them in wonder. Why should she be mocked or punished?
She felt no repentance; only bitter resentment that it should have been so brief.
Her husband had beaten her. A man, young, strong, and good to look upon, had come and kissed her with passionate tenderness.

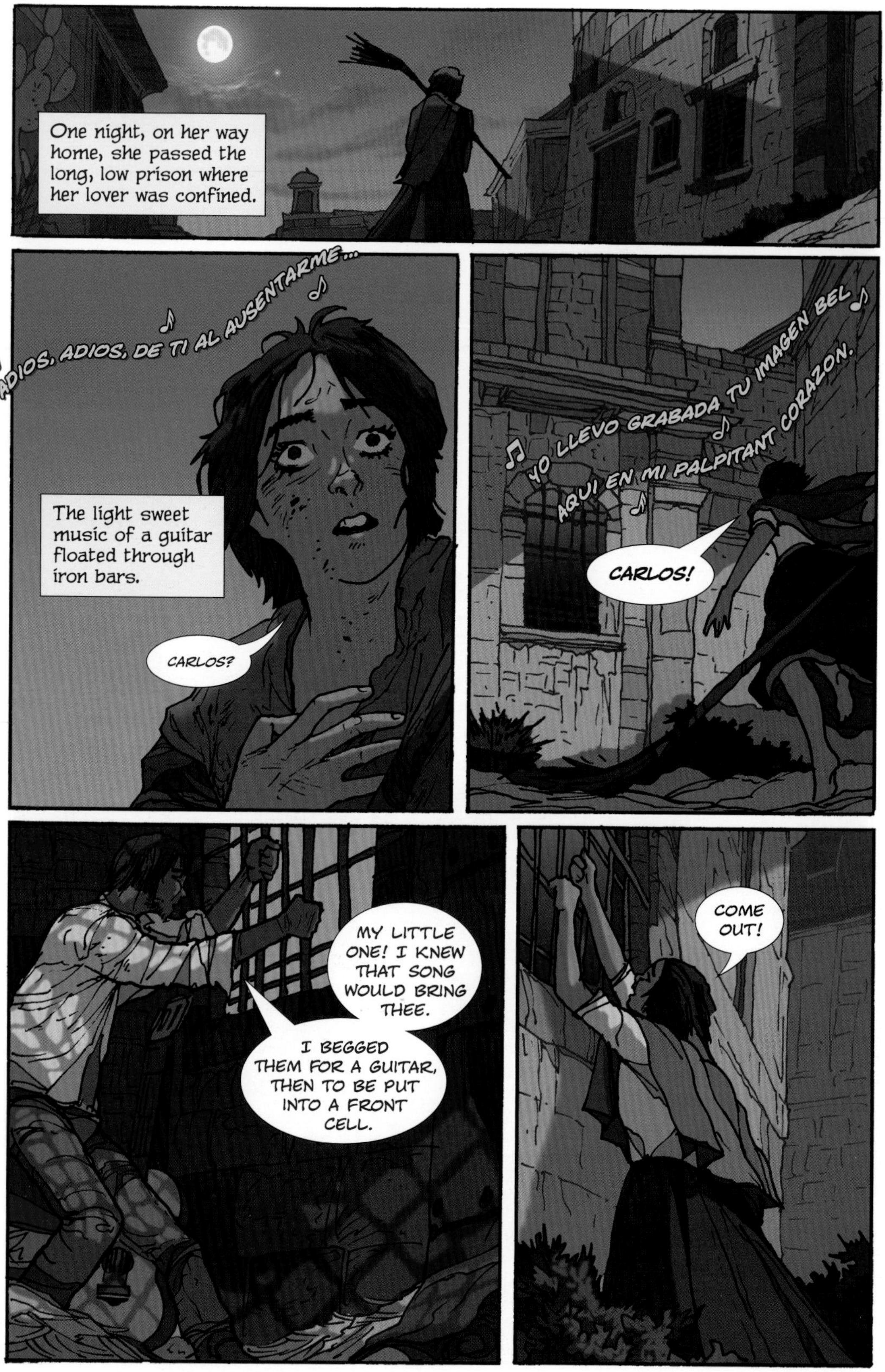

One night, on her way home, she passed the long, low prison where her lover was confined.
♫ ADIOS, ADIOS, DE TI AL AUSENTARME... ♪ ♪
The light sweet music of a guitar floated through iron bars.
CARLOS?
♫ YO LLEVO GRABADA TU IMAGEN BEL ♪ ♪
AQUI EN MI PALPITANT CORAZON. ♪
CARLOS!
MY LITTLE ONE! I KNEW THAT SONG WOULD BRING THEE.
I BEGGED THEM FOR A GUITAR, THEN TO BE PUT INTO A FRONT CELL.
COME OUT!

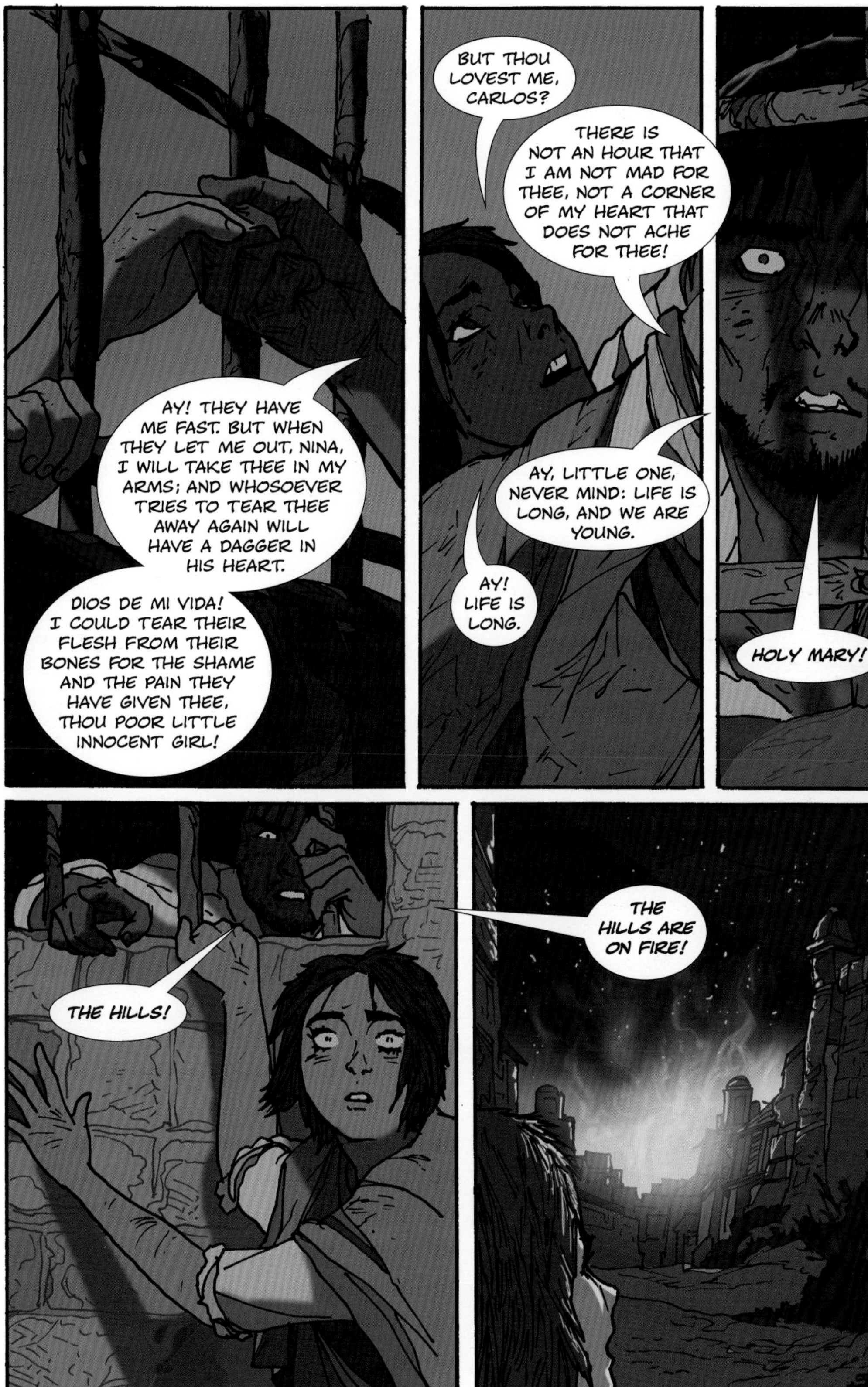
AY! THEY HAVE ME FAST. BUT WHEN THEY LET ME OUT, NINA, I WILL TAKE THEE IN MY ARMS; AND WHOSOEVER TRIES TO TEAR THEE AWAY AGAIN WILL HAVE A DAGGER IN HIS HEART.
DIOS DE MI VIDA! I COULD TEAR THEIR FLESH FROM THEIR BONES FOR THE SHAME AND THE PAIN THEY HAVE GIVEN THEE, THOU POOR LITTLE INNOCENT GIRL!
BUT THOU LOVEST ME, CARLOS?
THERE IS NOT AN HOUR THAT I AM NOT MAD FOR THEE, NOT A CORNER OF MY HEART THAT DOES NOT ACHE FOR THEE!
AY, LITTLE ONE, NEVER MIND: LIFE IS LONG, AND WE ARE YOUNG.
AY! LIFE IS LONG.
HOLY MARY!
THE HILLS!
THE HILLS ARE ON FIRE!

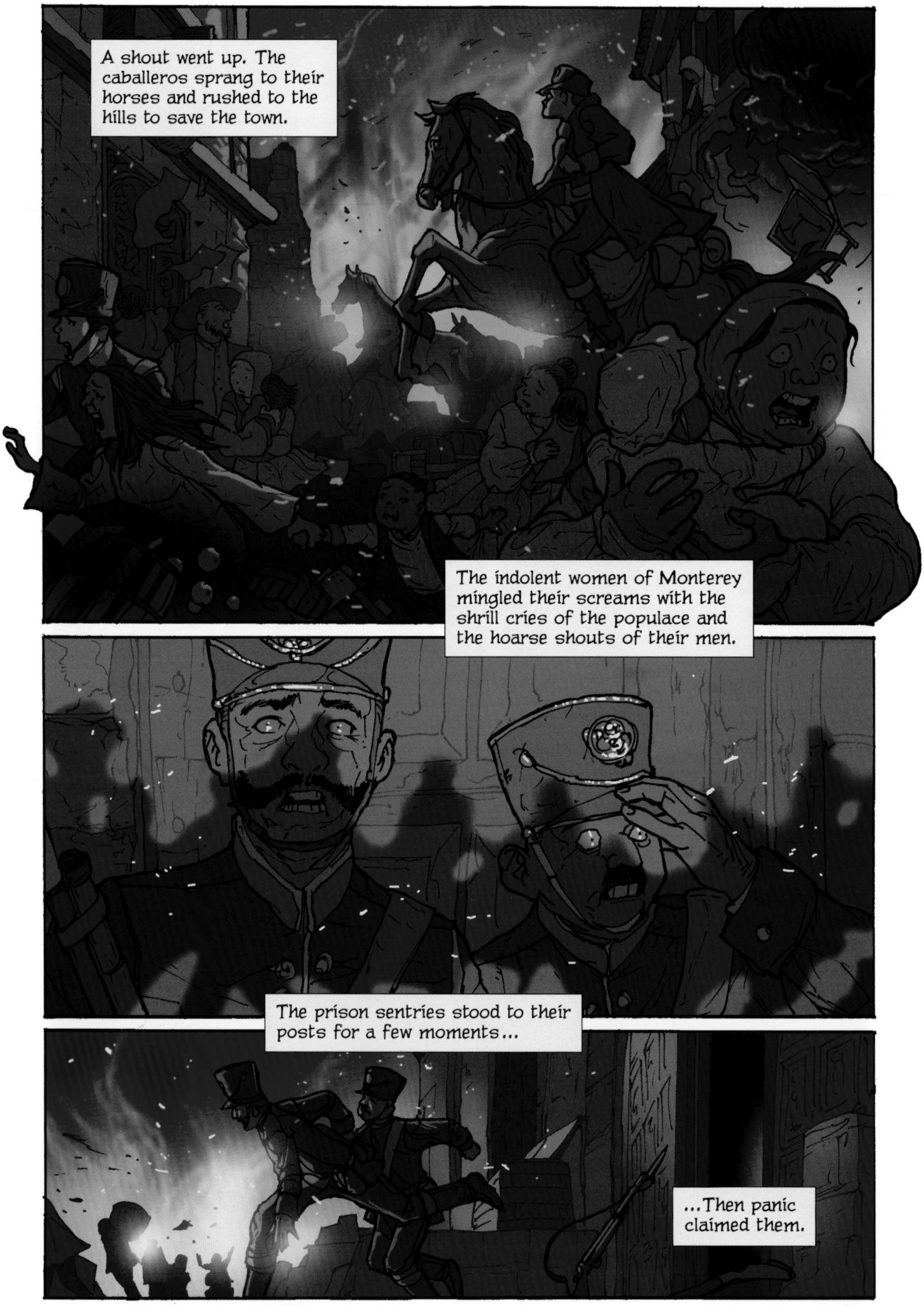
A shout went up. The caballeros sprang to their horses and rushed to the hills to save the town.
The indolent women of Monterey mingled their screams with the shrill cries of the populace and the hoarse shouts of their men.
The prison sentries stood to their posts for a few moments...
...Then panic claimed them.

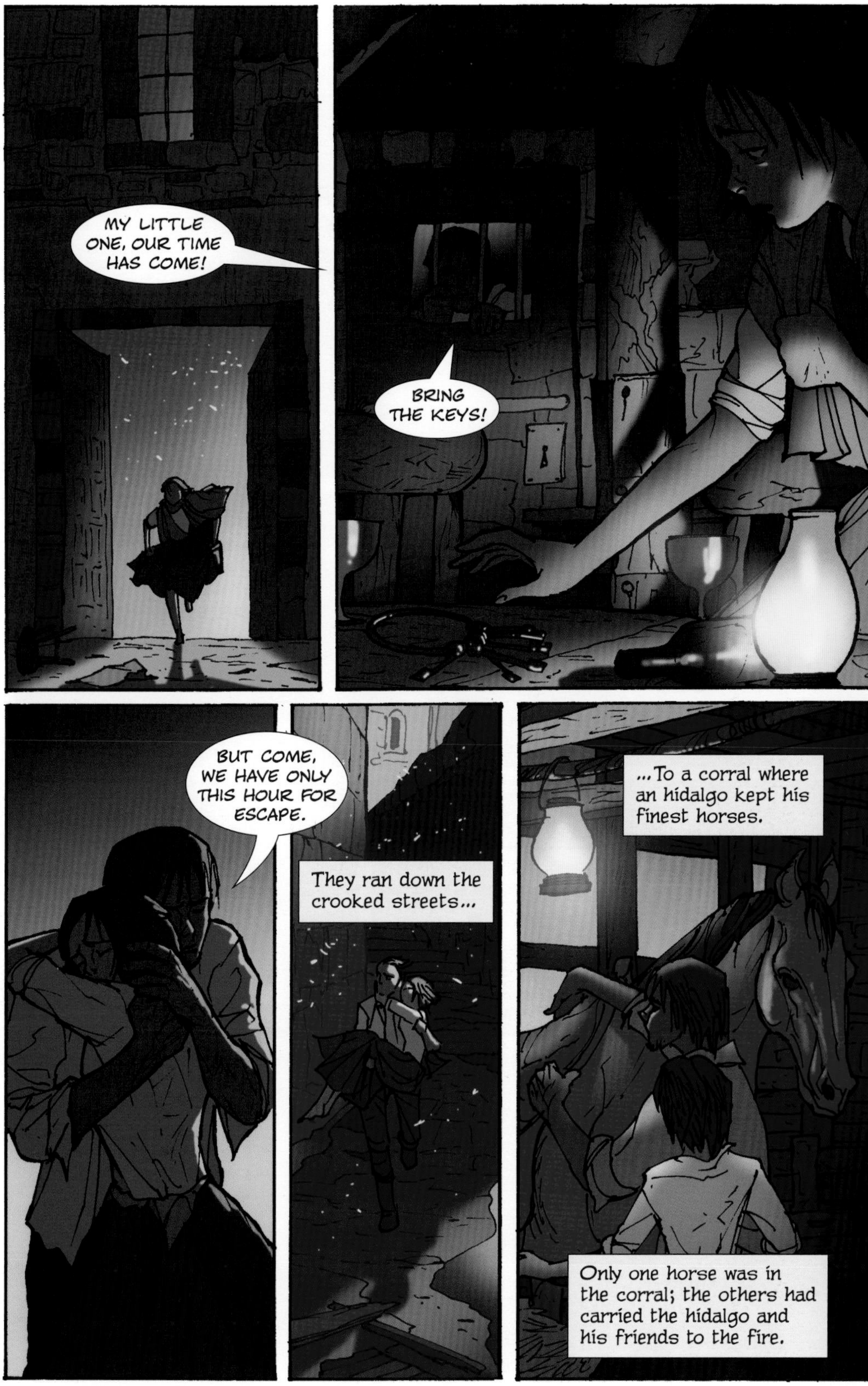
MY LITTLE ONE, OUR TIME HAS COME!
BRING THE KEYS!
BUT COME, WE HAVE ONLY THIS HOUR FOR ESCAPE.
They ran down the crooked streets...
...To a corral where an hidalgo kept his finest horses.
Only one horse was in the corral; the others had carried the hidalgo and his friends to the fire.

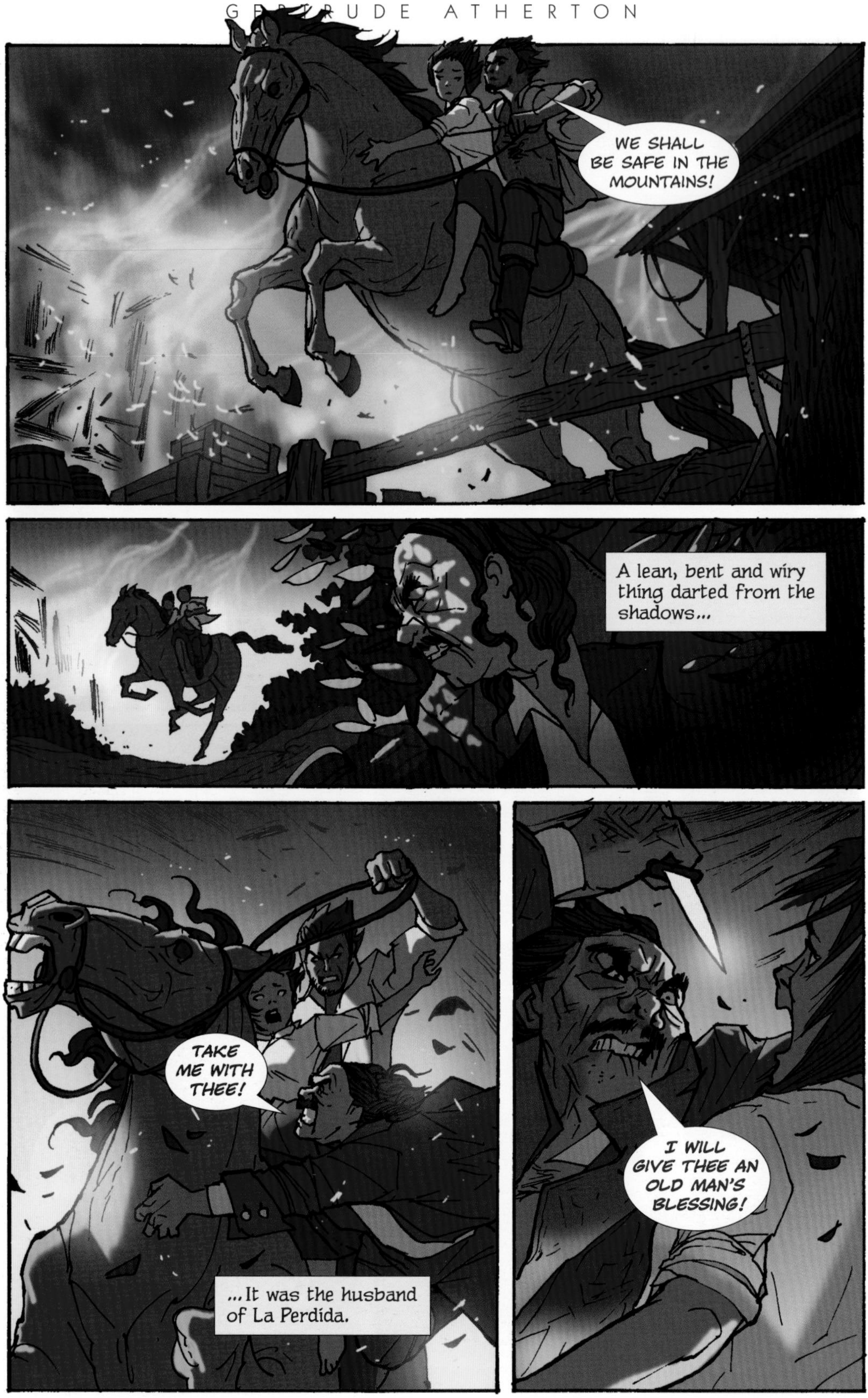
WE SHALL BE SAFE IN THE MOUNTAINS!
A lean, bent and wiry thing darted from the shadows...
TAKE ME WITH THEE!
...It was the husband of La Perdida.
I WILL GIVE THEE AN OLD MAN'S BLESSING!

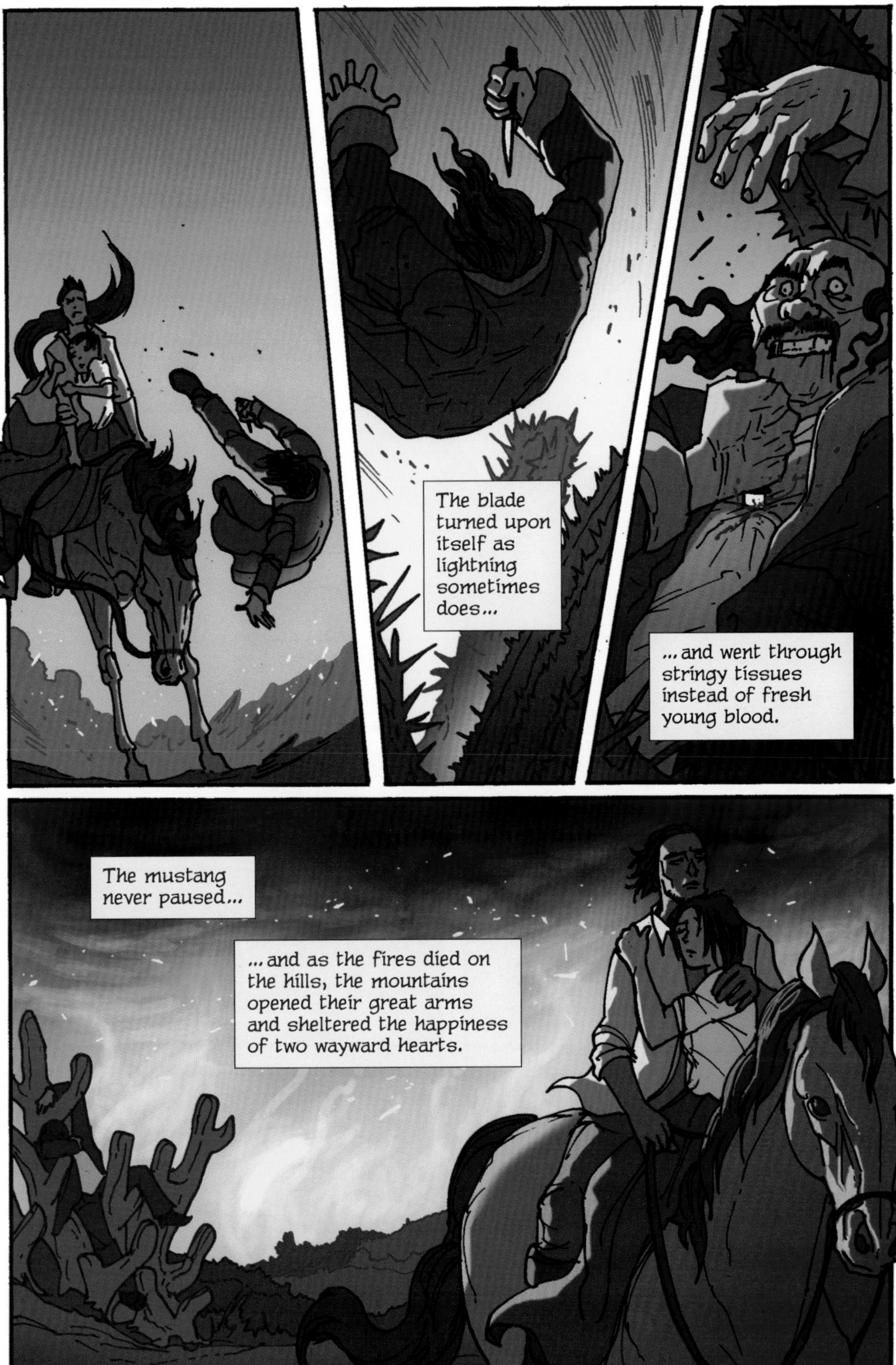
The blade turned upon itself as lightning sometimes does...
...and went through stringy tissues instead of fresh young blood.
The mustang never paused...
...and as the fires died on the hills, the mountains opened their great arms and sheltered the happiness of two wayward hearts.

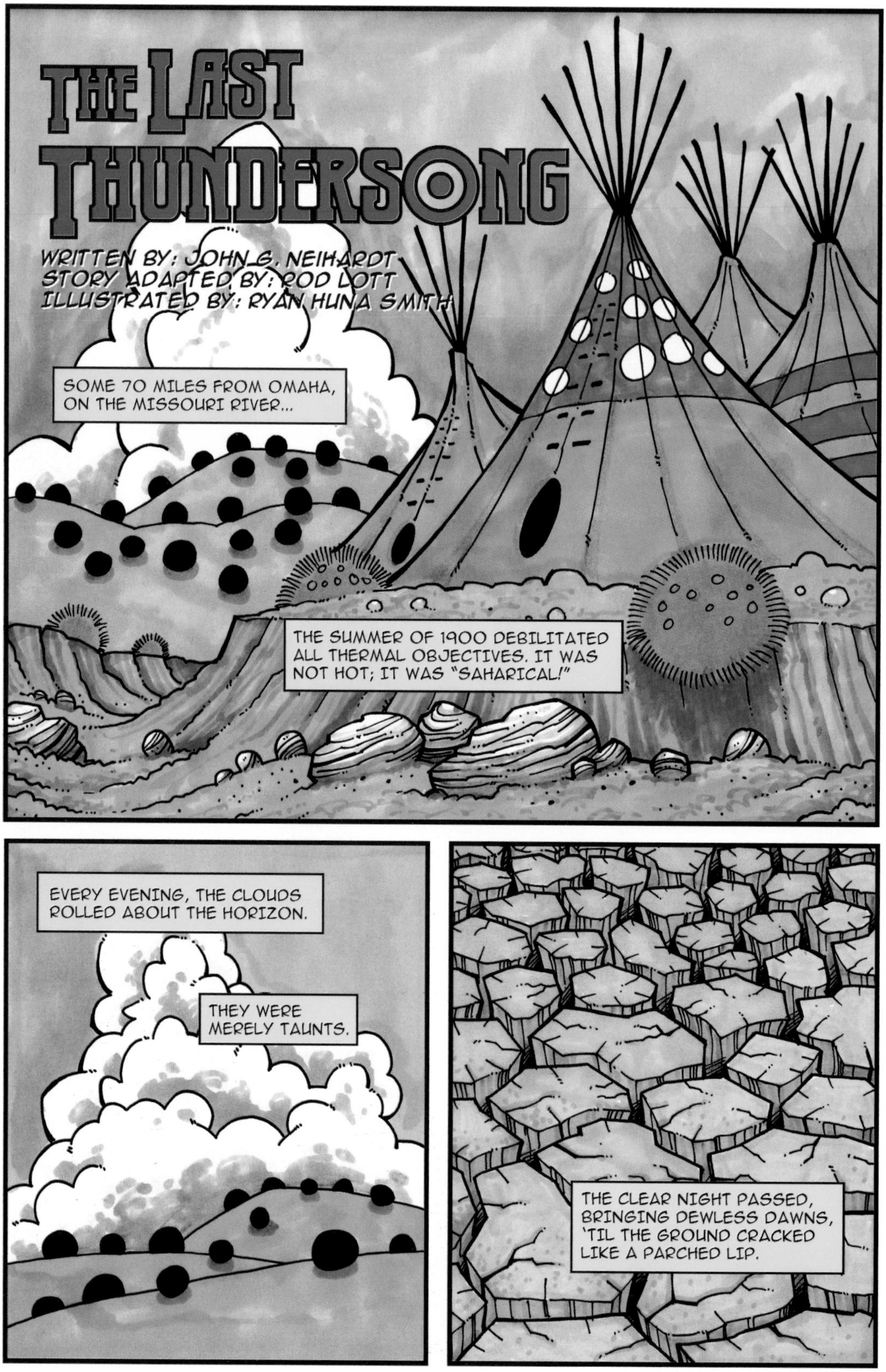
THE LAST THUNDERSONG
WRITTEN BY: JOHN G. NEIHARDT
STORY ADAPTED BY: ROD LOTT
ILLUSTRATED BY: RYAN HUNA SMITH
SOME 70 MILES FROM OMAHA, ON THE MISSOURI RIVER...
THE SUMMER OF 1900 DEBILITATED ALL THERMAL OBJECTIVES. IT WAS NOT HOT; IT WAS "SAHARICAL!"
EVERY EVENING, THE CLOUDS ROLLED ABOUT THE HORIZON.
THEY WERE MERELY TAUNTS.
THE CLEAR NIGHT PASSED, BRINGING DEWLESS DAWNS, 'TIL THE GROUND CRACKED LIKE A PARCHED LIP.

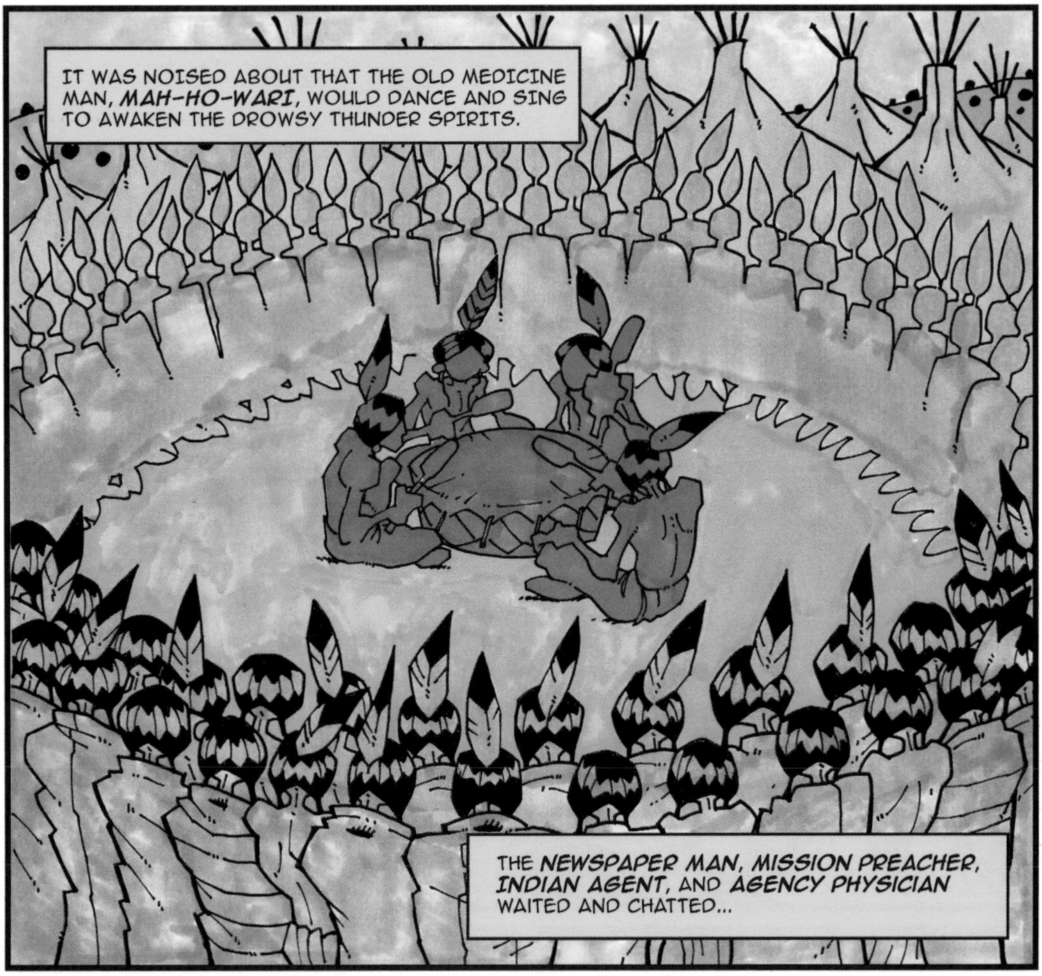
IT WAS NOISED ABOUT THAT THE OLD MEDICINE MAN, ***MAH-HO-WARI***, WOULD DANCE AND SING TO AWAKEN THE DROWSY THUNDER SPIRITS.
THE ***NEWSPAPER MAN***, ***MISSION PREACHER***, ***INDIAN AGENT***, AND ***AGENCY PHYSICIAN*** WAITED AND CHATTED...

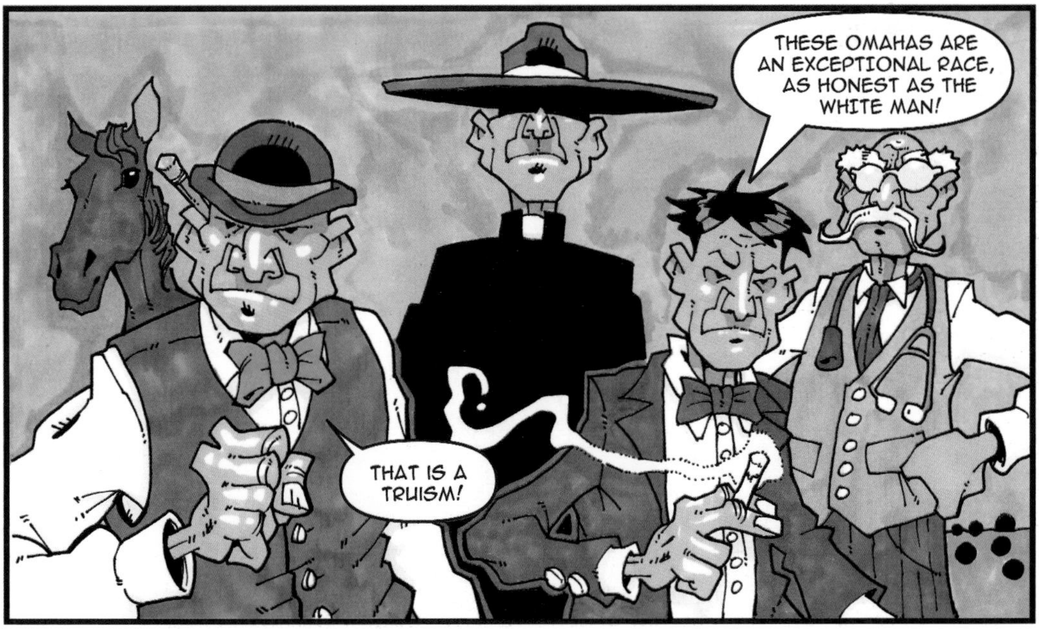
THESE OMAHAS ARE AN EXCEPTIONAL RACE, AS HONEST AS THE WHITE MAN!
THAT IS A TRUISM!

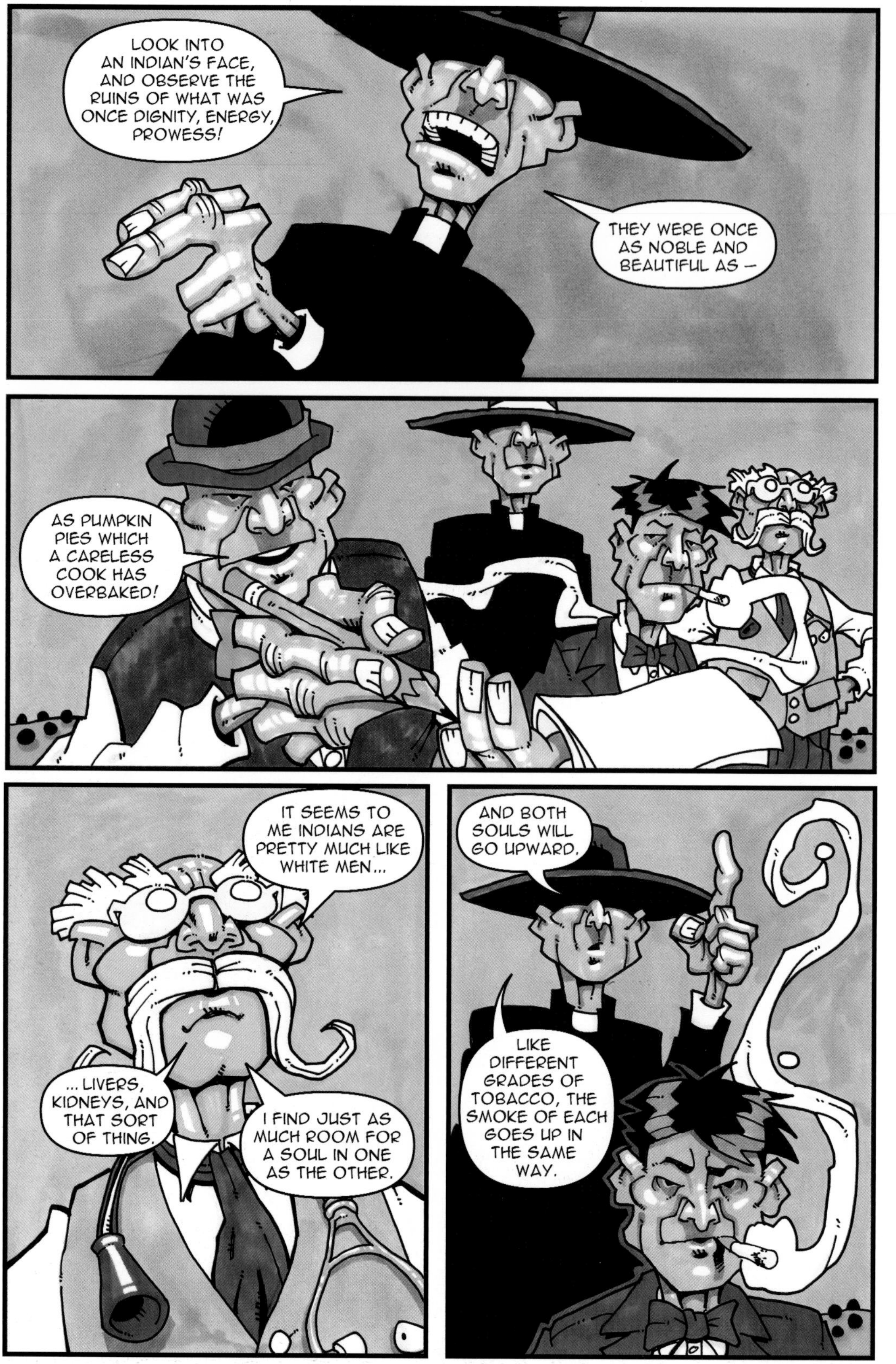
LOOK INTO AN INDIAN'S FACE, AND OBSERVE THE RUINS OF WHAT WAS ONCE DIGNITY, ENERGY, PROWESS!
THEY WERE ONCE AS NOBLE AND BEAUTIFUL AS —
AS PUMPKIN PIES WHICH A CARELESS COOK HAS OVERBAKED!
IT SEEMS TO ME INDIANS ARE PRETTY MUCH LIKE WHITE MEN...
... LIVERS, KIDNEYS, AND THAT SORT OF THING.
I FIND JUST AS MUCH ROOM FOR A SOUL IN ONE AS THE OTHER.
AND BOTH SOULS WILL GO UPWARD,
LIKE DIFFERENT GRADES OF TOBACCO, THE SMOKE OF EACH GOES UP IN THE SAME WAY.

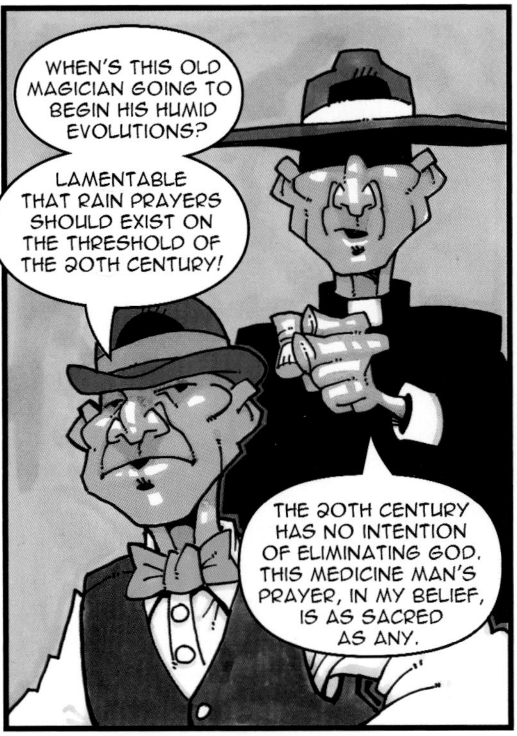
WHEN'S THIS OLD MAGICIAN GOING TO BEGIN HIS HUMID EVOLUTIONS?
LAMENTABLE THAT RAIN PRAYERS SHOULD EXIST ON THE THRESHOLD OF THE 20TH CENTURY!
THE 20TH CENTURY HAS NO INTENTION OF ELIMINATING GOD. THIS MEDICINE MAN'S PRAYER, IN MY BELIEF, IS AS SACRED AS ANY.

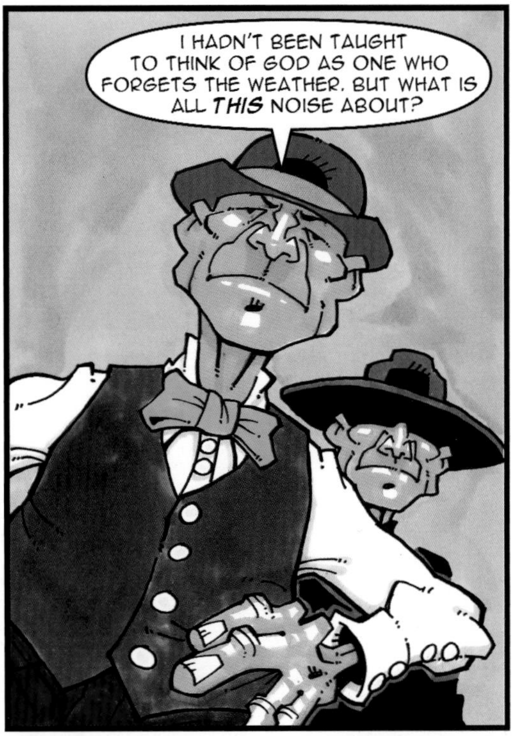
I HADN'T BEEN TAUGHT TO THINK OF GOD AS ONE WHO FORGETS THE WEATHER. BUT WHAT IS ALL *THIS* NOISE ABOUT?

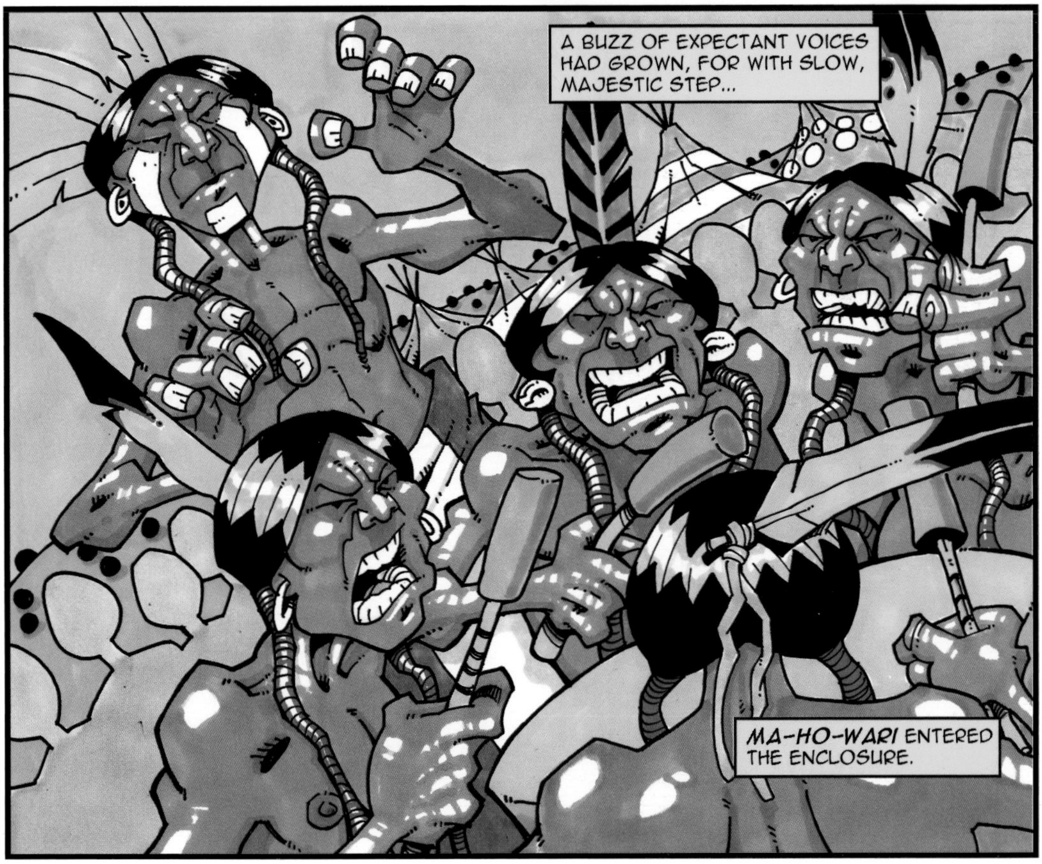
A BUZZ OF EXPECTANT VOICES HAD GROWN, FOR WITH SLOW, MAJESTIC STEP...
MA-HO-WARI ENTERED THE ENCLOSURE.

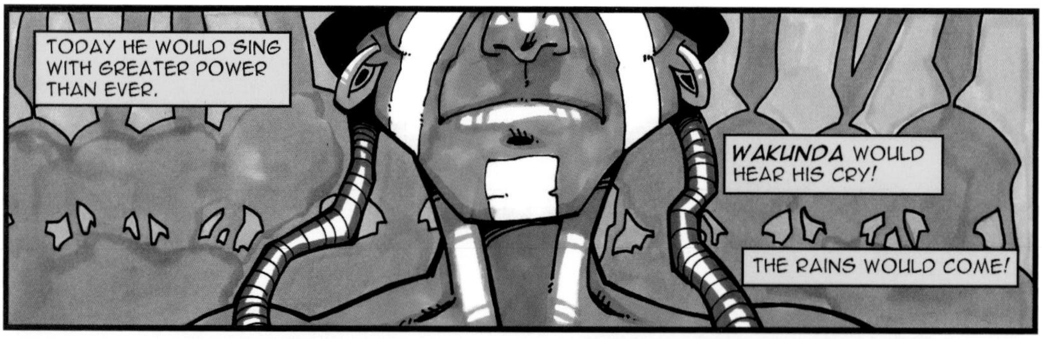
TODAY HE WOULD SING WITH GREATER POWER THAN EVER.
WAKUNDA WOULD HEAR HIS CRY!
THE RAINS WOULD COME!

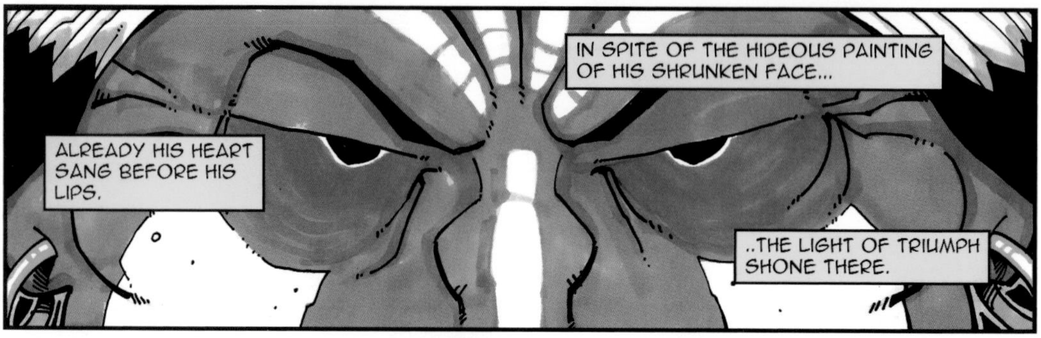
IN SPITE OF THE HIDEOUS PAINTING OF HIS SHRUNKEN FACE...
ALREADY HIS HEART SANG BEFORE HIS LIPS.
..THE LIGHT OF TRIUMPH SHONE THERE.

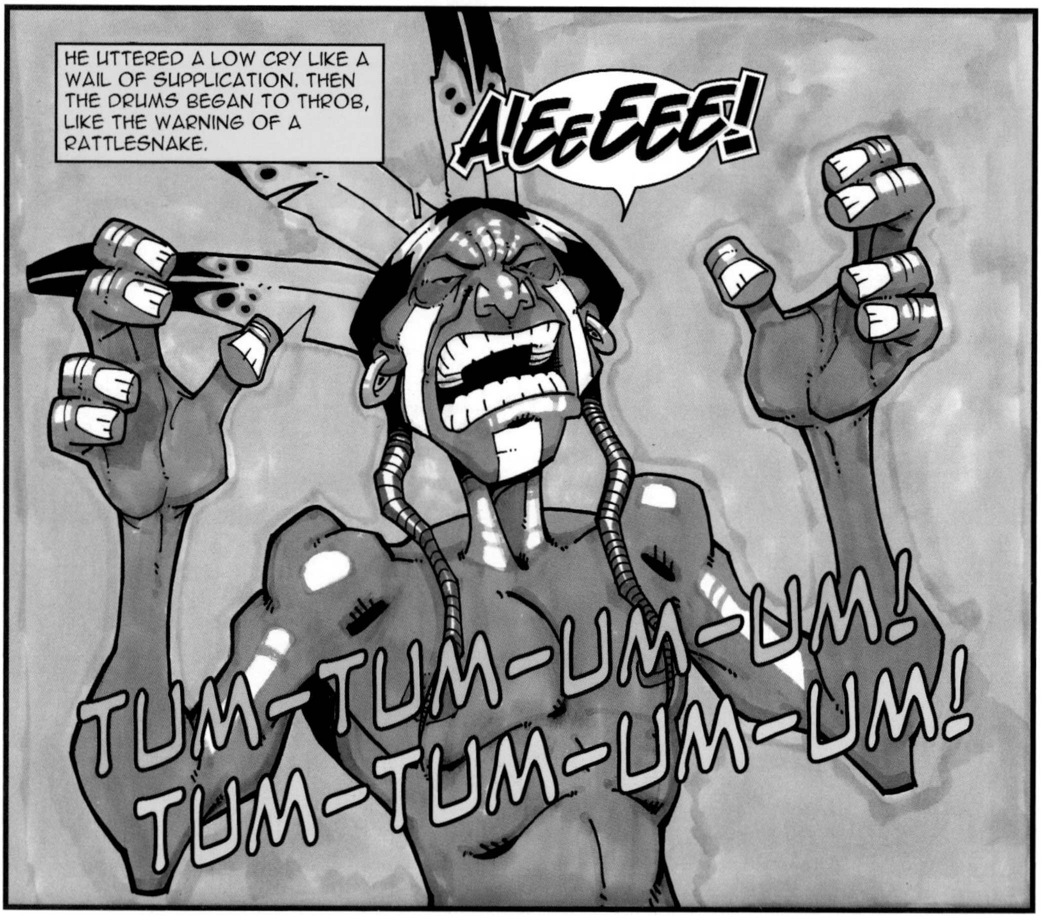
HE UTTERED A LOW CRY LIKE A WAIL OF SUPPLICATION. THEN THE DRUMS BEGAN TO THROB, LIKE THE WARNING OF A RATTLESNAKE.
AIEEEEE!
TUM-TUM-UM-UM!
TUM-TUM-UM-UM!

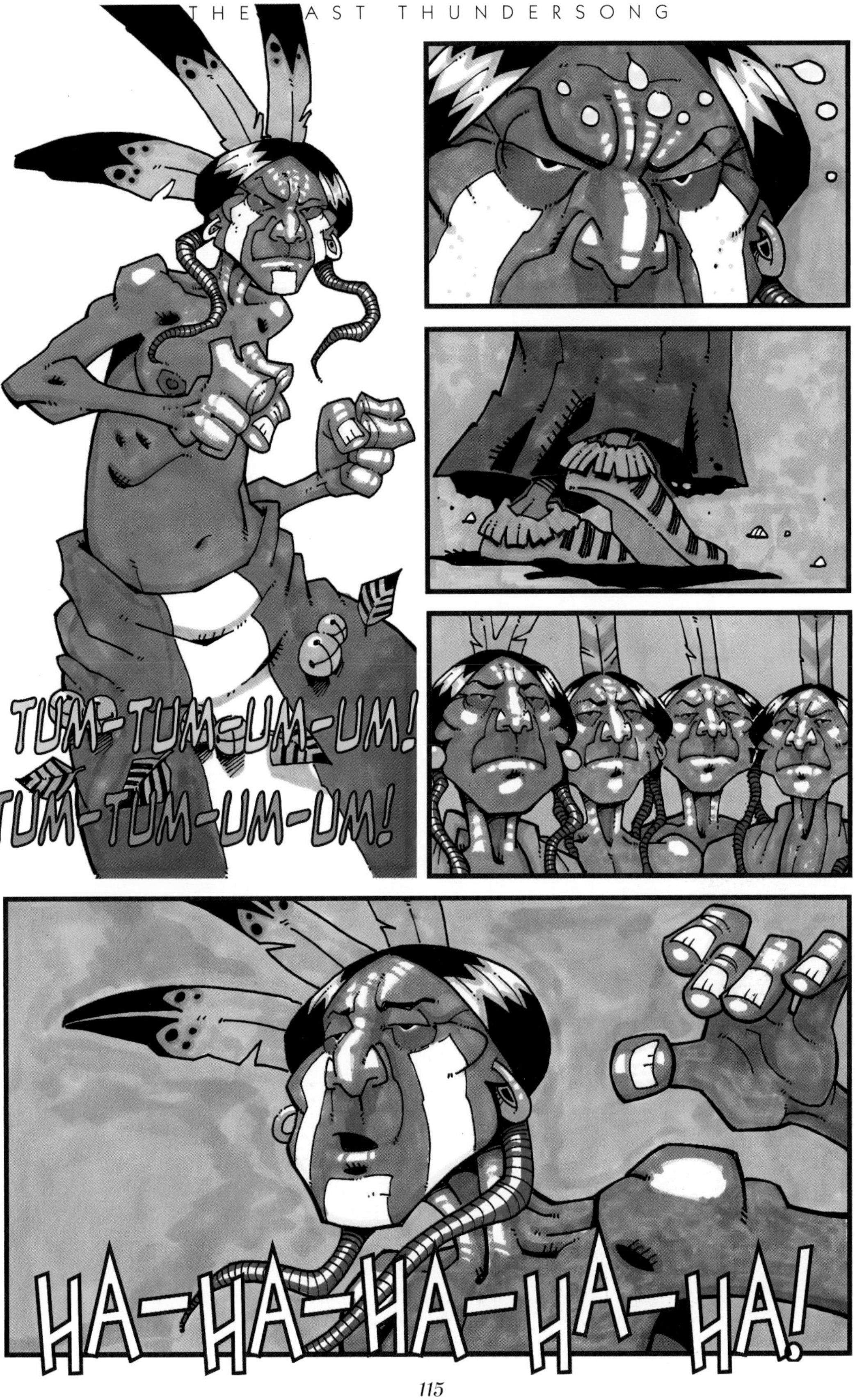
TUM-TUM-UM-UM!
TUM-TUM-UM-UM!
HA-HA-HA-HA-HA-HA!

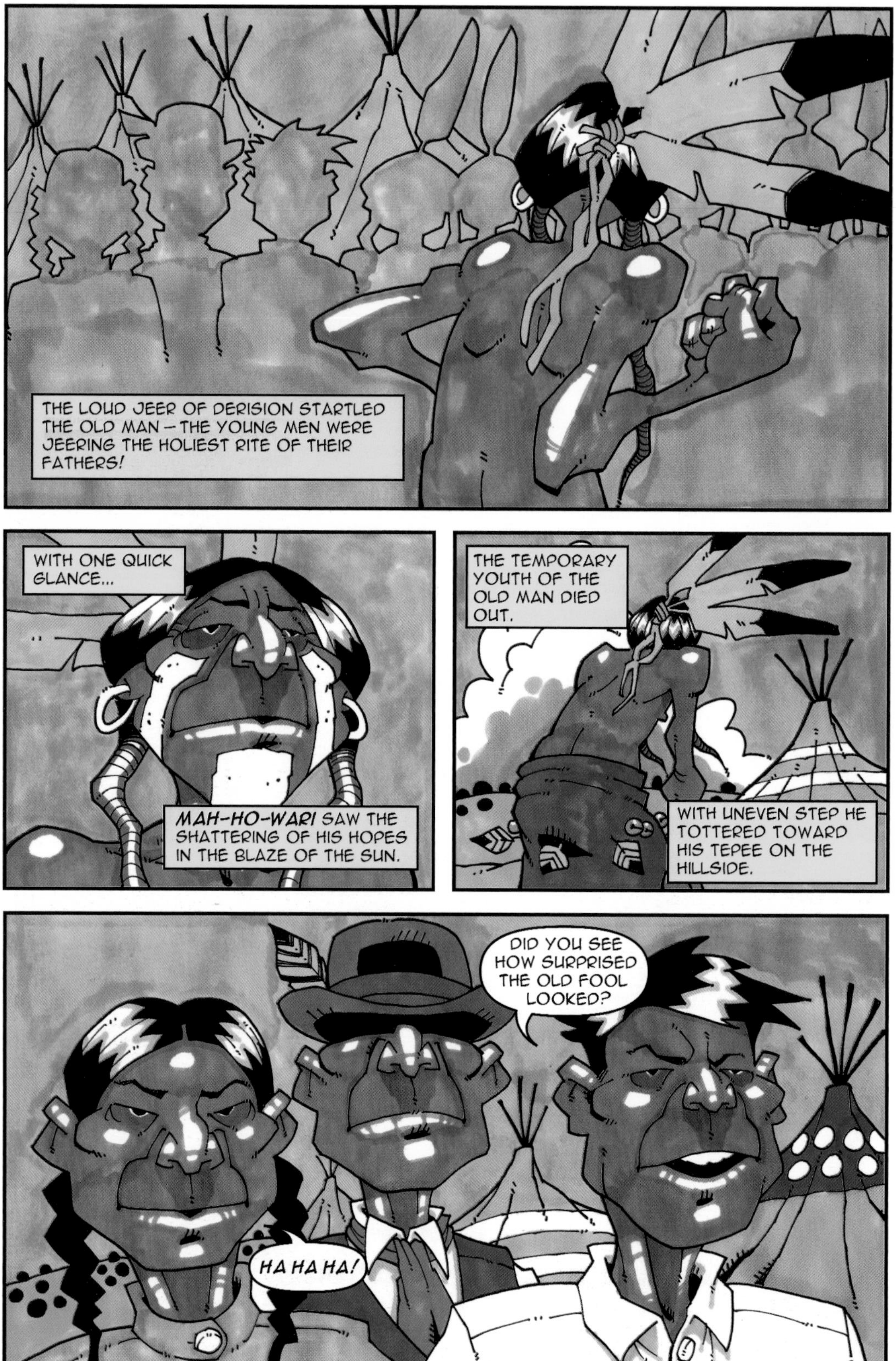
THE LOUD JEER OF DERISION STARTLED THE OLD MAN – THE YOUNG MEN WERE JEERING THE HOLIEST RITE OF THEIR FATHERS!
WITH ONE QUICK GLANCE...
MAH-HO-WARI SAW THE SHATTERING OF HIS HOPES IN THE BLAZE OF THE SUN.
THE TEMPORARY YOUTH OF THE OLD MAN DIED OUT.
WITH UNEVEN STEP HE TOTTERED TOWARD HIS TEPEE ON THE HILLSIDE.
DID YOU SEE HOW SURPRISED THE OLD FOOL LOOKED?
HA HA HA!

BUT THERE WAS NO LAUGHTER IN THE MINISTER'S HEART AS HE RODE TOWARD *MAH-HO-WARI'S* TEPEE THAT EVENING.

IF THE WHOLE FABRIC OF MY BELIEF WERE SUDDENLY WRENCHED FROM ME, WHAT THEN?

HOW!

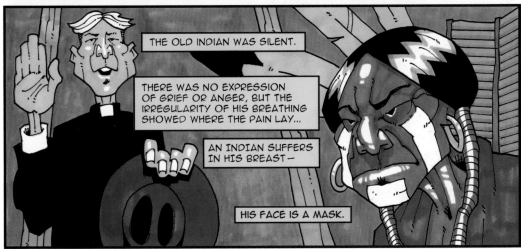

THE OLD INDIAN WAS SILENT.

THERE WAS NO EXPRESSION OF GRIEF OR ANGER, BUT THE IRREGULARITY OF HIS BREATHING SHOWED WHERE THE PAIN LAY...

AN INDIAN SUFFERS IN HIS BREAST—

HIS FACE IS A MASK.

117

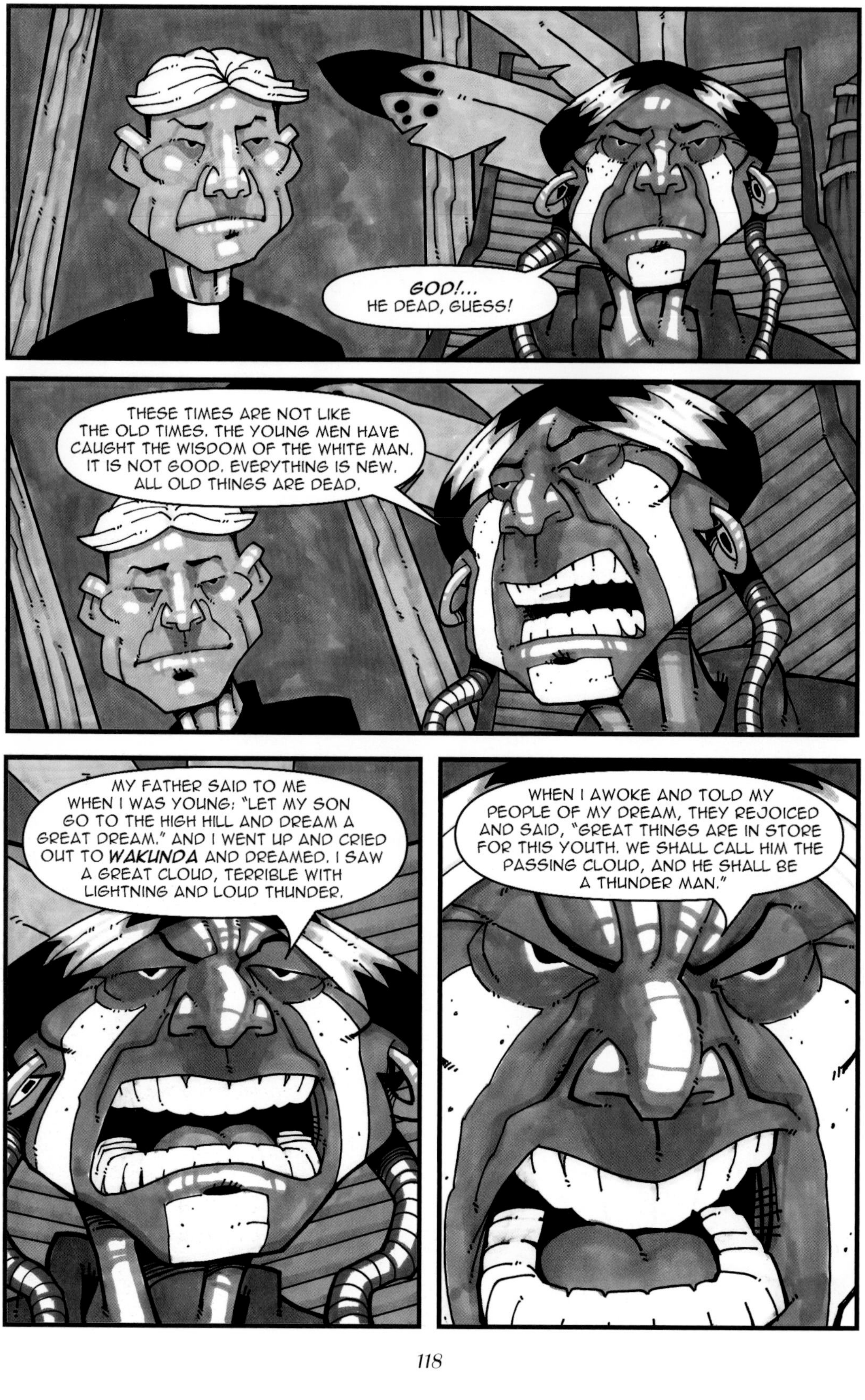
GOD!...
HE DEAD, GUESS!
THESE TIMES ARE NOT LIKE THE OLD TIMES. THE YOUNG MEN HAVE CAUGHT THE WISDOM OF THE WHITE MAN. IT IS NOT GOOD. EVERYTHING IS NEW. ALL OLD THINGS ARE DEAD.
MY FATHER SAID TO ME WHEN I WAS YOUNG: "LET MY SON GO TO THE HIGH HILL AND DREAM A GREAT DREAM." AND I WENT UP AND CRIED OUT TO WAKUNDA AND DREAMED. I SAW A GREAT CLOUD, TERRIBLE WITH LIGHTNING AND LOUD THUNDER.
WHEN I AWOKE AND TOLD MY PEOPLE OF MY DREAM, THEY REJOICED AND SAID, "GREAT THINGS ARE IN STORE FOR THIS YOUTH. WE SHALL CALL HIM THE PASSING CLOUD, AND HE SHALL BE A THUNDER MAN."

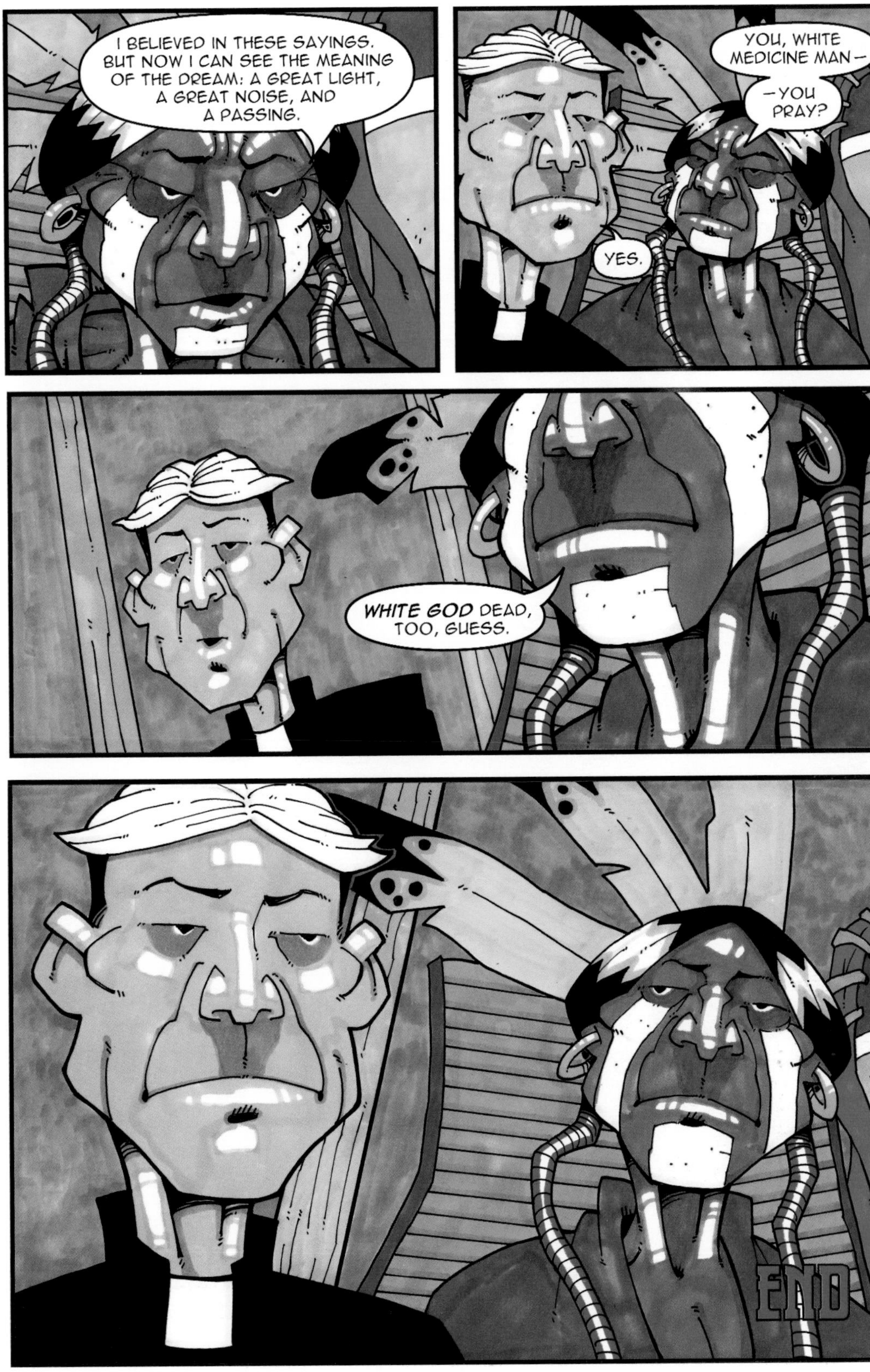
I BELIEVED IN THESE SAYINGS. BUT NOW I CAN SEE THE MEANING OF THE DREAM: A GREAT LIGHT, A GREAT NOISE, AND A PASSING.
YOU, WHITE MEDICINE MAN—
—YOU PRAY?
YES.
WHITE GOD DEAD, TOO, GUESS.
END

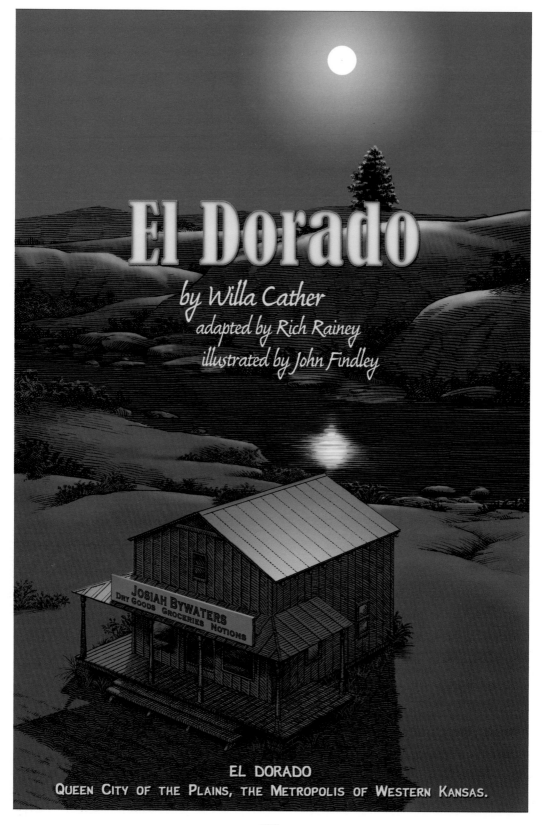

El Dorado

by Willa Cather
adapted by Rich Rainey
illustrated by John Findley

JOSIAH BYWATERS
DRY GOODS   GROCERIES   NOTIONS

EL DORADO
QUEEN CITY OF THE PLAINS, THE METROPOLIS OF WESTERN KANSAS.

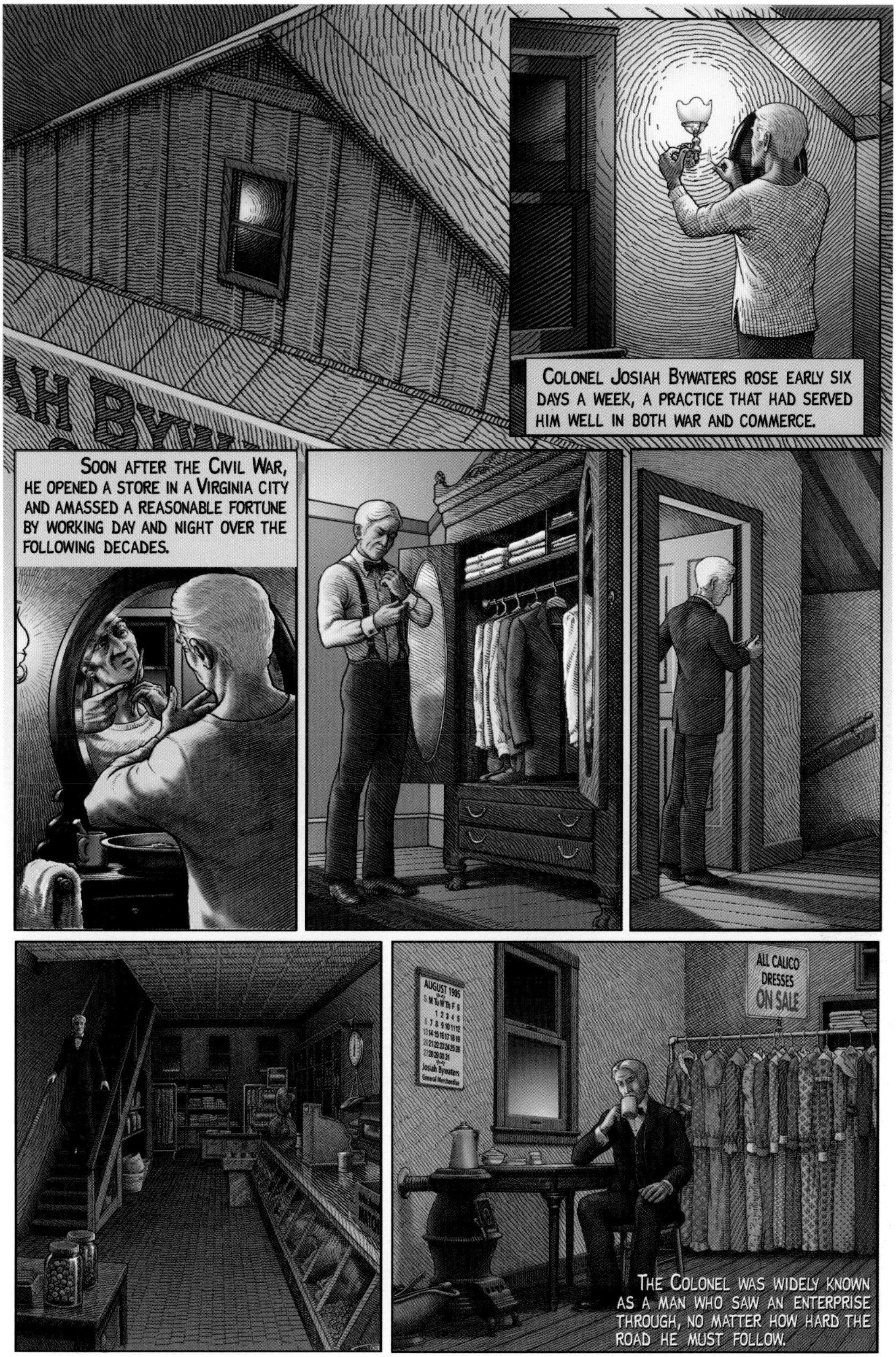
COLONEL JOSIAH BYWATERS ROSE EARLY SIX DAYS A WEEK, A PRACTICE THAT HAD SERVED HIM WELL IN BOTH WAR AND COMMERCE.
SOON AFTER THE CIVIL WAR, HE OPENED A STORE IN A VIRGINIA CITY AND AMASSED A REASONABLE FORTUNE BY WORKING DAY AND NIGHT OVER THE FOLLOWING DECADES.
AUGUST 1905
Josiah Bywaters
General Merchandise
ALL CALICO DRESSES ON SALE
THE COLONEL WAS WIDELY KNOWN AS A MAN WHO SAW AN ENTERPRISE THROUGH, NO MATTER HOW HARD THE ROAD HE MUST FOLLOW.

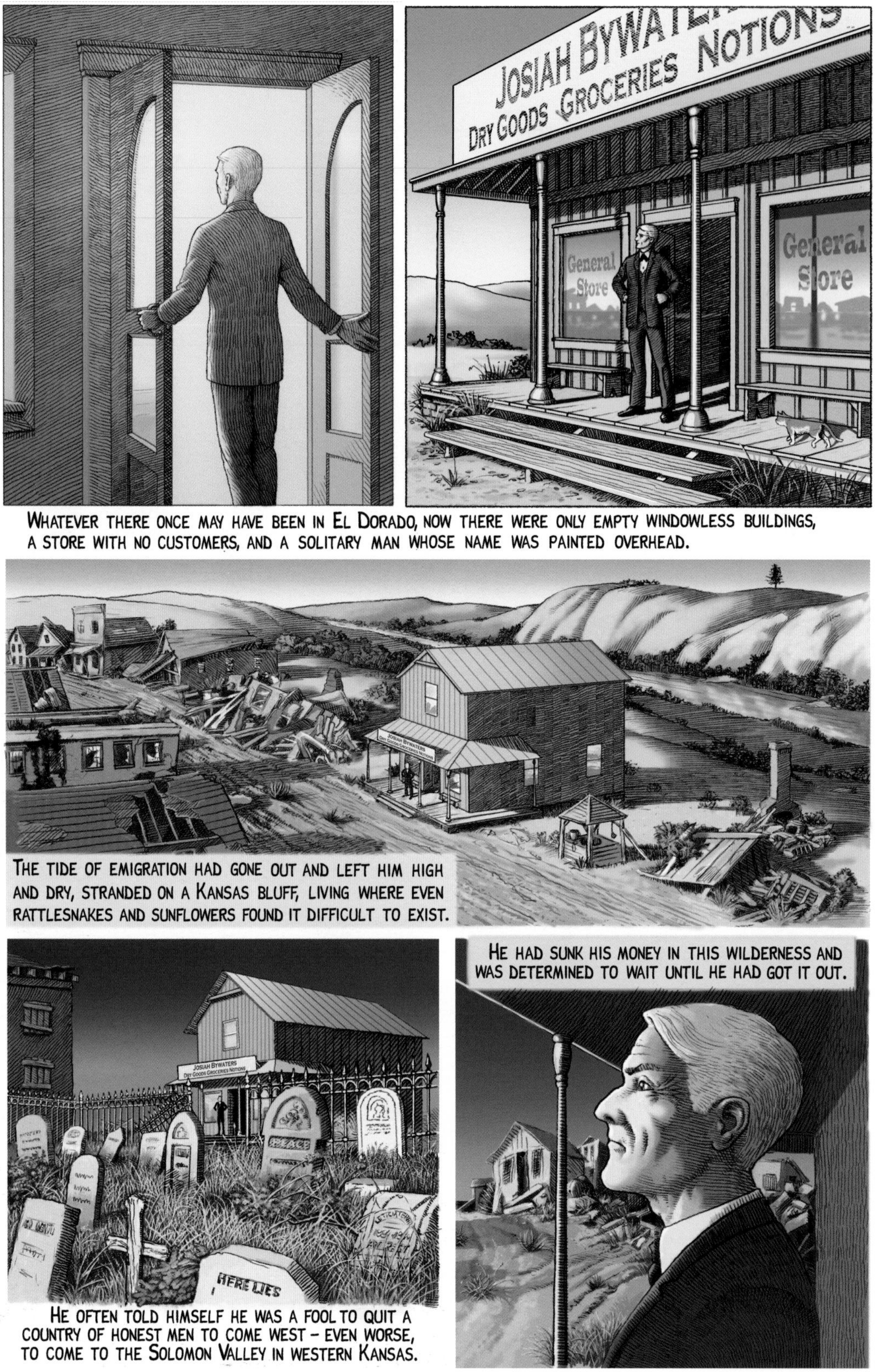
JOSIAH BYWATER
DRY GOODS GROCERIES NOTIONS
General Store
General Store
WHATEVER THERE ONCE MAY HAVE BEEN IN EL DORADO, NOW THERE WERE ONLY EMPTY WINDOWLESS BUILDINGS, A STORE WITH NO CUSTOMERS, AND A SOLITARY MAN WHOSE NAME WAS PAINTED OVERHEAD.
THE TIDE OF EMIGRATION HAD GONE OUT AND LEFT HIM HIGH AND DRY, STRANDED ON A KANSAS BLUFF, LIVING WHERE EVEN RATTLESNAKES AND SUNFLOWERS FOUND IT DIFFICULT TO EXIST.
JOSIAH BYWATERS
PEACE
HERE LIES
HE OFTEN TOLD HIMSELF HE WAS A FOOL TO QUIT A COUNTRY OF HONEST MEN TO COME WEST – EVEN WORSE, TO COME TO THE SOLOMON VALLEY IN WESTERN KANSAS.
HE HAD SUNK HIS MONEY IN THIS WILDERNESS AND WAS DETERMINED TO WAIT UNTIL HE HAD GOT IT OUT.

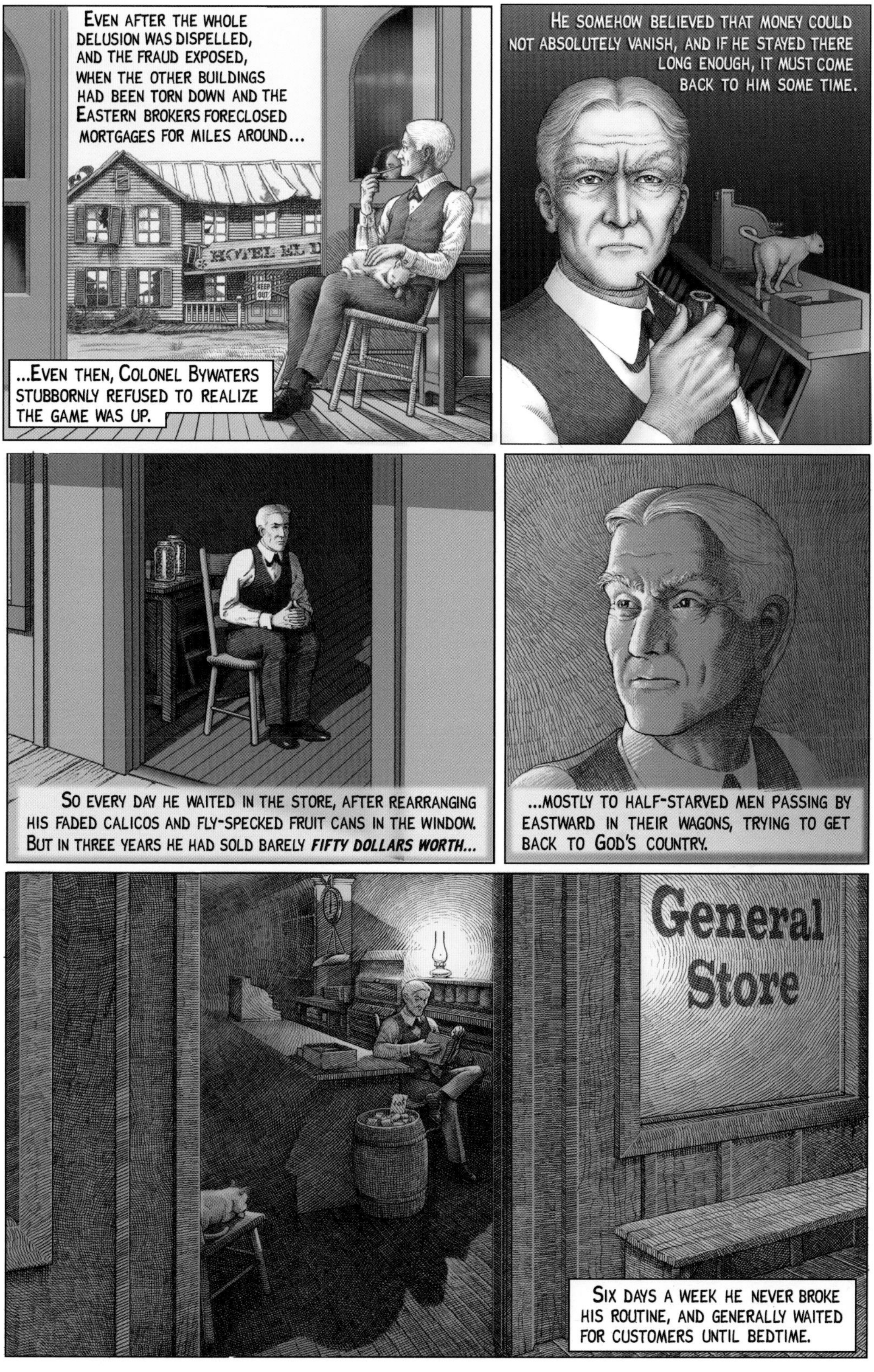
EVEN AFTER THE WHOLE DELUSION WAS DISPELLED, AND THE FRAUD EXPOSED, WHEN THE OTHER BUILDINGS HAD BEEN TORN DOWN AND THE EASTERN BROKERS FORECLOSED MORTGAGES FOR MILES AROUND...
HOTEL EL D
KEEP OUT
...EVEN THEN, COLONEL BYWATERS STUBBORNLY REFUSED TO REALIZE THE GAME WAS UP.
HE SOMEHOW BELIEVED THAT MONEY COULD NOT ABSOLUTELY VANISH, AND IF HE STAYED THERE LONG ENOUGH, IT MUST COME BACK TO HIM SOME TIME.
SO EVERY DAY HE WAITED IN THE STORE, AFTER REARRANGING HIS FADED CALICOS AND FLY-SPECKED FRUIT CANS IN THE WINDOW. BUT IN THREE YEARS HE HAD SOLD BARELY FIFTY DOLLARS WORTH...
...MOSTLY TO HALF-STARVED MEN PASSING BY EASTWARD IN THEIR WAGONS, TRYING TO GET BACK TO GOD'S COUNTRY.
General Store
SIX DAYS A WEEK HE NEVER BROKE HIS ROUTINE, AND GENERALLY WAITED FOR CUSTOMERS UNTIL BEDTIME.

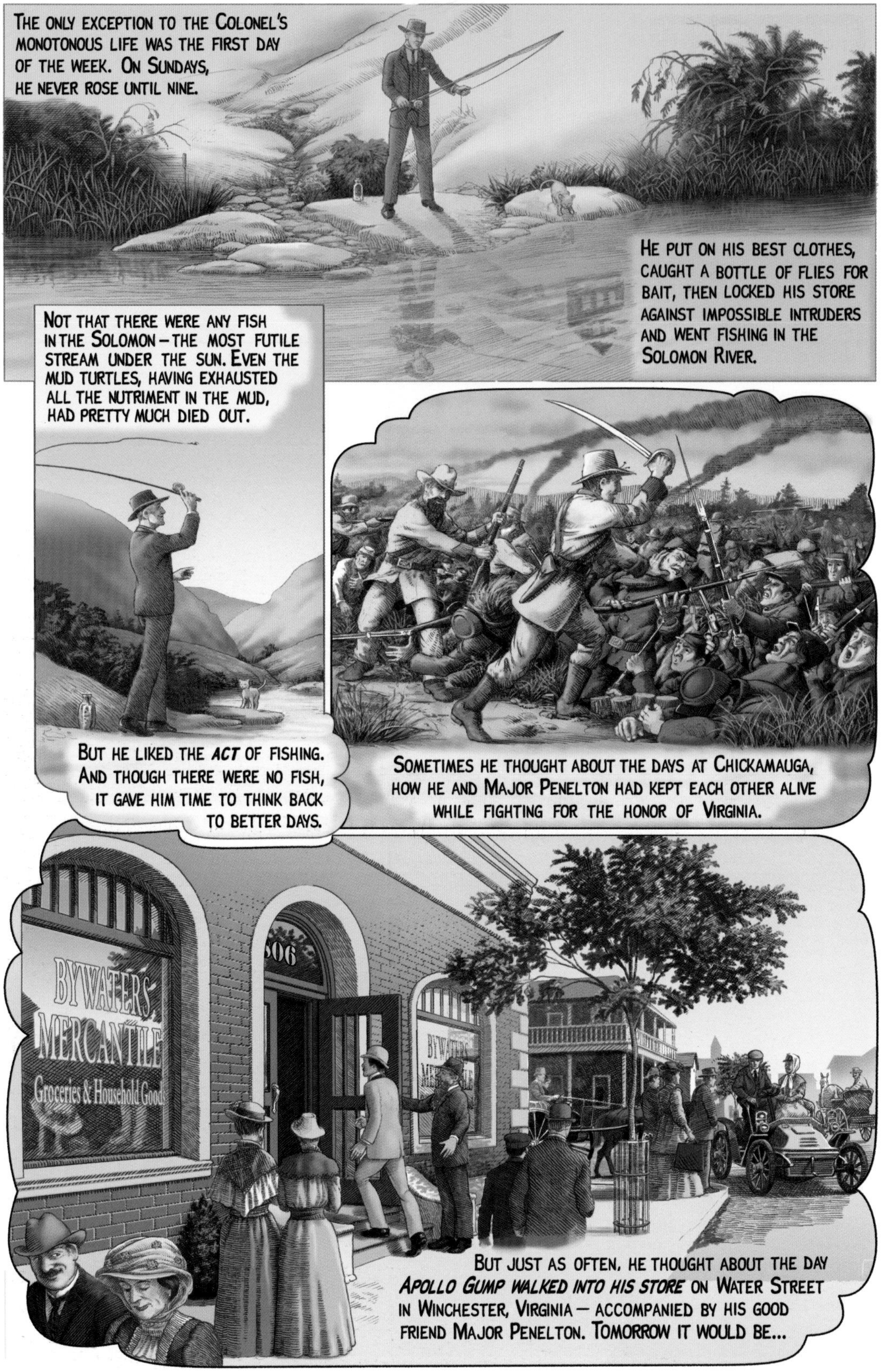
THE ONLY EXCEPTION TO THE COLONEL'S MONOTONOUS LIFE WAS THE FIRST DAY OF THE WEEK. ON SUNDAYS, HE NEVER ROSE UNTIL NINE.
HE PUT ON HIS BEST CLOTHES, CAUGHT A BOTTLE OF FLIES FOR BAIT, THEN LOCKED HIS STORE AGAINST IMPOSSIBLE INTRUDERS AND WENT FISHING IN THE SOLOMON RIVER.
NOT THAT THERE WERE ANY FISH IN THE SOLOMON – THE MOST FUTILE STREAM UNDER THE SUN. EVEN THE MUD TURTLES, HAVING EXHAUSTED ALL THE NUTRIMENT IN THE MUD, HAD PRETTY MUCH DIED OUT.
BUT HE LIKED THE *ACT* OF FISHING. AND THOUGH THERE WERE NO FISH, IT GAVE HIM TIME TO THINK BACK TO BETTER DAYS.
SOMETIMES HE THOUGHT ABOUT THE DAYS AT CHICKAMAUGA, HOW HE AND MAJOR PENELTON HAD KEPT EACH OTHER ALIVE WHILE FIGHTING FOR THE HONOR OF VIRGINIA.
506
BYWATERS MERCANTILE
Groceries & Household Goods
BUT JUST AS OFTEN, HE THOUGHT ABOUT THE DAY ***APOLLO GUMP WALKED INTO HIS STORE*** ON WATER STREET IN WINCHESTER, VIRGINIA – ACCOMPANIED BY HIS GOOD FRIEND MAJOR PENELTON. TOMORROW IT WOULD BE...

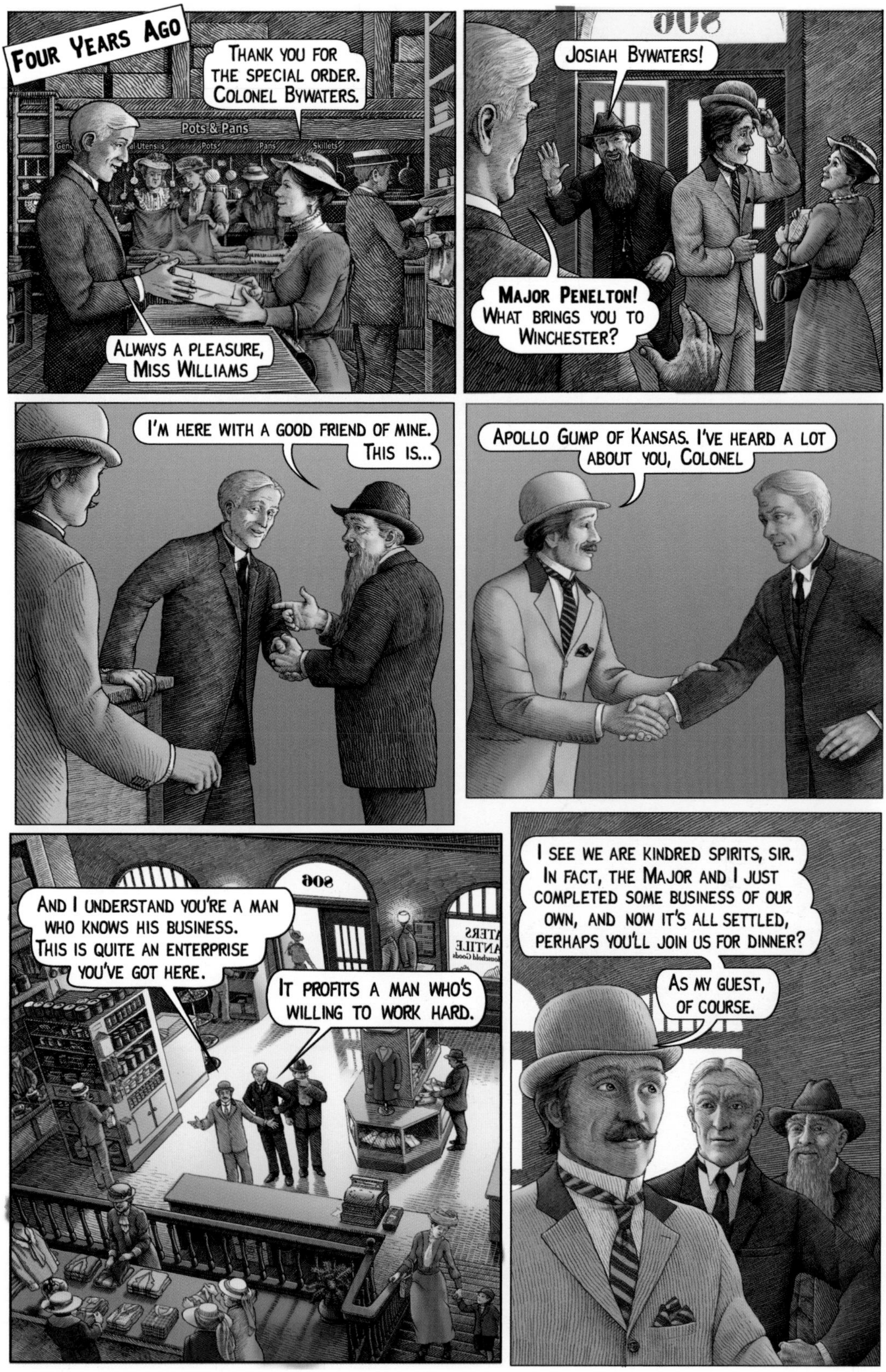
FOUR YEARS AGO
THANK YOU FOR THE SPECIAL ORDER. COLONEL BYWATERS.
Pots & Pans
Pots
Pans
Skillets
ALWAYS A PLEASURE, MISS WILLIAMS
JOSIAH BYWATERS!
MAJOR PENELTON! WHAT BRINGS YOU TO WINCHESTER?
I'M HERE WITH A GOOD FRIEND OF MINE. THIS IS...
APOLLO GUMP OF KANSAS. I'VE HEARD A LOT ABOUT YOU, COLONEL
AND I UNDERSTAND YOU'RE A MAN WHO KNOWS HIS BUSINESS. THIS IS QUITE AN ENTERPRISE YOU'VE GOT HERE.
IT PROFITS A MAN WHO'S WILLING TO WORK HARD.
I SEE WE ARE KINDRED SPIRITS, SIR. IN FACT, THE MAJOR AND I JUST COMPLETED SOME BUSINESS OF OUR OWN, AND NOW IT'S ALL SETTLED, PERHAPS YOU'LL JOIN US FOR DINNER?
AS MY GUEST, OF COURSE.

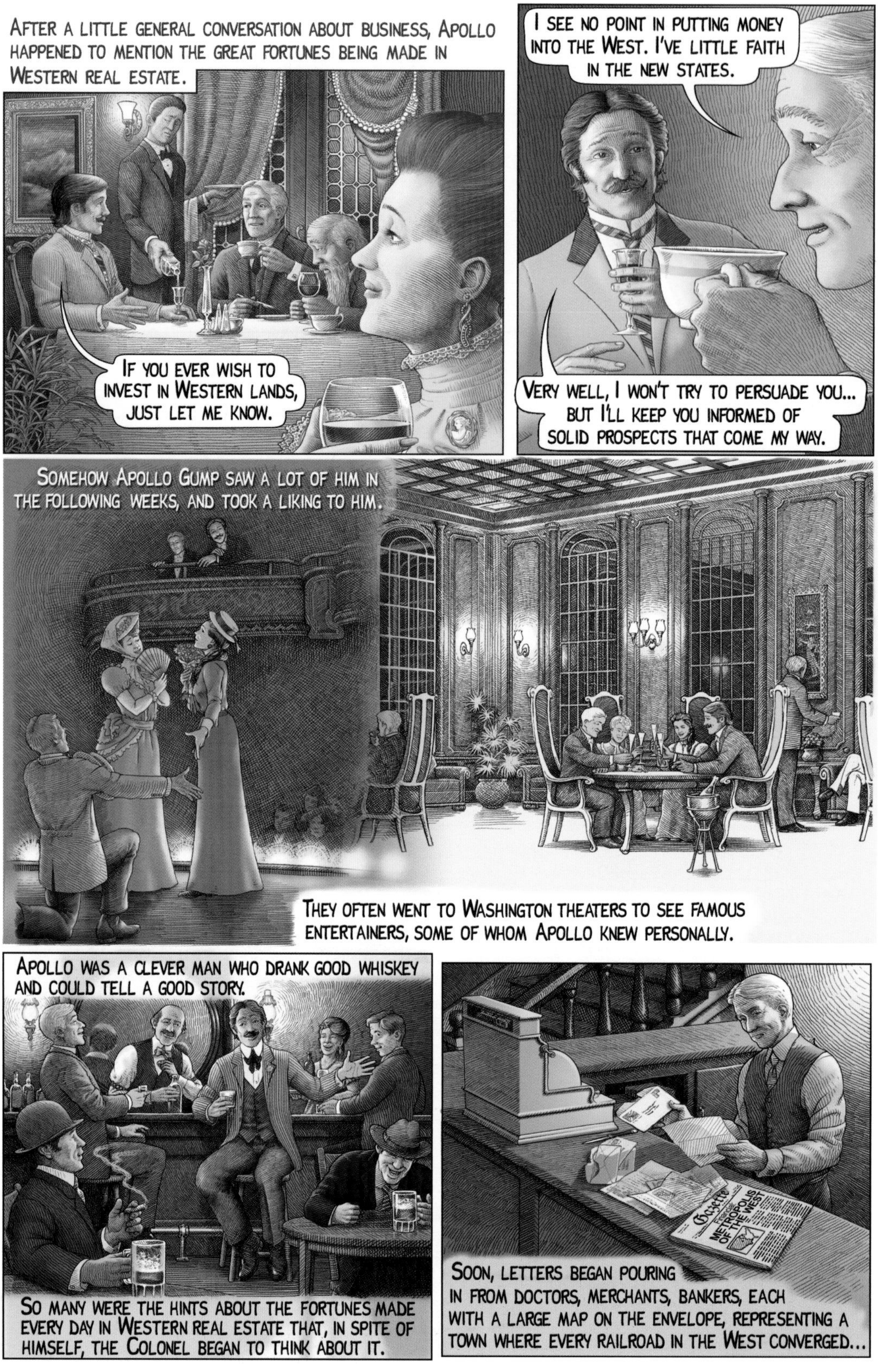
After a little general conversation about business, Apollo happened to mention the great fortunes being made in Western real estate.
If you ever wish to invest in Western lands, just let me know.
I see no point in putting money into the West. I've little faith in the new states.
Very well, I won't try to persuade you... but I'll keep you informed of solid prospects that come my way.
Somehow Apollo Gump saw a lot of him in the following weeks, and took a liking to him.
They often went to Washington theaters to see famous entertainers, some of whom Apollo knew personally.
Apollo was a clever man who drank good whiskey and could tell a good story.
So many were the hints about the fortunes made every day in Western real estate that, in spite of himself, the Colonel began to think about it.
Gazette
METROPOLIS OF THE WEST
Soon, letters began pouring in from doctors, merchants, bankers, each with a large map on the envelope, representing a town where every railroad in the West converged...

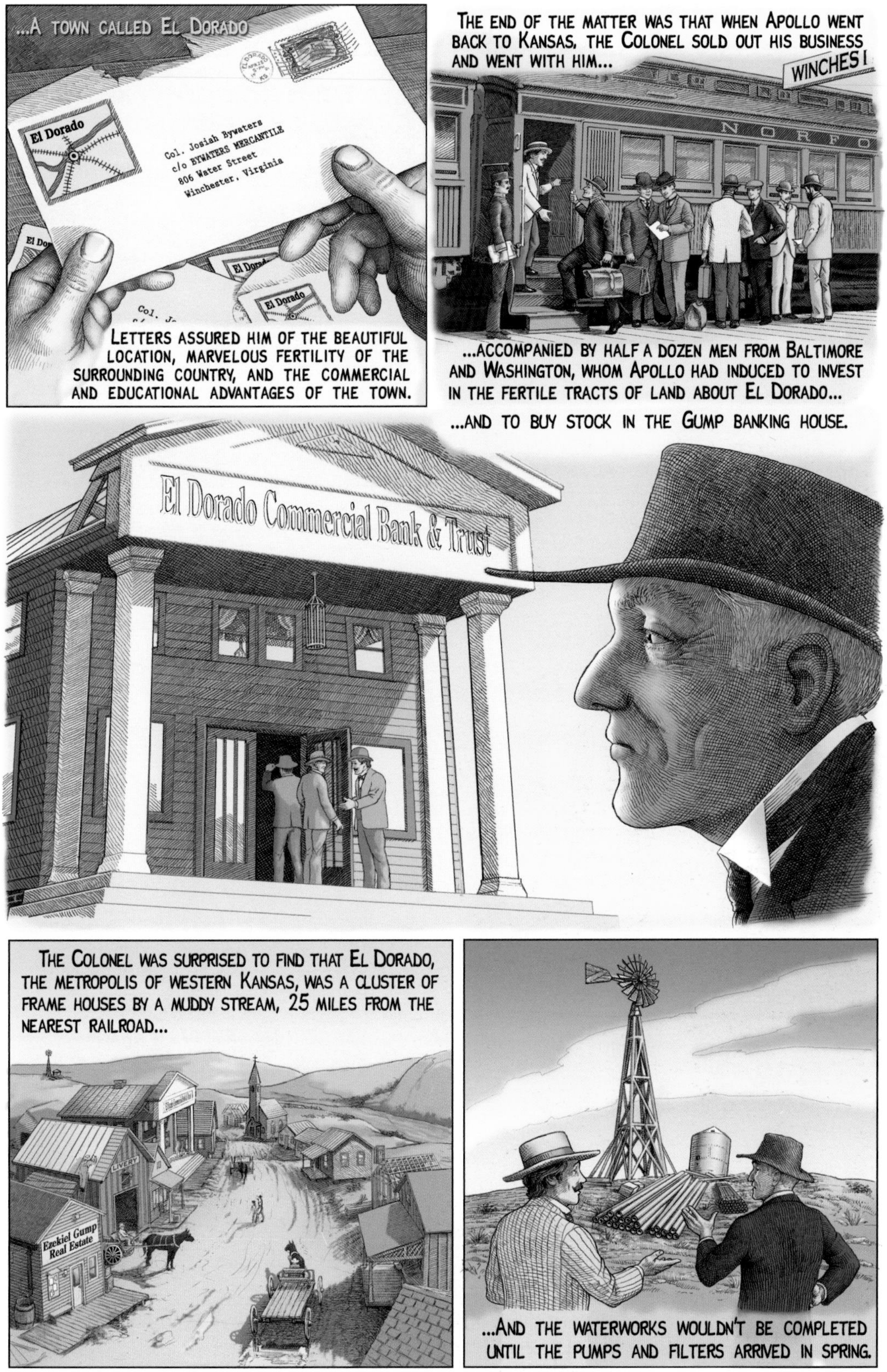
...A TOWN CALLED EL DORADO
El Dorado
Col. Josiah Bywaters
c/o BYWATERS MERCANTILE
806 Water Street
Winchester, Virginia
LETTERS ASSURED HIM OF THE BEAUTIFUL LOCATION, MARVELOUS FERTILITY OF THE SURROUNDING COUNTRY, AND THE COMMERCIAL AND EDUCATIONAL ADVANTAGES OF THE TOWN.
THE END OF THE MATTER WAS THAT WHEN APOLLO WENT BACK TO KANSAS, THE COLONEL SOLD OUT HIS BUSINESS AND WENT WITH HIM...
WINCHES
...ACCOMPANIED BY HALF A DOZEN MEN FROM BALTIMORE AND WASHINGTON, WHOM APOLLO HAD INDUCED TO INVEST IN THE FERTILE TRACTS OF LAND ABOUT EL DORADO...
...AND TO BUY STOCK IN THE GUMP BANKING HOUSE.
El Dorado Commercial Bank & Trust
THE COLONEL WAS SURPRISED TO FIND THAT EL DORADO, THE METROPOLIS OF WESTERN KANSAS, WAS A CLUSTER OF FRAME HOUSES BY A MUDDY STREAM, 25 MILES FROM THE NEAREST RAILROAD...
LIVERY
Ezekiel Gump Real Estate
...AND THE WATERWORKS WOULDN'T BE COMPLETED UNTIL THE PUMPS AND FILTERS ARRIVED IN SPRING.

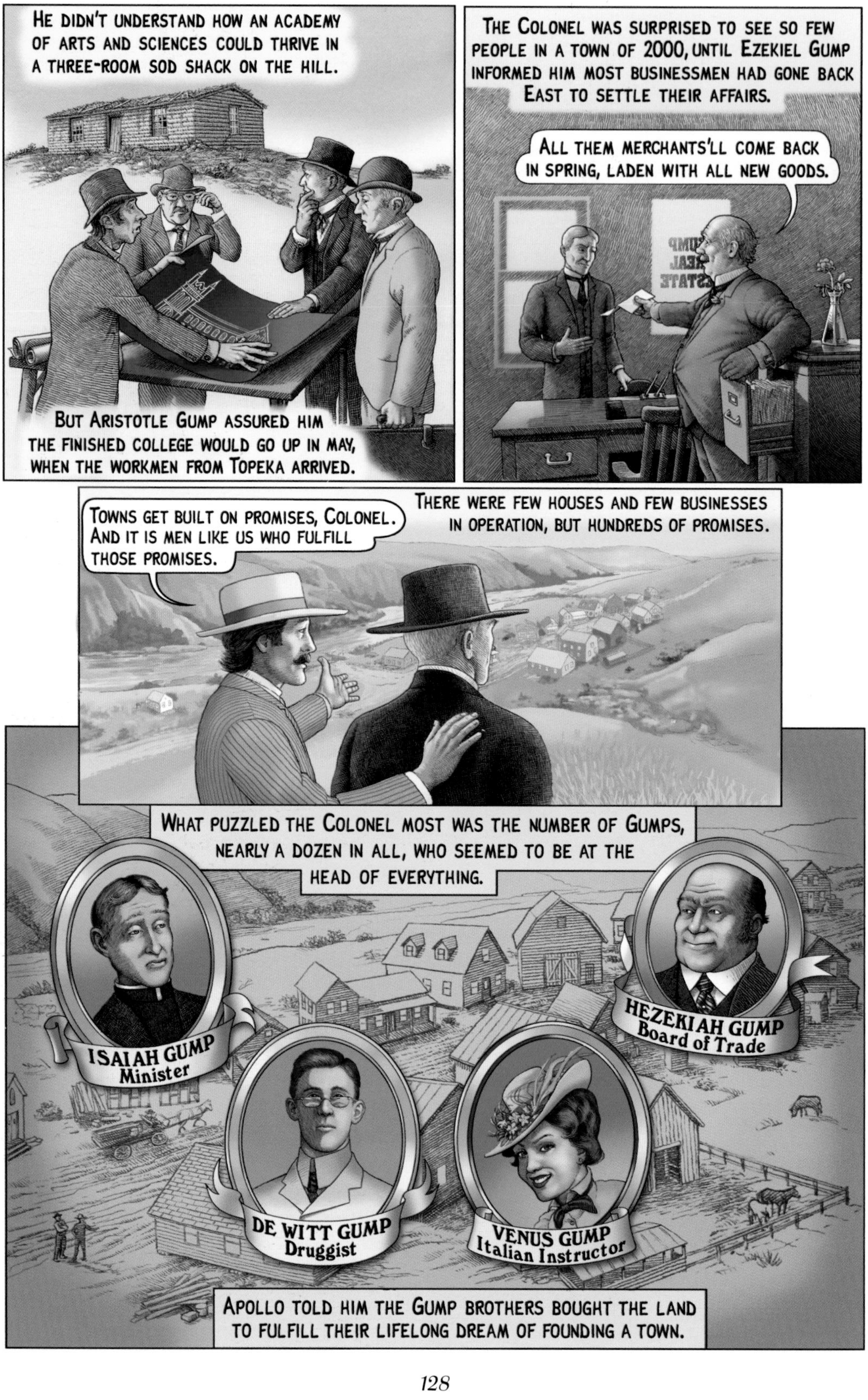
HE DIDN'T UNDERSTAND HOW AN ACADEMY OF ARTS AND SCIENCES COULD THRIVE IN A THREE-ROOM SOD SHACK ON THE HILL.
BUT ARISTOTLE GUMP ASSURED HIM THE FINISHED COLLEGE WOULD GO UP IN MAY, WHEN THE WORKMEN FROM TOPEKA ARRIVED.
THE COLONEL WAS SURPRISED TO SEE SO FEW PEOPLE IN A TOWN OF 2000, UNTIL EZEKIEL GUMP INFORMED HIM MOST BUSINESSMEN HAD GONE BACK EAST TO SETTLE THEIR AFFAIRS.
ALL THEM MERCHANTS'LL COME BACK IN SPRING, LADEN WITH ALL NEW GOODS.
TOWNS GET BUILT ON PROMISES, COLONEL. AND IT IS MEN LIKE US WHO FULFILL THOSE PROMISES.
THERE WERE FEW HOUSES AND FEW BUSINESSES IN OPERATION, BUT HUNDREDS OF PROMISES.
WHAT PUZZLED THE COLONEL MOST WAS THE NUMBER OF GUMPS, NEARLY A DOZEN IN ALL, WHO SEEMED TO BE AT THE HEAD OF EVERYTHING.
ISAIAH GUMP
Minister
HEZEKIAH GUMP
Board of Trade
DE WITT GUMP
Druggist
VENUS GUMP
Italian Instructor
APOLLO TOLD HIM THE GUMP BROTHERS BOUGHT THE LAND TO FULFILL THEIR LIFELONG DREAM OF FOUNDING A TOWN.

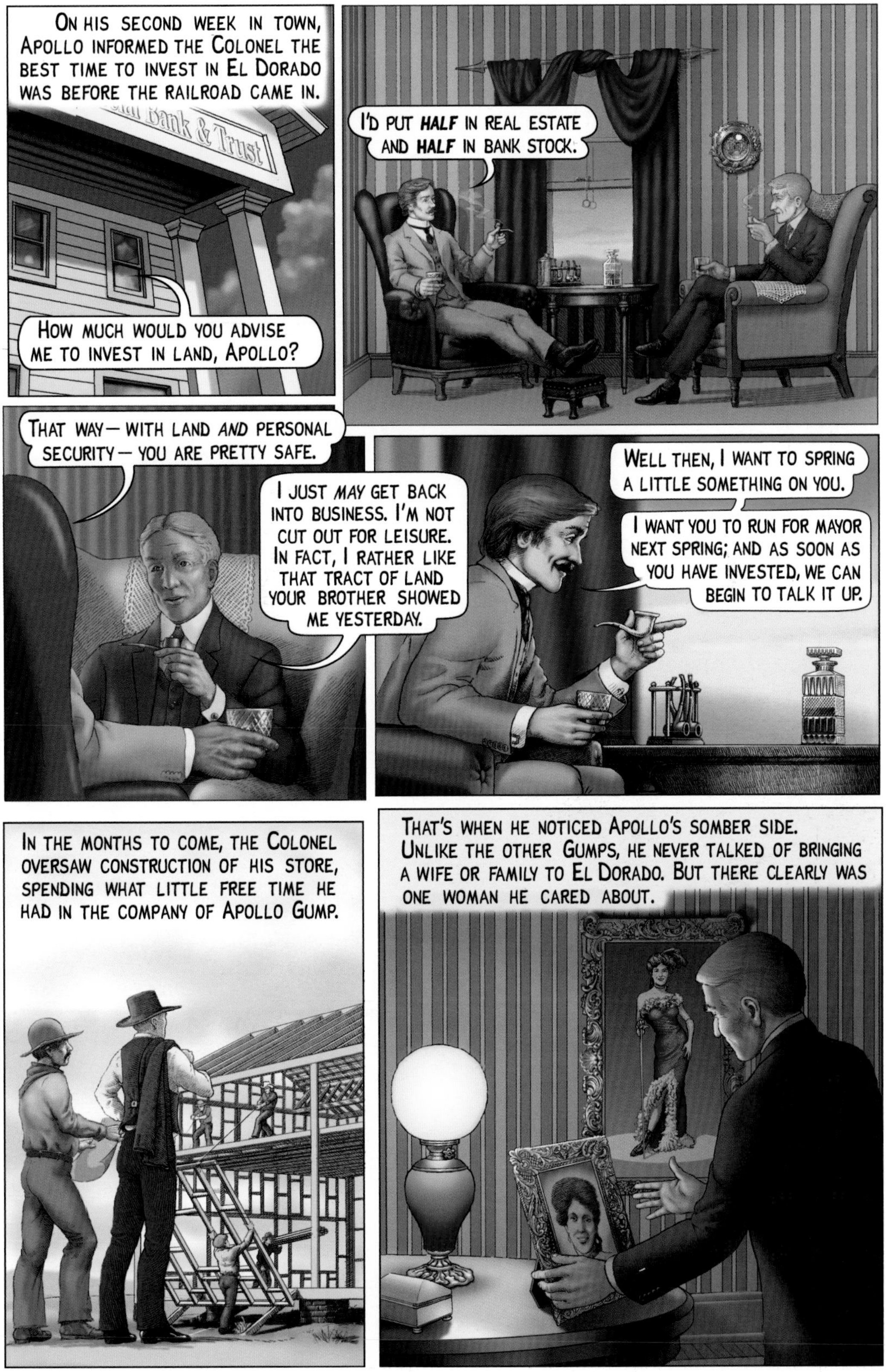
ON HIS SECOND WEEK IN TOWN, APOLLO INFORMED THE COLONEL THE BEST TIME TO INVEST IN EL DORADO WAS BEFORE THE RAILROAD CAME IN.
Bank & Trust
HOW MUCH WOULD YOU ADVISE ME TO INVEST IN LAND, APOLLO?
I'D PUT **HALF** IN REAL ESTATE AND **HALF** IN BANK STOCK.
THAT WAY— WITH LAND *AND* PERSONAL SECURITY— YOU ARE PRETTY SAFE.
I JUST *MAY* GET BACK INTO BUSINESS. I'M NOT CUT OUT FOR LEISURE. IN FACT, I RATHER LIKE THAT TRACT OF LAND YOUR BROTHER SHOWED ME YESTERDAY.
WELL THEN, I WANT TO SPRING A LITTLE SOMETHING ON YOU.
I WANT YOU TO RUN FOR MAYOR NEXT SPRING; AND AS SOON AS YOU HAVE INVESTED, WE CAN BEGIN TO TALK IT UP.
IN THE MONTHS TO COME, THE COLONEL OVERSAW CONSTRUCTION OF HIS STORE, SPENDING WHAT LITTLE FREE TIME HE HAD IN THE COMPANY OF APOLLO GUMP.
THAT'S WHEN HE NOTICED APOLLO'S SOMBER SIDE. UNLIKE THE OTHER GUMPS, HE NEVER TALKED OF BRINGING A WIFE OR FAMILY TO EL DORADO. BUT THERE CLEARLY WAS ONE WOMAN HE CARED ABOUT.

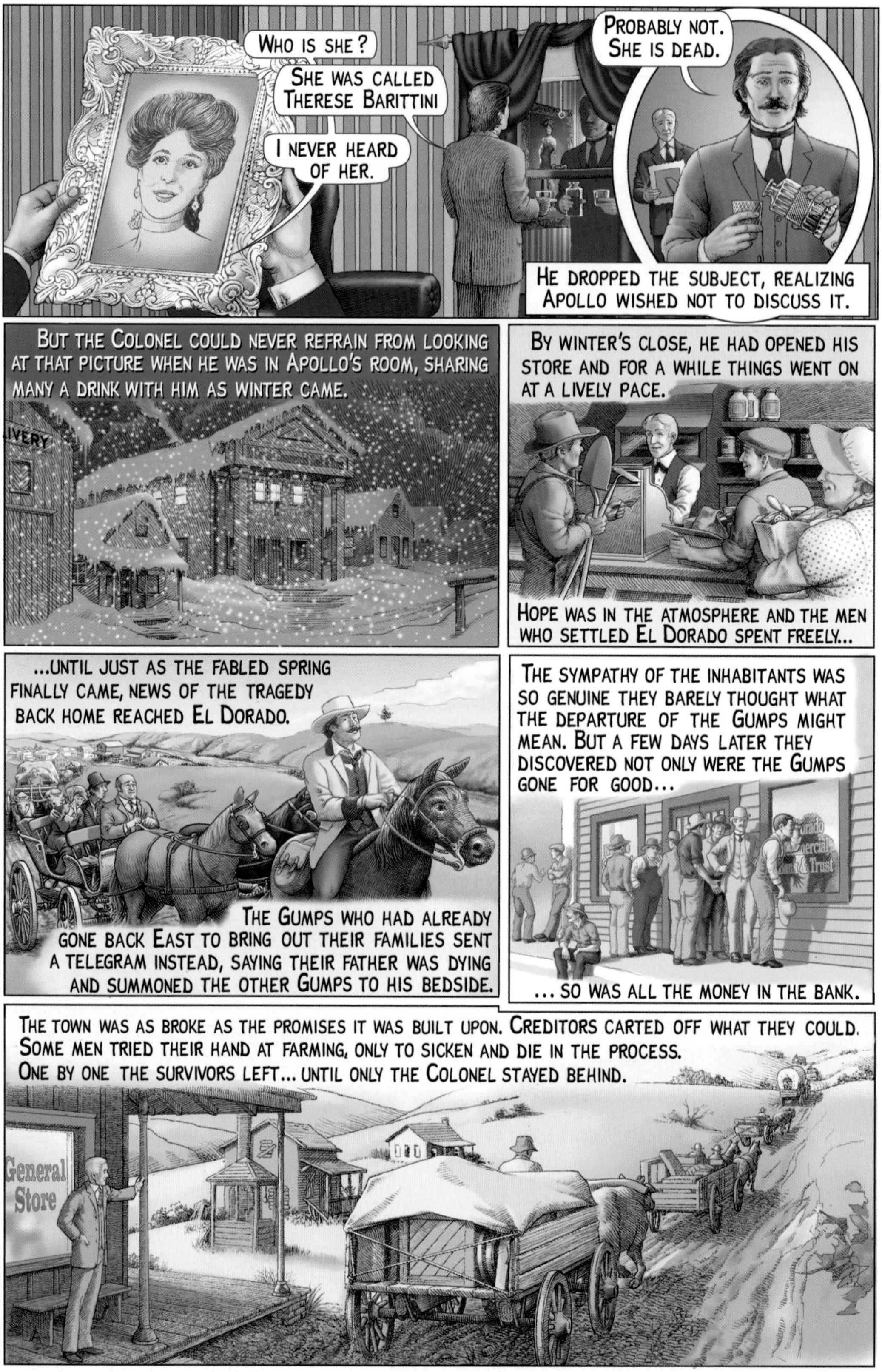
WHO IS SHE?
SHE WAS CALLED THERESE BARITTINI
I NEVER HEARD OF HER.
PROBABLY NOT. SHE IS DEAD.
HE DROPPED THE SUBJECT, REALIZING APOLLO WISHED NOT TO DISCUSS IT.
BUT THE COLONEL COULD NEVER REFRAIN FROM LOOKING AT THAT PICTURE WHEN HE WAS IN APOLLO'S ROOM, SHARING MANY A DRINK WITH HIM AS WINTER CAME.
BY WINTER'S CLOSE, HE HAD OPENED HIS STORE AND FOR A WHILE THINGS WENT ON AT A LIVELY PACE.
HOPE WAS IN THE ATMOSPHERE AND THE MEN WHO SETTLED EL DORADO SPENT FREELY...
...UNTIL JUST AS THE FABLED SPRING FINALLY CAME, NEWS OF THE TRAGEDY BACK HOME REACHED EL DORADO.
THE GUMPS WHO HAD ALREADY GONE BACK EAST TO BRING OUT THEIR FAMILIES SENT A TELEGRAM INSTEAD, SAYING THEIR FATHER WAS DYING AND SUMMONED THE OTHER GUMPS TO HIS BEDSIDE.
THE SYMPATHY OF THE INHABITANTS WAS SO GENUINE THEY BARELY THOUGHT WHAT THE DEPARTURE OF THE GUMPS MIGHT MEAN. BUT A FEW DAYS LATER THEY DISCOVERED NOT ONLY WERE THE GUMPS GONE FOR GOOD...
... SO WAS ALL THE MONEY IN THE BANK.
THE TOWN WAS AS BROKE AS THE PROMISES IT WAS BUILT UPON. CREDITORS CARTED OFF WHAT THEY COULD. SOME MEN TRIED THEIR HAND AT FARMING, ONLY TO SICKEN AND DIE IN THE PROCESS. ONE BY ONE THE SURVIVORS LEFT... UNTIL ONLY THE COLONEL STAYED BEHIND.
General Store

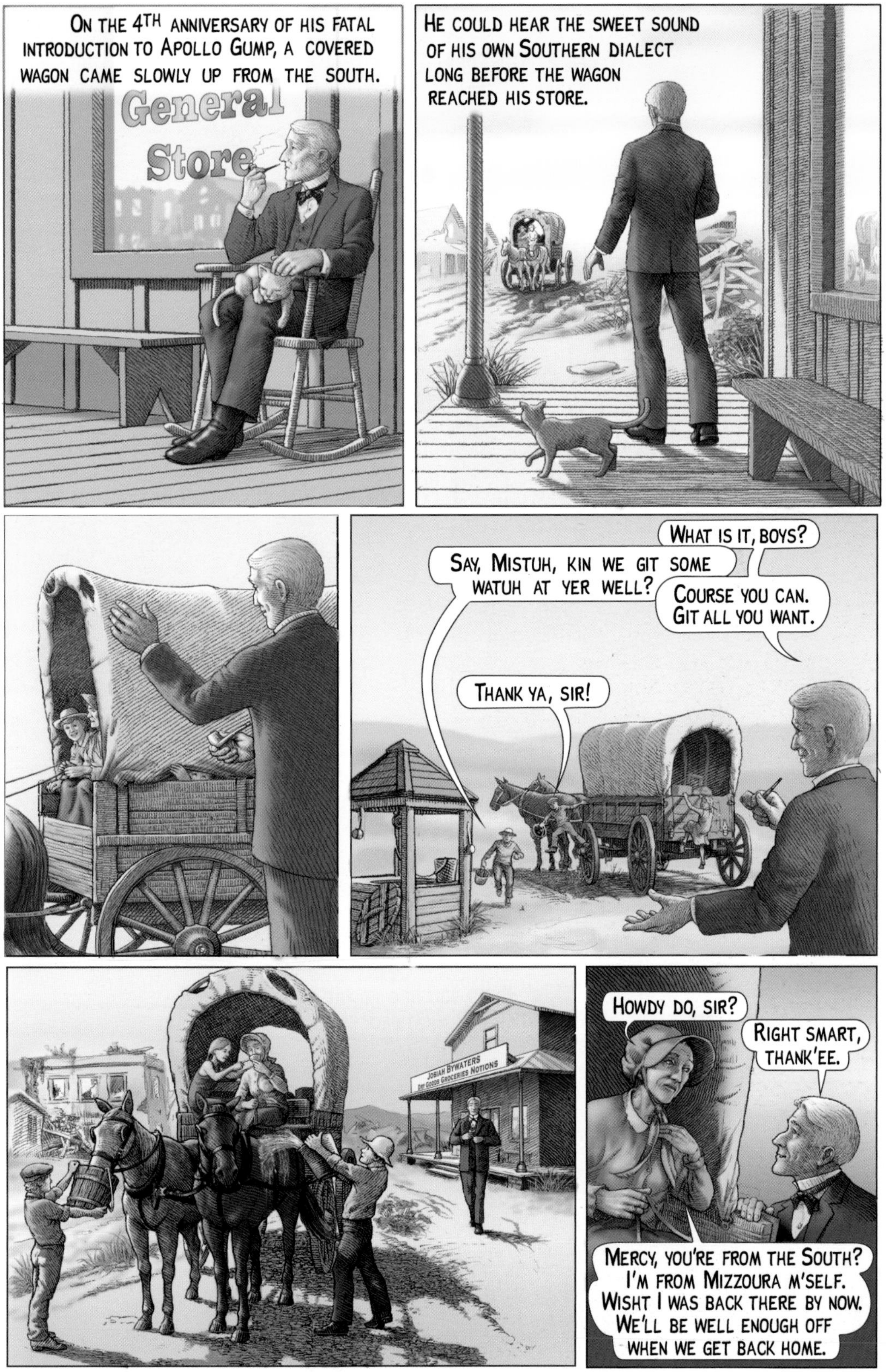
On the 4th anniversary of his fatal introduction to Apollo Gump, a covered wagon came slowly up from the south.
General Store
He could hear the sweet sound of his own Southern dialect long before the wagon reached his store.
What is it, boys?
Say, Mistuh, kin we git some watuh at yer well?
Course you can. Git all you want.
Thank ya, sir!
Josiah Bywaters
Dry Goods Groceries Notions
Howdy do, sir?
Right smart, thank'ee.
Mercy, you're from the South? I'm from Mizzoura m'self. Wisht I was back there by now. We'll be well enough off when we get back home.

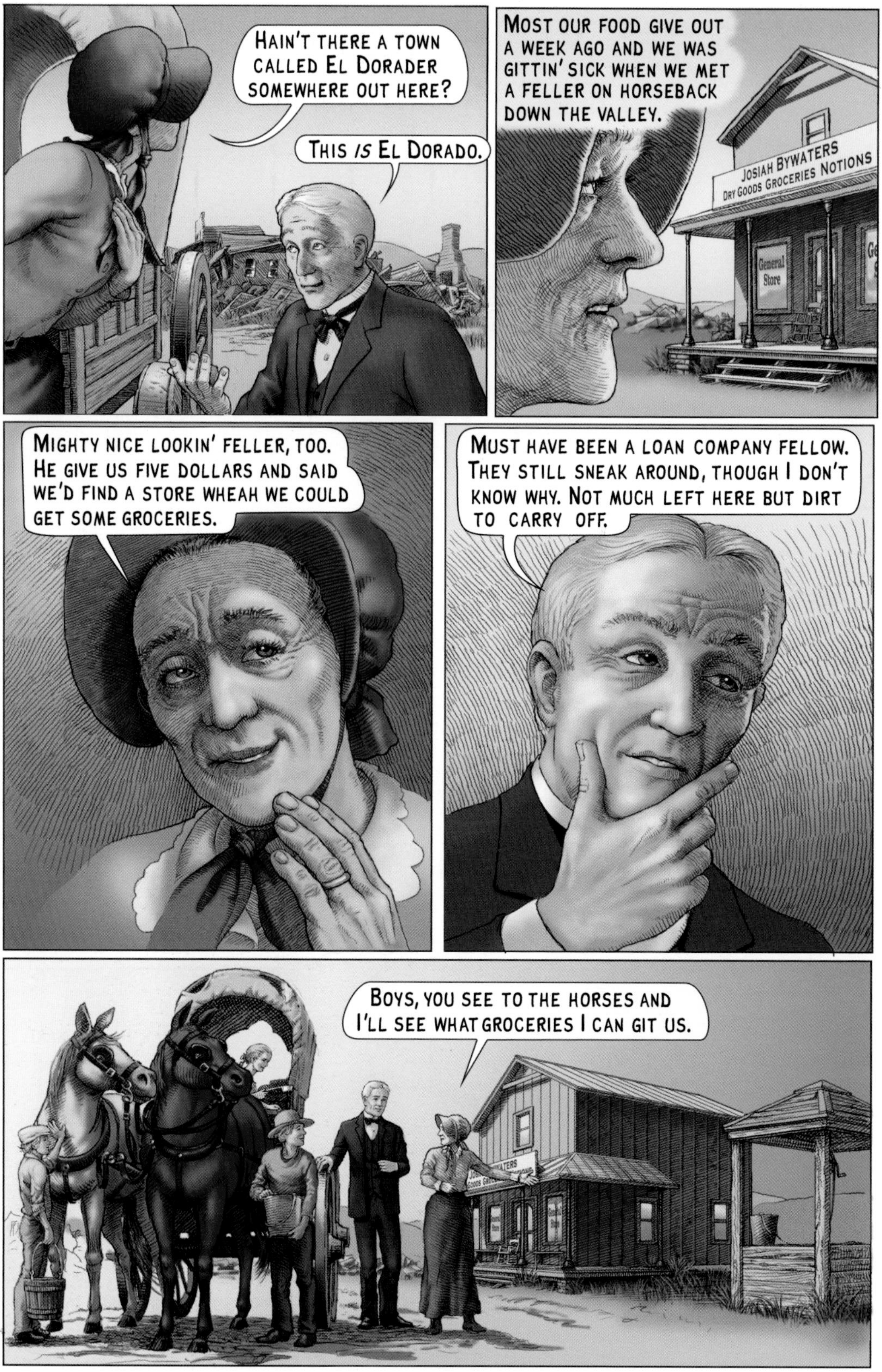
HAIN'T THERE A TOWN CALLED EL DORADER SOMEWHERE OUT HERE?
THIS *IS* EL DORADO.
MOST OUR FOOD GIVE OUT A WEEK AGO AND WE WAS GITTIN' SICK WHEN WE MET A FELLER ON HORSEBACK DOWN THE VALLEY.
JOSIAH BYWATERS
DRY GOODS GROCERIES NOTIONS
General Store
MIGHTY NICE LOOKIN' FELLER, TOO. HE GIVE US FIVE DOLLARS AND SAID WE'D FIND A STORE WHEAH WE COULD GET SOME GROCERIES.
MUST HAVE BEEN A LOAN COMPANY FELLOW. THEY STILL SNEAK AROUND, THOUGH I DON'T KNOW WHY. NOT MUCH LEFT HERE BUT DIRT TO CARRY OFF.
BOYS, YOU SEE TO THE HORSES AND I'LL SEE WHAT GROCERIES I CAN GIT US.

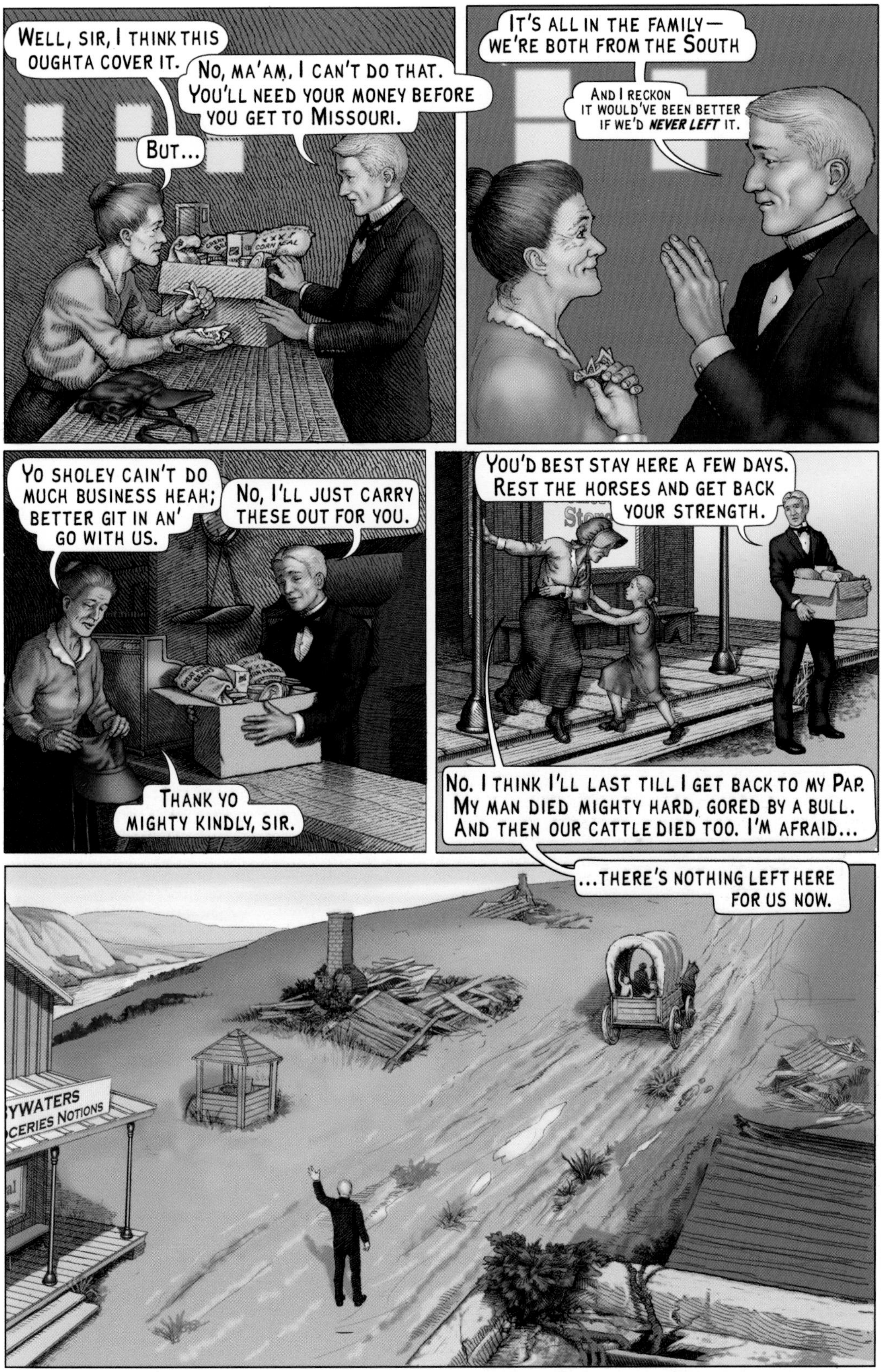
WELL, SIR, I THINK THIS OUGHTA COVER IT.
NO, MA'AM, I CAN'T DO THAT. YOU'LL NEED YOUR MONEY BEFORE YOU GET TO MISSOURI.
BUT...
IT'S ALL IN THE FAMILY— WE'RE BOTH FROM THE SOUTH
AND I RECKON IT WOULD'VE BEEN BETTER IF WE'D ***NEVER LEFT*** IT.
YO SHOLEY CAIN'T DO MUCH BUSINESS HEAH; BETTER GIT IN AN' GO WITH US.
NO, I'LL JUST CARRY THESE OUT FOR YOU.
THANK YO MIGHTY KINDLY, SIR.
YOU'D BEST STAY HERE A FEW DAYS. REST THE HORSES AND GET BACK YOUR STRENGTH.
NO. I THINK I'LL LAST TILL I GET BACK TO MY PAP. MY MAN DIED MIGHTY HARD, GORED BY A BULL. AND THEN OUR CATTLE DIED TOO. I'M AFRAID...
...THERE'S NOTHING LEFT HERE FOR US NOW.
YWATERS
CERIES NOTIONS

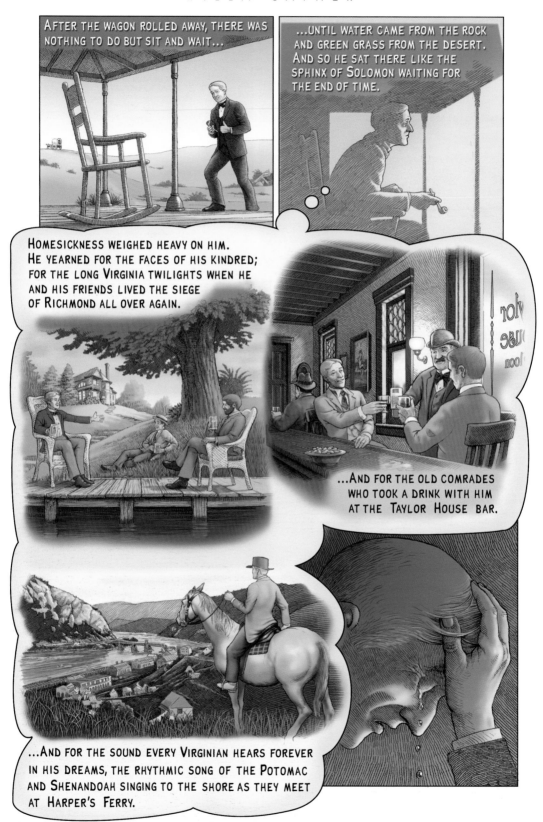

AFTER THE WAGON ROLLED AWAY, THERE WAS NOTHING TO DO BUT SIT AND WAIT...

...UNTIL WATER CAME FROM THE ROCK AND GREEN GRASS FROM THE DESERT. AND SO HE SAT THERE LIKE THE SPHINX OF SOLOMON WAITING FOR THE END OF TIME.

HOMESICKNESS WEIGHED HEAVY ON HIM. HE YEARNED FOR THE FACES OF HIS KINDRED; FOR THE LONG VIRGINIA TWILIGHTS WHEN HE AND HIS FRIENDS LIVED THE SIEGE OF RICHMOND ALL OVER AGAIN.

...AND FOR THE OLD COMRADES WHO TOOK A DRINK WITH HIM AT THE TAYLOR HOUSE BAR.

...AND FOR THE SOUND EVERY VIRGINIAN HEARS FOREVER IN HIS DREAMS, THE RHYTHMIC SONG OF THE POTOMAC AND SHENANDOAH SINGING TO THE SHORE AS THEY MEET AT HARPER'S FERRY.

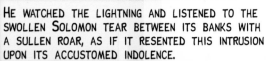

That night a violent storm set in, a drenching rain that came long after the barren summer waned into a fruitless autumn.

He watched the lightning and listened to the swollen Solomon tear between its banks with a sullen roar, as if it resented this intrusion upon its accustomed indolence.

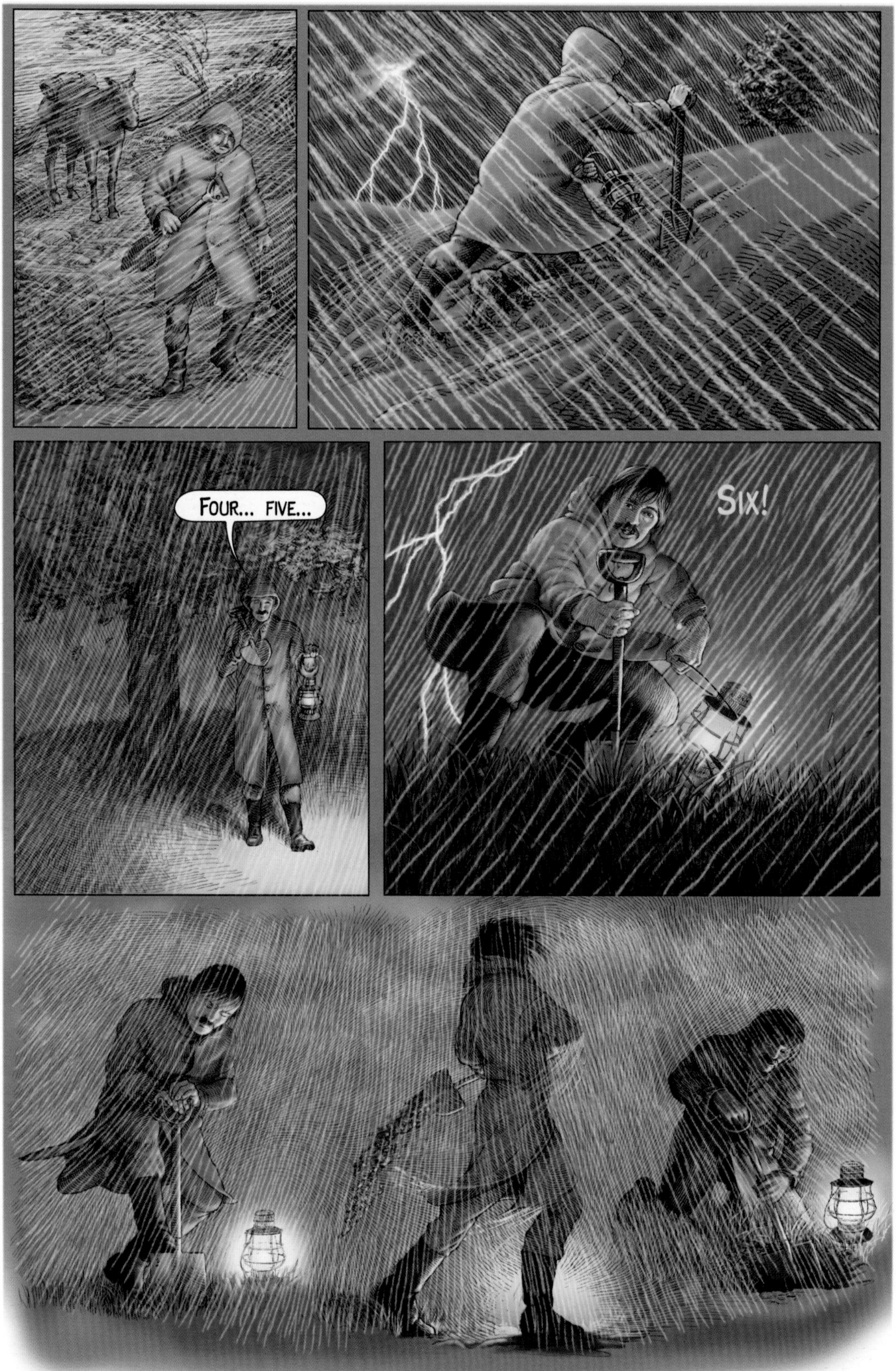
FOUR... FIVE...
SIX!

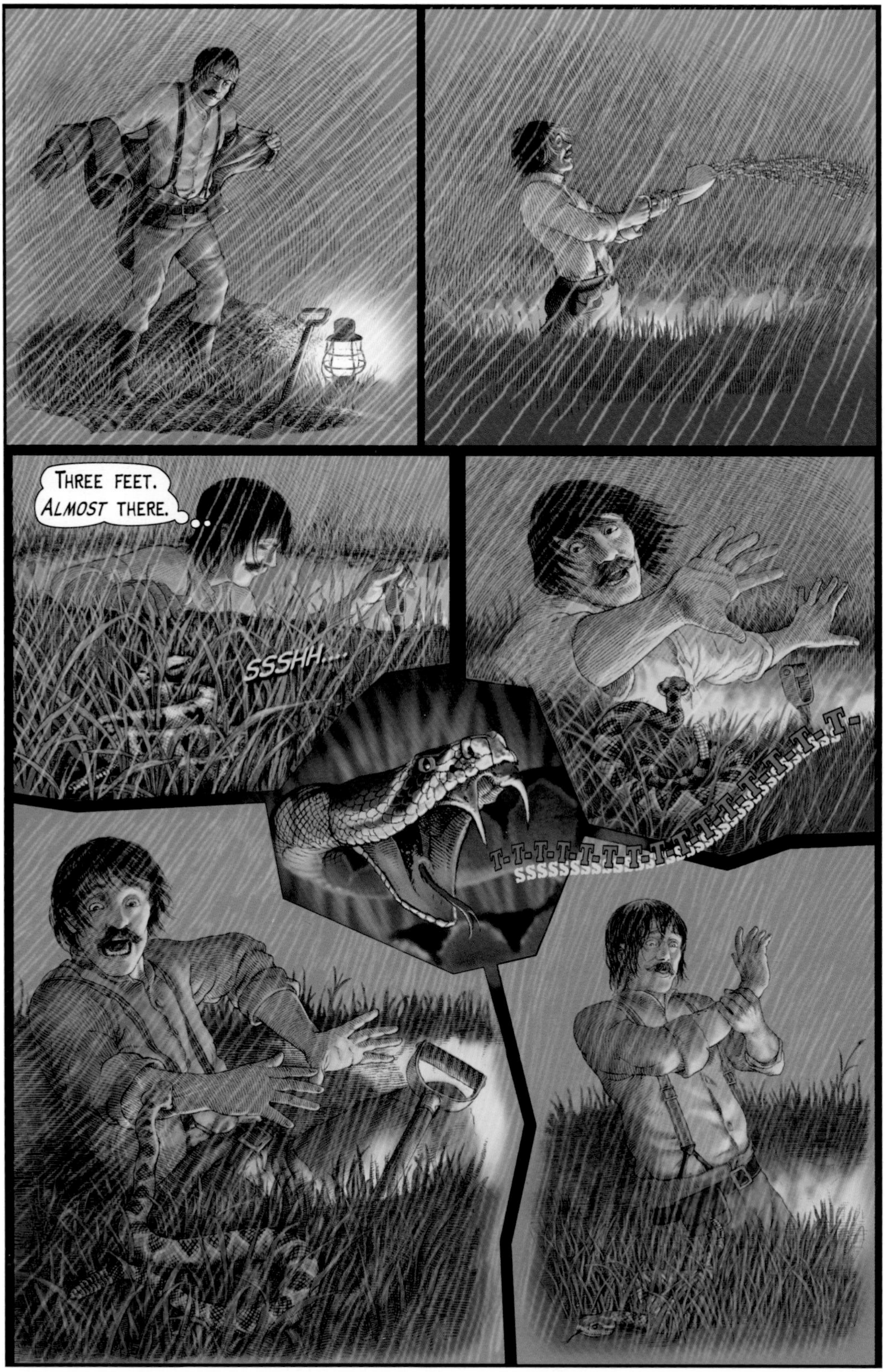
THREE FEET.
ALMOST THERE.
SSSHH....
T-T-T-T-T-T-T-T-T-T-T-T-T-T-T-T-T-
SSSSSSSSSSSSSSSSSSSS

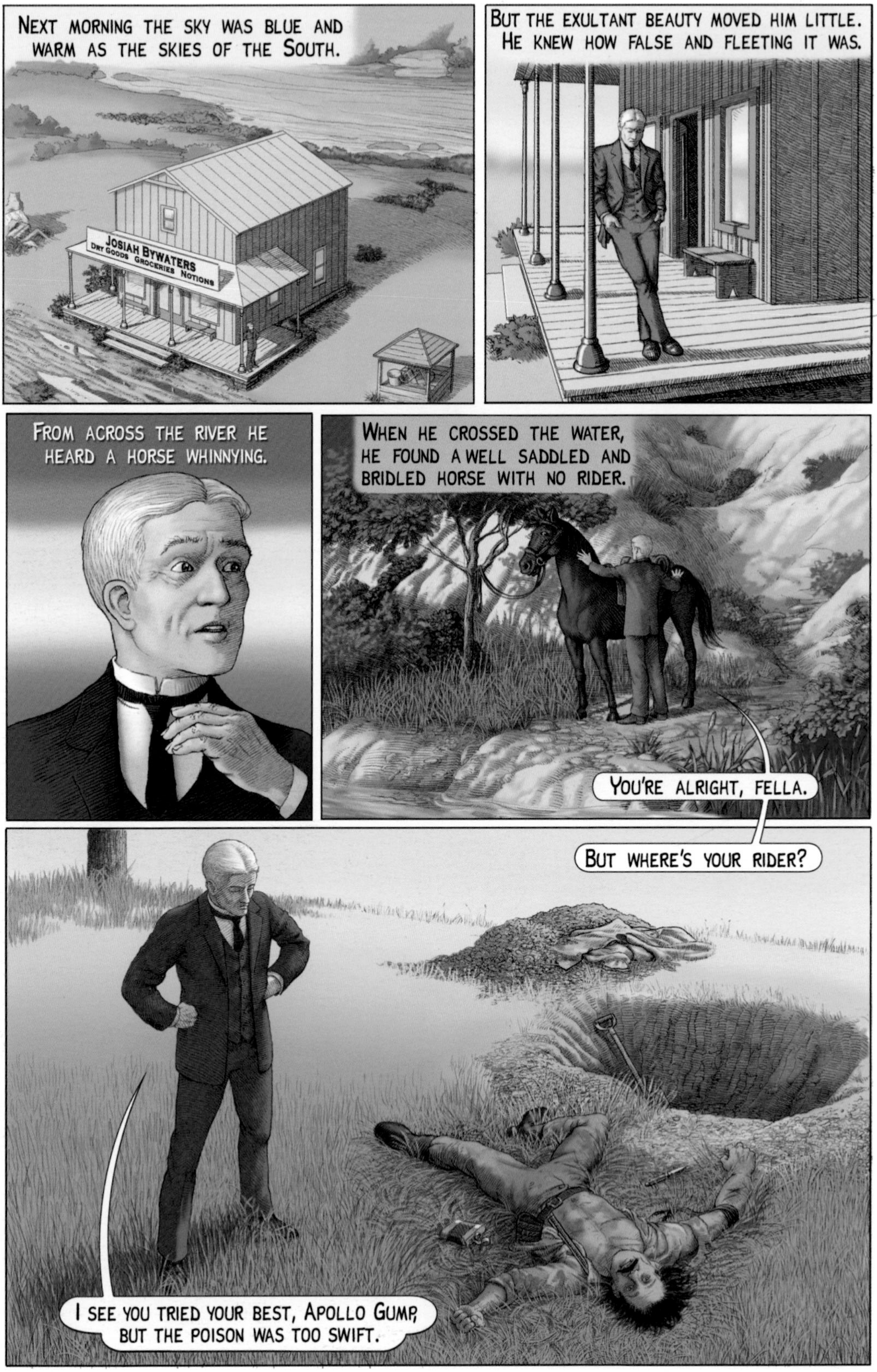
NEXT MORNING THE SKY WAS BLUE AND WARM AS THE SKIES OF THE SOUTH.
JOSIAH BYWATERS
DRY GOODS GROCERIES NOTIONS
BUT THE EXULTANT BEAUTY MOVED HIM LITTLE. HE KNEW HOW FALSE AND FLEETING IT WAS.
FROM ACROSS THE RIVER HE HEARD A HORSE WHINNYING.
WHEN HE CROSSED THE WATER, HE FOUND A WELL SADDLED AND BRIDLED HORSE WITH NO RIDER.
YOU'RE ALRIGHT, FELLA.
BUT WHERE'S YOUR RIDER?
I SEE YOU TRIED YOUR BEST, APOLLO GUMP, BUT THE POISON WAS TOO SWIFT.